something like aututmn

D1519720

Jay Bell Books
www.jaybellbooks.com

Did you buy this book? If so, thank you for putting food on our table! Making money as an independent artist isn't easy, so your support is greatly appreciated. Come give me a hug!

Did you pirate this book? If so, there are a couple of ways you can still help out. If you like the story, please take the time to leave a nice review somewhere, such as an online retail store (my preference), or on any blog or forum. Word of mouth is important for every book, so if you can recommend this book to friends with more cash to spare, that would be awesome too!

Something Like Autumn

by Jay Bell

A special "thank you" to my crew of supporters who make me look much more clever than I really am: Andreas, Claire, Kati, Kira, Linda, Mom, and Zate. Thank you guys for all being part of my big book family.

This book is dedicated to anyone who has stood on the brink and found the strength to turn back. To live is to love.

Part One:
Missouri, 1990

Chapter One

My name is Jace Holden, and today is the day I die. Words have always come easy for me, which makes it strange that I struggle with them now. Knowing that my time is coming to an end, there's so much I want to say. Mom, Dad, I want you to know that this isn't your fault. You've always given me everything I needed, and I always felt loved, but you don't know who I am. I hid the truth from you. I'm sorry for that and for what I'm about to do... have done, by the time you read this. But you need to understand that it's better for me to die now when, as odd as it might seem, I am still happy. I think about the future all the time, when you've both passed away and my sister has a family of her own. And you better, Michelle! You fall in love, have a slew of kids, and never look back. That's what I want, but I also know this means I'll end up on my own. I'll get old, and sick, and die alone, because that's what happens to people like me. All I want is someone to love, someone who will love me back. I don't understand why that person has to be another man. I can't explain that to you, but I'm sure you'll agree this is an impossible dream. So I'm leaving now, while I still have a wonderful family that loves me and will forgive me for anything, even for being selfish. Or for being gay. I'm just sorry I couldn't tell you in person.

Jace wiped his nose on his jacket sleeve, folded up the note, and placed it inside the plastic baggie. He probably should have double-bagged it, since the letter would have to survive being submerged in water, but at least the baggie had a trusty Ziploc seal. *Yellow and blue make green!* After some deliberation, Jace decided the note was safest in the front pocket of his jeans, shoved it in there, and turned his attention to the Blackwater River.

As a kid, Jace had imagined he could hop into the river, be swept out of this podunk Missouri town and up to Canada where his grandparents lived. Later, when a drunken hobo had fallen off this very bridge, Jace had learned that the river could take a person to a completely different destination. Whether that was Heaven or Hell he wasn't certain, but he was determined to find out. Placing his hand on the wrought-iron rail, which felt cold in the late October air, Jace considered the waters below. How would this kill him, exactly? Didn't Olympic divers jump from these same heights? Maybe he should have chugged his father's whisky, got himself nice and drunk like the bum who had died here years ago.

1

Jace's eyes scanned the river, the waters swollen by a week's worth of storms, and wondered if the hobo's body was still there, lurking beneath the surface. The bobbing light of a night fisher in the distance caught his eye. Jace pictured the fishing hook snagging waterlogged flesh. He *was* sure about doing this, wasn't he? Jace reached for the letter again before stopping himself. He'd read it enough times to have it memorized. And to know that what he'd written was right. There was no future for a person like him. He knew everyone in this town, more or less, and not once had he heard of an old gay couple enjoying retirement together or elderly lesbians celebrating their fiftieth anniversary. Such things simply didn't happen. Not on TV. Not in real life. So Jace had spent quite a long time trying to figure out what *did* happen to gay people, turning to history for answers.

Oscar Wilde's biography had given him hope. For all its imperfections, the relationship Oscar had with Bosie did resemble love, but Jace concluded those feelings were one-sided at best. Oscar Wilde had died a broken man, far from home, and with no family or a lover at his bedside. Walt Whitman passed away under the care of his housekeeper, not a loving husband. Emperor Hadrian's lover Antinous had drowned in the Nile, either by accident or on purpose. Jace had thought long and hard about that one, wondering if even being loved was enough to avoid this fate. By the end of his days, Hadrian had tried to take his own life many times. Was he chasing after Antinous?

Each gay biography Jace had read told him he wasn't alone— the homosexuality often only alluded to, hidden between the lines. Jace had initially reveled in each discovery. Eventually, all he did was despair. History proved he wasn't the only gay person, but it also assured him that he would die alone.

As he was about to do now. If only someone were with him, some shy and handsome guy from his school, gripping his hand tightly. Their forbidden love would drive them to take this plunge together to the one place where society couldn't tear them apart. But as Jace glanced beyond the lonely bridge, all he saw was a dusty gravel road and his car parked to one side of it, windshield partially obscured by fallen leaves. If he stood out here deliberating any longer, he would freeze to death.

Jace laughed, remembering this was his goal. It was time to go. Seventeen years of a happy life was much better than decades and decades spent searching for the impossible, yearning for what he couldn't have, growing older, sadder, and more bitter with every passing year. Like Antinous, Jace would let the waters take him while he was still young. He believed Antinous did so because love was too painful. What Antinous didn't know was that living without love could hurt even more. Clenching his jaw, Jace placed two flat palms on the rail and swung his legs over.

Gravity did the rest.

Air whipped around his clothing as Jace plunged toward the water much too quickly for his life to flash before his eyes. There wouldn't have been much worthy of seeing anyway: hanging out in the backyard with his sister on long summer nights, laughing and acting up so much that it irritated their parents. Or his father trying to get him interested in cars, Jace covertly yawning when his father ducked beneath the hood to examine the engine. Or his mother and her endless cats that would appear from out of nowhere when she clicked her tongue, eager for food, games, or affection. No, Jace's life hadn't been all that interesting, but in its own boring way, it had been wonderful.

Fuck.

Regret hit Jace the same time the water did. His body had tumbled sideways in the air, giving him newfound respect for those Olympic divers. The river felt solid when Jace smacked into it, forcing the air from his lungs in one painful wheeze. When he tried to breathe again, water poured in, not air. Jace panicked, kicking and waving his arms, hoping to move toward the surface but no longer knowing which way was up. The ache in his lungs intensified into agony. He had thought drowning would be painless and peaceful, the chilled river water luring him into a gentle sleep. Instead his insides felt searing hot.

Jace's head broke the surface. Desperate to gulp air into his lungs, he opened his mouth, heaving out water in a never-ending supply. Finally he coughed. Before he could take a proper breath, his head bobbed under again. Feeling weakened from the cold and lack of air, he fought to keep his head above water. When he did manage to take in air, it was only in tiny gasps. Ears buzzing and limbs stiffening from cold, he turned his face upward to an overcast sky. It would have been nice to see the stars again, one last time.

The buzzing in Jace's ears grew painfully loud, snarling

before ceasing entirely. Then something clamped onto his shoulder. A hand? Maybe. He couldn't feel much of anything now, that numbness he had dreamt of finally taking over. Only when he was spun around did he understand. The side of a boat filled his vision; over the edge of it a heavily wrinkled face twisted up with effort.

"Raise your arms. Come on now! I can't do this alone!"

"Help!" Jace squeaked, his lungs tighter than ever. "Help me!"

"Give me your goddamned hand!"

Jace's brain kicked in. Even though it made him bob dangerously, he stopped paddling with one of his arms just long enough to thrust it in the air. The old man grabbed his wrist, then his forearm as he pulled. Grunting with effort, he managed to get Jace's arm over the boat so he was hanging on at the elbow.

"Now the other one."

The process was repeated, and soon Jace was draped over the boat's edge. A new surge of adrenaline shot through him as he scrambled in an attempt to climb aboard, making the little fishing vessel rock.

"Easy!" the old man shouted. "You'll tip the whole damn boat! Stop your squirming and just breathe."

Jace tried to calm down despite feeling like he was freezing to death. He locked wide eyes with the old man, trying to communicate his despair. But he couldn't speak. The old man was right. He needed to breathe.

"Okay. Good. Okay." The old man rubbed the white scruff on his chin, looking between Jace and the deck. "I'm too old to haul you out. When you're ready, I want you to work your way to the back of the boat. Slowly."

Jace started right away. He feared that if he didn't, his arms would give out and he'd slip back into the river. Bit by bit, he inched his way to the rear of the boat. The entire time, the old man moved with him, walking on his knees and keeping a hand on Jace's jacket collar.

"That's it. You'll have an easier time getting in from back here. Think you can step onto the motor?"

The idea sounded dangerous, but silence meant the engine wasn't running. Jace kicked his leg up a few times until he felt it hit the motor. Then, pulling himself up with his last ounce of strength, he managed to get his foot on top. The water pulled at his clothes as he strained, like the river didn't want to give up the sacrifice it had been offered. Finally, just when he thought he'd never be free, Jace toppled over the edge of the boat and—embarrassingly—fell onto the old man.

There was some grumbled swearing until Jace rolled to the side, but he was too exhausted to apologize. Instead he curled up on his side—gasping, coughing, and shaking. Then the motor kicked into life, buzzing them down the river. The breeze made Jace wince. Just when he thought he couldn't get any colder!

Their trip was mercifully short. He felt the boat's prow slide onto earth and forced himself to sit up, eager to get back on land. The old man was sitting just behind him, hand resting on the motor's tiller. "Think you can climb out on your own?"

Jace nodded.

"Go ahead then. That's my place just over there. We'll get you inside and warmed up."

Jace glanced at the shore, seeing a recreational vehicle parked not far away. Once he stumbled onto land, he made straight for the RV, not looking back until he was at the door. He felt desperate to get inside.

"Move over," the old man said so he could unlock the door, cursing a bit under his breath.

Jace took a good look at him for the first time. He wasn't a tall man, probably five foot eight at best. Of course a lot of people looked short to Jace ever since he had shot up to six foot two. The old man had a prominent beer belly and a head of thinning white hair. Despite having just saved his life, he didn't look particularly friendly. Right now he was jerking his thumb, signaling Jace to get inside.

The interior had the old-man smell that filled his grandpa's workshop, spiced with a touch of fish from the small kitchen corner. In the light of a single lamp, Jace couldn't see much that wasn't practical. A table for dining was covered in newspapers, a half-finished crossword puzzle on top. A small couch curved around this table. Farther back was a bed, the two doors near it probably opening into closets or a toilet.

"What's your name?" the old man asked, shutting the door behind him.

Jace turned toward him but didn't answer. Now that he no

longer feared for his life, he was starting to wonder how much trouble he was in.

"Mine's Bernard," the old man said, thrusting out a hand. "Most people call me Bernie, which I hate."

Jace took his hand and shook it, but still didn't say a word. After a few quick pumps, Bernard pulled away. "Jesus, boy! You're freezing! Strip off your clothes. You won't get any warmer wearing those. You can heat up in the shower."

A hot shower? Jace didn't need encouraging. He took off his jacket and held it awkwardly, water dripping on the floor. Now that he noticed, he was getting water all over the place.

"Sorry," he said, teeth chattering.

"It's fine." Bernard took Jace's jacket and laid it across the table, the newspapers turning dark as they drank in the water. "Just throw it all here. The shower's right behind you. Towels are in there too."

With that, Bernard turned around and took a great interest in the ceiling. Jace kept shooting glances in his direction as he struggled to get off his shoes, then his jeans, but Bernard might as well have been a statue. When Jace was down to his underwear, he opened the door behind him and stepped inside.

The little room was barely bigger than a porta-potty, complete with toilet. At first he thought he chose the wrong door, but then he noticed the showerhead on the wall and the drain in the floor. There was also a sink and mirror to one side. Jace caught sight of himself. His blondish-brown hair clung to his forehead, his face more gaunt than usual. His high cheekbones looked more skeletal than attractive, like death had already gotten a grip on him and wasn't letting go.

Jace found the shower water handle and turned it. Even the cold water that first came out felt warm to him. When it started to steam, his skin stung, but he forced himself to stand beneath the flow until feeling and color returned to his skin. When he shut off the water, he heard a voice shout from the other room.

"Towels are in the drawer!"

Jace pulled at a handle in the wall, a drawer sliding open with bone-dry towels inside. He would have found the entire arrangement clever if the situation wasn't so embarrassing. Or horrible. Jace rubbed at the fog on the mirror and stared at himself. He looked human again, but his blue eyes were haunted, and he knew why. One of his schoolmates had tried killing herself during their freshman year and had been sent to a psychiatric hospital afterwards. Jace struggled to remember if he'd ever seen her again.

No, he might not have ended his life, but he sure had screwed it up. And for what? Despite the revelation that he wasn't ready to check out just yet, he still faced the same dreary future. Now it was likely to get a whole lot uglier. Sighing, Jace wrapped the towel around his waist and left the bathroom.

Bernard was sitting at the small table where Jace's wet clothes had been, except now they were bundled up in a trash bag. On top of this sat his wallet. And the baggied suicide note. The trusty Ziplock seal was no longer green. Had Bernard read his letter? Even worse, Jace's driver's license sat to one side.

"Feel better, Jason?" Bernard said, standing and grabbing a flannel blanket off the couch.

"Most people call me Jace," he replied, "and I actually like that."

The old man grunted, thrusting the blanket at him. "Here. Wrap yourself in this or you'll catch a chill. This RV is colder than a well digger's ass."

Jace took the blanket gratefully, glancing around the interior. "Do you live here?"

"Only on the weekends." Bernard sat back down with a grimace. The expression didn't leave even when he was settled. "What the hell were you playing at, son?"

Jace nodded toward his belongings, in particular the suicide note. "You already know why."

"Like hell I do! It's the letter I don't understand. What sort of stupid reason is that for wanting to kill yourself?"

Jace's chin jutted out. "I'm gay. That's not reason enough?"

"No," Bernard spat, "it isn't. And I wasn't referring to that. You're happy now but worry you won't be one day? Jesus, man! At least wait until you're miserable before you go leaping off a bridge. And next time choose one that's taller!"

Jace laughed. He couldn't help it. The entire evening had been insane. Part of him wondered if he *had* succeeded in killing himself and ended up in this strange purgatory.

"You've lost your mind," Bernard said, waving a hand dismissively.

"I think maybe I have," Jace admitted.

"Well, at least I know you won't be trying that again soon. The look on your face as you were crying for help convinced me of that." Bernard glared at him. "Of course you damn near killed me instead. I almost had a heart attack!"

"Sorry," Jace said. "And thank you."

Bernard sniffed and then nodded. "Have a seat. I'd offer you a drink if you were older."

Jace sat, readjusting the blanket around his shoulders. Unable to make eye contact, he stared at his belongings instead. "Are you going to tell my parents?"

Bernard was quiet a moment. "I don't know. Seems to me you have a lot of problems you need to talk over with them."

"I will." Jace raised his head. "But I'll do that on my own."

Bernard sized him up. "You better. Maybe they can talk some sense into you. There's a lot worse that can happen to a man than him ending up alone."

"I know," Jace said sheepishly.

"You don't," Bernard said, "and that's not your fault either. But you'll learn. Eventually."

"I'm not completely clueless," Jace said. "I've read plenty of history books. Biographies too. I know what can happen to a person."

"Reading about something and living through it are two different things." Bernard peered at him. "No, I can guess the worst problem you face."

"Oh really?"

"Yup. Free time. You know that saying about how idle hands are the devil's tools?"

"Yeah."

"Well, I don't believe in any devil, but there's plenty of truth to that saying. No man is happy for long when he doesn't have work to occupy his time and mind. Without a purpose, a man doesn't have any sense of worth. You seem to think your life is worthless or you wouldn't have tried throwing it away."

"I go to school," Jace said. "That keeps me busy."

Bernard crossed his arms over his chest. "If that were enough, I wouldn't have had to drag your ass out of the river tonight. You able to work nights?"

"If I wanted to."

"You want a job?"

"Doing what?" Jace asked. "Fishing?"

Bernard scoffed. "This is my hobby, not my livelihood."

The pieces came together. "Wait, you're *the* Bernie! As in Bernie's Stop and Shop." Jace made him sound like some kind of celebrity, but in a small town like this one, owning the local gas station was halfway there.

"I could use another man on the night shift. Not the whole thing. Not at your age, but you'd come in after dinner and be done before bedtime."

Jace blinked and wondered if the night could get any weirder. "Why?"

"I told you why. If you expect me not to tell your parents, then I should at least keep my eye on you. Besides—" Bernard stopped and shook his head, then scowled hard at the soaked crossword puzzle.

"Okay," Jace said, if only to bring him out of the sudden mood change. "If you really think it'll help, I'll give it a shot. Uh, I'll get paid, right?"

Bernard looked up at him incredulously and cracked a grin. "Well, I did save your life. Surely that's worth a week's pay. You'll have to wear that blanket home too, since I don't have a dryer here. That's not free either."

"You can have the blanket back later," Jace said, "and as you know, I already consider my life worthless. The way I see it, that makes us even."

Bernard barked laughter. "Very well. Work hard, and I'll see you get paid. Deal?"

Jace nodded. What did he have to lose?

"Deal."

Jace pulled into his neighborhood, thankful for once that it was sleepy, dark, and quiet. That could describe all of Warrensburg, Missouri. A visiting cousin had once expressed excitement that Warrensburg was a college town, throwing out terms like "liberal paradise" and "cultural oasis." That enthusiasm soon diminished when she actually visited. Jace figured that college life here wasn't so different than grade school had been or high school was. Ancient brick buildings, worn-out wooden desks, and teachers old enough to remember when the schools and equipment had been new. Everything in Warrensburg felt old and tired to Jace. Only the nights had potential, when it was too dark to see the truth and still possible to imagine anything.

Right now, Jace was fervently imagining himself getting caught sneaking back inside. His clothes were still soaked and tied up in the trash bag, looking like a sad black pumpkin on his passenger seat. All he had on was the blanket Bernard had given him, burnt orange in color. Another downside to being tall was that the fabric didn't cover nearly as much of him as he'd like. Draped in the blanket, Jace had felt like a Hare Krishna when walking back to his car, carefully driving the speed limit the whole way home so he wouldn't have to explain himself to a bored police officer.

"Evenin' officer! Just driving around naked, except for this oversized washcloth. I do this every Saturday night. Don't you?"

Now he turned off the headlights before pulling into the driveway of his family's home. After killing the engine, he checked the windows one by one. The house was mostly dark, except for a dim light in the kitchen his mother always left on. Jace considered entering through the front door and dashing to his room, but if his mom or dad came downstairs for a midnight snack...

No, Michelle's room was his best bet. Jace eyed the trash bag of soaked clothes but decided to leave it behind. He needed both his hands on the blanket unless he wanted to add 'unintentional flasher' to the night's list of transgressions. Closing the car door as quietly as possible, he hurried across the lawn to the side of the house.

Jace's bedroom was on the top floor, down the hall from his parents. His sister Michelle had a lot more privacy. Down one set of stairs to the kitchen and living room, and down another flight to the family room, Michelle's bedroom was tucked away in a corner of the house. Most of it was underground, except for two high-set windows. Jace knew for a fact these windows acted as an entrance and an exit—sometimes for Michelle, sometimes for her boyfriends.

Jace squatted, adjusted the blanket to make sure his junk wasn't showing, and tapped on the window. The light inside the bedroom turned off before the window slid open.

"Brett!" Michelle said, grinning while peering into the dark. "You're so bad!"

"It's me, stupid!" Jace hissed.

Michelle's smile faltered. "Ew!"

"Ew, indeed. Now let me in."

"What are you doing out there?" Michelle squinted. "And what are you wearing?"

"I'll explain later. Just get out of my way. And turn around."

"What? Why?"

"Because I'm half-naked."

"Ugh!" Michelle retreated into the dark.

When Jace hopped into the room, she had her back to the window, hands over her eyes. He shook his head ruefully, turning on the bedside lamp. "I said half-naked. Not naked."

Michelle spun around, peering between her fingers before she dropped her hands and laughed. She kept laughing while Jace glared at her. Michelle was a year younger than he was, and with her tall build and blondish-brown hair, many people mistook them for fraternal twins. They often told people they were. Michelle had even talked Jace into growing out his hair. It wasn't as long as hers, not yet reaching his shoulders. Michelle's tumbled halfway down her back, but him having longer hair did help solidify the illusion.

Not only did they look alike, but they were kindred spirits as well. They might not share every hobby and interest, but they got along like best friends. Other siblings they knew were in constant competition with each other or always squabbling. Not them. He and Michelle were as close as could be.

"What's her name?" Michelle asked, "and what did you do to end up like this? Did her boyfriend chase you off? Oh god, it's not a married woman, is it?"

Jace swallowed. Okay, so maybe their closeness didn't extend to every area of their lives. "Why would Brett be at your window?" he asked, changing subjects. "I thought you two broke up."

"We did." Michelle studied him. "God, you're so naïve. And here I thought you finally had a girlfriend." She grinned again. "Do you?"

"No. I was out for a hike and was crossing a river. There was this log, like a fallen tree, and I slipped and fell into the water."

Michelle's eyebrows rose. "And then you hit your head and became a shitty liar. What really happened? Where'd you get that blanket?"

Jace sighed. "Can you just get me some clothes from upstairs? Please?"

"And then you'll tell me the truth?" Michelle looked disappointed.

He didn't blame her. Normally they were honest with each other. He supposed that was all he could be now. "I don't want to tell you." Jace swallowed. "It's embarrassing. And stupid."

Now Michelle looked concerned. "Are you okay?"

"Yeah. I'm fine." Jace pulled the blanket tighter around himself. "I'll tell you," he said. "Just not now. I need time."

"For what?"

"To figure out how to say it."

Michelle studied him, looking for any hint of the truth. "I'll be right back," she said finally, hurrying from the room.

Jace sat on the edge of the bed and sighed. She loved him. His parents did too. He didn't doubt it in the slightest. That was the problem. The worst thing about being loved is how vulnerable it makes you. If coming out made that love falter… Jace couldn't bear the thought. For a fleeting moment, he wished he had succeeded, had shrugged off Bernard's grip and allowed himself to sink into the Blackwater River.

"Fashion time," Michelle said, causing him to jump. She had an old pair of jeans and a T-shirt draped over one arm. "I was tempted to bring that horrible suit Mom bought you for their anniversary."

Jace grimaced. "My skin itches just thinking about it."

"Which you would deserve," Michelle said with menace. "Lying to your own sister!"

"I know," Jace said, taking the clothes. "I suck. Sorry."

Michelle gave a half-hearted shrug. "I didn't bring any underwear. Digging through that drawer would have been gross."

"It's all right," Jace said, keeping his eyes on the clothes. "I just want to put these on and go up to bed." He glanced over at her to make sure she understood. There wouldn't be any big discussions tonight.

Michelle's room had its own bathroom, which he ducked

into to get changed. Jace couldn't even look at himself in the mirror as he dressed, the bitter taste of guilt in his mouth. Once he was done, he said a quick goodnight to his sister and headed upstairs. He was almost to his room when his mother surprised him in the hall.

"Jace! I didn't hear you come in!"

Dressed in a nightgown, clutching the front closed with one hand, she looked happy to see him. Was it a mother's instinct that kept her up? Had she felt her son nearly take his own life?

"Just got in," he mumbled.

With her free hand, his mother toyed with the braid of gray hair that hung over one shoulder, a dead giveaway that she was worried. "Did you have fun?"

"Yeah!" Jace said, trying to sound chipper. "Just went for a drive. You know how I love that. Probably would have bored anyone else to tears."

"Okay." His mother looked somewhat relieved. "As long as you're fine."

He nodded. "I am. I love you."

"I love you too. Sweet dreams."

Jace kept the smile plastered on his face until his bedroom door was shut behind him. Then he exhaled. Leaving the light off, he threw himself across his bed. What now? Deciding to kill himself meant not having to make decisions about the future. Now what was there to look forward to? A part-time job with a grumpy old man? Seeing the hurt on his sister's face when she learned the truth? A lifetime spent alone while he watched everyone his age fall in love and build a family?

Jace growled in frustration and shoved himself up and out of bed. He walked to the window, looked out at the sleepy suburb. He knew every neighbor, every married couple residing on this street. Some of the older people had lost their spouses, but even they had children and grandchildren to help fill the void. Jace looked at the sky, wishing he could see the horizon, see a town or city beyond this one. Somewhere out there, no matter how far away, had to be someone else like him. Someone just for him, his own Bosie or Antinous.

Clenching his jaw, Jace swore an oath to find him. No matter what he had to do, how far he had to search, he would find that person. Together, maybe they could prove the history books wrong.

Chapter Two

Jace stumbled to the breakfast table wearing a pair of pajama bottoms and the same T-shirt his sister had picked out for him the night before. Michelle was already there, stabbing at a bowl of cereal. Next to her, their father thumbed through a copy of *Reader's Digest*, ignoring his eggs and toast. The number of people who mistook Michelle for his twin was trivial compared to the number who thought Jace's parents were his grandparents. His father was bald down the middle of his head, white hair combed over from the sides to compensate. Thick glasses perched on the end of his nose, but he looked over them instead of through them to read.

"Fried egg?" his mother asked from the stove.

"No thanks," Jace said, heading for the cabinet with the cereal bowls.

His mother turned back to the pan. Only a year younger than her husband, Serena had tried for years to have children until moving to Missouri. Here the family doctor—fresh out of a university—convinced her to give *in vitro* fertilization a try. Obviously it had worked. Michelle hated being a test-tube baby, but Jace loved it and told anyone who would listen. The other kids at school would look at him like he was a clone or a mad scientist's experiment, which always cracked him up.

"What did you do last night?" his father asked as Jace sat.

"Nothing."

His father licked his finger and turned a page. "That's not what I heard."

Jace glanced over at Michelle, who gave a barely perceptible shake of her head. She hadn't betrayed him. "I just went for a drive, that's all."

"Oh, *that's all*."

"Bob," Jace's mother said warningly.

"Serena," he shot back. "We talked about this last night. He's putting miles on the car for no good reason."

Jace rolled his eyes and shoved cereal into his mouth.

"A car," Bob continued, setting down the magazine, "that you have to share with your sister. That's not fair to her, is it?"

"I don't care if he goes driving," Michelle said.

Their father frowned.

"What?" she replied. "You gave us that car and said it was our responsibility. Is it or isn't it?"

"It is, but I expected you to actually *be* responsible with it." Bob picked up his *Reader's Digest* again. After a moment of silence, he said, "The ice caps are melting. Pretty soon we'll all be living in swimming pools."

Just like that, the topic was over. Jace rolled his eyes at his sister. Then they both smirked. Neither of their parents were big on discipline. Their father doled out the occasional guilt trip, and their mother kept them in line with her love. Or by making them feel like they were still toddlers. Case in point: A plate of fried eggs was placed next to Jace's cereal bowl.

"You're a growing boy," his mother explained.

"Don't forget to burp him when he's done eating," Michelle murmured.

Jace moodily worked his way through the cereal, letting the eggs get cold in protest, but eventually he ate those too. He hated being treated like he was a child and took some delight in having very grown-up news to share.

"I got a job," he announced.

"What?" His father turned his thick lenses on him again. "Why would you do that when I've been asking you to work at the store for years?"

"The store" referred to either of the dry cleaning locations that his father owned. One catered to the university, the other to the general public. From what his mother said, they could easily sell the stores and retire, but for now his father still enjoyed running the business.

"You always say I should be independent," Jace countered.

His father lifted a wiry eyebrow. "I certainly have not!"

"No," Serena chimed in, "that's definitely not something your father would say. Where is this new job?"

"At Bernie's. I'll be working part-time after school."

"You'll be working for Bernie Hudson?" his father asked.

Jace shrugged. "I guess so."

Now his father appeared smug. "Well, Bernie is a client of mine, so I always make sure to fuel up at his place. I even buy my whisky there. I guess we'll be seeing plenty more of each other!"

His father cackled as Jace cleared the table and pretended

his family didn't exist. And to think he had felt so soppy toward them last night! Jace rinsed the dishes and left them in the sink, retreating upstairs for some quiet time and then a shower. He hated small towns. Of course Bernard knew his father! The worst part was that Bernard might say something to his parents. Unless he kept his part of the bargain. Jace would keep his, being a good little worker as long as his suicide attempt stayed secret.

Once clean and dressed, Jace headed out on foot. Today was his sister's turn to have the car, and he knew his father would be hounding him about the new job. Or his dream of Jace taking over the family business one day. Fat chance! The last thing Jace wanted was to be trapped in Warrensburg the rest of his life. As soon as he graduated from high school, he'd choose a college somewhere far away and never look back.

For now, Greg's place would be his only sanctuary. Jace didn't have far to walk. Behind his family's house, the land sloped downward into a small valley. No fence separated their yard from the property directly behind theirs, a house situated atop the ascending slope. This was the home of the Trouts, close family friends. Greg had been there for every one of Jace's birthdays and vice versa, as far back as he could remember. Not that they had much in common. During childhood, living nearby is enough to seal a friendship, but Jace would have liked Greg regardless. They'd had their fallings out over the years, but nothing serious.

Jace pounded on the back patio door that led to the living room, where he knew Greg would be watching one of the many action films constantly on repeat. Luckily, Jace wouldn't have to suffer through another viewing of *Rambo III* today. Greg had gotten an archery set for his birthday—their main diversion as of late.

Once Greg put on his shoes, they headed down the valley toward the small lake that nestled there. They walked around its edge and entered the woods, where they had nailed a target to a tree.

"You wanna go first?" Greg asked.

"Sure."

"Too bad!" Greg snickered and unsheathed an arrow from the homemade quiver he wore on his back. That he wasn't shirtless and wearing a red bandana like Rambo was a small miracle. As Jace watched Greg's arm muscles tense and flex with the effort of pulling the bow string back, the image was annoyingly erotic. Jesus, he needed to get laid!

Greg unleashed a set of arrows, cussing when each one hit the target, no matter the result. "Shit!" meant his aim was off. "Fuck yeah!" indicated that he had struck near the center. All around them leaves fell as squirrels scampered away, just in case they became a more interesting target.

"What did you get up to last night?" Greg asked.

"Nothing," Jace said, knowing his best friend wasn't prying but looking for an excuse to brag.

"I had Angie over," Greg said, walking to the target to pull his arrows free. "Watched some movies up in my room. Mom was drinking wine and didn't care for once, thank god."

"Which movie did you guys watch?"

Greg spared him a glance that said he wasn't making sense. Jace was used to those. "Some stupid chick flick. The point is, she let me feel her up. *And* down."

"Wow!" Jace said, feeling a little uncomfortable, but he managed to match Greg's leering grin as the bow was shoved into his hands. "Lucky you."

"Yeah." Greg watched him shoot the first arrow. "She has a sister. A couple of years younger than us, but she has a birthday coming up. Not ideal, but you know."

Jace did know. He was perpetually single, which was starting to draw attention. A single freshman or sophomore was one thing, but junior and senior year brought added pressures. Like prom. No doubt Greg would have a date, even if it wasn't Angie by then. Greg always had a girlfriend these days. And like their birthdays or first days of school, the Trouts and Holdens would come together, their parents nudging each other, smiling, and taking photos of their sons in rented tuxedos. If Greg had a prom date and Jace didn't, eyebrows would be raised and might not ever come down again.

"Is her sister pretty?" Jace asked, buying for time. He didn't need to listen to Greg's response because he didn't care. This sort of pressure made him sick to his stomach. Enough that he often considered telling everyone the truth. Not having to pretend anymore, to fake interest in the big-boobed costars of Greg's action movies, or flirt ineptly with his sister's friends—all of that would go away if he just told the truth. Jace only wished he had some way of knowing what everyone's reaction would be ahead of time. He supposed he could find out, as long as he was clever about it.

Jace made small talk while they took turns shooting arrows, putting distance between the discussion of relationships. "So I've been reading this book about Leonardo da Vinci," he said eventually.

"Oh yeah? Any good?"

Jace knew that Greg couldn't care less, but it was the job of any good friend to feign interest. Jace faked enthusiasm every time Hulk Hogan won another wrestling belt, and Greg listened with practiced attention when Jace felt like talking about historical figures.

"Yeah. Pretty good. A little weird though." Jace made a face. "The author thinks that da Vinci was gay. I guess he was accused of sodomy once and—"

"Sodomy?" Greg smirked. "You mean butt sex?"

"Yeah." Jace chuckled and cocked an arrow. "He also had a male pupil, Salaì, and there seemed to be something going on there too."

"Huh." Greg watched the arrow strike the target. "Well, that explains why the Mona Lisa is so ugly."

"What?"

"I mean, if da Vinci dug chicks, he would have found someone prettier to paint." Greg thought for a moment. "That's a weird thing to read in a history book."

"Yeah." Jace laughed, mostly because he was nervous. "Then again, gay people have always been around. That sort of makes it normal."

Greg took the bow from Jace and went to retrieve the arrows. "I wouldn't say *normal*. Personally, I think they should all be shipped off to an island somewhere."

Jace's stomach sank. Suddenly he was very glad that Greg was facing away. "Really?"

"Yeah." Greg returned to Jace's side and fired off a few arrows. "You know," he said thoughtfully, "I have an aunt who's a lesbian."

"You do? Have I ever met her?"

Greg shook his head. "Don't think so. We don't see her much. She lives out in California with her girlfriend."

"Oh." God how Jace would love to have a gay uncle! That would show him exactly how the family would react, and if not positively, would give him a place to go. "So do you wish she'd been shipped off to an island?"

Greg fumbled his shot, the arrow burying itself in the ground. "No! Jesus, dude! She's my aunt!"

"But you said—"

"I mean the gay guys. I'm okay with lesbians. It's kind of hot. Not my aunt, of course, but you know."

This was yet another mystery to Jace, as were Greg's double standards. "So what do you have against gay guys?"

Greg's bow arm went slack. "Nothing. I just don't want them looking at me like I'm a piece of meat."

The funny thing was, Jace never did look at Greg like that. Not usually, which was ironic since Greg was a good-looking guy. The consummate Eagle Scout, Greg had returned from each Boy Scout camping trip tanner and more toned than before. His brown hair was honey-colored from so much sun, his arms and legs thick from scaling up trees or whatever the hell Boy Scouts got up to. Greg laughed a lot too, which made it hard to stay in a bad mood around him. They hadn't been swimming together this year, but Jace could imagine how impressive Greg's body had become, the muscles more defined, maybe even a little hair sprouting on his chest.

"Yeah," Greg said. "Exactly like that. Stop it, dude! You're creeping me out!"

Greg laughed and punched him playfully on the arm. Jace made sure to laugh back, to chuckle long and hard in support of it being a clever joke and nothing more. But he found, as they continued their target practice, that he couldn't let the subject drop. That his best friend was such a homophobe made him sad. And a little angry.

"So basically, because you're worried a bunch of gay guys will have the hots for you, you think they should all be sent to an island to die."

Greg winced. "That's a little harsh. I didn't say anything about killing them."

"What then? They just take a lifelong vacation to some tropical island?"

"Sure." Greg shrugged. "Let them all hang out there and be

gay together. We'll build a nice resort for them, maybe a golf course. Do gay people play golf?"

"No idea," Jace said. "So how will they survive on this island of yours?"

"They'll live off the island's bounty," Greg said with surprising flourish. "I'm sure there will be plenty of banana trees." Greg nudged him while grinning. "Know what I mean? A bunch of gay guys all snacking on bananas?"

Jace fought down a grin. "Yeah, I get it. Maybe you can send shipments of fat juicy sausages there as well."

Greg guffawed, Jace soon joining him. Laughing about his sexuality felt better than constantly stressing over it, and he supposed Greg's reaction could have been worse. Far from ideal, but not terrible. Regardless, Jace wouldn't be coming out any time soon.

"You piece of shit!"

Michelle stood in the doorway to Jace's room, cheeks red and covered in tears. In one hand she held a trash bag full of wet clothes. In the other she held a letter. And it was open.

Jace's stomach sank. The day had been so nice! After his tense conversation with Greg, they had gone for a hike and later went back to Greg's place for a movie. For the first time in weeks, Jace had felt almost normal. And now—

"Shut the door," Jace whispered. "Please."

His sister looked like she was about to explode, but she clenched her jaw, dropped the trash bag on the floor, and quietly shut the door. When she turned around, her face was crimson and her voice came out as a growl.

"How could you do this to us?" she hissed, holding up the letter.

Jace sighed, almost feeling a mad sort of relief. Now she knew. And she would tell his parents and they would tell everyone. She knew he was gay, and she was furious at him because of it, but at least he wouldn't be hiding or lying anymore.

"What the hell is wrong with you?" Michelle said, stomping over and throwing the letter at him. When it fluttered harmlessly to the ground, she slapped at his chest. Her eyes looked crazy, her teeth grinding together. Jace hadn't expected this much hate!

"It's who I am," Jace said. "I'm gay. I can't help it."

His sister's eyes widened in shock. "Jace, I couldn't care less who you sleep with! You tried—" Michelle's face crumpled and she began sobbing.

Jace moved toward her, tentatively placing a hand on her shoulder, worried she'd explode again. When she didn't, he took her into his arms and let her cry. What he really wanted to do was question her. Had she meant what she said? Did it really not matter to her? Then he felt a surge of guilt, because he finally understood what she was upset about.

"It was a dumb mistake," Jace murmured. "I regretted it the second I tried."

"Suicide!" Michelle pushed away from him. "You would have killed us! Do you understand that? Mom and Dad are old. They wouldn't survive the shock, and as for me—" Michelle shook her head, huffing a few times to get herself under control. "I can't even talk about it. I can't! It's just too fucked up. If you ever think of doing that again, just remember that you're killing us too."

"Okay!" Jace said. "I'm sorry!"

Michelle wiped her eyes and went to sit on the edge of the bed. She picked up the letter on the way, shaking her head at it. "Why didn't you tell me?"

"About the gay thing?" Jace swallowed. "I can't stand the idea of losing you guys either."

Michelle looked at him like he was being silly. "We love you, stupid. Do you think something like this matters to us?"

"I don't know." Jace went to sit next to her. "I really don't."

His sister exhaled and leaned toward him, their shoulders touching. "Gay or straight, I love you. You're my brother and that will never change. Why would you ever think otherwise?"

Jace shrugged. "Remember when I told you about Elton John?"

"You mean when he came out?"

"Yeah. You said 'ew,' like it was disgusting."

"That's because Elton John looks like the Pillsbury Doughboy wearing a toupee. The idea of him sleeping with anyone grosses me out."

"Fair enough."

"But I still love his music," Michelle continued. "I wouldn't if I had a problem with gay people."

"Okay."

"Mom and Dad won't mind either. I promise." Michelle nudged him. "You have no idea how often Mom has asked me about you."

"About me being gay?"

His sister nodded.

"Am I that obvious?"

"You don't lisp or anything but come on! You're seventeen years old, never had a girlfriend, and just look at you!"

Jace blinked. "What?"

"Ugh. You're going to make me say it, aren't you?" Michelle batted her eyes. "Fine. My big brother has grown up so pretty!"

Jace chuckled. "You think so?"

"Oh, go look in a mirror. Anyway, Mom isn't going to be shocked. At least I don't think so. Dad maybe, but he'll be all right. You've got nothing to worry about."

"Will you tell them for me?"

Michelle shrugged. "If you want. Or we can do it together."

"I'm a big wimp, aren't I?"

"Kind of." Michelle grew somber. "You have to promise me something. If you ever feel suicidal, come talk to me."

"I won't ever try killing myself again. Seriously."

"But just in case you feel tempted, promise you'll talk to me."

"Okay." Jace put his arm around her. "Don't worry, I'm fine now. Great, actually. You have no idea how relieved this makes me feel."

"Does anyone else know?" Michelle asked. "Does Greg?"

Jace shook his head. "No. I think he's a homophobe. A well-meaning homophobe, maybe. You're the first to know."

"Oh. I thought you might have someone. I still don't get why you showed up in a blanket last night."

Jace took a deep breath and explained everything about his ill-conceived suicide attempt and the strange events that followed it. When he was finished, Michelle digested his words for a moment.

"So basically you jumped off a bridge and ended up getting a job."

"Yup!"

Michelle shook her head. "Sounds about normal for you." She stared at the carpet, thinking for a moment. "So if you never had a boyfriend, how do you know you're gay?"

"Same way that you know you're straight, I guess. Did you have to kiss a guy before you knew you wanted to?"

"God no! Remember my crush on Michael Jackson?"

Jace laughed. "Exactly. And the one time I did kiss a girl, it didn't do anything for me."

Michelle crinkled her nose. "That's right. I made you play spin-the-bottle with my friends, and you ended up kissing Sheila."

"All I remember is that she smelled like cabbage."

"She always did." Michelle turned to him with an expression of exaggerated concern. "Do you think her cabbage kiss turned you gay?"

Jace nodded. "Probably. It's all your fault."

Michelle sighed. "Well, there's no turning back now. I have a gay brother, and he's still hopelessly single."

"Don't remind me."

"Hey, you think this old guy has the hots for you?"

"Bernard?" Jace grimaced. "Why would you say that?"

"Well, he did pull you from the river and then offered you a job. That's not exactly normal."

He considered this and sighed. "Great, my first boyfriend and he's eighty years old."

Jace sat in the back room of Bernie's Stop and Shop, trying to fight down a case of the jitters. He wasn't used to sitting still. At least not for two hours in a row. So far all Bernard had wanted to do was talk, or be talked to. As soon as Jace had shown up for work, Bernard walked him through a storage area lined by cardboard boxes, familiar junk food logos printed on each side. In a back corner, fenced off by walls made of these boxes, was a desk.

For the first hour, Jace sat on one side of the desk and was grilled with questions. Bernard wanted to know how Jace did at school and what his home life was like. He mentioned knowing Jace's parents, but made no threat to tell them about the other night. Bernard seemed more interested in assessing how he was doing. Jace did his best to make all his answers sound cheerful and optimistic.

Then Bernard really started talking, apparently determined to tell Jace his life story. Considering how old he was, the entire night could pass in this fashion. Jace tried to pay close attention and nod or laugh at all the right places, but in the back of his mind, he wondered if this was a date. Not that he could honestly picture being with someone so ancient, but there were always stories of old rich guys marrying twenty-year-olds. Maybe this was the small town equivalent.

"Best days of my life, the Navy," Bernard was saying. "Hard work, but you also make lifelong friends. I'm still in touch with most of my shipmates, those who are still alive. There's a reunion every year, and seeing them is like being twenty-one and on shore leave again." He chuckled to himself before looking wistful. "My son was in the Marines. You think he'd be eager to follow in his daddy's footsteps, but Brian can out-stubborn a mule."

Son? Okay, so that was one strike against Bernard being gay, although it didn't count him out. Maybe he'd had a wife and kids before coming to terms with himself.

Bernard nodded at Jace. "You ever consider joining the service?"

"Yeah," he said, "but only as a way of escaping this town."

"Don't care for Warrensburg?"

Jace shrugged. "I want to see more."

Bernard grunted. "Good for you. A young person should see the world. No need to put down roots just yet. The Navy can give you an excellent start. You'll see more continents and countries than most men ever do."

"Actually, I was thinking of going to college."

"I thought you said you wanted to leave?"

"I do. I won't be going to CMSU."

Bernard raised an eyebrow. "You have a college in your hometown and you won't be going to it? I'd love to see the faces of your folks when you explain that to them. You know how much out-of-state tuition costs? And housing. It won't be cheap!"

Jace smiled. "Then it's a good thing I have a job."

"Fair enough!" Bernard pushed himself up and out of his chair with a groan or two. "All right. Time to show you the store."

The main area of Bernie's looked like any other gas station. There was the front counter, manned by a middle-aged guy named Dan who didn't seem very friendly. Then there were the miniature grocery store aisles, stocked with anything salty, sweet, and unhealthy. "You won't have to worry much about these," Bernard explained. "I take care of restocking when I do inventory, but if you get a bunch of stoners who buy up all the Doritos, just duck in back and grab a few more bags. Mostly I want you out here and aware."

The back wall of the store was made of refrigerators with glass doors. Aside from ice cream and some frozen food, the fridges mostly held drinks. "You won't be selling any beer. Let Dan do that, or whoever you're working with that night. I won't schedule you alone for that reason. Cigarettes too. If someone comes in here wanting booze and smokes and your coworker is out on break, they'll just have to wait or go without. You don't smoke, do you?"

Jace shook his head, withering under Bernard's stare until they moved on. Of course he had smoked before. Michelle liked it more than he did, depending on who she was dating. If the guy was a smoker, so was she. At least when she could get away with it. Jace didn't see the appeal, but he'd tried a few times just to be sure.

Next Bernard led him to the fountain drinks. "Welcome to your own personal Hell. I call this area the mess—not out of nostalgia for my Navy days, but because it's always a goddamn mess. You'll have to wipe up over here every ten minutes. People always try to fill their cups to the brim and end up spilling. Then there's the nacho cheese over here, and the microwave, which is always splattered with meat shrapnel. You'll be waging a never-ending war against people who don't give a shit."

As bad as Bernard made it sound, Jace felt he could handle it. He was shown how to change out the drink syrup when it was running low. Then Jace spent the rest of the night standing behind Dan, learning how to work the cash register. His first impression was right. Dan was mean and impatient, making Jace wish Bernard was doing the training, but he had retreated back to his office.

Jace was on break, standing out front and getting some fresh air, when Bernard came outside.

"Heading home now," he said. "You'll be okay?"

"Yeah," Jace answered, feeling that Bernard meant more than just the job. The old man had a hard shell, but he obviously cared. Maybe Michelle was right. Time to go fishing for some info. "Anyone you're heading home to?"

"Nope, just my dog Maxie."

Ah ha!

"Oh, and my wife," Bernard added with a wink. "Almost forgot about her. I keep trying, but she always finds ways of reminding me she's still around."

From the way Bernard smiled, this was lighthearted humor. There wasn't any animosity in his voice. In fact, his happy expression remained as he got in his car and drove away. Not gay, then. Jace's shoulders drooped. He wasn't interested in Bernard, of course, but it would have been nice to have someone to talk to. Someone to make the world feel a little less lonely.

"That seemed to go well," Jace said.

He was lying next to Michelle on her bed, staring up at posters on the ceiling that hadn't changed since she was fourteen: *The Cure, Sixteen Candles, Depeche Mode,* and one of Corey Haim looking sad and vulnerable. That had been Jace's favorite. Sometimes he had snuck into her room just to take a peek at it, but now Corey looked too young. Maybe he should buy her a newer poster of him. Hell, now that his parents knew the truth, he could put it on his own ceiling.

"Dad didn't say a word," Michelle pointed out. "That was nice. You should have come out sooner."

"Do you think he's upset?"

"A little. I don't think he knew what to say. Like he was worried about saying the wrong thing."

"I hope so." Jace sighed. "Mom looked surprised. I thought you said she knew."

"Yeah, that was weird. She asked me if you were gay plenty of times before." Michelle thought about it a moment. "I guess she wasn't sure, but she's going to be okay. How many times did she say she loves you?"

"About a million." Jace laughed. "Like she developed a nervous tick or something."

"She just wants to make sure you know." Michelle elbowed him. "Probably so you don't do something stupid like try to kill yourself."

Jace had kept that from his parents. They had enough to think about. He didn't want them or anyone else to ever know. He had even burned the suicide note so there wasn't any chance of it being found again.

"Now that you're out, you can start dating."

"I wish it was that easy," Jace replied.

"What kind of guy would you want? If you could design the perfect guy, who would it be?"

The idea seemed so impossible, so unlikely, that Jace struggled to answer. "I don't know."

"I want a guy who's obsessed with me. Like a stalker." Michelle giggled. "I want him to be so enamored with me that he feels he can't breathe unless he kisses me every hour. I wouldn't be into him though. Not at first. But one night he would climb through my window and I'd give into his passion—"

"Spare me the details," Jace pleaded.

"Your loss. Anyway, after our night together, I would finally feel his love—in more than one way."

Jace groaned.

"Then I'd let him have my heart." Michelle pointed to a *21 Jump Street* poster. "And he'd look just like Johnny Depp."

"Of course he would." Jace considered her fantasy. It didn't appeal to him at all, which made it easier to come up with his own answer. "I'd want my guy to be my friend. Someone I know really well and am comfortable with. I wouldn't even know I was interested until one day when I just sort of noticed him. Like seeing him for the first time."

Michelle rolled over on her side to face him. "That happens," she said. "People are friends growing up until suddenly it changes one day."

"Yeah." Jace nodded. "I'd want him to be my best friend."

Michelle was quiet before she asked, "Do you have a crush on Greg?"

"What?" Jace looked over at her. "No! At least, I don't think so."

"Hm, maybe you just need to 'see him for the first time,'" she said dramatically.

Jace laughed before grabbing a pillow and thwacking her with it. "At least I'm not deluded enough to think Johnny Depp is obsessed with me."

"It's not actually Johnny Depp. My lover just *looks* like him, that's all."

"Oh, right. Well, he'll have to wait in line behind all your other boyfriends."

Michelle smirked. "Jealous?"

"Totally. One hundred percent."

"Don't be," Michelle said softly. "You'll find someone. Just give it time."

Jace looked longingly at all the beautiful faces staring down at him and hoped with all his being that she was right.

Chapter Three

"I don't know why Bernie hired you," Dan sneered.

That's all Dan ever did. He sneered at customers, he sneered at Bernard behind his back, and when it came to Jace, he was on a sneering marathon. A shame, because Jace was starting to agree with Bernard: Keeping busy *did* make him happier. The last couple of weeks had been too full for him to get angsty about anything. If Jace wasn't at school or working, he was hanging out with Michelle or Greg. That left no time to feel mopey about his lack of a love life.

Getting his first paycheck was nice too. The amount wasn't much, but it was all his. He could blow it on anything he wanted without having to answer to his parents. So far he had taken Michelle out to eat and Greg out to a movie, spending most of the rest on a pair of overpriced sunglasses he felt made him look older.

Maybe this was his future. No kids, no loving partner, but tons and tons of cash. Jace could compensate for his loneliness by climbing corporate ladders and making money hand over fist. Hard to feel sorry for yourself when you're driving around in a Jaguar. Of course that was all still far away. Humble beginnings and all that. Jace tuned back into Dan's rant.

"I never needed help before, and if anything, Bernie comes around *more* now that you're here. That's stupid, because now there are two of you hanging around doing nothing."

Except it was Dan who stood around picking his nose, literally, until a customer came in. Jace was the only one to clean up spills, put abandoned candy back where it belonged, or wipe out the microwave. He was happy to since it meant being farther away from his coworker. Speaking of which, Jace headed over to the drink station to restock the cups.

While he was doing so, a chime rang, signaling a customer had walked through the door. From the nasal voice that rang out, he didn't need to turn around to see who it was. Dan had a girlfriend. Jace didn't know her name, had never said a single word to her. All he knew was that she and Dan were a match made in Heaven. While Dan sneered at him, she pulled back her lips at Jace, as if he were a feces-covered weasel or something. In contrast, when Dan and this woman looked at each other, they became repulsively affectionate.

Jace tended to stay out of the way when they were together, like he did now, keeping busy until Dan came over to him with an almost friendly expression. Jace sighed inwardly. He knew what was coming.

"Hey, champ," Dan said. "Cover for me, okay?"

"Fine," Jace said, glancing over at the clock. "Don't be long. My shift ends in half an hour."

Dan nodded, already having turned away before Jace had finished speaking. At least his work day would end on a positive note. Jace moved behind the counter, happy to be on his own. He helped the few customers who came in, but soon he began staring at the clock. The end of his shift came and went. He didn't panic. Dan usually came back after an hour, which only meant staying half an hour extra. Bernard would probably praise him for putting in overtime.

Except the hour hand kept moving upward, until two hours later when it passed the twelve and began its descent again. Not cool. Already there had been one pissed-off customer who wanted beer that Jace couldn't sell. That sucked enough, but he also had school in the morning, and had no idea if Dan was coming back at all. He darted into the back room to check the schedule. The next person didn't begin her shift until two in the morning.

He considered calling Bernard, but that would probably mean waking him up. Besides, Jace didn't want to be the kind of person who ratted out a coworker. Instead he returned to the cash register, resigned to being stuck there for now. Ironically, the night shift wouldn't be so bad if he didn't have school. There were hardly any customers. In fact, the store was silent until almost one in the morning.

That's when the werewolf showed up.

A mane of brown hair, tall pointed elf ears, and a long snout with an open mouth of red glistening teeth. Just a mask, of course, but disguises and gas stations didn't have the best history together. Jace glanced outside. No cars were at the pumps. The person in the werewolf mask didn't browse or glance around. Instead he headed straight for the counter where Jace was. At first he thought Dan might be playing a trick on him, but the body in the green army surplus jacket lacked the necessary potbelly.

The hair on the back of Jace's neck bristled with fear. His first night in the store alone, and he was getting robbed.

Or was he overreacting? The werewolf had stopped in front of the counter and was just staring at him. Jace stared back. The eyes were human, ruining the monstrous illusion, but they were still upsettingly mismatched. One eye was brown, the other green. Jace had never met anyone with two different-colored eyes before, which meant this wasn't a joke. Greg wasn't beneath the mask, nor was one of his sister's boyfriends, or anyone he knew from school.

"Halloween isn't for another couple of days," Jace said, throat dry.

"Never too early to start trick-or-treating," the werewolf replied in a muffled voice.

Jace licked his lips. "You want candy?"

"Cigarettes. Give me a carton."

This time the voice sounded firmer. No doubt about it, Bernie's was being robbed. "I'm not old enough to sell cigarettes," Jace said, buying for time. He moved his hands below the counter, felt around for what Bernard had only mentioned in passing, but what Dan had delighted in taking off the shelf and waving around. Jace's fingers brushed against cold metal and a wooden stock. He didn't know how to fire a gun, aside from what he'd seen in movies, and he sure as hell didn't know how to handle a shotgun, but maybe it would be enough to scare away this guy.

The mismatched eyes searched his before moving down his body. With both hands hidden beneath the counter, Jace felt sure it was obvious what he was doing. The werewolf raised an arm, and even though he saw no weapon, Jace grabbed the shotgun, trembling hand slick with sweat on the metal barrel. Jace kept the gun hidden from view, but beneath the counter was a thud as the wooden stock bumped into something. The werewolf hesitated, but then moved his arm higher and pulled off the mask.

A stranger. Definitely a stranger because Jace would have remembered seeing him. He noticed the hair first, a brown so dark it could be mistaken for black, but the fluorescent lights revealed all. His head was shaved on each side, the remaining strip of hair too wide to be a mohawk. Instead Jace thought of a skunk, maybe because of the bristled hair or because the word rhymed with punk. That's what this guy was. A punk. No one looked healthy in the store's stark lighting, but this guy's olive skin tone fared better than most, his face flushed and sweaty from wearing the mask.

Heart still thudding, Jace gripped the gun tighter. The mismatched eyes bored into his, as if reading his every thought and intention.

"My name is Victor." He tossed the werewolf mask on the counter. "It doesn't matter that you're too young to sell cigarettes because I'm too broke to buy them."

"So?" Jace said, the word coming out as a challenge. Was he being robbed or not?

Victor considered him a moment longer and then smiled. "So I'm shit out of luck."

Jace didn't reply, watching for any sudden moves.

"Penny for your thoughts," Victor said.

Jace frowned. "I thought you didn't have any money?"

"So I'll owe you."

Okay. Why not? "What you are doing here?"

Victor exhaled and glanced around the store. "Bored. Lonely. Desperate." Mismatched eyes met his again. "You know the feeling?"

Jace lifted his hands off the gun. "Yeah."

"Yeah." Victor pressed his lips together, eyeing the display of cigarettes behind the counter. "So… You smoke?"

"Of course." Jace winced inwardly. Why had he said that? Maybe because there was something undeniably cool about Victor. If Jace could start over in a new school and reinvent himself, he'd probably copy a lot of what Victor had going on, although he might wimp out on the three silver loops piercing one ear's cartilage.

"Well—" Victor read his nametag, " —Jason, do you mind if I bum a cigarette?"

"Jace," he said. "Uh, I'm sort of out."

Victor glanced meaningfully back at the display.

"Oh. Right!" Jace turned around to face rows of cardboard boxes that favored red, green, and gold. Every day was Christmas to a smoker. "What kind do you like? They're all the same to me."

Why the hell was he doing this? As Victor verbally guided him to the right brand, Jace started to get angry at himself. Hell, werewolf-boy could be reaching over the counter right now, grabbing for the shotgun while Jace's back was turned. He spun around, pack of cigarettes in hand. Victor was right where he'd left him. The mismatched eyes lit up at the sight of the smokes, and for some reason Jace felt like smiling. Oh crap! He *was* smiling!

"Let's go out front," Victor said. "Unless there's a swanky lounge in back or something."

Jace shook his head, grabbing one of the cheap lighters from the counter. Already he was adding up a list in his head. He should have enough cash on him to pay for these things. Bernard would never know that a customer hadn't come in and bought them as long as the money was in the register.

Outside, Jace was reminded of just how small their town was. No cars were in sight, no boom of a nightclub or whatever other noises a real city might have. The ethereal sound of a train in the distance was the sole indication that he and Victor weren't the only people left on earth.

"May I?" Victor gently took the pack of cigarettes from Jace, slapping the top of the container against his palm to "pack the tobacco," as one of his sister's boyfriends had once explained. Jace had thought it was bullshit then, but now it seemed kind of cool.

Once the package was open, Victor held out the box to him. Jace took one, trying to remember the last time he smoked. He usually did okay. Sometimes he coughed. He prayed this wouldn't be one of those times. He raised the lighter, but Victor had pulled out a silver Zippo. When he flicked open the lid, a flame sprang to life. Victor leaned forward to offer him the gift of fire, a white cancer stick bouncing up and down between his lips that he then lit second.

Jace choked, but managed to hold it in, eyes watering. Victor sucked deep on his cigarette, smirking a little before he exhaled through his nose. "Sweet, sweet tobacco!" he said with a sigh.

More like sour! Maybe Jace could just hold his cigarette until it burned down. Together they leaned against the brick wall next to the gas station's entrance. Jace stole little glances at Victor as he puffed away. A hint of dark stubble shaded his chin, but he didn't seem too much older than Jace. "What school do you go to?"

Victor stared at a distant streetlight. "I don't."

"Already graduated?"

"No."

"Oh." Jace covertly checked him out. The army jacket was hanging open, some sort of concert T-shirt beneath, but it was too loose to tell what sort of body Victor had.

"I take it you're still in high school?" Victor asked.

"Yeah. Senior. I'll graduate in the summer."

Victor smirked. "That's usually how it works."

Ugh. Coolness meter dropping to critical! Jace took another drag, wishing they made these things in bubble gum flavor. At least this time he managed not to gasp or wheeze, but now he was hurriedly trying to think of something that didn't sound lame. "What sort of career path are you planning on?" What the hell? Now he was channeling his father!

Instead of answering, Victor looked over at him and nodded at the cigarette. "You don't have to pretend. It's already cool that you got me these." He held up the pack. "I'm assuming you don't want them?"

Jace shook his head, dropping the cigarette on the ground and grinding it out with his foot. He felt like giving up and going back inside, but he still felt oddly drawn to this person. Victor had gotten what he wanted and would soon disappear back into the night, but before he did, Jace wanted to know who he was. Instead of trying to play it cool anymore, he simply let loose. "Who are you? I don't get what you're doing here or why you were wearing that mask. And if you're not in school, then how old are you, because you make it sound like you dropped out. If you did, what are you going to do?"

Victor exhaled, watching the smoke on the air before he grinned. "I'll give you three questions. One at a time. I promise to answer them truthfully, although it will probably be the last time I'm ever honest with you."

Jace shook his head. "This is so weird. *You're* weird."

"Three questions. Take it or leave it."

Okay. Jace didn't need long to come up with the first one. "What's your name? Like your whole name." This way he could ask people about him, could maybe find him again.

"Victor Nathaniel Hemingway. And no, I can't write, so the name is very ironic."

Can't write anything, or can't write prose? Jace shook his head. Only two questions left. He wanted to know how old Victor was, and if he had dropped out of school, but if he played it right, he could figure out both. "If you were still in school, what grade would you be in, if you would be in a grade at all?"

Victor snorted. "Clever."

"Thanks. Uh, you have to answer."

"If I hadn't dropped out of high school, and assuming I had the money and inclination, I'd be a freshman in college now."

A year older than he was, then. The last question was probably the most burning, although Jace wasn't sure he really wanted to know. Maybe it was as superficial as his appearance, or maybe because he was actually interesting, but Jace wanted to give Victor the benefit of the doubt. The answer to the next question could make it very hard for them to be friends. "Were you going to rob me?"

Victor flicked away his cigarette, turning to face Jace and leaning against the wall. "I don't know."

"You said you'd be truthful."

"I am." Victor's lips twitched. "I was thinking about it before I came in, yeah. But then I didn't."

The revelation made Jace feel threatened. "Are you armed?"

"You're out of questions." Victor looked him over and frowned. "But no. I'm not armed, and I wouldn't have hurt you. I just would have grabbed something and ran. Would you have chased after me?"

"I don't know," Jace said, relaxing a little bit. "How fast can werewolves run?"

"Pretty damn fast."

Jace laughed, and soon Victor joined him. This was all so surreal, but he liked it.

"So tell me something about you," Victor said.

A sobering request. What was there to say? High school student with a job at a gas station. That's all Jace's life was. Victor already knew everything about him. Except one thing.

"I'm gay," he blurted out.

Those mismatched eyes searched his. Victor didn't ask if he was serious or kidding. He didn't even look surprised. Jace was used to feeling like he'd known everyone for their whole lives, because in many cases, he had. Now, for the first time, he felt like someone knew everything about him, even though he couldn't possibly.

A semi-truck pulled into the parking lot, brakes hissing as it came to a stop in front of the pumps. The trucker hopped out and waved.

"I have to turn on the pump," Jace said, heading for the door.

"I'm going to take off," Victor said.

"Oh. Okay." What else would he do after Jace dropped a bombshell like that?

"Thanks again for the smokes." Victor pushed off the wall and headed across the parking lot toward the street.

Jace watched him a moment, his stomach sinking, before he turned and opened the door.

"Hey!"

Jace spun around. Victor was halfway to the pumps, hands stuffed in the old army jacket. He nodded in Jace's direction. "You want to go trick-or-treating with me?"

"For real?"

Victor shrugged. "I like freebies."

"Okay!"

Victor grinned, spun around, and headed into the night. Jace stared after him until he noticed the trucker looking less than patient. Then he hurried inside to authorize the pump. Once he had, he noticed the werewolf mask still sitting on the counter. At least Victor wouldn't be robbing anyone else tonight.

The front door of the house creaked loudly, or so it seemed in the heavy silence. At half past two in the morning, Warrensburg had gone from sleepy to stone dead. Jace hadn't seen another car on the drive home. The woman who'd come to relieve him from duty hadn't seemed surprised that Dan was absent. Apparently it had happened before, even without someone there to run the store. Jace was much too tired to worry about any of that now. He was heading up to his room when the hall light switched on.

He blinked against the brightness. His mother stood at the top of the stairs, illuminated like an angel by forty watts worth of heavenly light.

"There you are," she whispered. "Did you just get home?"

Jace nodded, trudging up the stairs to her. "One of my coworkers bailed on me. It was either stay late or abandon the store."

Serena nodded her understanding, but the worry on her face didn't disappear.

"I'll be fine," Jace said. "Five hours sleep is enough to get me through the day."

"You could stay home."

This took him aback. His mother had a razor-sharp instinct for when he was playing sick. Jace hadn't missed a day of school in his life without good reason. Of course, skipping tomorrow would mean not being able to ask around about Victor. He glanced down at the Halloween mask in his hand, drawing his mother's attention to it.

"Is that what you're wearing this year?" she asked.

"No. It's my friend's."

"Greg?"

Jace didn't answer the question directly. "I need something that compliments it. What goes with a werewolf? A dog catcher?"

His mother smiled. "Are you asking me to make you a costume? And here I thought you were growing up too quickly."

Jace chuckled. "You don't have to make something. You never had to. Everyone else's parents bought things off the rack."

"Oh, but I loved making costumes for you and Michelle! We weren't being cheap, you know. It usually ended up costing more."

"And they were usually better," Jace said wistfully. It did seem like a long time ago. "Except for the year I wanted to be He-Man, and you made me go as a generic knight."

Serena raised her eyebrows. "It wasn't He-Man. You wanted to be the girl version."

"She-Ra? Really?" Jace broke out into a grin. "That's right! I guess that should have been your first hint."

The worried expression returned to his mother's face. Obviously she still wasn't comfortable with the subject. "You should get some sleep," she said.

Jace stayed where he was. "I'm still me, you know. Nothing has changed. I just like guys."

"It's not that." Serena pressed her lips together.

"What then?"

She took a deep breath. "I worry. That's a mother's job, but now I worry even more. Being gay *is* a big deal to a lot of people. I'm concerned about you getting hurt. All it takes is one stupid person—" Serena shook her head, unable to continue.

"I'll be careful," he said. "I promise."

"I also think about the sort of life you'll have. I always pictured you with a wife and children. I can let go of that, but I want you to have someone."

"You and me both," Jace murmured.

"Do you think it's possible?"

"Yeah, I guess." Jace shrugged. "At least I hope so."

"Good. Life can be hard, but every burden is easier to bear with someone at your side. That's what I want for my baby. Someone to watch out for him."

Before Jace could respond, his mother wrapped him in her arms. She kissed his cheeks, then his forehead, before wishing him sweet dreams. When he was alone again, he went to his room and sat on the edge of the bed. He stared down at the werewolf mask before putting it on. In the reflection of the bedroom window, he could just barely see himself, the eyes of the wolf blue now. He blinked, sighed into the latex, and pulled off the mask.

Two more days until Halloween. Two more days until Victor. Jace flopped over onto his side and with his clothes still on, allowed himself to dream.

"Victor Hemingway," Jace repeated.

Across from him at the lunch table, Greg was hammering a plastic-wrapped sandwich with his fist, smooshing it down. This was his daily ritual. Ever since he was a kid, he preferred his sandwiches as compressed as possible. This did nothing to change the flavor, but he claimed the texture was better. As Jace watched him devour half of it in two bites, he wondered if the procedure was really about getting more food into his mouth at once.

"Mm-mm," Greg said as he chewed, shaking his head. After he swallowed he added, "Never heard of him. Why?"

"Just wondering. He showed up at the store last night and —" And all kinds of things, but luckily Greg seem preoccupied by his own thoughts.

"What are we going to do for Halloween?" he asked between bites.

Uh oh. Jace hadn't thought of that. He couldn't remember a Halloween without Greg. Now he couldn't picture one with Greg tagging along. Jace barely knew what to expect as it was. "What did you have in mind?" he asked.

"Angie was saying we should drive to Kansas City, check out some of the big haunted houses. We haven't done that since junior high."

"With your dad." Jace smiled at the memory. "That was fun, but this year I was thinking about doing my own thing."

Greg looked incredulous. "Like what?"

"Well, I have to work," Jace said. In truth, he planned on asking to leave work early, but he still had to be there because the gas station was the only place where Victor knew to find him. Not for the first time, Jace wondered if he was being naïve. Maybe Victor had only been joking. It's not like they exchanged phone numbers or made solid plans about when and where to meet.

"You can't get the night off?" Greg asked. "Angie was planning on bringing her little sister."

Oh. Right. "Bummer," Jace said, sounding unconvincing even to his own ears.

"You'd probably like her if you met her," Greg said.

"Maybe some other time. I'll be working part of the night, and it would suck if you guys had to hang around waiting for me."

"I guess so." Greg tackled his chips, looking sullen as he ate them one by one instead of inhaling them.

"Sorry," Jace said.

"It's okay. Really. I'm just trying to figure out if I can get Angie to ditch her little sister. It's a nice long drive out there and back, and Angie will probably want to rest her head on my lap." Greg leered suggestively.

Jace laughed. His best friend had been a horndog ever since they were twelve, dragging Jace along to check out his dad's stash of Playboy magazines, or channel surfing soft porn movies during their sleepovers, desperate for a glimpse of boob. It sounded like Jace would have been cramping Greg's style by tagging along, which made him feel a lot less guilty.

When they were headed off to their separate classes, Jace caught sight of his sister in the hall and made his way over to her. He'd slept late and skipped breakfast, so this was the first he'd seen of her. He made the two-word inquiry that he'd been putting to anyone who would listen.

"Victor Hemingway."

Michelle shrugged and shook her head, but the person

walking with her—a freckled-faced girl named Julie—looked thoughtful and said, "Wasn't that the weird guy with the long dark hair?"

"Could be," Jace said. "You know him?"

"Not really." The tip of Julie's tongue appeared in the corner of her mouth for a second. "Wait, wasn't he the one who got kicked out of school?"

"I thought he dropped out," Jace said.

"No, I'm sure he was kicked out because... because..."

Jace was practically salivating.

"Because of some big deal. I can't remember."

"Do you think you can find out?" Jace said. "If you do, come find me. Or better yet, call me. Same number as my sister's."

The girl's cheeks flushed. Oops! Jace grinned nervously, then turned to Michelle.

"My brother, boy detective," she said. "What's this all about?"

Now Jace's cheeks grew warm. Luckily, nothing was lost on his sister.

"Never mind," she said. "Come on, Julie. We're going to be late."

Jace would explain later, but no doubt she had figured out most of it already. She'd only need the details about how he and Victor met. And the news of their big date. Jace backpedaled mentally. He was probably—no, absolutely—making a big deal out of nothing. Some guy had shown up, nearly robbed him, and wandered away afterwards. Not exactly wedding bells, but he'd take what he could get—even if it was a hopeless fantasy.

Chapter Four

Jace showed up at work in costume, feeling silly despite the great job his mother had done. His childhood costumes had mostly been innocent, never terror-inducing, but this year his mother hadn't held back. Jace was a bloody, gory mess. His clothing was shredded, his face marred by fake wounds, his hair matted with blood. Where one of his arms should have been was a tangle of real meat and bone—his mother had splurged on some sort of meat cuts, shaping them into a mutilated limb before binding it in plastic wrap. All Jace had to do was hold his arm behind his back to make it look like a werewolf had been munching on his appendage.

As awesome as his costume was, Jace wasn't looking forward to Dan sneering at him even more than usual. Once in the gas station, he instantly felt relieved. Bernard was there, decked out from head to foot in Army-type camouflage. His face was covered in green and brown makeup, an old dinged helmet on his head. A couple of kids were pestering him for candy, Bernard happily scooping handfuls into their bags from a plastic witch's cauldron set in the middle of the store. Jace had a vague memory of his father getting gas one Halloween and scoring some candy himself.

When Bernard saw him, he grinned broadly. "Oh, good! You dressed up!"

"Yeah," Jace said. "So that's what they wear in the Navy?"

Bernard grimaced. "I lost a bet and a whole lot more playing poker with one of my buddies. He was an Army grunt and we're always ribbing each other— Well, anyway, this is my punishment."

Jace glanced over at the counter where Dan was looking even more annoyed than usual. "Looks like Dan dressed up as a sociopath."

Bernard chuckled, shaking his belly and looking like a militant Santa Claus. "Oh, that's good! I told him to wear a costume, but you know how some people are. My son always loved Halloween when he was little. Even more than Christmas or his birthday, which I thought was unusual."

"Definitely. I'll take presents over candy any day." Jace bit his lip. "Although I wouldn't mind scoring some free chocolate tonight. Do you think I can take off early?"

Bernard waved dismissively. "Of course. Have fun!"

"Uh, and do you think I can put my arm in the freezer until then? I'm not sure how long it'll keep."

"Sure, sure." A tiny witch and a princess had walked in with their parents, drawing away Bernard's attention.

Jace headed in the back and stashed his fake arm in a chest freezer, leaving his backpack on the closed lid to guard it. Then he went to work, spinning around every time the door chime went off and hoping to see Victor there. Eventually he started paying more attention to the clock. *When* Victor was going to show up became *if* Victor would show up at all. Jace was just starting to feel like the biggest idiot in the world when the door chimed again.

This time when he turned around, Victor was there. When he saw Jace he smiled—really smiled—like they were old friends. Jace beamed back at him, before gesturing that Victor should wait. Jace ran to the back room, grabbed his backpack and reattached his meaty appendage. "I'm out of here!" he announced, heading straight for the door so Victor would follow. He wanted to be alone with him, to finally start their night together.

"Looking good, Jace," Victor said appreciatively. "What are you supposed to be? Car wreck victim?"

"No." Jace dug in his backpack and pulled out the werewolf mask, handing it to Victor.

"Oh, cool! You remembered my costume."

"It's important, because I'm your victim. Or at least the werewolf's victim."

Victor grinned. "Nice!"

Jace nodded. "Especially since that's what I was supposed to be the other night. Victor's victim."

"Now you're making me feel guilty!"

"Really?"

Victor shook his head. "Nope."

Jace laughed and nudged him, delighting in the contact. "So, where to? You promised me free candy."

Not far from downtown Warrensburg was a neighborhood of tiny one-story houses. They walked toward this area together, Victor pulling on his werewolf mask, which Jace found oddly thrilling, like they were about to rob a bank together. Victor's costume wasn't totally convincing. He still wore the same Army-surplus jacket, and a pair of jeans torn at the knees. Those fit the part, he supposed, but Jace wished he'd had his mom whip up some hairy gloves. At least he'd remembered to bring pillow cases to hold their loot.

"When's the last time you did this?" Jace asked.

"Are you kidding?" The werewolf blinked at him. "Every year since I was a kid. I'll never stop, even if people are starting to get pissy about it."

"What do you mean?"

"Wait and see."

Everything went fine at the first house. A middle-aged woman gave them a couple of miniature Snicker's bars, but at the next house, an old man answered. After looking them over, he slammed the door.

"What the hell?" Jace asked.

"Ageism," was Victor's muddled reply. "He thinks we're too old to do this."

"That sucks," Jace said, looking down at his pillow case which now held one pathetic candy bar.

"Who cares?" Victor said, already moving to the next house. "They won't all be like that."

"Yeah, but it kind of ruins the fun."

The next three houses were fine. At the fourth, an unshaven, unshowered man stared at them. His heavy gut made him look like he drank for a living.

"What do you want?" he said.

"Trick-or-treat," Jace repeated.

The man spat a glob of brown liquid onto the porch. Jace smelled chewing tobacco on his breath when he said, "Halloween is for kids."

"Trust me," Victor said. "We're very immature."

"Fuck off. You're too old."

"I don't understand, sir," Victor said in cordial tones. "Why do you want me to be more grown up? So I can screw your wife? Can't get it up for her and hoping I can help out?"

Veins popped out on the man's neck. Jace grabbed Victor's arm and started pulling him away. The man stepped out onto the porch like he was aching for a fight, but in the end he shouted something unintelligible and slammed the door.

Jace's heart was thudding but Victor howled with laughter as they returned to the street. "Did you see his face? I thought the douche bag was about to have a heart attack!"

"Yeah." Jace forced himself to chuckle, but felt his brow knitting together. "What an asshole! We're not that old! Would it have killed him to give us some stupid candy?"

"Only if we were lucky. Ready for the next one?"

"Seriously?" Jace scowled. "I'm already pissed off enough as it is. I can't handle dealing with any more jerks like that."

The werewolf's eyes looked disappointed. "I figured you weren't the kind of guy who cares what others think. I mean, you're gay. Stupid people hate you for no reason." Victor gestured to the street. "And stupid people here don't want us to have fun. There's no point in getting angry at people you can't change. All it does is make you feel like crap. That's exactly what they want. We can't let them win."

Now Jace's heart was thumping for another reason. Victor didn't have a problem with him being gay. He hadn't said anything the other night, but now he had drawn a line in the sand and was standing on the right side. And Jace *loved* the sound of that *we*. "Let's keep going," he said. A group of kids passed them on the sidewalk, giving him an idea. He nodded in their direction. "We'll tag along with them. People will think we're their older brothers or something. Not that I care what anyone thinks, but we'll get more candy this way."

"Yeah, all right."

Jace couldn't be sure, but he felt like there was a smile in that voice. Feeling proud of himself, he and Victor caught up with the gaggle of kids, waiting behind them when they rang the doorbell. He even pretended to be miserable, as if escorting the kids against his will. The woman at the house smiled at him like he was a good brother as she gave him candy—way better than being told to go away.

They covered the next couple of blocks in this manner, but then the kids started backtracking.

"Where are you going?" Victor asked them. "There are plenty of houses left."

"We aren't allowed to go that far," one of the Ninja Turtles said.

"You can if you stick with us," Victor said. "We're adults. Aren't we, Jace?"

"Yeah. Just think how much more candy you'll get."

The kids locked greedy eyes before agreeing. Now they really were going from house to house as a group. Victor was good with the kids, playing different games with them. First he got them to start saying treat-or-trick, which threw people off, and then he had them take turns saying it, one after the other like a pint-sized barbershop quartet. One time Victor had them all stand perfectly still and say nothing, an effect that was surprisingly creepy. His games had the kids laughing and screaming as they covered another couple of blocks. Then he and Jace led them back to their own neighborhood.

"Here," Victor said, holding out his filled-to-the-brim pillowcase to the Ninja Turtle. "You guys did so good I'm going to let you have this, but you have to split it up evenly, okay?"

There was no false modesty with children. They grabbed the offered prize and raced off into the night.

"Dude, sorry!" Victor said. "I should have asked you about the pillowcase."

"It's okay," Jace said. "It was old. I don't think they need any more candy, though."

"Nah." Victor pulled off the werewolf mask, his hair damp with sweat. His cheeks were flushed and he looked happy. "It's never enough at that age. I used to keep going until my sack was full. Then I'd head home, dump it out, and hit the streets again. One time I went so far that I got lost. I was about their age at the time and didn't make it home until one in the morning."

"You must have been scared," Jace said as they began the walk back to the Stop and Shop.

"No way! I loved it." Victor wiped the sweat from his brow. "I felt really grown up being out that late. For the first time I was on my own. No one was looking out for me or telling me what to do. I just kept walking and snacking on my candy as more and more houses turned their lights off. Eventually there wasn't anyone on the sidewalk or any cars on the street, and I felt like I owned everything. The whole town was mine."

Jace glanced sidelong at him. "I kind of know what you mean. I like driving around late at night and... Never mind, it sounds weird."

"Go on. Tell me."

"Uh. Okay. Sometimes I'll just park outside a random home, staring at what I can see through the windows. But not in a pervy way, like a peeping Tom. I just sit there and try to imagine what kind of life goes on inside. I take the details I can see—decorations and stuff like that, or occasionally I'll catch sight of someone— and all of that will add to the story."

"So what do you usually imagine?" Victor asked. "I bet there's a theme. What comes up the most?"

"A few things. Sometimes I think of that person being alone, and like you said, that can feel good. You can be yourself when it's just you, even more so than with your closest friends or family. And then—" Jace laughed in embarrassment. "—I usually imagine that person finding someone, or maybe just sitting there and yearning for the right person to show up."

"How romantic." Victor grinned at him. "And do they find that person?"

"Occasionally. Other times I get bored and imagine them having an accident, like falling down the stairs and dying, only for some grief-crazed relative to bring them back with voodoo." Jace stuck out his arms in front of him and moaned like a zombie. "And the sick thing is, the relative keeps them around as an undead butler, making them vacuum and do the dishes and stuff."

Victor stared at him. "You're serious, aren't you?"

Jace dropped his arms. "Yup. It's how I get my kicks."

"Well take me with you next time. It sounds fun."

"Deal. Where should we go now?"

"I'm hungry." Victor swiped the pillowcase from Jace's hands. "Let's find somewhere to divvy this up and eat."

"You can snack on my meat arm." Jace sniffed. "Actually, I need to find somewhere to ditch this thing. And I need something real to eat. Let's grab a burger."

"No money," Victor said, already tearing open a tiny pack of M&M's.

"Then it's on me. Oh! That reminds me…" Jace swung his backpack off and unzipped the front pocket, taking out a small shrink-wrapped box that he offered to Victor. "For you."

"You got me some smokes?" Victor's eyes shone as he took them. "Man, thank you! I wish I had known earlier. I would have cut a hole in my mask. A smoking werewolf! How cool would that have been?"

"You'll huff and you'll puff," Jace said, "but your lungs won't manage to blow any houses down."

"True enough. It's a terrible habit." Victor winked, a filter already trapped between his lips. "Block the wind for me?"

"Oh."

Jace stepped close, taking in the details of Victor's face as it was illuminated by the flame—the dark eyebrows, the mismatched eyes, the dimple above his mouth. This attention didn't go unnoticed, but Victor seemed more amused than anything. When he exhaled, the scent of chocolate was mixed with the smoke.

Jace grasped for something to say. "Uh, did you drive to the gas station tonight?"

"Nope. No car, no license. I assume you have both with all the night driving you do."

"Yeah." Jace resumed walking down the sidewalk, suddenly lost for words. He listened to Victor breathing in and blowing out, the smell reminding him of when the Holdens and the Trouts would team up to rake the valley behind their homes, making piles of leaves that were then set alight in a controlled burn.

Victor seemed content with their silence, the sound of children's voices babbling from elsewhere in the neighborhood as they continued to beg for candy.

Jace wondered, for a moment, if something was wrong with him. He had known Victor for a handful of hours, and in that miniscule amount of time, Jace had decided he liked him. More than that, in fact. Surely love didn't come this quickly, but *something* was definitely there. He wanted to stare at Victor, had trouble keeping his eyes averted. He wanted Victor to talk nonstop just so he could listen, no matter what he had to say. And Jace wanted to touch him, to finally see what another guy's body felt like. He wanted to smell his skin, taste his lips, anything he could get away with. Did he fall easily? Or was he living up to the promiscuous gay stereotype?

"What about this house?" Victor said, stopping and pointing up a walkway.

"Huh?" Jace looked in the pointed direction, seeing a small home that was a little rundown. The porch light was on and a jack o' lantern sat on a step, inviting trick-or-treaters. "Don't we have enough candy?"

"No, I mean, if you were out driving around at night, what story would this house tell you?"

"Oh!" Jace looked at the house anew. It definitely needed maintenance. A fresh lick of paint and maybe some groundskeeping. No man in the house, or not enough money. Or both. "It belongs to an old widow. She's on welfare, and everyone thinks she's poor, but that's not the truth."

"No?"

"Nope. The thing is, she's addicted to jewelry. Like hardcore. She can't get enough of it. When her first husband died of a heart attack, she cashed in his life insurance policy and went wild, buying all the gold and jewels she ever wanted. When the money ran out, well, she had to find herself another husband, didn't she?"

"I see. A black widow."

"Yup. Three men have given their lives to feed her insatiable appetite for precious minerals. Her home is just as rundown inside, unless you see the cellar, which looks like a dragon's horde."

Victor snorted. "How does such an old lady lure in so many unwitting victims?"

"She's got great legs," Jace said with certainty. "I mean phenomenal! Guys propose just to get their hands on them."

Victor shook his head ruefully. "I think I'll pass."

They snacked on candy all the rest of the way back. At the gas station, Jace tossed the mutilated meat arm into the dumpster. Victor pretended they were burying an old friend, making them each say parting words before they unceremoniously slammed shut the dumpster lid. Once Jace had Victor in the passenger seat of his car, they headed to a fast food joint on the edge of town.

"Inside or…?"

"Let's eat outside."

Jace pulled up to the drive-thru window, picked up some burgers and fries, then parked the car. He imagined they would eat right where they were, but Victor got out and went around to the trunk, sitting there. Jace joined him. With their backs to the neon cathedral of grease, they were facing an empty field. A faded plastic sign advertised that the land was for sale.

"Man, that smells good," Victor said as Jace passed him a cheeseburger wrapped in paper. "First real meal I've had all day."

"Why's that?"

Victor shrugged. "Just haven't been home much of late."

"Oh." Jace took a bite and chewed in silence. If Victor didn't have school or a job, what could he do besides be at home? Unless he had a good reason for avoiding it. Jace pictured a stern man like the one Victor had mouthed off to earlier, a man who threw empty beer bottles at Victor anytime he messed up. "Do you not like being there?"

"At home?" Victor sounded surprised at first, but laughed when he read Jace's face. "It's not like that. I'm not abused. It's just me and my mom, and I try not to be such a burden to her. I don't expect her to support or take care of me."

"So what do you do?" Jace said. The more Victor talked, the less he felt he understood him.

Victor shrugged and worked on his food. Jace let him eat, puzzling over it all. Did Victor just wander the streets, stealing when he needed something? He snuck a few peeks and found Victor staring straight ahead at the field as if he saw something there. When he was finished eating, Victor nodded in that direction.

"Things like that just kill me," he said. "Forget your black widow and her sexified legs. What seduces me is wondering what's over there. If I get up and just start walking now, where will I end up?"

"It's an empty field," Jace said.

"Yeah, but those dark trees on the edge. What's in there?"

"More trees? Bugs?"

Victor shook his head and hopped off the car. "Come on. I'll show you."

They walked across the field together, the soil damp beneath their feet, the plants they trod on yellow and wilting. A strange transition occurred as they left the artificial lights of Warrensburg. The trees were a dark curtain, a barrier they could pass through. Jace wanted to stop and consider their options, but Victor walked right in. All Jace could do was follow.

The world beyond was one of shadows. He followed the sound of Victor's passage more than his outline, which he could barely see, and almost bumped into him when Victor came to a stop.

"Right here," he said, as if they had reached a specific destination. "Sit down on the ground with me."

Jace worried about his jeans getting wet but did what he was told. Victor didn't instruct him further, except when Jace tried to ask a question.

"Just listen. Take it all in. Look around you."

The first couple of minutes, Jace struggled with his confusion. Then he started looking and listening. His eyes adjusted now, the world around him remained dark, but there was contrast. The trees were solid, their branches like dark veins against a sky heavy with clouds. The trees groaned in the breeze, their wooden fingers clutching and clattering against each other. The ground beneath them was gray, sometimes reflecting dim light where leaves cupped water. Occasionally Jace heard small movements, little creatures that began their day when the sun went down.

Victor sat across from him, the details of his features lost in shadows. "No one ever comes here," he said, his voice barely louder than a whisper. "Hundreds of people pulled into that parking lot or went through the drive-thru today, but hardly any of them looked at this field, and none of them got out of their cars and walked into these trees. They're like ants, running along the same path every day, driving the same roads, eating the same foods, watching the same shows. Why?"

"I don't know." Jace swallowed. He couldn't see Victor's eyes, but he could imagine them looking right through him, as they always seemed to, and seeing one of those boring ants.

"I like your stories," Victor said. "The way you can imagine all these interesting lives people have. I see the opposite. I look around and I see them sleepwalking, doing what they do because that's all they've ever done. It's like we hypnotize ourselves into perceiving only a fraction of the world around us."

"What can you do?" Jace asked. "I get what you're saying, but we can't all return to the trees. What would we eat? How would we survive?"

"I don't know." Victor sighed. "Maybe I'm just full of shit, but I want to try. I don't want to be part of the system or fall into line. That feeling I had all those years ago when I got lost trick-or-treating, it's right here. These woods, this weird little world, it comforts me. I used to think I wanted to live outside of it all, creeping along the edges of the real world, but look behind you."

Jace glanced over his shoulder. Through the trees, he could see a hint of the orange parking lot lights, a sliver of the fluorescent tubes illuminating people as they sat there and shoved food into their mouths. And it seemed so distant, so absurd and small. Now he understood.

"*This* is the real world," Jace said. "All that's just what we created for ourselves."

"Exactly!" Victor sounded proud. "I knew you'd get it."

But Jace didn't, not entirely. Philosophically, Victor's ideas were appealing, but from a practical standpoint Jace still didn't see how it would work. "Where do you sleep at night?"

"I have a tent. Sometimes I crash with friends. Mostly I camp out somewhere. When it rains it gets trickier. There used to be this old train car, but that's gone now." Victor sounded frustrated. "I know I'm still living off the system. None of those things would exist if it wasn't for capitalism. I don't have all the answers, but I won't figure out anything if I don't try. That's what I want to do. It's not a job, I'm not making any money, but this weird experiment is what I want to do with my life. We can be *anything*. Not just a lawyer or a burger-flipper. Be a freaking cowboy if you want, you know? Steal yourself a horse and take off into the wilderness." Victor chuckled. "What do you want to be?"

Your boyfriend. The thought came so quickly it almost reached his tongue, but Jace hesitated. "I don't know," he said. "I need to think about it."

"That's fine too. We can be nothing, we can be everything. Sometimes we're both in a matter of minutes."

Jace smiled, but part of him felt sad. "Are you homeless?"

"No," Victor said. "Everything I told you about my mom is true. She's always there for me, and I'm always there for her. That's how it is. That's my home, if I need it. But I don't want to need it."

Jace thought about this, tried to imagine all of his structures falling away. Without school, his job, or his family around, he would be left with the barest essence of his self. Who would that person be? Could he do it? Could he give it all up, run away into the woods with Victor? Maybe that would distort who he was, influencing him just like school and his job did. Maybe a person had to be alone to discover who they really were. If so, Jace wasn't interested, because he didn't want this to end. He wanted to sit out here with Victor forever. Or at least keep seeing him every day.

"I don't suppose you have a phone in that tent of yours," he said.

"Huh?"

Jace licked his lips, glad for the darkness that hid him. "I like you. I mean, I like hanging out with you."

"Are you asking me for my digits?" Victor's voice held an edge of amusement.

"Well, yeah." Jace cleared his throat. "What if I want to shower you with free burgers and cigarettes and can't find you? I'm not always at the gas station, you know."

The trees swayed above them for a moment.

"Tell me where you live," Victor said. "It'll give me somewhere else to find you."

"We're sort of on the edge of town," Jace said. "It would be a long walk."

"You'd be surprised where these legs have taken me."

"Oh. In that case, it's probably best if I show you how to get there."

As they left the line of trees, the fast food restaurant—cars swarming around it like bees on a hive—almost appeared threatening. Victor was right. The life they lived was so far divorced from nature as to be almost absurd. It was understandable why he'd want to disappear into the dark. He just hoped Victor didn't disappear completely, or if he did, that he would take Jace with him.

Chapter Five

Jace's family lived on the southwest edge of town, which in Warrensburg wasn't any great distance. Biking into town was possible, he and his sister having done so often enough before they learned to drive. A walk seemed too far, especially in this weather. Jace couldn't remember a single Halloween when it hadn't rained, and this year was no exception. The sluggish clouds had finally let loose, the slow drizzle becoming a steady downpour. Victor wouldn't be walking home in this. Jace would drive him back into town. Better yet, he had another idea.

"Nice," Victor said as they cruised past a small lake circled by trees.

"The yard of my house runs right down to that lake."

"You guys rich?"

"No." Jace laughed. "It's not *our* yard. It just sort of feels that way. There's a valley that a bunch of houses are built along. Anyone can go out back and walk down to the lake. It's small, but you can fish, and there are some woods you can hike through."

They pulled into the subdivision, which was only four or five blocks linked together. His father always joked that some developer had built their neighborhood as an escape from the fast-paced life of downtown Warrensburg.

"This is it," Jace said, pulling into the driveway. "Uh, what do you think about crashing here tonight? I could drive you back into town tomorrow when I go to school."

"Think your parents will mind?"

"Hopefully they won't notice."

Victor leaned forward, considering the house through the windshield. "Sure. Why not?"

Jace shut off the engine, got out of the car, and led the way inside. The house was dark and quiet. He thought they would make it to his room undetected, but the hall light turned on just as they were at the door. For an older woman, Serena sure had good hearing!

"You look even scarier with the makeup running," she said before noticing Victor. "Who's this?"

Jace made the introductions. Victor seemed comfortable enough, offering his hand and smiling. "Is it okay if he stays over?"

"It's a school night," his mother said. "I thought you were out with Greg?"

"No. He had plans with his girlfriend." Jace put on his best "please please please!" face. "We'll go straight to bed. I'll be up even later if I have to drive him back into town."

His mother looked reluctant, but in the end she nodded. "Wash that makeup off your face and then straight to bed!"

This made Jace feel eight years old, but he was too happy to complain. He showed Victor to his bedroom, which suddenly felt a little awkward. He didn't have his own television like Greg did, or anything he expected Victor would find very interesting. He had a decent music collection, but they couldn't listen to anything right now.

"Uh, I gotta take a shower real quick. Think you'll be okay?"

"Yeah." Victor tossed their candy on the bed. "I'll check for razor blades or something."

"Okay." Jace didn't want to leave the room, but once he was in the bathroom, he groaned. He looked like hell. Of course he was supposed to, but he'd mostly forgotten how gory his makeup was. Victor had been staring at a ghastly face all night.

Jace rushed through his usual shower ritual, dried off, and threw on a clean T-shirt and pajama bottoms. When he returned to his room, Victor was stretched out on the bed, flipping through an old comic book. He had taken off his shoes. The Army jacket too. For the first time, Jace could see a lot more of his body. Victor wasn't ripped or anything, his build on the thin side, but Jace's interest was piqued.

"You a big Batman fan?" Victor asked, setting aside the comic.

Jace shook his head. "Just one of those things that I've had around forever."

"Oh. I always liked the old television show. Cheesy, but fun."

He couldn't remember much about it, unfortunately. Instead, Jace was worried about the sleeping arrangements. He and Greg had grown up together, so sharing a bed didn't seem awkward. And besides, the mattress was queen-size, so there was plenty of room.

"My best friend is straight and we sleep together," Jace blurted out.

"Sounds like you should be on a talk show."

Jace's face started to burn. "Not like that. I mean we share the bed, but if that makes you uncomfortable, I'll take the floor."

Victor grinned. "It's fine. If your best friend can handle it, so can I."

"Oh, okay." Jace hesitated. "Are you tired?"

"Yeah. Let's call it a night." Victor stood and started unbuttoning his jeans. Jace forced himself to look away and shut off the light. Then he crawled into bed, keeping his back to his guest. Once Victor was under the sheets with him, Jace mumbled good night, closed his eyes, and remained absolutely rigid for the next half hour. Part of him didn't want to accidently brush against Victor and give him the wrong impression, mostly because that would be the exact right impression.

Sleep felt far away, so Jace listened to the sound of Victor's breathing as it deepened, took in the subtle scent of his body, and felt amazed at the warmth next to him. No wonder Michelle always let guys sneak through her window at night! Once Jace was sure Victor was asleep, he rolled over. In the dim light, he could see Victor's bare shoulder, his messy punk hair. He stared at these simple things, yearning to reach out his hand, to touch him. It wouldn't have to be sexual. Sure, Jace wanted that as well, but even more he wanted to hold another man, or maybe be held. He just wanted to be close to someone.

Eventually, eyes burning from exhaustion, Jace rolled back over and went to sleep.

Sunlight streamed through his bedroom window, bathing his room in light. When Jace woke up, the first thing he did was make sure he wasn't dreaming. He'd had quite a few in the night, none of them satisfying. Most revolved around trying to pull the blankets off Victor, but they wouldn't budge, like they were made of cement. As Jace eyed Victor's sleeping form next to him, this frustration remained. Of course now he *could* pull down the blankets and see what he was missing, but Jace wasn't ready to sink that low.

Instead he lay on his back and tried to think of anything boring to get his morning wood to subside. Algebra, the dirty microwave at Bernie's Stop and Shop, Dan's ugly face... That last one did it. Jace crawled out of bed, grabbed some clean clothes, and hit the shower. Sure he'd taken one the night before, but sleeping always made him feel grubby, and last night he had sweat much more than usual.

When he returned to his room, Victor was awake and sitting up, the sheets scrunched up around his waist. Jace had never seen him in daylight before. Nor had he seen this much of him. "Did you sleep well?" he mumbled as he stared. Victor was thin—not surprising if he skipped meals so often. Dark hair was sprinkled across the very top of his chest, his torso below smooth until the hair returned in a narrow trail just below his belly button. When Jace realized that Victor hadn't answered, he looked up to find him smirking.

"I don't know how to tell you this, man," Victor said, "but I think you might be gay."

"Ha ha." Jace rolled his eyes and busied himself with straightening up his room. "Do you want to take a shower?"

"Aaaand that confirms it."

"Not with me!" Jace said, body tensing. When he saw Victor's grin he relaxed.

"Yeah, a shower sounds good. If there's still time."

"There is." Jace turned his back when Victor started getting out of bed. "Uh, my family usually eats breakfast together. I don't know if you're up for that. I wouldn't blame you for sneaking out."

Victor laughed. "I'm good. You know me and free food. I can't say no."

"Okay. Well, there are fresh towels beneath the sink."

"Okay."

The room was silent. Victor didn't seem to be moving. Jace could sense him standing not too far away, but he kept his focus on arranging the socks in his dresser.

"What do I call your parents?" Victor said eventually. "Here I am in your room, wearing nothing but my underwear, and I don't even know your last name."

"Holden."

"Mr. and Mrs. Holden. All right."

The room was quiet again, although Jace was sure he could hear the frantic beating of his own heart.

"Jace?"

"Yeah?"

"It's okay to look. I don't mind."

After some hesitation, Jace turned around. Victor was

standing there, the window behind illuminating him like the sexiest saint ever conceived. Jace noticed for the first time the thin dark line around one of Victor's arms. A tattoo? His attention didn't remain there for long. Jace followed the teasing trail of hair down to the maroon briefs. Victor was thin, but this only made his bulge appear all the more pronounced. Before Jace's tongue flopped out and he started panting, he looked upward, his gaze traveling back to those mismatched eyes.

"Anyone would be lucky to have you look at them like that." Victor smiled, but it was gentle, not mocking or amused. "You remember that."

Jace didn't think that would be a problem. He wouldn't forget a single detail of this moment. Ever!

Victor asked him where the bathroom was, then excused himself. Even though Jace had found sexual relief in the shower, he had no doubt he was up for another round. Rather than risk getting caught, he sat on the edge of the bed and considered the implications.

Was Victor simply being nice? Or was it more than that? His package had been impressive, and yet Victor hadn't been hard. If he was interested in Jace, wouldn't he have been? Surely Victor now knew Jace was interested, since like everything else, his thoughts and feelings seemed completely transparent to him.

A smile crept over Jace's face. Whatever it all meant, having a nearly naked man let him stare was pretty damn awesome. His good mood remained intact, even when Victor returned—dressed in yesterday's clothing—and they joined his family at the breakfast table. He imagined Victor squirming in discomfort, eager to escape back to the wild world he came from. Instead he was right in his element. Victor ignored the surprised or curious stares and happily chatted with all of Jace's family, even Michelle, whose jaw was practically resting on the table. Of course Victor was still weird. He began telling them of the chicken farm a family friend owned, about the battery cages and miserable living conditions of the egg-laying hens. By the end of breakfast, most of them had uneaten eggs on their plates, except for Jace's father, who happily gobbled up the leftovers.

When it was time to go, Michelle allowed Victor to ride shotgun while Jace drove. "I insist," she said. Having overcome her surprise, she donned a patient expression. Despite it, Jace knew she'd be grilling him the second they were alone.

"You can let me out here," Victor said once they were downtown.

Jace pulled over, watching Victor in the rearview mirror. He had a lot of questions, but he couldn't ask most of them, especially in front of his sister. "Are you coming by Bernie's tonight?" he asked.

"If you're working. Sure."

Thank you, sweet baby Jesus! Jace practiced restraint, managing a fairly detached, "Okay. Cool."

"Everything," Michelle said as they pulled away from the curb. "I don't care if you have to drive in circles for the next three hours. I'm not getting out of this car until I know everything."

Jace laughed and filled her in on the basics. He didn't tell her about the strange moment in the woods last night, or Victor in his underwear this morning. Those things were private, treasures he would hoard greedily, like his fictional black widow did jewelry.

"What do you think?" he asked when finished with his story.

"Well, it's obvious you like him. So much for the slow realization fantasy."

"No kidding. If you weren't in the car I probably would have proposed."

Michelle giggled. "I can't believe Mom and Dad let you have a boyfriend over."

"It's not like that," Jace said. "We're just friends."

"Yeah, for now." Michelle considered him. "So is Victor—"

Jace sighed. "I don't know. How am I supposed to tell?"

Michelle shrugged. "Just ask him, I guess. You said he's totally cool with you being gay, so I don't think he'd find the question offensive."

Jace mulled this over as they pulled into the school parking lot. Why not? When Victor showed up at Bernie's tonight, he'd simply ask him.

Jace and his sister rarely ate together, despite having the same lunch period. As close as they were, they remained siblings, and this meant getting sick of sharing the same roof. So when Michelle approached his table, Julie blushing along behind her, Jace knew he was in for an awkward conversation, especially since his sister seemed amused.

"Hi," Julie said, practically squirming as she sat down.

"Hello there!" Greg replied, happy to flirt with any girl.

Julie barely looked at him. Instead she stared at Jace, not saying a word. Okay, maybe he could understand why Victor had him so figured out, especially if Jace behaved anything like she did. He felt like offering her a napkin in case she drooled.

"Julie here has something to tell you," Michelle said.

Julie blinked. "I do?"

"About Victor." Michelle said helpfully.

Jace perked up. "Really?"

"Oh my god, I can't believe I forgot!" Julie's shyness melted away as she delved into gossip. "Victor Hemingway is a hero! You know who Mr. Collins is?"

"Yeah, the health and fitness teacher," Jace said. The course was a requirement for all sophomores, focusing on nutrition, exercise, and anything else relating to staying fit.

"He's also one of the PE coaches," Greg said. "I was unlucky enough to have him for both classes that year. The guy is a total jerk. He was always going on about priming the pump. 'If you want to get anywhere in life, you have to prime the pump.'"

Jace laughed. "I remember that. What he really meant is that we were supposed to kiss his ass."

"Everyone hates him," Julie agreed. "The guy is a total Nazi. He made so many girls in my class cry."

"I had Mrs. Sheridan," Michelle said. "What's so bad about Mr. Collins?"

"He's a dick," Greg said frankly. "One time he talked about how peeing in the shower isn't a big deal, because urine is sterile. He asked people to raise their hands if they'd ever done that, which of course was every guy there. Then Mr. Collins told us how disgusting we all were and called us animals."

"Like he's never done it!" Jace said.

Michelle snorted. "Hell, even I pee in the shower sometimes."

They all laughed, but Jace had an even worse story that made him somber. "Did he do that body-check thing with you guys? With us he called three people to the front, each with a different build. One was skinny, one fat, and one was some perfect guy on the football team."

"Mr. Collins loves his jocks," Greg interjected.

"Yeah, they're the only ones he was nice to. Anyway, Mr.

Collins praised the jock's body, practically worshipping him before totally humiliating the other two guys. He made the skinny one show his ribs, then measured his arms and compared them to the jock's muscles. The overweight guy had it even worse. Mr. Collins measured his waist, which was bad enough, and then made him lift his arms to point out all the flab beneath. It was cruel."

Julie nodded. "He did that to the girls too. I know some parents complained, but he's still teaching. My dad blamed tenure, whatever that means. Anyway, it was something like that which set Victor off. All I know is Mr. Collins was being his usual horrible self and Victor snapped and slammed him up against the chalkboard."

"Oh yeah!" Greg said excitedly. "I heard about that! He had his arm pressed against Mr. Collins's throat in some sort of Chuck Norris move."

"The best part is what he said," Julie continued. "Victor asked Mr. Collins if he went home and primed his pump every night while thinking about students' bodies. His face turned bright red, so now everyone's sure that Mr. Collins was ashamed of the truth. He's totally a perv."

Or he couldn't breathe. Either way, Jace felt a swelling in his chest.

"Mr. Collins took time off, didn't he?"

"He was being investigated," Julie said in conspiring tones. "Victor was kicked out of school for assaulting a teacher, and no one has heard from him since."

"That's not quite true," Michelle said. "He was in our car this morning."

"No way!" Greg and Julie said in unison.

Michelle looked at Jace to back her up.

"Yeah, we've hung out a few times," he said bashfully. "It's not a big deal."

"What's he like?" Julie breathed, her crush on him forgotten.

"Nice," Jace said.

"Nice?" Greg repeated incredulously. "That's it? The guy who had Mr. Collins begging for mercy is *nice*?"

"Okay, so he's kind of wild," Jace said, thinking of how Victor smart-mouthed the potbellied man while trick-or-treating. "But only when provoked. Otherwise, he's nice."

And that's all they'd get out of him. Julie and Greg hammered him with questions, but Jace just shook his head and kept changing the subject until the bell rang. The word "hero" was bandied around a lot.

Jace liked that. Victor was a hero.

The fluorescent lights hummed, one of them occasionally flickering. In their cold light, even the brightly colored chip bags and candy wrappers seemed sucked clean of life. Or maybe it was just the foul mood that had followed Jace since yesterday. Victor hadn't shown up last night. Jace had even worked an extra hour after his shift had ended, which wasn't easy since Dan was being especially rude to him. That came mostly from Bernard hanging around the store longer than usual, which Dan blamed on Jace. He was probably right. Bernard only seemed interested in visiting with him, chatting about his son for as long as Jace was willing to listen. That part he hadn't minded. He admired how much Bernard loved his kid. It was only later in the evening, when Dan kept sneering at him and Victor didn't show, that Jace had become despondent.

Tonight wasn't looking hopeful. Bernard wasn't around, which Dan took advantage of to once again leave early. In a way Jace was glad, since working late into the night gave Victor more opportunity to show up, but his shift was coming to an end. He was scowling at a cardboard cutout of a bikini-clad model, her tiny hand wrapped around a bottle of beer, when a familiar voice greeted him.

"Jace, my man! How's it going?"

His head shot up, but it was only Greg. His best friend noticed his disappointment.

"Not happy to see me?"

"I am. Sorry." Jace rubbed his eyes. "It's been a rough night."

Greg leaned over the counter, nodding sympathetically. "I can tell. Do you always work this late?"

"No. I'm covering for someone." Now that he noticed, Greg seemed worn out too. "How about you?"

"Oh, man. Angie and her sister got in this huge fight. I mean massive!" Greg looked exasperated. "I was sitting there most of the night, letting her talk it out. She kept crying too. Just when it got better, her sister barges in and they're at each other's throats again. Once they were finished, I was back to comforting her, like one hellish rerun."

Jace winced in sympathy. "You know what? That sounds worse than my night."

"Glad to hear it, for your sake. Anyway, tomorrow I definitely need some guy time. You up for it?"

Jace glanced at the parking lot one more time. Empty, except for Greg's car at one of the pumps. "Yeah," he said. "You know me. I never have any plans."

Missouri was having second thoughts about fall, the chilly gray weather chased away by blue skies and the warmth of the afternoon. The perfect day for being outside, to make up for all those squandered summer days that should have been spent in nature's splendor. Too bad, then, that Greg was so set on shopping, seemingly desperate to find the perfect gift for Angie. At the third store, Jace started rolling his eyes.

"I thought you wanted guy time," he said, gesturing at the sea of bras and underwear surrounding them.

"Sorry," Greg said. "I didn't think it'd take this long."

"What's the big occasion anyway? Birthday?"

"No." Greg turned big innocent eyes on him. "I'm ready to take things to the next level."

Jace snorted. "More like you want to get laid."

Greg grinned shamelessly.

"You're my best friend, but this isn't how I want to spend my day." Jace meant that in more than one way. He looked out the window to the sidewalk, hoping to see punky hair walking by.

"Okay, I'll hurry." Greg swiped a pair of panties from a rack, lacy yellow things that wouldn't cover much.

"Seriously?" Jace took the panties and hung them up again. Then he led Greg to the front of the store where cheap jewelry was displayed on columns. He spun one until he found a bracelet decorated with pink beads and silver hearts, grabbing a matching pair of earrings too. He handed them to Greg.

"You think so?" Greg frowned. "I wouldn't like these."

"That's exactly the point."

Angie wouldn't swoon, but she'd appreciate the gesture. Jace watched as Greg paid for the items and sighed. It's not like Greg really needed any help. Those puppy-dog eyes had gotten him

into plenty of beds before. The gift-buying tactic was new. Maybe
Angie really did mean something to him.

"What now?" Greg asked, still beaming from his big romantic
purchase.

"Anything outside," Jace said.

"Archery?"

"Sure."

Jace was driving, so they went back to his house to drop off
the car. His mother made a fuss about them not having eaten.
Whenever she saw him and Greg together, she acted like they
were little kids still begging for mac and cheese. Of course his
treacherous stomach went along with her, grumbling at the idea.
Afterwards, more daylight was lost as Greg asked to use the
phone. Upstairs in his bedroom, Jace watched with puzzlement as
Greg checked in with Angie. Is that what he'd be doing now if he
had Victor's number? If life was different, would Jace have been
out shopping for a silly present before rushing home to call him?

Maybe. As dopey as it all looked from the outside, he bet it
was nice.

The "quick call" stretched on and on. Jace tried to make his
peace with the day being a lost cause, but he still snapped at his
mom when she came in the room without knocking.

"What?"

"Your other... friend is here," she said, eyebrows raised
disapprovingly at his tone. "Should I send him up?"

Jace bolted upright. "Of course! Why not?"

His mother looked between him and Greg. Oh. Were his
feelings for Victor that obvious? "You know what? I'll come down
with you. You're not my servant."

"That's news to me!" his mother said.

Greg kept chatting into the phone, oblivious when Jace
gestured that he'd be back. He found Victor waiting in the
entryway by the front door, looking out one of the small windows
as if eager to get back into the nice weather. Jace could relate.
His heart still raced at the sight of him. For a moment, Jace just
stood there staring. Then he remembered his mother. One sour
look sent her on her way, but the grumpiness Jace felt wasn't
meant for her.

"Where were you?" he said.

Victor turned around, those damn eyes reading him like a

book. "I didn't forget about you. Star rolled into town. I meant to bring her by Bernie's so you could meet, but things got carried away."

Jace felt a lump in his throat. "Carried away how?"

Victor didn't answer the question. Instead he addressed the problem. "I like you, Jace. I wouldn't be here otherwise. But I never promised I'd be reliable."

"You said you'd be there the other night," Jace said, fighting to keep the whine from his voice. "We had plans."

"I said I'd swing by. I didn't leave you sitting at a restaurant. You were working, and a friend of mine dropped in for a surprise visit."

Jace didn't want to argue. He wanted to hang out with Victor, to have this dreadfully boring day be saved, but his feelings were still hurt, and he barely understood why. "You could have called," he pressed.

"I could also get a boring job, a crappy apartment, and a phone number just for you to reach me on." Victor's voice was surprisingly calm. "But what would that make me?"

Normal. Not the weird person Jace felt so drawn to. Not the most interesting thing that had happened to him in years.

Victor put on a playful expression. "I'm flattered that you missed me so much."

"I didn't say I missed you," Jace answered with a huff, but he returned the smile.

Victor nodded toward the door. "Let's get out of here."

Jace took a couple of steps before he remembered Greg. "Uh, actually, I'm hanging out with my best friend today."

Victor shrugged. "Bring him along."

How could someone so complicated be so easy? Part of Jace wanted Victor to complain, to demand that they be alone, but once again Victor had him gleefully tap-dancing across eggshells.

Victor waited outside while Jace went to fetch Greg. His friend was just hanging up with Angie, but not before unleashing a barrage of pet names and kissy noises. Pathetic. But Jace couldn't help feeling a little envious.

"Dude! I'm sorry," Greg said, pointing to his crotch. "Blame him, not me."

"Right. Anyway, a friend of mine is here and wants to hang out with us."

Greg looked puzzled. "Your sister?"

"No! I have other friends besides her."

Realization dawned. "You mean that Victor guy? No shit?"

Jace smiled, feeling oddly proud. "No shit."

They found Victor smoking underneath the tall oak tree out front. He nodded casually at Greg when introductions were made. Greg, on the other hand, wasn't quite as cool.

"Wow! You're really him? I thought you'd be bigger!"

"Bigger?" Victor asked.

"Well, yeah. Mr. Collins used to be a quarterback, so..."

"Oh, that." Victor smirked. "You'd be surprised what a little military training can do."

"What did I tell you?" Greg said, nudging Jace. "Chuck Norris!"

Jace just shook his head. Earlier in the week, Greg hadn't even know Victor's name. Now he acted like he was an expert. Or a fan who happily trotted alongside his idol as they headed into the valley behind the house, asking Victor to teach him moves and asking what other fights he'd been in.

They were heading toward the lake, which prompted Jace to ask, "Where are we going?"

Victor seemed relieved at the change of subject. "I set up camp not far away. This weather is supposed to hold all week."

"Really?" Jace asked. "You're staying here?" He felt sure music would have swelled, that they would have tumbled into each other's arms, if Greg hadn't been walking between them.

"We should get drunk!" his best friend suggested.

"I had something else in mind." Victor patted a jacket pocket mysteriously.

That made Jace a little nervous, but his thoughts soon returned to Victor being near for the next couple of days.

From out of the woods, a small creek wound its way through an empty field before spilling into the lake. This is what he and Greg always followed to start their hikes. As Victor led them along this same path, Jace wondered if he had noticed their archery target. Had they come out here sooner instead of shopping, they might have met. But Victor led them much farther into the woods than they normally ventured. The sounds of leaf blowers faded away into the distance until that familiar feeling returned. The suburban world behind them—*that* was the dream. Reality was right here.

Victor stopped and gestured. Jace had pictured a simple pup tent, but instead saw a small shelter built from branches and boughs of pine. Propped up between two trees, the structure reminded him of the forts he and Michelle used to make from sheets and blankets. Even those provided more cover. This was little more than a wall leaning forward, the angle enough to cover the sleeping bag laid out horizontally beneath it.

"Nice lean-to!" Greg exclaimed, rushing forward to check it out. "Of course pine isn't the best choice when it comes to keeping water out and heat in. What do you usually do for a fire?"

Victor picked up a small axe and gestured with it toward a circular area that had been cleared of leaves and debris. "I still need to gather wood, if you want to help."

"Totally, although a circular fire in the middle is no good this time of year. A long fire will keep your whole body warm at night."

Jace stood back and watched the proceedings. Victor might have more experience living off the land, but Greg was the consummate Boy Scout. He knew the official handbook inside and out. Jace had often joked that if civilization came to an end, he'd follow Greg around like a puppy. He'd know what to do in any situation.

Victor seemed to take the critical feedback in stride. In fact, he seemed happy to take Greg's advice. Soon both he and Jace were following the Eagle Scout's directions. In a few short hours, they had a fire prepped, the lean-to insulated with moss, and enough wood gathered or cut to last the weekend. Greg even had a cooking area set up at one end of the fire, arranging sticks so a small blackened pot could be hung from them.

"That won't last forever, but it'll stop your soup from burning too easily."

"I usually just toss the pot straight into the embers," Victor said.

Greg shook his head as if this was unthinkable. "This is better. You know, we *could* build a second lean-to on the other side to reflect heat. Or a nice A-frame shelter—"

"How about we enjoy what we've done?" Jace said, not hiding his exasperation.

"Oh. Right." Greg looked a little embarrassed, but not much.

"It just so happens," Victor said, "that I have the perfect way to celebrate."

From an inside pocket, he pulled out a bag of weed. Jace only recognized it from the anti-drug films they were shown in school, although those usually included pre-rolled joints as well, maybe with pills thrown in for effect. This appeared much more innocent. Victor took a small metal pipe from the same pocket and began filling it. He looked up at their silence.

"First time?" he asked.

Guilty as charged. Michelle had smoked it a few times with one of her boyfriends, but she didn't care for it. Jace wondered if he would. As for Greg doing something like this, Jace just couldn't imagine it. He glanced over at his best friend to see shiny eyes. Okay, so maybe Greg would jump off a cliff if Victor asked him to. He supposed that made two of them.

Jace wondered if his attraction to Victor was just that— admiration. Sure he found his body enticing, but he checked out Greg too, and there definitely weren't any feelings there. He probably wouldn't recognize love, even if he felt it. The realization was sad, but he didn't stew on it, since Victor was demonstrating how to smoke.

"Just like a cigarette," he was saying, lighting the pipe, "but take it slower. Just a little bit at a time."

He made it look easy, but when Jace took his turn, he coughed for two solid minutes. Greg looked smug until he tried. Soon they both sounded like they were trapped in a burning building. Eventually they got the hang of it. The pain of Jace's raw throat became distant as everything changed. He'd always imagined pot clouding his mind, making it hard to think. Instead the world around him seemed to intensify. Everything was interesting, not just Victor or Greg, but the shape of the leaves above and the sound of the wind sailing through them. Every thought seemed to last a small eternity, each a realization of incredible depth.

"I really like camels," he said.

His friends burst out laughing, and after a moment of bewilderment, Jace joined them.

"Seriously! Everyone focuses on the humps, but have you ever looked at their lips? The way they move their mouths… I dunno. I'm sure they could talk if they wanted to."

"They have funky expressions too," Victor said. "Like a rich old countess who's way past her expiration date but still thinks she's hot shit."

"What's a countess, anyway?" Greg asked. "Aren't they just some made-up monster, like a vampire's wife?"

Jace pinched the bridge of his nose. "Of course they're real. You've just never met one because you don't live in medieval Europe. Wait, did you say vampire?"

"Yeah!" Greg appeared dead serious. "Like on Sesame Street. Remember the Count? He was a creepy vampire."

"Terrifying," Jace said, shaking his head. "It's a miracle you manage to sleep at night."

"I don't like blood-suckers," Greg said, sullenly slapping at his neck.

"One!" Victor said, doing his best Transylvanian accent. "One dead mosquito, ah ah ah!"

"Both of you shut up." Greg glared at them. "What are you guys scared of?"

"Like our worst fear?" Jace asked.

"Yeah."

"Well it's not Big Bird."

"I was little." Greg glowered before cracking a smile. "Come on. Out with it!"

Jace shrugged. "I don't know."

"You do," Victor said. "Don't be shy. I'll spill my guts right after you."

Jace looked him square in the eye and understood. This was a challenge. Was Jace one of the herd, afraid to be himself? He thought of the suicide note, of the fear that was enough to make him want to quit, and before he could stop himself he confessed. "I don't want to die alone."

There was a moment of silence that Greg seemed eager to fill. "You don't have to worry about that. Chances are you'll be in a hospital with your family there, or even if you're in an ambulance, there will be a paramedic. Of course if you get mauled by a bear in the woods, I guess you'd be alone. Except for the bear."

Jace nearly smiled. Greg meant well, like he always did. "I don't mean it like that. Although I guess that's part of it, yeah. Mostly I don't want to go through my whole life watching everyone fall in love and have kids, be these perfect little couples while I sit on the sidelines wondering what's wrong with me."

Greg put a hand on his shoulder. "I keep telling you, man, there are all sorts of girls for you. Maybe Angie's little sister is a dumb idea, but that Julie chick was giving you the eye. You just have to come out of your shell."

Jace needed to come out of something, or these little pep talks would never end. Victor caught his eye, but his puzzlement didn't last for long. Jace wondered if this disqualified him, made him someone who just wanted to fit in, but it wasn't as simple as that. Victor didn't know about Greg's island for gay people, or just how much losing his best friend would tear Jace up inside. He kept his eyes locked on Victor's, wondering if he could silently communicate all of this.

"My worst fear," Victor said, looking away, "is losing my mother."

"Oh man!" Greg said. "Is she—"

"No." Victor's smile was reassuring. "She's not sick or anything like that. We're on our own, that's all. My dad ran off when I was little, and from what she's told me, we're better off without him. Of course we have distant relatives, but—" Victor considered them. "I don't have any siblings, but do they feel closer to you than a cousin or an uncle? I mean, is the bond stronger?"

"Totally," Jace said, Greg nodding in agreement. "I love my grandparents, my aunts and uncles, but I'd take a bullet for my parents or my sister without a second thought."

"Dude," Greg whispered, "you wouldn't take one for your granny?"

"No one's going to shoot my grandma," Jace said dismissively.

"That's good to know," Victor said. "I mean that the family bond is stronger with immediate family. Maybe it's even more intense for my mom and me because we're all each other has. When I was growing up, she worked her ass off to support me. When she was at home, she gave me all of her time, made me feel loved and special."

Victor's face grew dark. For the first time, as far as Jace had seen, he appeared angry. It wasn't a pretty sight. "Mr. Collins." Victor said the name with a growl. " He decided to lecture the class about single parents, how insufficient they are, how sons grow up limp-wristed or daughters turn out promiscuous like their mothers. A vicious cycle, he called it. Only after he finished his ignorant rant did he think to ask if any of us had single parents. I was pissed enough to raise my hand, but when three other students followed suit, the idea of them having to listen to the same bullshit set me off."

"And so you pinned Mr. Collins to the chalkboard?" Greg asked in transparent admiration.

"Yeah. And for all his big talk, he was terrified. I told him that my mother was hard working and respectable, not some pervert who primes his pump while drooling over the pretty boys in his classes."

"Do you think he really does that?" Greg asked.

"Probably," Victor said.

"Sick."

Jace's stomach grew tight at the sound of that one word. It was all too easy to imagine Greg directing it at him and not at Mr. Collins. Jace could feel Victor's eyes on him, but he kept his focus on the ground.

"It's only sick," Victor said, "because Mr. Collins is one twisted motherfucker. Even if he liked women his own age, it would be sick, because no one like him should reproduce. Or be loved. But there's nothing wrong with being gay."

Greg snorted, but then sounded puzzled. "Are you serious?"

"Absolutely. It doesn't matter if someone loves a guy or a girl. What matters is who they are inside."

Jace raised his head, but Victor's focus was on Greg now. That was good. Unfortunately, what was said next nearly gave him a heart attack.

"What if Jace was gay?" Victor challenged. "Would you stop being his friend, just because he'd rather be with a guy?"

Greg was stunned. He stared at Jace, mouth agape, like the idea was impossible. Or like he'd missed the obvious all this time. When he spoke, his voice sounded terse. "Are you?"

Maybe it was the pot, or maybe he was tired of feeling it, but the fear inside Jace vanished. One nod. That's all it took to confirm the truth.

Greg continued to stare, but eventually he looked back to Victor. "And you?"

Victor smirked. "I am nothing, and I am everything."

What the hell was that supposed to mean? Greg looked at

Jace, as if he could explain, but he only shrugged.

"It's getting dark," Victor said, standing and brushing off his rump. "I'll get the fire started."

Jace rose to help him, even though he didn't know how, but at least it allowed him to turn his back on Greg. He walked to the edge of the clearing to escape the tension, was considering walking home when a hand grabbed his wrist and spun him around. Greg stood there, a look of grim determination on his face. For one terrifying moment, Jace thought Greg was going to deck him.

"You're my best friend," he said instead, his lips forming a line, nostrils flaring. "I don't care if you get a sex change and marry a freaking goat! You'll always be my best friend."

Before Jace could respond, Greg threw his arms around him and squeezed. Jace wanted to say thank you, but instead all that came out were tears. His body shook and his nose ran, but the funny thing was, he hadn't felt happier in years. When Greg finally released him, it was clear that he had been crying too.

"Must be the marijuana," Jace murmured, wiping at his eyes.

"Totally," Greg said, grateful for the excuse. "Real men don't cry. Even gay ones."

Jace chuckled. "That's right. Uh, thanks. For being cool, I mean."

Greg nodded, cheeks red. "I better help Victor with the fire."

"Yeah. Before he burns down the lean-to."

They laughed nervously, and when Greg went to help, Jace stayed where he was, watching them work. Funny how they could grow up together, be friends their entire lives, and despite being so close, both fail to see the truth. Jace needed someone—but Greg hadn't understood who, or at least what gender they would be. And his own oversight felt even greater, because Greg had more love in his heart than Jace had ever guessed.

Chapter Six

The fire crackled and spat, creating shadows that danced and leapt around the edge of the clearing. Greg disappeared into these, Jace watching him go until he could no longer be seen. Even half-stoned and in the dark, Greg would find his way home. All he had to do was follow the creek, but he'd be cold by the time he made it back. As nice as the day had been, the evening warned of winter's approach.

"He's all right," Victor said. Sitting in front of the fire, he stared into its light. "A lot smarter than he looks."

"Yeah, that's true," Jace said, taking a seat next to him. "He's easy on the eyes too."

He was hoping for some sort of reaction to this bait. Jealousy or shared interest, but there was none. Once everything had calmed down, Jace found time to consider the conversation from a clearer perspective. In retrospect, he was thrilled that Greg had asked Victor if he was gay too. If only the answer had been clear. The topic of sexuality hadn't returned once they had lit the fire. They smoked more pot and let their tongues lob silly and absurd words at each other. Later they heated up and shared a can of soup, dipping stale bread into it until it was soft enough to eat.

Now Greg had gone home, leaving Jace alone with Victor, and all those unanswered questions were bubbling to the surface. "Did you do it on purpose?"

Victor glanced at him, then back to the fire. His dark hair reflected the light, giving it orange highlights. "Outing you? No. I really didn't. I wanted you to see that Greg would accept you, but he surprised me when he put all the pieces together like that. As I said, smarter than he looks."

"But you knew he wouldn't have a problem with me being gay?"

"Yeah."

Jace shook his head. "Don't laugh, but are you psychic? Every time you look at me, it's like you can read my mind. *And* you knew Greg would be cool, which sort of pisses me off, because I've known him my whole life."

To his credit, Victor kept a straight face. Mostly. "No, I'm not psychic. I've always been a good judge of character. Like I knew you would've shot me that night at the gas station if I tried anything."

"I wouldn't have!"

Victor nodded. "Yes you would. You just wouldn't have aimed for the head."

Jace considered it. "Maybe I would have taken out a leg, just to slow you down until the cops got there."

Victor grinned. "See? It was either be your friend, or walk with a limp the rest of my life."

Except Jace didn't want to be just friends. Forget any fantasy about taking it slow. What he needed most, right now, was to know if he had a chance. "What did you mean when you said you're all or nothing?"

"Nothing and everything," Victor corrected. "We kind of touched on this the other night."

"That doesn't mean I understood," Jace said.

"Probably because it's silly." Victor shook his head. "It's not important."

"Tell me anyway."

"Okay, let me put it to you this way. If you go to college and get your medical degree, you'll be Dr. Holden. For the rest of your life, that's what you'll be. A doctor. Everyone will look at you that way. If someone says, 'Jace who?' the other person will answer, 'You know, the doctor.' Are you with me so far?"

"I think so."

"Good. But if you don't go to school, don't limit yourself to one career choice in life, you'll always have the potential to be anything. By never choosing one path, you're free to walk all of them."

Jace frowned. "But that doesn't mean you can be *everything*. You can't be a doctor if you don't go to medical school."

Victor shrugged. "Why not? There are medicine men, or faith healers, or people who use folk remedies. My mom puts half an onion on a bee sting. In that moment, she's performing the role of a doctor."

Jace thought about it. "But she still has another job, and whatever that is, it doesn't limit her from being a doctor when the situation warrants it. And besides, Greg asked if you were gay, and I'm pretty sure that's not a profession."

Victor studied him. "You drive me crazy sometimes."

"In a gay way?"

After a chuckle, Victor shook his head and said, "It's a philosophy, that's all. I told you it was silly. Greg wanted to know who I am, and I refuse to limit myself to any one thing. That's why I don't like titles. I don't need them, especially when it comes to love."

Jace was momentarily thrilled, until Victor added.

"That's why I'm not interested in relationships."

Was he asexual? How torturous if true! But Jace had his own psychic flash when Victor had first mentioned Star. Maybe he was learning to read people too, because something about the way Victor said her name had felt affectionate. "That girl you were with the other night, were you *with* her?"

"I'm starting to detect a theme here."

"Seriously," Jace said, surprised at how vulnerable he felt.

Victor shrugged. "We've slept together before, yeah. But we didn't this week."

"Oh. When's the last time you did? I mean, do you love her?"

"Why does it matter?"

Jace wanted to say it, more than anything, but the words caught in his throat. Victor watched him a moment longer before he got up to tend the fire. Why did this have to be so hard? All he wanted to know was if there was hope, or if he should give up now. One thing was for sure. Jace wasn't going home tonight. Not without knowing.

Jace stood, feeling a little dizzy. "It matters because if she means something to you, there's no room for me." Victor turned around to face him, which made it harder to speak, but he pressed on. "I'm crazy for thinking I have a shot at being someone special to you, aren't I? If so, tell me now so I can get over it. Don't talk in riddles or try to soften the blow. Just tell me so I can deal with the truth."

Victor tossed some kindling into the fire and came closer. "You aren't crazy. But I meant it when I said I'm not into relationships. I don't want a girlfriend, a boyfriend, a wife, or anything else. There's no need."

"There is for me," Jace said, his lip beginning to tremble. "Lately that need is all I feel."

"Why?" Victor asked, his voice gentle. "If I was your boyfriend, what would you do?"

Jace felt on the verge of tears, so he steeled himself and answered. "I'd kiss you."

Victor opened his arms wide. "There's nothing stopping you."

Jace didn't hesitate, not even for a second. He stepped forward and kissed Victor, his lips forgetting their sorrow the second they made contact. And this wasn't a joke because Victor kissed him back, wrapped his arms around Jace, which prompted him to do the same. Jace held on to him with desperation, just in case this was the last time another guy let him do something like this. Just in case this was his one brush with love.

The kiss broke as Victor pulled away. "Why are you crying?" he asked.

Jace wiped at the tears, surprised they were there at all. Then he shook his head. "If there's finally something you don't understand about me, I'm not about to explain it."

"Fair enough." One of Victor's hands remained on the back of Jace's head, toying with his hair. "Do you see what I mean now? We can be anything we want to each other. I'm not scared to admit who I'm interested in, or ashamed to have feelings for anyone, but I'm also not eager to label myself."

"Why not?" Jace said jokingly, but he was glad he got an answer.

"If I had told myself I was straight, limited myself that way with a title, I would have missed out on that awesome fucking kiss just now."

"Which would have been bad?"

"Devastating."

"But I mean," Jace ran a thumb along Victor's jaw, eager to taste his lips again, "you can still feel things for me. Even without putting a title on it, you can still—"

"No limits," Victor promised. "We can take it further than all those boring old married people, feel things they haven't discovered and never will."

"Like what?" Jace asked, eyes wide.

Victor smirked, moving in for a kiss. "Let's find out."

Jace woke with the sun warming his face, his bed a pile of soft leaves, his room for the night a forest glen filled with birdsong. Birdsong that sounded suspiciously like Patsy Cline. Jace raised his head, the last remnants of his dream fading away, replacing the tranquil scene with his bedroom. His mother's music crooned from the kitchen downstairs. At least the sunlight was real, causing his hair to glow as it warmed his face.

Rubbing his eyes, Jace looked at the clock and groaned. Past noon already. He didn't usually sleep so late, but then he hadn't gotten home until three in the morning. Smiling at the memory, he touched his fingers to his lips. He and Victor had kissed for hours, or at least it had felt that way. Jace's body had been begging to go further, but that was one giant step, and he wasn't sure if he was supposed to make that move, or if Victor was, or if they had to talk about it first.

Jace laughed at himself. He wouldn't find out by staying here! Rolling out of bed, he headed across the hall to the bathroom. His whole body smelled hickory-smoked from the campfire, so he hit the shower. He was still wildly horny from last night, but he abstained on the off chance that he'd find release tonight. Once he was clean and dressed, Jace headed downstairs to the kitchen.

His mother's music was still playing, but she wasn't in sight, so Jace raided the pantry. He was munching a peanut butter and honey sandwich held in one hand while using the other to toss canned goods into a backpack. He wanted Victor to be well-stocked during his stay in the area.

"Collecting for a food drive?" his mother said from behind.

"Sort of," Jace said. When he turned around, he could see she already knew.

"You were out late, so I called the Trouts. Greg told me everything."

Jace doubted that. Besides, Greg didn't know the half of it, although it did remind him that they had plans today. "Has he come by?"

Serena shook her head. "I was surprised you were in your room this morning. I thought you were camping out."

"No," Jace said, although he loved the idea. "But tonight I am."

"On a school night?"

"It's Sunday," he countered.

"You know what I mean. You have school in the morning."

Jace defiantly tossed a can of ravioli in the backpack. "It's not like I'll be far. I'm practically in the backyard. I'll take a battery-powered alarm clock with me and be at the breakfast table the same time I always am."

His mother pursed her lips.

"I'll literally be five minutes away," he said. "Please."

"Ask your father."

Yes! That was as good as having permission. All he needed to tell his dad was, "Mom says it's fine if I camp out tonight. Is it okay with you?" Worked every time. Once he was loaded up with supplies, he paid his father a short visit. He was in the living room, watching golf on TV, which made it even easier. Jace could have said he was moving to Istanbul and his father would have nodded.

That just left Greg. Jace telephoned his house, but there wasn't an answer. Thinking Greg might be on his way over, he went out on the back porch but didn't see him anywhere. Greg was usually so reliable. Could it be that, sober and in the light of day, he wasn't feeling supportive of Jace's sexuality anymore? Jace found that hard to believe. The things he had felt while high last night hadn't changed now. Pot hadn't made him a different person, like alcohol seemed to. And yet, Greg was nowhere to be seen. In the end, Jace decided to head down to the campsite. Greg would know to find him there. Hell, maybe his best friend was there already, lecturing Victor on further improvements he could make.

Jace had stood and was walking away from the house when the back door slid open.

"Car keys!" his sister called, chasing after him.

"Oh, right." Jace dug in his pocket and fished them out, tossing them to her.

"Thanks," Michelle said, deftly catching them. "I want to get some Christmas shopping done today."

"For real?" Jace gestured around him at the unseasonal weather. But he wasn't surprised. His sister was Christmas crazy.

"Don't make me cross you off the list," she teased. "Hey, any progress with Victor?"

Jace didn't have to answer. He just smiled.

"What? You're shitting me!" Michelle slapped his arm playfully. "Oh my god, tell me everything! On second thought, don't!" She considered the implications. "My big brother has a boyfriend!"

"Kind of. He's uh—" Wonderful. Sexy. Mysterious. "Complicated."

"Oh. But you guys are, you know, getting friendly in a physical way?"

Jace bit his lip and nodded rapidly.

"Good for you!"

"Thanks. Although it's kind of hard to tell how serious he is."

Michelle looked sympathetic. "Welcome to the fun part. You know he likes you, but you don't know if he *really* likes you. Remember Dave? Ten months together, all those presents, the horrible poetry, and I still wasn't sure. Guys are dogs; they'll say or do anything to get—and keep getting—what they want."

Jace didn't hide his surprise. "Wow. I didn't know you were so jaded."

"Me? No! I love the game. Believe me when I say I'm getting what I want too." Michelle's face softened. "But I don't mean to make it sound cold. The wondering and hoping, that's all part of love. That's what keeps you on your toes and makes it so damn exciting. Just try to enjoy it. If he makes you feel good about yourself, and if you can do the same for him, that's all that matters."

"I'm getting you an extra present for Christmas this year," Jace promised.

"Score!"

"All right. I'm headed out to see him now."

"Have fun," Michelle said. She was at the sliding door when she turned around. "Hey! One more piece of advice. No matter how big his thingy is, act like it's huge. Guys love that!"

Jace looked repulsed, causing his sister to cackle with laughter. Hopefully that was the last advice she'd ever give him in that department.

When Jace reached the campsite, Victor was sitting under the lean-to, legs pulled up to his chest. His hair was sticking up, looking even more punky than usual. Victor's eyes sparkled when he spotted Jace, inviting and welcoming, which made him feel brave. Without hesitation, he went to Victor and bent over, placing a finger under his chin to lift it so they could kiss.

And just like last night, Victor kissed him right back. At first, anyway.

"I feel scuzzy," he said, dodging Jace's next attempt.

"I don't care," he said honestly, crawling onto the sleeping bag. Why had he left last night? Now that his head was clear, his body rested, he was ready to go further. He leaned forward to kiss Victor's neck.

"Seriously," Victor said, gently pushing him away. "Wait until I get cleaned up."

"Want a tongue bath?" Jace said with a grin.

Victor eyed him. "I can see that you're going to be a handful. But no. I have a better method of getting clean. I'll show you later today. Right now I need to scrounge for any leftovers."

"There aren't any," Jace said. "Blame the munchies. Luckily you have me."

He dragged the backpack close and started emptying the contents, naming each and trying to put an exotic spin on them. "Fresh garden vegetables left to simmer in a delicate broth," he said, handing over a cheap can of vegetable soup. "Italian dough pockets stuffed with minced veal," he said, setting down the can of ravioli.

"And this?" Victor asked, holding up a lowly can of pork and beans.

"That, my friend," Jace said, taking on a tone of wonder, "is more precious than rocket fuel. Why, that is the very meal that propelled the settlers across this great nation. Almost literally, I imagine."

Victor feigned awe. "These must have cost you a fortune."

"I took out a five-year loan," he said dismissively.

"Seriously though, thank you." Victor picked up and frowned at a box of crackers. "There's got to be a better way. If I'm going to do this, I don't want to keep mooching off you. Greg mentioned sustainability yesterday, which was cool. People used to live off the land. Settlers ate more than just pork and beans."

Jace raised an eyebrow. "Planning on hunting buffalo?"

Victor chuckled. "No, but there are fruit trees, if you know where to look. Or I could fish. If I knew how."

"I could teach you," Jace said.

Victor looked surprised. "Really?"

"Of course! I've lived next to a lake my entire life." He considered the sky. "Today's the perfect day for it too. I can run back to the house and pick up some equipment."

Victor grinned, which felt like the greatest prize in the world. "All right. Let's do it."

"Let's eat something first," Jace said. "We'll starve before we yank anything out of that lake."

After sharing a meal of soup and crackers, Jace returned to the house, Victor staying behind to get the evening's fire ready. They met where the creek spilled into the lake, Jace guiding them to an unmaintained and rarely visited dock on the far side. Here they would have privacy. Jace didn't care much for fishing. He received his own rod and tackle box one year for his birthday. All the different lures and methods kept him interested for a month or so before he moved on to other distractions.

"Worms are way better," Jace said. "If you buy nightcrawlers, you'll have a fish in no time. I've never had much luck with lures, but we're going to use them anyway. Unless you want to go digging for worms."

Victor rifled through the tackle box. "We can try these. I like this one." He held up a rubbery lure resembling a tadpole—aside from being bright yellow and having a giant eyes painted on each side of the head. "What's this supposed to be?"

Jace shrugged. "I've never used that one. Let's see what happens."

Fishing wasn't complicated. Teaching Victor the basics of the rod didn't take long. They practiced casting the line into the water and reeling it back in a few times. After that, the true skill came into play—patience. They sat on the dock, the sun already making its descent. Only an hour of light, at most, remained.

"What do we do once we catch one?" Victor asked, jiggling the pole.

"Hand it to Greg," Jace said. He wasn't joking. Even taking the hook out of a fish's mouth made him squeamish. "If you really plan on eating one, there's this club thing you can whack them over the head with. It's called a priest, believe it or not. Greg always jokes about it giving fish their last rites. Then he makes a cut so they bleed out. Or you can leave them to suffocate, but that can take a really long time and seems cruel."

"Think he'd be willing to show me this stuff?" Victor asked.

"Yeah!" Jace said, but then he looked across the lake toward Greg's home. When fetching their fishing equipment, he'd asked if Greg had called or stopped by. He hadn't.

"What's wrong?"

"I don't know," Jace said, picking at the splintering wood of the dock. "I was supposed to hang out with Greg today, but he didn't show."

"And you think he's not okay about you being gay?" Victor nudged him. "Trust me on this. He's fine. Just give it time."

Jace looked up. "Maybe I should stop by his place a little later."

"Give him space. It'll be fine. You'll see."

"You sure?"

Victor winked. "I'm psychic, remember?"

As the day steadily grew darker, they made small talk, joking with each other or telling stories from their past. Sometimes, as Jace listened to Victor and watched the different expressions play out on his face, his breath would feel short, like he couldn't get enough air. That he had kissed this person, would do so again, felt miraculous. The idea of being able to touch another guy, even in ways that were simple, like when he placed his hand over Victor's, seemed amazing. Maybe straight people always expected this, saw it as something obvious and inevitable, but to Jace it felt like he'd achieved the impossible.

"I felt something!" Victor said, his body tense as he watched the bobber in the water. Then he scrambled to his feet. "Shit! Okay! Uh..."

Jace tried to explain what to do but kept laughing at how panicked Victor was. Eventually he got the hang of it, slowly reeling in the line. With a splash of water, a shiny speckled fish burst into the air.

"Oh my god!" Victor said, reeling it in with a look of wonder.

"It's crappie!" Jace said, intoning one of the oldest fishing jokes in the world.

"Looks good to me!"

"That's the species name," Jace said. "Crappie. You can definitely eat one of those. Crappie taste good, not crappy."

A protruded golden eye seemed to focus on them momentarily as the fish spun on its line, jerking occasionally. The fish and its captors considered each other in silence.

"I want to let it go," Victor said, voice terse.

"Yeah, okay." Jace grimaced. He hated this part and had only done it once or twice. He bent down and got his hands wet in the lake water, just like Greg always did. "Swing the line around so I can grab it."

Victor practically smacked him in the face with the fish, but after ducking and a bit of fumbling, Jace had it in hand. Scowling in concentration, he grabbed the hook in the fish's lip. The rest was a matter of jiggling it free, which still made his brow sweat since he didn't want to hurt the poor thing. Ironic, since their goal from the beginning had been to hook it. Once the metal barb slipped free with minimal damage, he knelt and placed the fish in the water. It disappeared beneath the murky surface.

"That was intense," Victor breathed.

"Yeah." Jace washed his hands in the water. "Obviously I'm not very experienced."

"Are you kidding? You did great!"

Jace smiled and stood. "You're the one who caught his first fish."

"Yeah." Victor looked to where the fish had disappeared. "I'm not sure this is for me. I felt bad."

"I know what you mean. But if you're doing it to survive..."

"True."

"Just have Greg with you next time. He's so smooth that the fish look like they're having fun."

Victor laughed. "I'll keep him in mind." He considered the horizon. "It's getting dark."

"Should we head back?"

"Not yet. There's still this."

From out of his jacket pocket, Victor produced a bar of soap. "About time to get freshened up," he said.

Jace stared at him. "Here?"

"Why not? No one will see. You'll love it."

That depended on what Victor meant. Jace would love to sit on the dock and watch Victor bathe himself on the shore, but he didn't plan on joining in. "I took a shower this morning."

"But that fish got its smell all over you." Victor shook his head. "Nope. I'm afraid you're going swimming with me."

Jace finally understood. "You want to go skinny dipping? With all those houses right over there?"

Victor didn't seem concerned. "You've lived here your whole life. How many neighbors do you run into down here? Besides, I thought you'd be into this. Me and you, naked in the water together."

"Well, when you put it that way." Jace considered the settling dusk. "Just wait a little while longer, when it's really dark. Then I'll do it."

Victor was smug. "Looks like I just caught my second fish."

Chapter Seven

They sat side by side on the dock, warm where their arms and shoulders pressed against each other. The light fled from the day, leaving them alone, the water disturbed only by the bugs dancing across its surface as if it were made of glass.

Victor leaned close, brought his lips to Jace's ear. "Time to take off your clothes."

Jace laughed and pulled away. "You first."

"No," Victor said, getting to his feet. "Together. No hesitating, no dipping a toe in the water first. We rip off our clothes and jump in."

"Okay," Jace said, a fluttering in his chest. He stood, stripping off his shirt first. Glancing over, he saw Victor had done the same and was working on his jeans. The sky was clear, but the night was dark, the moon a tiny sliver. Jace sat again to take off his shoes, wishing he hadn't been shy earlier when he could have seen so much more in the dwindling light. Then again, maybe it was for the best, since Jace was having enough trouble controlling his body.

"Come on, slow poke," Victor said. He stood over Jace, wearing nothing but his underwear.

The second Jace had his shoes off and jeans unzipped, Victor started pulling at the legs, Jace kicking and laughing in protest. After tossing Jace's pants farther down the dock, Victor offered his hand. Jace took it and was pulled up, brought close enough that he thought they would kiss.

"Ready?" Victor said, thumbs already beneath the waistband of his underwear.

"Yeah," Jace said, doing the same.

"Now or never! Go!"

Victor ripped his underwear down and Jace did the same, but he didn't have time to gawk, because Victor took him by the hand. Together they ran and leapt off the end of the dock, fingers losing their grip as they plunged into the water.

Cold! The first thing Jace thought of was his suicide leap into the Blackwater River. For a moment, he wondered if he was still there, all of this a mad fantasy produced by his oxygen-starved brain. But as his head broke the surface, he saw stars above him. Gasping for air, he felt a hand seek out his, a leg brush against his own.

"It's freezing!" Jace said.

"I think the right term is 'bracing,'" Victor said, eyes wild. "Come on. Keep moving and you'll warm up."

Victor headed for the middle of the lake, pulling Jace along until certain he would follow. Then they released each other and started swimming properly. Victor was right. It wasn't so bad, the two days of sun having tempered the water. Not that Jace had ever taken a bath in water this cold, but he wouldn't need any old fisherman to save his life this time.

Victor stopped swimming, turning in the water with glee. Jace didn't stop swimming until he was on top of him, Victor angling back in the water to accommodate.

"Now you're all freshened up and don't have an excuse," Jace said, stealing a kiss.

Victor kissed him back, their bodies touching beneath the water, but only fleetingly as they paddled in place. An arm bumped against a hip, or legs brushed against each other before sweeping away. If they did stop moving and pressed against each other completely, they would sink to the bottom. Jace thought it might be worth the sacrifice.

Oddly enough, Victor was having similar thoughts. "How deep do you think this lake is?" he asked before sucking in air and disappearing beneath the surface. Jace was alone. He spun in the water, searching for some sign of his friend, and noticed how different the lake looked. His whole life he'd been standing on the shore, never even taking a boat on the lake since it seemed too small to be worth it. But now that he was out here, he saw the other side of the picture he'd been missing: The ring of trees, the small docks, and the gentle way the valley was lit by porch lights.

Something grabbed his ankle, causing him to yelp.

Victor's head popped up next to his. "Didn't manage," he panted. "You try. You're taller."

Jace nodded, taking a deep breath before bringing his limbs close to his body. He plunged down through the darkness like a torpedo, feeling a little scared of the things around him that he couldn't see. He was picturing the fish they'd caught chasing after him, seeking revenge, when his feet touched muddy ground. Jace kicked off this, bouncing upward again, lungs growing tight. Then he burst into air, Victor's face expectant.

"Well?"

"Easy." Jace said.

"I'll try again."

But Jace grabbed him before he could dive, hugging their torsos together and kicking extra hard to keep them afloat. He pressed his lips against Victor's, the temperature in his body rising a few degrees. He was moving his hands down Victor's back when something splashed at the shore, scaring him.

"Just a frog," Victor said. "All your neighbors are locked up in TV land, don't worry."

"Is your life always like this?" he asked.

Victor looked wistful. "No, this is just the dream. So far at least. Why? Think you could get used to it?"

Jace thought about the comforts of home: a hot shower, a warm bed, and a cold refrigerator. "No," he said honestly, "but I sure like visiting."

They swam together a little longer, but even Victor had to admit the truth.

"This isn't the right time of year for this," he said. "Let's head back to the dock so I can wash up."

Once there, Jace climbed out. They didn't have any towels, so he did his best impression of a dog and shook off the water. Then he hurriedly got dressed, out of necessity more than humility. He was cold! His clothes helped to soak up the remaining moisture, but already he was shivering.

Victor sat on the edge of the dock while Jace was dressing, lathering the soap and washing before plopping back in the lake. His back was turned during all of this, and despite the little that Jace could see, he felt like drooling. Geez, maybe he *was* turning into a dog!

When Victor got out of the water, Jace didn't want to appear perverted, so he busied himself with packing up their fishing equipment.

"Let's hurry back to camp," Victor said. "The fire will get us warmed up again."

Victor usually walked the easy, carefree stroll of a person with all the time in the world. Now he practically sprinted back to the campsite. Jace kept pace right behind him. The outside temperature was steadily dropping, their damp clothes clinging to their skin and absorbing any heat. Victor skidded to a halt in front of the campfire and worked on getting it lit. He'd built another long fire like Greg had instructed, which would be heavenly once roaring.

"Get in the sleeping bag and warm up," Victor said. He glanced over when Jace had one leg in. "Take your clothes off first or they'll never dry out."

The idea of being even more exposed to the elements seemed bad, even if temporary, but Jace did what he was told. Victor was too busy with the fire to watch him anyway, and he supposed it was silly to feel shy after swimming naked together.

The camp site was soon illuminated by the fire, warmth returning to the world, but Jace was still cold and Victor's teeth were practically chattering. He took one look at Jace and started tearing off his clothes without the slightest bit of shame. Jace stared. He couldn't help himself. The lake had been dark, but now the fire revealed all. He'd seen quite a bit of Victor's body already, except for —

The underwear came off. Angels should have played trumpets to mark the occasion. Victor wasn't hard, but in this weather, Jace didn't take that personally. What he noticed most was the raven-black pubic hair, a stark difference to the blondish-brown of his own. Victor's package bounced its way toward him. Jace tore away his eyes, seeing an expression that looked desperate, but not with lust.

"Coooold!" Victor whined. "Make room for me!"

The sleeping bag was definitely not built for two. They had to unzip it down to Jace's waist so Victor could squeeze in, and then Victor had to press his back against Jace to get it zipped up again. This left absolutely no room for privacy, which meant his reaction to seeing Victor nude was all too apparent. Even worse, the stupid thing kept twitching of its own accord.

"Uh, sorry," Jace said.

Victor laughed. "Hey, at least it's warm!"

With their combined body heat and the radiating heat from the fire, Victor soon stopped shivering. "How do you usually survive winters?" Jace asked, but he didn't hear the answer. He was staring at Victor's neck, where the wide stripe of hair ended. He nuzzled this mane with his nose and then kissed Victor's neck. Jace had his arm around him to help warm him, but now his hand was itching to explore. He moved it experimentally.

"Can I —?"

"No limits," Victor reminded him.

Jace didn't need any more encouragement. He slid his palm

across Victor's chest, feeling the tickle of hair. Then he started kissing Victor's neck more intensely, moving his hand south. Sometimes Jace wondered if Victor really felt the same way that he did, or if this was all part of him trying to be different, to not define himself. Kisses were one thing, but if Victor was really attracted to him…

Something hot and hard bumped against his hand as he explored. The breath caught in Jace's throat as he wrapped his fingers around it. *He likes me!* Jace held back a laugh, and started pumping instead. Victor let out a moan, but he didn't remain stationary.

"Hold up," he said.

After some shifting and squirming, Victor managed to roll around to face him. Jace attacked his lips hungrily, his hands searching out his prize again. He wanted to throw off the sleeping bag, see everything laid bare, even if they would freeze. Before he could suggest it, Victor took hold of Jace's cock, and he was pretty damn sure those angels were nearby after all, because it felt like heaven.

"Taller than me *and* bigger," Victor said with faux frustration.

Jace tightened his grip. He didn't have any complaints about what he was holding! "Kiss me," he said.

Victor did. Rolling onto him a little, his tongue twisted around Jace's, their hands working in unison beneath the sleeping bag. Jace kept holding back, not wanting it to end, but it was so damn exciting! Another guy, letting him do things he'd barely even dreamed of. And there was so much more he wanted. His body tensed.

Victor stopped kissing him, pulling back and fixing those mismatched eyes on his own.

"Maybe we should—" Jace whimpered, barely able to speak. "Uh, we should get out of the sleeping bag or I'll make a mess."

"I promise you I'll make a bigger one," Victor said.

The thought pushed Jace over the edge. He was groaning and shooting and writhing in ecstasy, but he kept his arm pumping until Victor joined him. Then they released each other, panting for breath, but Jace hated even that small separation. He wrapped his arms around Victor, pressing their bodies together again, kissing him until Victor started laughing.

"What?" Jace asked.

"I don't know," Victor said. "You make me happy."

Jace grinned in response. "If that did the trick, then I'm willing to make you happy any time you want!"

"Deal." Victor touched his forehead to Jace's. "Now let's get out of this sleeping bag. We'll dry off by dancing around the fire like a couple of lost boys."

"You be Tinker Bell, I'll be Peter Pan," Jace teased.

Victor pushed himself up and onto Jace. One eyebrow cocked, his face was deeply shadowed by the fire's light. He looked like a scoundrel. "You be Peter," he said, and then he thrust his hips meaningfully. "I'll be Captain Hook."

Jace swallowed. Perhaps he had bitten off more than he could chew!

The light in the clearing was soft, the embers of the fire still smoldering, sending wisps of smoke up into the treetops. Jace licked his dry lips, taking stock of his situation. An arm was wrapped around his neck in the softest of headlocks as Victor snored steadily into his ear. Their bodies were pressed together as they had been all night, and though they had put on some clothes to stay warm, he could feel Victor's hardness pressing against his back.

Despite being uncomfortable, thirsty, and desperate to pee, Jace lay there as long as he could, enjoying every second. Only when absolutely necessary did he untangle himself from Victor, waking him. Unzipping the sleeping bag, Jace stumbled to the edge of the clearing. When he came back, Victor was sitting up, sipping from a canteen that he offered to share.

Jace enjoyed the first two swigs, but nearly spit the third out. "Shit! What time is it?"

He handed back the canteen and kneeled, digging through his backpack for the travel alarm clock that he had packed and then forgotten. Eleven in the morning! Jace groaned and rolled over onto his butt.

"Trouble?" Victor asked.

"I'm dead," Jace said. "It's a school day."

Victor shrugged, like it didn't matter.

"Don't start," Jace said. "You may have escaped the system, but I'm still subject to its rules. In particular, my mother's."

"Yeah, there's no getting away from a mom," Victor said with sympathy. "So I guess you're leaving?"

"Have to," Jace said. He looked at Victor sitting shirtless under the lean-to, the sleeping bag crumpled up around his hips, half an inch of his pubic hair peeking over the edge. "In a few minutes."

"I'm sure you'll be fine," Victor said. "People sleep-in all the time. She'll understand."

"Maybe," Jace said, but thoughts of his family were far from his mind as he continued to check out his boyfriend. Victor might not like titles, but Jace already thought of him that way. "Is that a tattoo?" he asked, nodding at dark line around one arm.

"Yeah," Victor said, raising his arm to examine it. "Did it myself."

"Seriously? How?"

"All you need is a needle and some ink. And skill, which I'm sadly lacking."

"I think it looks cool," Jace said.

Victor didn't seem convinced. "I wanted the line to be thicker and darker. Then I wanted a fox running along it."

"Why a fox?"

Victor grinned. "Because I might not be the smartest, the biggest, or the strongest, but I'm clever."

"Are you?" Jace teased. "I hadn't noticed."

"Yeah, well, which one of us is in trouble?"

"Good point." Jace sighed. Time to face the music. "I have to work tonight. Want to come by? You can ride into town with me."

Victor shook his head. "I'm not ready to face civilization just yet."

"Okay." Jace hesitated. "I'll try to come see you. After work. Is that okay?"

"You don't need my permission," Victor said, spreading his arms and flopping onto his back. "This is the *real* land of the free."

"Well, in that case…" Jace crawled over to Victor and kissed him. Victor reciprocated, pulling Jace down on top of him, tangling his fingers through Jace's hair.

"I love it," Victor whispered, pulling away to better see. His eyes darted around the edge of Jace's face.

"My hair?"

Victor nodded. "Even now when it's a goddamn mess!"

Jace did his best to look offended, sitting up and trying to tame the unruly mop, but mostly he felt glad that Michelle had made him grow it out. Victor sat up to kiss him again, and it took more willpower than Jace knew he had to pull his lips away and stand.

"Hopefully that will go down before you get home," Victor said, nodding at Jace's jeans.

Lost for words, he blushed and started gathering his things.

"Just tell your mom the clock battery died," Victor suggested.

"No, you were right the first time. She'll understand."

Jace stared at Victor, wishing he could take a photo to preserve this memory forever. When Victor winked, looking amused, Jace forced his eyes away and turned to leave. He was only minutes away when a yearning filled his chest, and although he couldn't be certain, Jace didn't think the feeling would cease until he saw Victor again.

His mother was home. Of all the ill omens that could have awaited him, this was the worst. Jace had expected an angry letter, or maybe a passive-aggressive pickle loaf sandwich—the kind he hated—in his lunch bag, but instead his mother was sitting at the kitchen table. Not for long. She stood up so quickly that the chair toppled over behind her. Her features were crinkled with enough concern that Jace thought he'd be okay, but once she looked him over, the worry turned to anger.

"Where were you this morning?"

"Camping," Jace said. "I slept in."

"You're missing school! I trusted you to come home when you said you would. I treated you like an adult, and this is how you repay me?"

"It was an accident!" Jace said, his voice rising. "It's not like I woke up on time and sat around the woods just to piss you off."

Serena's cheeks grew red. "Watch your mouth! Did you even bring an alarm with you?"

"Yes, but—"

"But what?"

"I forgot to set it." Jace regretted his honesty instantly. His mother launched into a tirade, the word "responsibility" being the most repeated. He should have lied and said the battery had died, just like his clever fox suggested. Jace took the brunt of the lecture, occasionally shouting in his own defense, but his mother wouldn't listen. Instead, she passed judgment.

"For the next week, you aren't going anywhere but work and school. I'll be driving you to school in the morning, picking you up in the afternoon, and will do the same for your work. You're grounded from the car and you're grounded from seeing anyone."

"That's bullshit!" Jace yelled.

"No," his mother said, eyes narrowing. "That's fact, and if you don't want to be grounded for *two* weeks, you'll button your lip!"

Jace fumed on the car ride to school, hatching a million schemes in his mind. As soon as he was home again, he would gather all the food he could carry and run straight down the valley and back into Victor's arms. No one would ever see Jace again. The system wanted to punish him for an honest mistake? Fine. In that case, he wouldn't play the game anymore.

But as he walked into the school building, Jace was plagued with doubt. He knew he couldn't do it, because it wouldn't work. Victor's plan didn't make sense. He couldn't live off the land anymore than Jace could. Without the food from his parent's cupboard, or handouts from strangers, Victor wouldn't make it. Unless Jace continued to support him, took responsibility for him. Doing so would mean working a stupid job and putting up with unfair rules, but if it meant getting to keep his lost boy, letting him remain wild and free, Jace knew he could bear the burden.

Lunch period was ending as Jace arrived. He spotted Greg in the hall, but his best friend averted his eyes. The anger rose anew in Jace's chest, so much that he swiped at a student-made poster on the wall, tearing it down. The hallway cleared around him as students give him wide berth. Good! Jace hoped he looked as crazy as he felt. Let them see just how maddening he found this stupid world!

Jace glowered his way through classes, not answering in calculus when the teacher called on him. He managed to stay silent until the end of the day, but by then his anger had simmered into frustration and eventually lost all potency, leaving nothing but misery. He spoke briefly to Michelle before dinner, telling her about the injustice he was suffering. She was sufficiently sympathetic. After dinner, Jace's mother drove him to work. There at least he felt slightly better because Victor might show up, needing cigarettes or company. Being alone in the woods all day had to get boring. Jace pictured Victor sitting there for an entire week, waiting for him to return. Maybe he could get Greg to go down and tell him what had happened.

But no, all of that was messed up too.

"Everything all right?" Bernard asked.

Jace flinched in surprise. He was in the back room fetching more jumbo-sized cups for the soda fountain and hadn't seen Bernard sitting at his desk.

"Fine," Jace said.

"You don't look fine."

Jace almost snapped that Bernard should mind his own business, but the older man's expression was genuinely concerned. Unlike the other adults in his life, Bernard had never betrayed his trust, despite having more reason to than others. Hell, Jace would probably be in a psych ward now if Bernard hadn't agreed to keep his suicide attempt a secret.

"I can always tell when my son's had a bad day because his face gets flushed like yours. Looks like geysers of blood want to come shooting out of your ears!"

Jace managed a small smile. "It was a shitty day. I'll live." He meant this as a figure of speech, but he supposed it told Bernard what he needed to know.

"What do you think of the job so far?" Bernard tapped a bunch of envelops against the desk's surface, straightening them. "You seem happy here, aside from today."

"I like it," Jace said. "You were right. It's hard to feel sorry for myself when I have so much to do." Except for today.

Bernard cocked his head. "How do you like working with Dan?"

Jace answered the question carefully. "I probably wouldn't invite him to my birthday party."

Bernard cracked a smile. "Yeah, he doesn't make a good first impression. Or second or third. He's a good worker though, right?"

Jace hesitated. As much as he disliked Dan, he didn't want to rat him out, or be responsible for him losing his job. He pictured someone wearing a werewolf mask, rushing the counter and grabbing the shotgun before he could get to it, except when the mask came off, this time it would be Dan's sneering face.

"He does his thing, I do mine." There. That wasn't a lie, exactly.

Bernard studied him, then nodded. "I better get home to the missus. You know if you need anything, my phone number is taped on the desk here." He tapped a finger on the metal surface. "You write it down, put it in your wallet. Never know when it might come in handy."

Jace stared. What had he done to deserve the star treatment? Was Bernard this nice to everyone? Jace walked with him to the door and wished him a pleasant evening. After Bernard's car had driven away, he went up to Dan.

"I'm grounded," he said.

Dan snickered.

"Yeah, real funny. But before you laugh too hard, my mom is picking me up after work every day. If you don't come back from your break, I won't be here to cover for you."

The smile slipped off Dan's face. "Did you say something to Bernard? Did he ask?"

"No and no. But he'll find out if you try anything like that again."

Mostly because Jace would go home and the store would get robbed, but he let Dan interpret this as a threat. Releasing a little of his anger felt good. Maybe this would be the new him, stomping through life and raging at the machine. Screw his dumb coworkers and his homophobic friends. Jace would growl at the whole world! Aside from those moments when he was alone with Victor. Then he would purr.

Victor didn't show up during his shift, but Jace wasn't expecting him to. When Dan was on one of his short breaks, Jace took a couple packs of cigarettes, some beef jerky, and a bag of trail mix, leaving money for it in the cash register. Maybe he could sneak out of the house later and deliver it.

As it turned out, his mother seemed willing to go without sleep to keep him in line. Jace waited until midnight before opening his bedroom door. A few seconds later, his mother turned on the hall light and just stood there watching him. He pretended he needed to use the restroom. Thank goodness he was still in his pajamas, only wanting to see if the coast was clear. Obviously it wasn't.

Figuring his mother would continue her unrelenting vigil,

Jace made peace with not seeing Victor. Until tomorrow. He didn't care if he had to make a break for it in the middle of dinner. One way or another, they would be together again.

Jace leaned against a pillar in the cafeteria, watching Greg as he unpacked his sack lunch. As per his usual ritual, he set out every item on the table, nice and orderly. Then he started pounding his sandwich flat. Strange, but Jace liked him that way. Or used to. Or would again, if Greg would stop being an asshole. They still hadn't talked since the weekend, Greg having avoided him in the halls yesterday. Jace was surprised to see him at their usual table now. Scowling, he marched toward it. Jace could eat with his sister instead, but why should he have to? Plopping down across from Greg, he dumped his lunch on the table. Greg considered him with transparent surprise before lowering his eyes.

Jace huffed in response. "Find somewhere else to eat if you have a problem with me."

Greg glared at his lunch. "I'll go. But not because I have a problem with you."

Jace stopped clenching his jaw long enough to ask, "Then why?"

"Because I don't deserve to be your friend." Greg looked up, and Jace realized his anger was directed inward. "After that night with you and Victor, once my head was clear again, I thought about what I'd said before. How gay people should all be shipped off to an island. I think back on that conversation now, and I feel like a prick. You were opening your heart to me—"

"I wasn't," Jace said, shoulders relaxing. "I was just trying to gauge your reaction."

"And I showed you," Greg said. "The sick thing is that I meant it. Back then, at least. I'm so fucking stupid! You've been my best friend my entire life, and I didn't have a clue. Not only that, but then I go and say something awful."

"It was a nice island," Jace said. "If I remember right, there were a lot of bananas there."

"That's not funny," Greg said. "Not anymore. And you know what? It shouldn't have taken my best friend coming out for me to realize that."

Jace exhaled. "You're human. It's not a big deal. And if the idea of you hurting me makes you feel this angry at yourself, then I love you. In a totally non-gay way, of course."

Greg's brow unknotted. "You mean that?"

"Yes!" Jace laughed. "Seriously. I thought I scared you off!"

"No." Greg shook his head. "Not me. I love gay people." He repeated himself, but this time he shouted it to the whole cafeteria. "I LOVE GAY PEOPLE!"

"Okay," Jace said, pinching the bridge of his nose. "We're good. Just… stop."

Greg chuckled madly. "Is this what coming out feels like? Because that felt good." His twinkling eyes grew hard. "I've got your back, man. You know that? If anyone messes with you, I'll kick their ass."

Jace sighed. For one fleeting moment, he wished he was a girl, because Greg was definitely marriage material. "I'll be fine," he said. "I just want things to be like before. Nothing has changed. I'm still me."

"All right." Greg still looked concerned. "I guess you've got a Chuck Norris boyfriend looking out for you anyway. He is, right? You guys are an item?"

"Victor and me?" Jace smiled. "We're together. In a way."

"Like how? Tell me everything!" Greg ripped apart his smooshed sandwich, stuffing half in his mouth.

"Everything?" Jace asked.

"Hell yeah," Greg said after swallowing. "How many times did you listen to me ranting about all the pussy I get? It's payback time!"

He didn't have all that much to tell, at least not when it came to sex, but it felt good not to hold back. Of course there were some stares from other students at their cafeteria table, but screw them. With Victor and Greg on his side, Jace didn't fear a thing. If worst came to worst, Michelle was an absolute beast in a fight.

"Sounds like one weird dude," Greg said as they walked toward their classes. "Which makes you perfect for each other."

"Weird how?" Jace asked.

Greg shrugged. "I like camping as much as the next guy, but I don't want to do it for a living."

"Yeah, I know. I think Victor is just trying to figure out everything. Can you blame him? If we didn't have college next year, what would you do with your life?"

Greg looked momentarily terrified. "Hide in the woods with Victor, I guess."

"Exactly. I'm sure he'll figure out what he wants eventually. By then, I'll already be a major part of his life."

"And in the meantime…" Greg made an "O" with one hand and repeatedly jabbed a finger through the opening with the other. Then, after a moment of puzzled thought, he started jabbing two fingers together. "More like that, huh?"

Jace rolled his eyes. "From guilt-ridden to demeaning in the blink of an eye!"

"I like to move fast," Greg replied. "Speaking of which, are you the guy or the girl? Know what I mean?"

"I know," Jace said patiently, stopping outside his class.

"Because Victor is smaller than you, but then again, he's the guy who threw Mr. Collins around, so I can't really imagine him bending over and—"

"No need to paint a picture," Jace said. "Or for us to discuss this further."

"Out of the closet but still a total prude." Greg punched him playfully on the arm and sauntered off down the hall.

Jace shook his head. "Am I the guy or the girl?" he muttered to himself. Wasn't it obvious? As he took his seat in class, he tried to imagine both scenarios and couldn't. No, it really wasn't obvious at all!

Chapter Eight

When the school day came to an end, his father's car awaited him at the curb. Jace was glad. His mom had been ferrying him everywhere the past few days, and they still weren't on good terms. He clammed up whenever they were together, only answering with the absolute minimum to avoid getting into more trouble. Not that it would matter tonight. He was determined to see Victor, even if his mom caught him on his way out of the house.

"How's my favorite son?" his father asked once Jace was in the car.

"Fine," he answered, feeling uneasy. His father was a good guy, but not the type for forced joviality. He had to put on the happy mask for customers all day, so when he was home, Bob tended to be more outspoken. If something was bugging him, like when Jace and his sister got too rowdy, he would tell them to shut up before he went insane. His father would say this in a pragmatic way, devoid of aggression, that made it the simple truth. And it was, except right now his father's customer service mask was still on when it shouldn't be.

"How was your day?" Jace asked, testing the waters.

"Great! The weather was nice enough to leave the store door propped open, which you know I like. Beautiful weather!"

Jace eyed him. He definitely preferred the other Bob. Being told to go outside because his father wanted to pretend he was childless was a lot better than this grinning scarecrow.

"Mom tired of picking me up?"

"No." Bob's grin faltered, just as he turned away to check his blind spot. "I don't think she can find enough excuses to be around you. Not with you graduating so soon."

Jace rolled his eyes. "Well I can't wait. It'll be nice to be on my own."

"Not for us, it won't." There he was. The real Bob. "We'll miss having you around, even though you drive us crazy."

Jace snorted, turning to look out the window. "The feeling is mutual." Outside, the brick buildings of downtown had been left behind, replaced by small houses. "Do you think it's fair? I didn't sleep-in on purpose. I forgot to set the alarm, but Mom acts like I did it just to defy her."

"No, it's not fair," his father said, "but that's life. You still get a speeding ticket, even though you didn't mean to go over the limit. A police officer doesn't care if you simply forgot to watch the speedometer. Honest accidents happen, but you still have to pay for them."

"But she didn't *have* to punish me. It's not her job like it is for a cop."

"Her job—at least one of them—is to make sure you turn out right." Bob exhaled. "Maybe she's been overdoing it lately. She can't even sleep until she knows you're home and safe. Did you know that?"

"Lucky me," Jace muttered.

"I need you to forgive her," Bob said. "Especially tonight, I need you to set it all aside."

"She's the one who should forgive me," Jace muttered. Then he caught his father's meaning and tore his eyes away from the window. "Wait, is everything okay?"

His father didn't answer. He just kept driving, all the way to the edge of town. They were on the road leading up to their neighborhood, the one that passed by the lake, when he pulled the car to the side of the road. Bob took off his glasses and wiped his eyes.

"Dad?"

"I'm sorry, son. It's your grandmother. She passed away today."

Jace just stared. When he tried to speak, his voice was weak. "How?"

"Aneurysm." His father replaced his glasses and tapped the side of the head. "A blood clot in the brain. It's a quick and painless way to go. We shouldn't be surprised. She was ninety-six, and you know your parents will go someday. That's how it's supposed to be, but it still hurts like hell when they do. When I lost my mother, well, I was barely older than you and…" His father looked over, as if embarrassed at his rambling. "I'm sorry."

A dam broke inside Jace, releasing all the anger he'd been feeling, all the little concerns and worries. None of it mattered anymore. Instead his thoughts turned to a frail old woman with a raspy laugh, boney hands, and an easy smile that never seemed to fade. The smell of her home, the little glass birds that sat in her kitchen window, the way she always winked at Jace while talking with other adults, like her being serious was all pretend.

"That's it, let it out."

Jace didn't realize he had been crying, or that his father had unbuckled his seat belt to reach over and hug him.

"She was a good woman, and we're all going to miss her."

Jace cried a little longer, and when they drove the rest of the way home, his father didn't have to ask him to be civil. All was forgiven. Jace only wanted to hug his mom, thankful that she was still there. He found her sitting at the kitchen table. Michelle was there too, eyes puffy and red. His sister cried first, which set them all off again. All but Jace. He clamped down on his tears, wanting to be strong for his mother.

"I'm sorry," he said. "For everything."

"It's okay," Serena said soothingly. "Everything is fine."

But he knew it wasn't. Not for her.

A little while later, Michelle pulled him into the other room. "Horrible, isn't it?"

Jace nodded, lost for words.

"I hate it," his sister said, tearing up, "because I think about how old Mom and Dad are, and—"

"Don't go there," Jace said firmly. "Please."

Michelle nodded and tried to get herself under control. "I think we should cook dinner."

"Will Mom want to eat anything? I don't feel like eating."

"Neither do I, but she'll worry about us being hungry."

Working together they made a meal of instant stuffing, some canned green beans, and leftover chicken. Whether it was appetizing or not, they didn't discover, since they only picked at their plates. When it all went cold, Michelle started clearing the table.

"I'm supposed to be at work soon," Jace said, feeling ashamed for even broaching the subject.

"I'll call Bernie and explain," his father said. "I have his number in the office."

This left Jace alone with his mother. She looked tired. "Is there anything I can do?" he offered.

Serena shook her head, half-distracted before she looked at him. "No, I'll be fine. We're catching a flight tomorrow afternoon. Someone needs to be there for your grandfather. You and Michelle will be okay for a couple of days, right?"

"Yes," Jace said. "I promise I won't mess up this time. I mean it."

His mother looked puzzled for a moment, like their argument was part of a previous life. "I know you won't. Is your friend still camping by the lake?"

Jace nodded. "I think so."

"Go see him. This is one of those times in life I was talking about when it helps to have someone." His mother's smile was sad. "You like him, don't you?"

"Yeah," Jace said.

His mom nodded and returned to her thoughts. Jace stayed long enough to help Michelle clean up. He wanted to see Victor, but the idea of doing something for fun seemed wrong. Then again, maybe his mother was right. Maybe it would help ease the ache in Jace's heart.

When he got to the clearing, the fire was already blazing. Victor sat in front of it, knife in hand as he carved at a piece of wood.

"Hey," Jace said.

Victor was startled, but over the fire, those wide eyes read him. "You all right?"

"No. My grandma—" Jace's face crumpled, and he spun around to wipe away the tears that managed to escape. He didn't want to cry in front of Victor again, didn't like to cry in front of anyone. He felt hands on his shoulder, and when he turned around, Victor wore a worried expression.

"Did you lose her?"

Jace nodded, not trusting himself to speak.

Victor wrapped an arm around his waist. The other reached around his back, pulling him close, holding him near. Victor didn't offer any words of solace. No hokey speeches about better places or God needing angels. He just held Jace until the pain felt manageable. Then he led Jace to the little shelter, sat down, and offered his lap as a pillow.

"I'm sorry," Victor said, running his fingers through Jace's hair. "I'm here for you. Or if you want me at the store to support you, I can do that. Hell, I'll enroll in school again if you want me to."

Jace managed a smile. "You mean it?"

"Yeah. Of course."

"My parents are going to be gone for a while. That means I can stay here with you."

"Is that what you want?"

Jace's hips already hurt from the hard ground below the sleeping bag. "No. Come stay with me at the house. Or at least visit for as long as you can stand it."

"I haven't gone completely feral just yet," Victor said. "I can handle being just about anywhere if it'll make you feel better."

Jace reached up to take Victor's hand. He didn't stay long after that, wanting to show his mom he could be responsible. And he needed to be alone in his room, where he could be free to cry, if need be. Once he was there, he discovered what he wanted most was to remember, so Jace grabbed a shoebox of old photos from his closet and lost himself in memories.

"I invited Victor to stay over," Jace said. He had meant to tell Michelle in the morning during the drive to school, but guilt had silenced him. Now, on their way home, he had no choice since she'd soon find out. "I'm terrible, aren't I?"

"Hell no! You think Grandma would want us to stop being happy?" Michelle bit her lip. "Besides, Brett is coming over too."

"Are you guys back together?"

His sister shrugged. "Just keeping each other company."

Jace was starting to feel like his views on relationships were outdated. Victor disliked titles, and his sister—despite being boy-crazy—seemed nonchalant about what form love took. Jace wanted a good old-fashioned commitment. He wanted to throw words around like "always" and "forever" and "only you." Wasn't that what everyone wanted, the assurance that someone would be there, even if such promises couldn't always be kept?

"Hey hey!" Michelle said. "Looks like there's a package for you on the front step."

Jace looked over and couldn't help his dopey grin. Victor was sitting sideways on the steps, back pressed against the house as he calmly smoked a cigarette. When he saw their car, he didn't smile, wave, nod, or react at all. He just coolly watched them park.

"He's got the bad-boy thing down." Michelle sounded impressed. "Nice catch, big brother."

"Thanks." Jace thought of the way Victor had held and

comforted him last night. He wasn't a bad boy. When they were together, Victor was soft.

"You might want to stop staring and get out of the car," Michelle said pointedly.

Groaning in embarrassment, Jace unbuckled his seatbelt and hopped out, fetching his book bag from the backseat and messing with it until the heat left his cheeks. Michelle reached Victor first. She was thanking him for his condolences when Jace approached. Both carrying a pack over one shoulder, he and Victor eyed each other as Michelle unlocked the front door. Were they supposed to kiss? This was another reason Jace wanted to define their relationship. Of course boyfriends kiss when meeting again! That's what all couples do, right? But without the title, he was left navigating in the dark... In a storm-ravaged sea... Without a boat.

"Want to go to my room?" Jace asked him once they were inside. "Or do you want something from the kitchen?"

"Upstairs is good," Victor said.

Jace led him to his room, wondering what they would do to pass the time. He couldn't see Victor playing board games or anything so mundane.

"How are you holding up?" Victor said, tossing his pack on the bed.

"Fine," Jace said, sitting next to it. Like Victor, it smelled strongly of campfire smoke. "Really good. I still feel sad, but mostly for my mom. And my grandpa. I keep thinking what he must be going through. My loss is nothing compared to his. You expect to lose your grandparents eventually, but losing a wife..."

"Yeah, that's true." Victor stood in front of him, arms crossed over his chest as he frowned. "There should be some deal when you get married that if one person dies, the other does too."

"At the same time? That would be nice." Jace thought about it for a moment. "How would it happen? If one person dies in a house fire, and the other is at work, would they burst into flames at the office?"

Victor tsked and shook his head. "You're always ruining my best lines."

"Yeah, well, you're no Hemingway. Oh wait!"

Victor humored him with a smile. "I'll let that one slide, but only because it's nice to see you doing better."

"I am," Jace said. "I'm glad you're here."

"Me too," Victor said. "To be honest, I about froze my balls off last night without you in the sleeping bag with me. And I need a shower. There was some guy from the city checking the lake water today, so I couldn't go for a swim."

"You let that stop you? I'm surprised you didn't invite him to join you."

"He wasn't my type. You have to work tonight?"

"No." When his father had called Bernard, he said Jace wouldn't be there for the next day or two. That gave him more freedom than he'd had all month, but now he had plenty to keep him busy.

"Okay. Towels in the same place?"

Jace nodded. Once Victor was in the shower, he straightened his room, wondering if he should swipe some candles from the dining room for later. Later! He sure hoped there was going to be a later in that way! Their night together in the woods had been fun, but being stuffed in the sleeping bag had limited what they could do. These thoughts were further fueled when Victor reentered the room wearing nothing but a towel.

"Does your family have a washer and drier, or is everything dry-cleaned?"

Jace grinned. "We wash our clothes like anyone else. You can do a load, if you need to, but you'll have to figure out the machine yourself."

Victor looked surprised. "You've never done your own laundry?"

Jace felt silly admitting it, but he hadn't. "I was saving that experience for college."

"I can teach you how."

Not exactly the thrilling evening Jace had just been imagining.

"Or I can strut around naked in front of your sister," Victor threatened.

"I don't think she'd mind," Jace said, but in the end he agreed.

Victor borrowed a shirt and boxers from him. The shirt was too large, and the boxers hung off Victor's butt more than his hips. That was awesome, and also distracting as Jace listened to Victor's lecture in the laundry room on reasons for separating his whites from the dark colors, and what water temperatures to use with each load.

"From woodsman to domestic goddess," Jace said, as Victor stuffed clothes in the washer. "Who would have thought? Wait a minute, you've got your whites mixed with your colors!"

"Because I'm not racist," Victor joked. "I'm doing my laundry quickly, not correctly. Otherwise I'll die of boredom."

Once the washer was running, they went downstairs to the family room, where his sister was hanging out with Brett.

"Nice outfit," he said when he saw what Victor was wearing.

"I'll let you borrow it sometime," came the casual reply.

Nothing ever seemed to faze Victor. In this case it was good, since Brett was an equal-opportunity asshole, acting rude to anyone he met, but he was good-looking enough that Jace understood why his sister put up with him. They ordered a pizza, flipping through the TV channels until it arrived. Victor moved his clothes into the dryer. They watched a movie while they ate, Jace occasionally glancing over at Victor. His eyes seemed unfocused as he stared at the screen. Jace thought of the endless movie nights he and Greg had shared, how much fun they always were. Now the idea of finishing the movie seemed torturous when he could be interacting with Victor. When the dryer buzzed, Jace followed Victor to the laundry room.

"Want to get out of here?" he offered.

Victor brightened. "What about one of those night drives? You promised to take me along."

"Deal!"

Victor pulled his clothes out of the dryer and got dressed in front of Jace, which was more erotic than he would have expected. Usually he imagined guys getting undressed, but this was hotter. All the parts Jace wanted to kiss and touch were flashed before his eyes and then hidden behind cloth and denim, his memory desperate to retain every fleeting detail. Once Victor looked more like his usual self, they hopped into the car and drove off into the night.

They cruised outside the city limits, taking small wooded roads past dark farmland. Jace hoped Victor would feel more comfortable here, like camping in motion. There weren't many street lights, not where few people drove during the day and even fewer at night. The only artificial light came from the dashboard. With the darkness pressing in from the outside, driving at night always made Jace feel like he was piloting a submarine.

"I can see why you like this," Victor said. He rested his arm on the back of the driver's seat, toying with Jace's hair.

This reminded him of the way Victor consoled him the other night, how comfortable he seemed with touching Jace and being close to him. "Have you ever been with a guy? I mean, besides me."

"Depends what you mean by 'been with,'" Victor said, but he seemed to understand. "There was only this friend of mine in eighth grade. We used to jack off together. He always acted like it was a contest to see who could come first, or last, depending on his mood. I didn't really need an excuse because I thought it was hot. We never touched each other. I'd watch him and, well, he'd mostly watch himself. Definitely an exhibitionist. That was the thrill for him."

"Sounds... kind of awesome," Jace said.

"Yeah, it was fun. Did you and Greg ever do anything like that?"

Jace practically hit the breaks. "No!"

"Why not?"

"Because we're friends!" Jace kept his eyes on the road, but he could hear the smile in Victor's response.

"And we aren't?"

"It's different," Jace said. "Greg isn't into guys. At all. Anyway, when you and this friend used to—you know—did you figure out that you were gay then?"

"I figured I was bisexual, yeah. It wasn't a revelation or anything. I already knew I liked girls, so I mentally added guys to the list."

"I guess being bisexual is easier since you can still fit in," Jace said. "You can choose to be with a woman and live a normal life."

"It's not any easier." Victor playfully tugged on Jace's ear. "We can't choose who we fall in love with. Besides, there's nothing abnormal about two guys being together. Nature made you the way you are and me the way I am. We're already living normal lives."

Jace glanced over at him. "You might believe that, but the rest of the world doesn't. They don't think being gay is normal."

"Maybe, but does it really matter what they think?"

Kind of, since it could make Jace's life difficult, but he didn't want to admit that to Victor. Instead he changed the topic. "Hey, open the glove box."

Victor did. A couple packs of cigarettes fell to the floorboard. Several more didn't. The whole glove box was stuffed. Victor chuckled. "Are you trying to kill me?"

"Too many?" Jace asked.

"No," Victor said, closing the glove box and fetching the packs that had fallen. "But you don't have to buy me anything. If I run out of smokes, I run out."

"And show up masked at a gas station."

Victor shrugged. "I was looking for a new experience, that's all."

Jace snorted in disbelief, but Victor seemed completely serious. "What if you'd been arrested?"

"Exactly," Victor said. "Wouldn't that be interesting? A lot better than being bored on a Monday night." After a moment he laughed, Jace joining him, still not sure how serious he was.

Tired of navigating the darkness, Jace drove them back into town. They prowled around neighborhoods, driving slowly and looking for interesting stories to tell about the houses they saw.

"This one looks good," Jace said, pulling over.

The house was large, two stories, and well-maintained. Even though it had a large garage, a cherry-red Porsche sat in the driveway.

"Who lives here?" Victor asked. "I'm picturing a really ugly guy with a hairy back."

"No," Jace said. "He's gorgeous. Porn-star hung, super-model good looks. Even straight guys want to get with him, but the thing is, he lives alone."

"Why?"

"Because he couldn't make up his mind. When he was younger, everyone wanted him and he wanted everyone, so he never settled down."

"Is this a cautionary tale?" Victor asked, sounding dubious.

Jace laughed. "No, not like that. This guy was like a kid in a candy store, taking a bite of everything before tossing it over his shoulder. Eventually, everyone who wanted this guy had their turn, but the truth was, he wasn't using and losing them."

"He wasn't?"

"Nope. Once the guy found someone he wanted to be with,

she didn't call him after the first time they slept together. That's when he realized the ugly truth: No one was coming back for more."

"Lousy in bed?" Victor asked.

"Horrible. Like, completely incompetent. 'Oops, I didn't mean to poke you in the eye with it.' That sort of thing."

"And now?"

"And now he sits in his castle with his pretty car parked outside, and he's still gorgeous as hell, but everyone knows he sucks in bed, because there's a lady with an eye patch who goes around telling everyone."

Victor cracked up as Jace put the car back in gear and drove away. "Hey, remember that crazy widow who hoards jewelry in her basement?"

Jace needed a moment to remember. "You mean the house we saw on Halloween?"

"Yeah. Think you can get us back there?"

"I don't know. Let's find out."

After driving up and down the streets they trick-or-treated on, Jace found the house and pulled over to the side of the road. "That's it, right?"

Victor nodded. "Yup. I remember the crack in the front window."

"Yeah, you're right!"

"Let's go check it out."

Jace stared. "What?"

"Let's see who really lives there. Aren't you curious to know if your stories are true?"

Victor was already getting out of the car. Jace followed, protesting the whole way up the walkway, his voice dropping to a whisper on the small front porch. "C'mon, let's go back to the car. Please!"

Victor paused, fist just inches from the door. "I'm sure a black widow would be happy to see two handsome young men like us."

Victor knocked and Jace groaned. The porch light turned on. Victor shoved Jace directly in front of the door as it opened, then dodged off to the side. The woman who answered had dark hair, slightly frizzled, as if she'd been lying in bed watching TV. The worn nightgown she had on played into this scenario, fabric crinkled up like the wrinkles on her face, which deepened in worry.

"Can I help you?" she said.

"I'm sorry," Jace replied. "I think I have the wrong house."

The woman looked him over. "Do you know Victor?"

They both turned their heads toward the nearby snickering. Victor strolled into view, the woman's face lighting up with delight.

"Hi, Mama," he said, embracing her.

"Why are you knocking on the door?" his mother said, swatting him after their hug. "You nearly scared me half to death!"

"Oh, nothing bad ever happens in this town," Victor said, stepping past her into the house. "That's my friend Jace," he called over his shoulder.

"I'm Victor's mom," she said, before looking uncertain. "Or Rachel. Or Mrs. Hemingway. Gosh, I don't know what I'm called anymore. Take your pick!"

She gestured for him to enter, which Jace did, feeling slightly overwhelmed but also excited. Victor had brought him to meet his mother! Even if he didn't stay here often, this was a *huge* part of his life.

"You have a lovely home," Jace said, taking in his surroundings. The house was small, the front door opening directly to the living room. While the outside could use maintenance, the interior had the sort of worn comfort that made any home welcoming. The living room didn't have a flashy entertainment center or a trendy sectional. Instead, each piece of furniture had personality, such as the threadbare couch partially covered by a quilt, or the pock-marked wooden coffee table in front of it.

"Get your friend something to drink too!" Mrs. Hemingway called.

Jace could see a kitchen through the doorway, Victor returning from it and handing Jace a can. "Hope you like diet soda."

"Yeah. Thanks."

Mrs. Hemingway gestured for Jace to sit. He took a seat on the couch, noticing a framed photo on the side table of a much younger Victor, chubby-cheeked but still looking just as mischievous.

"Where have you been staying?" Mrs. Hemingway asked, sitting in one of the chairs.

Victor remained standing. "Camping out. Jace's family has some property. I've been safe, don't worry."

But Mrs. Hemingway pressed a hand to her face. "I just knew you were outside somewhere! It's supposed to snow this weekend. Did you know that?"

"No." Victor frowned at his drink. "I'll grab some warmer clothes while I'm here."

"There are fresh sheets on your bed."

"I won't be staying long."

Jace felt awkward, like he should ask to use the restroom while they figured out everything. The wrinkles had returned to Mrs. Hemingway's face. He wondered if years of worry had etched them there.

"And you, Jace," she said, turning to him. "What a lovely name! Tell me about yourself."

"Uh…" Jace looked helplessly to Victor. "I'm a high school senior and work part-time at Bernie's."

"That's what he does, not who he is," Victor said. "Jace has a huge heart, is a sucker for the underdog, and likes to read books, probably as a way of escaping this dreary town. He'd also like me to propose to him, since he's fond of commitment."

"Oh, Victor!" Mrs. Hemingway laughed, shaking her head at her son. "Maybe I should tell him about you!" She thought for a moment, lips pressed together. "Victor likes animal crackers, but not the frosted kind because they give him diarrhea. He didn't sleep through a single thunderstorm growing up, and I used to check his pockets before leaving a grocery store because he was always stealing candy."

Jace grinned at this, Victor shrugging as if it didn't matter. "Does he ever get embarrassed?" Jace asked. "I've never seen him blush."

"Oh, there's an easy way to make him do that!" Mrs. Hemingway said.

"Okay!" Victor said loudly. "We're going down to my room now. You'll have to humiliate me some other day."

"All you have to do is call him Pooky."

"Mom!" Victor complained.

Jace laughed. "Pooky?"

"Remember Garfield?" Mrs. Hemingway said. "He had a little teddy bear named Pooky. Victor thought he was so cute that he wanted to *be* Pooky, and used to pretend he was."

"How do you pretend to be a teddy bear?" Jace asked.

"By sitting very, very still," Victor said with anything but patience.

Mrs. Hemingway clapped her hands. "Show him how you used to do it!"

"No," Victor said. "We're going to my room."

"Oh, fine. Are you hungry?"

"We already ate."

At Victor's insistence, Jace followed him down a set of stairs to the small basement. The concrete walls were painted maroon and had a few band posters taped to them, but there were also elements that were surprisingly juvenile. An old Star Wars toy in the corner—the robot-looking thing with four long legs. Or the lamp next to the bed that resembled a catcher's glove and ball. Some of the room felt like Victor, such as the plastic milk crates full of records, or the stereo next to them, but the rest of the room seemed like it belonged to a kid.

"I don't stay here much," Victor said dismissively, heading for the dresser. He pulled out sweatshirts and grabbed a battered bomber jacket off a chair. "Ready to go?"

"We just got here," Jace said.

"So? She's probably already up there trying to figure out what to cook. It's better if we leave now."

"Okay." Jace hesitated. "She seems to miss you."

Victor's eyebrows rose, like a father whose kid had talked back to him. Then he gestured with his head. "Come on. Let's go."

When they returned upstairs, Mrs. Hemingway appeared in the kitchen door, holding a can of tomato soup and an opener. "Oh! Are you leaving?"

"Yeah." Victor kissed her on the cheek.

"Okay. Well, come visit soon. I don't want you out somewhere when it snows."

Victor was turning to leave. "I know."

"Star called."

This stopped him in his tracks. "Really?"

"Yes. She said something about coming home for

Thanksgiving. You'll be here, won't you?"

Victor nodded without turning around. "Yeah. I will. Don't go crazy though, okay?"

Mrs. Hemingway ignored this and smiled at Jace. "It was nice meeting you!"

"You too," he said.

Once they were back in the car, Jace put the key in the ignition but didn't turn it. "She's really nice," he said.

Victor eyed him. "And I'm a dick for making her worry."

"I didn't say that!"

"You thought it." For once, Victor looked agitated. "There's a lot you don't know."

"Then tell me," Jace said. "No limits, remember? That includes keeping secrets from each other. Right?"

Victor stared through the windshield, nodding when he came to a decision. "You up for a longer drive? It'll make more sense if I show you."

"Yeah, okay. Where to?"

"Mexico."

Chapter Nine

The story went that settlers, traveling across Missouri, stumbled upon an old wooden sign. Pointing to the southwest, the sign read *Mexico*. Putting down roots at that spot, the settlers chose to name their town Mexico instead of taking down the wooden sign. Jace had read this anecdote when researching the city's name. He supposed it was meant to be charming, but to him it made the town founders seem lazy and not very creative. Then again, Columbia was a city in Missouri too, as well as Paris, California, Houston, Washington... The list went on and on. Maybe, like Jace, those town founders were eager to be anywhere *but* Missouri, and had to settle for pretending.

Mexico the town didn't resemble the country in the slightest. Like Warrensburg, many of the homes were small and uninspired, constructed in a quality that made them seem temporary, as if the builders never expected anyone to live there for long. At least that was the impression Jace got from the outskirts of the city. Victor had guided them not through the downtown area but along the fringes, his scowl deepening as they took a left turn.

"There it is," he said, venom in his voice.

A lawn ran along the side of the road, leaves blanketing the ground. What lay beyond reminded Jace of a university. A number of three-story rectangular brick buildings could have been anything from housing to classrooms. The most central building was domed, with four white pillars holding up the roof over the ornate entrance.

"*That's* the military academy?" Jace said, not hiding his surprise. Of course he'd heard of it. Depending on who you asked, The Missouri Military Academy either provided one of the best foundations a young man could receive, or was a dumping ground for troubled teens. One thing was certain: It cost money, a fact made plain as they drove past sculpted lawns and a lake that reflected yellow-lit windows of the building nestled against it.

"Pretty, isn't it?" Victor said, but he sounded repulsed. "You should see it in the spring. It's absolutely gorgeous."

The academy was much better looking than CMSU, the state university in Warrensburg. Jace had suspected the drive to Mexico had something to do with the military academy, but he doubted Victor went there. Being sent to the academy was a standard threat from parents in the area, but as Michelle once said, "Don't worry, you have to be fucked up *and* rich to end up there."

"Turn here," Victor said.

Past the lake and a much less scenic parking lot was a large sports field surrounded by a competitive running track. Victor instructed him to pull off onto a small dirt road just on the other side of the field. As they parked and got out of the car, Jace began to feel nervous.

"Will we get in trouble for being here?"

"Probably," Victor said, but he didn't sound concerned. He held out his hand, offering it to Jace. "Come on."

Jace accepted, intertwining their fingers together and shivering in the cool evening weather as they strolled across the field.

"I was a bad kid," Victor said. "I've never liked authority. I would talk back to teachers, break every rule at recess, and twist homework assignments to upset my teachers." He looked over at Jace and grinned. "My first book report was on Stephen King's *Carrie*. Everyone else was doing theirs on *Where the Wild Things Are* or *The Little Prince*. Me? I stood in front of the class and talked about a prom queen covered in pig blood. I hadn't even read the book, but I caught the movie on TV when my mom was working a night shift."

"I bet that went over well!"

"My mom thought it was funny. At first she was angry, of course, but later she asked me to perform the book report and laughed her ass off." Victor smiled at the memory. "That was about the worst of it. All the trouble I got into was just little-kid stuff—being a smart ass—until I was older and started hanging around with my cousin."

They stopped at the far end of the track. Where one playing field ended, another began, this one dedicated to football, judging from the goals. Jace could see tennis courts farther away, and the brick buildings they'd passed earlier. From the rear, the buildings looked more like an institution than part of a beautiful campus, which was probably Victor's reason for bringing them here.

"My cousin, Andrew, *he* was wild. I was tame by comparison. When he was eight, he stole the family car. He made it about five blocks before wrecking it. I think he hit a parked car or something. Andrew is four years older than me, so I was really little at the time. Do you want to sit? We're less likely to be noticed."

Jace nodded, reluctantly letting go of Victor's hand as they sat on the rubbery track surface. "So you and Andrew started getting into trouble together?"

"Yeah. I was in junior high. Hanging around someone his age felt cool, like I was already in high school. Andrew was a freaking mess, but he was popular and well-connected. That he welcomed me into his world felt like an honor. At that age you want to grow up quick. Andrew made that possible. I was thirteen years old, drinking, smoking pot, and getting laid." Victor took a deep breath and exhaled. "Of course one thing my family never had is money, but Andrew knew a number of ways to compensate."

"You started stealing."

"Yup. I was arrested for shoplifting when I was fourteen. We'd steal from any retail chain, drive to the next nearest location, and return the stuff for cash, like it was gifts we didn't want. Easy money. When they caught me, I had an air pistol shoved down my pants. This made me look violent, or like I was going to start holding up places. I only wanted the gun because it was expensive."

"So what happened?" Jace asked. "You can't get arrested when you're that young, can you?"

Victor shrugged. "I don't know. In my case, they called my mom. When she showed up they started with the threats, saying they could prosecute, have me thrown in juvenile hall, make her pay fines. I hated seeing her talked down to like that. She was angry with me, but even worse, she was sad. There had been other incidents, but this was the one that really got her scared. She thought I was spiraling out of control. When Andrew was arrested a few weeks later, she made a decision."

Jace followed his gaze to the military academy. "You were enrolled here?"

"Yeah." Victor sounded hoarse. "Freshman year. My head was shaved, and I hated the uniform, but the real battle took place inside here." Victor tapped the side of his head. "A sergeant here always said 'We break boys down and build them back up into men.' That was their philosophy. Whoever you were, whatever you wanted to be—all that had to be destroyed to make way for the new you. You can imagine how the kid who refused to do a proper book report took to a conformist environment like that."

"I bet you gave them hell!" Jace said, feeling proud, but the answer surprised him.

"No. I tried my best to comply. My mom sold her car to pay for tuition. She walked everywhere for three years after that, just to try and save me. So I tried my hardest, because I didn't want her sacrifice to be in vain, and I did okay for the first few months. I hated it, but I got by. Then—" Victor's jaw clenched. "There was this geeky guy, Kenneth, who the other cadets didn't like. I don't know why. He just didn't fit in, I guess. Anyway, one morning after our showers, they shoved Kenneth's face up against the mirror, telling him to look at how ugly he was, making fun of his zits. They pressed his face so hard against the mirror that his glasses broke in two, and they wouldn't let him go, even when he started crying. You can't—I'm no hero, but you can't just stand there and watch something like that. Not if you have a heart. So I shoved the other guys away."

"I'm glad you did," Jace said.

"Yeah, me too." Victor said, but he seemed uncertain. "The other guys turned on me then, but before anything could happen, our company commander walked in. When he asked Kenneth what had happened, Kenneth was so scared he pointed at me. Smart move. He knew the tide had turned, probably knew that I couldn't protect him. So he sold me out. I saved him, just not in the way I meant to. From then on, *I* was the scapegoat. I was beaten, called a faggot, anything my mom sent me was stolen… They made my life hell, and any time I tried to fight back, to defend myself, it was the word of all these other guys against mine. The staff started to hold it against me too. If there was trouble, I was in the middle of it, so they tried to make an example out of me."

Victor got to his feet, face red and breath heavy. "They came so fucking close to breaking me, but if they had, I don't think there would have been anything to build back up again. I took it every fucking day, thinking about my mother's sacrifice, and I swore to myself that when I got out, I'd never let them touch me again. Them or anyone like them."

Jace stood, put a gentle hand on Victor's shoulder, but he spun around.

"I don't know what I'm doing!" he shouted. "I don't know how to escape from it all, so I sit out there in the woods and feel grateful that I'm not part of the machine. It never lasts and I can't survive on my own, but it feels like coming up for air. And my mother, I love her so fucking much, but I won't let myself be a liability to her again. She's not walking through the snow after being on her feet all day just because I can't get my shit together. Not again. That's why I stay away, Jace. If I was smart, I'd stay away from you too."

"What?" Jace felt panic grip his heart. "Why would you say that?"

"Because I see the way you look at me, how you admire me, and it's probably the same way I looked at Andrew. You think I'm something special, but I'm not. We shouldn't see each other again. I'll only end up hurting you."

"Too fucking late!" Jace shouted. "You don't think it will hurt if I never see you again? I hurt just thinking about it, so shut up!"

Victor stared at him, his face slack before he smiled. "I keep telling you—there's no point in getting angry at someone you can't change."

"I don't want to change you." Jace grabbed Victor's hand. "You're stuck with me, whether you like it or not. I don't care how creepy that sounds."

"It doesn't sound creepy." Victor came in for a kiss, but something caught his eye. "Uh-oh. Somebody called out the cavalry."

Jace turned, adrenaline shooting through his veins, but saw only a single flashlight bobbing toward them. Better than a platoon of angry young men, but he didn't want to stick around. Still holding each other's hands, they raced back to the car, peeled out down the road, and didn't slow down until they crossed the Mexican border. Well, the city line, anyway.

The lights in Jace's bedroom flicked off. A moment later, car headlights cut through the darkness, capturing a few seconds of Victor lying in bed, still looking at where Jace was standing. Then the vision was gone, but he found he wanted it to return very badly. He flipped the light switch, illuminating the room again.

"Maybe I should get some candles," he said.

Victor smirked. "Here. We'll do this instead." Rolling over, he grabbed his jeans from the floor, pulling out the Zippo lighter. His thumb flicked open the lid and spun the wheel in one smooth motion, the flint sparking the wick into life. Then he set the lighter on the bookshelf next to Jace's bed. "Instant campfire."

Jace smiled and turned off the light again. Now he could still see Victor, but the light wasn't so bright that he would feel shy. He hoped. The shadows certainly did very little to help how short his breath felt. Stripping down to his underwear, as Victor had done minutes before, he crawled into bed and slipped beneath the sheets. Jace rolled over on his side, facing Victor who wore a slightly haunted look, as if speaking about the past had allowed it to catch up to him again.

"We'll buy a cabin," Jace said.

"Hm?"

"In the woods. Hidden away somewhere. We'll find a little cabin with lots of land and that will be our home."

Victor's eyes searched his. "How will we survive?"

"I'll get a job. Something full-time. Every night I'll come home to you, weary from being part of the machine, but seeing you will make it all worthwhile."

"Yeah?"

"Yeah. Eventually I'll have earned enough money so we never have to return. Except for shopping. And clothes. And maybe the occasional movie."

Victor chuckled. "How about we build the cabin together? And we clear away enough of the land to grow our own food."

"What about clothes?" Jace said.

"We won't need them." Victor fumbled beneath the sheets, his hands returning with a pair of underwear. "We'll live as God intended, naked as the day we were born."

"Okay." Jace pulled down his own boxers, kicking them off under the sheets. "And movies? What will we do for entertainment?"

"Oh, I'm sure we'll figure something out," Victor said as Jace scooted closer. "Judging by what just poked me in the leg, I'd say you already have."

"Sorry," Jace said, but of course he wasn't. Since their sleeping bag fumbling the other night, he'd dreamt over and over again of having another chance, one with more opportunity. That time was now. Jace started with Victor's chest, rubbing his palm across

118

his skin, over his nipples, and then up to his neck which he held on to while kissing him.

"Do you want me to be your toy?" Victor said, lips brushing against his.

"Yeah."

Victor rolled over on to his back, placing his hands behind his head, surrendering full control. Jace let his hand begin exploring again, fingers brushing along the hair on Victor's chest before tickling his armpit playfully. He covered Victor's mouth with his own when he tried to laugh. Then Jace stopped teasing himself, stopped holding back. Fingers arched, the tips slid across Victor's belly, leaving goose bumps in their wake until the head of Victor's cock halted their progress.

Jace moaned, as if touching himself, but it was the sheer idea that brought him pleasure. He could do whatever he wanted, and the prospect was almost overwhelming because he wanted everything at once. He hopped up on his knees, throwing back the covers, his modesty extinguished in a sea of hormones. Victor's body was finally exposed in the dancing light of the Zippo flame. Jace reveled in every part: the angular lines between his stomach and hips, the dark bush around his hard cock, the heavy balls, and the fine hair on his thighs. All meant to be secret but now laid bare for him.

Victor was looking him over too. "Damn," he said. "Now that's what I call blessed!"

Jace blushed at the compliment, but his own body was the furthest thing from his mind. All he wanted to do was taste Victor. Flopping onto his side, he was finally close enough to enact a fantasy that had plagued him for years. He took hold of Victor's cock, pumped it a few times and then moved forward, shoving it deep into his mouth.

Too deep, as it turned out, because he gagged, but he wasn't about to let that stop him. Being more cautious and keeping one hand on the base, Jace began moving his head up and down. Soon Victor's breath met his rhythm. When Jace pulled up—fist following the trail his tongue left—Victor breathed in. Then Jace's slick fingers slid down, Victor exhaling in a short burst, like a bull ready to charge. Jace picked up the pace when Victor's hand found him and began returning the favor.

"Get up here," Victor instructed. "Put your legs on either side of my head."

Jace did what he was told, not letting go of Victor, not missing a single stroke. He never wanted to stop. Ever. Only when he felt something warm and wet envelop him did he pause, gasping and looking down to see Victor's mouth rising and falling on him. Jace's world became a blur of pleasure. Some part of him knew to keep going, his body doing all it could to please Victor in return, while his mind reeled and writhed in ecstasy.

When Victor shoved Jace off him, he was momentarily confused, but soon Victor was straddling his hips. He thought the question of who played which role was about to be answered, but Victor had something else in mind. He grabbed Jace's wrist, guided his hand to his cock. "I'm close," he huffed.

That was enough to make Jace a whole lot closer. He started pumping, Victor reaching to do the same to him. Jace's entire focus was on Victor's body as it tightened, the expression on his face almost pained before it became one of bliss. Then Jace's eyes darted back down.

When Victor came, he came a lot. Jace let loose shortly afterwards, but Victor still had a few shots left, even after Jace was done. His chest and abs were totally soaked. Now he knew why the sleeping bag had gotten so wet!

Victor opened his eyes, took in Jace's look of shock, and laughed.

"Is that normal?" Jace asked.

"Hell if I know!"

They grinned dopily at each other before Victor stooped for a kiss. Sex had a strange way of going from being the most imperative urge to the least important thing in the world, all in the space of a few seconds. This time it was different. While the sexual urge faded, the need to be close to Victor, to touch, caress, and kiss him didn't. Even after they sacrificed a T-shirt in the name of getting Jace cleaned up, all he could think of was pressing their bodies against each other, of being as near as possible.

Victor held him from behind, kissing his shoulder occasionally, as they dozed in and out of consciousness. Jace wished this could last forever, that they had enough privacy every day to live like this.

"Where's our cabin going to be?" he asked.

"Near a lake," Victor murmured sleepily. "Or a stream. You'll need somewhere to bang laundry against rocks."

"Gee, thanks," Jace said. "No, I mean *where*. Not Missouri, I hope. Somewhere warm, where they don't have winter. Or maybe up in Canada. It's cold, but the forests are beautiful."

Victor was quiet, enough so that Jace thought he had fallen asleep. But eventually he spoke. "How about where I'm camping now? I'm sure if we ask Greg, he could whip us up a cabin in no time."

"Probably." Jace laughed. "Seriously, though. I won't stay here. Warrensburg isn't the place for me."

"It's not so bad." Victor yawned, then tightened his grip on Jace. "You know that old saying about home being where the heart is? I don't think that refers to your own. It's the hearts of other people, the ones you love, that makes a home."

Jace thought about this, was still trying to decide what it meant for his future, when the endorphins coaxed him into a blissful slumber.

Chapter Ten

"I'm sorry for your loss."

Like a secret phrase, this had been uttered throughout the day—from the teachers who had heard the news or the other students who wondered why Jace had been absent. Even Greg said it solemnly during lunch. Jace supposed Greg had heard the phrase when his grandfather died a couple of years ago. Jace only wished he knew the appropriate response. All he could think to say was—

"Thank you." He stood in the back room of the gas station, pen still in hand. He finished signing in and turned to face Bernard. "She was really old," he tried, hoping this would explain it all.

Bernard nodded sympathetically. "It helps when it's not totally unexpected, but still, I know how hard this must be for you."

Jace felt a surge of guilt. Since yesterday, his thoughts had been on Victor and Victor alone. He'd floated through the day thinking about him, not hearing or learning a thing in class, and barely making conversation at lunch. Victor had gone from being an unreachable mystery to the closest person in his life. Jace hated being away from him.

"You can take another night off, if you need to," Bernard prompted.

Jace shook his head, regaining his focus. "No, I'm all right. I think keeping busy will help." Besides, he didn't know where Victor would be. With Jace's parents having arrived home during the day, Victor couldn't stay over again, and it was getting colder by the minute. Even Victor didn't know where he'd be that night. At least that's what he said before Jace left for school.

"I truly believe we'll all be together one day," Bernard was saying, "in a place where we never have to say goodbye."

"That would be nice," Jace said.

"It would. That was one of the few comforts I had when I lost my son. I kept thinking—"

"What?" The fog lifted from Jace's mind. "When did your son pass away?"

"Eight years ago." Bernard broke eye contact. "I know. I talk about him like he's still alive. Drives my wife crazy, but it hurts too much to refer to him in the past tense, like he doesn't exist anymore. He remains a major part of my life. I think of him every day. I carry his memory with me, so to me he's still here."

"I'm sorry," Jace said. He stopped at adding the other three words, but he understood now what people meant. "What happened? I mean, if you don't mind me asking."

Bernard took a deep breath. "Suicide. But before you judge him, Brian fought in Vietnam. He was in the trenches and didn't like to talk about what he saw there, but it wasn't pretty. He came back from that war a changed man. Found his feet again though, became one of the best car salesmen there is. Was. Always outsold the other men at his dealership. He had put the war behind him, I think."

Jace wanted to ask what the reason was, if not the war, but it seemed inappropriate. Then he recognized what it must have been like for Bernard to drag him out of the water, to find his suicide note. Jace's face betrayed this realization, Bernard responding to it.

"The world has a funny way of teaching you a lesson," he said, clapping Jace on the shoulder. "Brian had a friend, Franklin, a handsome guy who could charm the socks off a centipede. They were in sales together for a while, in direct competition, until Franklin took a job in marketing. Once they were no longer competing, Brian invited him out, hit Franklin up for his sales tactics, since he wouldn't be needing them anymore. They became friends. More than that, really. They were inseparable." Bernard hesitated. "Brian came to me a year before he died, told me all of this. Of course I figured out the story before he finished. He and Franklin were lovers. Is that the right term?"

"It's fine," Jace said.

"Okay. Well, I cut Brian off before he could say too much. I told him I wanted no part of it, that I didn't want to hear about it and certainly didn't want Franklin under my roof... I still remember the hurt on his face. That year was the first Christmas that Brian didn't come home to visit." Bernard's jowls trembled before he steeled himself. "Of course now I wish I'd been proud of him, like I was in every other way. I should have insisted on meeting Franklin so I could shake his hand. As it turned out, I did, but only at Brian's funeral." Bernard's focus returned to

Jace. "But as I said, the world has a funny way of teaching you a lesson, or giving you a second chance. If there's anything you want to talk about, or if anyone gives you trouble for being gay, you come to me, son. I'm always there for you."

Jace didn't know what to say, couldn't find words to express how this made him feel, so instead he stepped forward and hugged Bernard tight. Of course Dan walked in, staring like he'd caught them in a compromising situation, but Jace glared at him over Bernard's shoulder until he went away. When they broke their embrace, Bernard turned. There was some sniffing and wiping, but when he faced Jace again, he looked like his old self.

"Come over to my desk. There's something I want to ask you about."

Jace followed him over, watching Bernard covertly as he settled into his chair. So much made sense now—why Bernard had gone out of his way to keep him close and keep an eye on him. Jace wouldn't let him down. Suicide was and would remain the furthest thing from his mind, but he'd also do his best to make Bernard proud. As it turned out, he wasn't off to the greatest start.

"Still like working with Dan?" Bernard asked.

"Oh." Jace hesitated.

Bernard nodded, as if this answer was sufficient. "I know he's taken off early a few times. We all have our problems, so I try not to judge, but my patience is running out."

"That's understandable," Jace said as neutrally as possible.

"There's something else. I did inventory recently, and there are items unaccounted for. Shoplifting is an expected loss, but we're talking things from behind the counter that customers can't reach. Like cigarettes."

Great. Bernard had poured his heart out to him, only to find out that Jace had been stealing. Except he hadn't. Not exactly.

"The thing is," Bernard continued, "that the register total keeps coming out too high, and the amount it's over is just about right to make up for anything missing."

"Like someone's been buying things but not ringing them up."

Bernard looked puzzled for a moment, then nodded. "I suppose that would account for it."

Jace studied the desk surface, body tense. "Don't be mad," he said. "I know I'm not old enough to buy cigarettes, and I don't smoke them. I have a friend who's old enough, and I buy them as presents. He could come in, I guess, but it's unpredictable when I see him, so I stock up. I know that sounds like a lie, but if I *was* lying, I'd come up with something better, I swear."

Bernard studied him. "And here I thought Dan was embezzling somehow. I know from that hug that you're not a smoker, so I believe you. I can show you how to do an employee discount. You don't have to pay full price, you know."

"I don't?" Jace thought about it. "Can I get a refund on what I've bought so far?"

"Not a chance."

They exchanged grins. "I didn't mean to deceive you."

"It's fine. Just make sure no one sees you pocketing cigarettes or I could get in trouble. And for god's sake, ring them up first so I can keep my books in order. Now get out there and get to work. Something about you seems to make Dan miserable, and that only makes me like you more."

Jace smiled and headed to the front room, ready to do battle with the ever-filthy microwave.

The second-worst thing about Star was how pretty she was. No, that wasn't quite right. Pretty is the sort of word used for little girls in Sunday dresses, or the first day of mild weather after a long hard winter. Star wasn't pretty. She was beautiful. Her long blond hair was silky, the highlights natural, or expensive enough to appear so. Her clothing was both casual and fashionable— hip-hugging jeans just worn enough to be comfortable, a pink blouse matching the color of her glossy lipstick. Star smelled like perfume and gum. She had a way of smiling when she talked that showed off her perfect white teeth.

But worse than her catwalk style and stunning good looks was the way Victor behaved around her. He practically danced into the gas station, bouncing with energy as he introduced his "firecracker princess." Jace didn't know what that meant, but he found himself suddenly eager for a pet name of his own. After he tossed Victor a pack of cigarettes, his boyfriend went outside for a smoke, leaving Jace and Star alone.

"Having to work on Thanksgiving must suck," she said, sounding genuinely sympathetic, but that smile never faded.

"I volunteered," Jace said. "I get paid double, which isn't bad, and aside from people fuelling up, I'm mostly just selling cans of cranberry sauce or boxes of stuffing mix."

He nodded to where Bernard had smartly stocked up on Thanksgiving food items and arranged them in an eye-catching display. Most customers who walked in looked so relieved to see whatever item they were missing that they overlooked the hiked-up prices.

Star didn't turn to see what Jace was referring to. Instead she peered at him, as if trying to figure something out. "So you and Victor," she said. "I won't call it a relationship, or else he'll throw a fit, but you guys are screwing, right?"

Jace didn't like how that sounded. Sure, they'd been having a lot of sex. Over the last couple of weeks, they went to all sorts of extremes to be together. For a while Victor was sleeping in Jace's car, and Jace had managed to sneak out for some backseat fun. A few times he had begged Michelle to let Victor enter through her window. In the morning, Victor would hide beneath the bed until everyone had left the house. So yes, they were having sex, but screwing made it sound cold, when really they were—

"Making love," Jace said without thinking.

Star opened her mouth, snapped it shut, then nodded as if in slow motion. "O-kay," she said. "Very romantic. I can see why Victor talks about you all the time."

"He does?" Jace said a little too eagerly.

"Yeah. Sometimes I wonder if he'll ever stop."

Her voice had an edge when she said this, barely detectable and probably not intentional, but it was there. Who the hell was she, exactly?

"So how did you two meet?" Jace asked.

"I used to live here. My father owned a business in town, and I was going through that phase where I wanted to upset him. As you can imagine, Victor was the perfect way of doing so. Not that I was using him." Star glanced out the window, Victor waving when he saw her, a smoldering cigarette trapped between his fingers. "Okay, so I was, but he was using me too. One day we sort of clicked, and it became affection instead of opportunity."

"So you guys were—"

"Screwing. Even I wouldn't call it making love."

Jace considered reaching for the shotgun.

"These days I'm the person he turns to when he feels like running away."

Yup! Definitely going to need that shotgun. Was it loaded? If not, he could smack her upside the head with it.

Star smiled, oblivious to her life being in mortal peril. "You should come along next time. I have a place in Kansas City. We could party together, and you'd see more of him that way. I know what it can be like when you want more and Victor keeps disappearing."

"That would be cool," Jace said, but with some reservation.

Star looked him over. "You have a better chance with him than I ever did. Victor likes to go against the grain, and two guys being together…"

"Definitely not the norm," Jace said with a chuckle. Star's smile widened, like she was happy for them both. Maybe he wouldn't need the shotgun after all. In fact, maybe Star could be an ally instead of a rival. "Any tips?"

"On keeping Victor happy and interested?" Star exhaled, as if this were a tall order. "Nothing you probably haven't figured out. Don't try to pin him down. I had him cornered for three months once. Wouldn't let him out of my sight, and it got ugly. That was a big mistake. Don't expect an explanation, either, when he reappears from one of his little sojourns."

"If you love someone, set them free," Jace said. "If they come back, don't ask where they've been."

Star laughed. "Exactly. Oh my god! You so have him figured out already!"

"I'm getting there," Jace said. "Bit by bit. Any other words of wisdom?"

"Just be yourself," Star said. "Victor will see right through any games you try to play. That's why he's still my friend, after all this time."

Jace wasn't sure what that meant. Before he could ask, Victor came back inside, a cocky grin on his face.

"Talking about me?" he asked. "I know you were because you both look like you could swoon at any second. I have that affect on all the ladies." Victor shot a wink in Jace's direction. "A few of the guys too."

"Are you still here?" Star said, sounding bored.

She was cool, especially since Jace's reaction nearly *had* been to swoon when he caught that wink. Maybe he could learn from Star—not just how to best handle Victor, but more about his past as well. He and Star had a history together, and Jace wanted to know more of it.

"We can't stay long," Victor said. "My mom cooks a whole turkey every year, even though it's just the two of us. You want me to bring some by after we eat?"

Jace thought about what Star had said. "Nope. You guys go have fun. If you get bored, you know where to find me."

Victor seemed—well, not taken aback exactly, but he obviously hadn't expected Jace to answer that way. Star snuck him a look that said she approved. Already her advice had paid off. Jace was definitely looking forward to seeing more of her around.

Later, when Jace was off work, and after he had stuffed himself at the table with his family, he lay in bed and read drowsily. He was nodding off when the doorknob to his bedroom turned much too carefully to be anyone but the person he wanted to see most.

"I think your sister is getting tired of me coming in through the window," Victor whispered.

"I'll increase her bribe money," Jace said, tossing aside the book as Victor crawled over his body. Victor kissed him once reaching his lips, not stopping until they were both truly exhausted.

As Jace dozed off, he wondered—even if it was unrealistic to expect Victor to be his completely—if it would be all right to belong to him entirely.

Jace had gotten his wish. Victor had settled down. Jace knew where to find him on any given night. More or less. Winter had blown across Warrensburg, encasing it in ice and decorating it with snow. The weather forecasters were calling it the worst winter in the last decade, and even the elderly conceded it was *at least* as bad as such-and-such storm from their childhood.

This meant Victor had very few options left. Even though Greg had helped him upgrade the lean-to in the woods to what he called an A-frame shelter, it was simply too cold for Victor to live outside. Aside from a few rare occurrences, Victor spent every night at his mother's house. In the evenings, he'd walk to Bernie's to keep Jace company. Once, when Dan complained that Victor needed to buy something or leave, Jace gave Victor money that he used to buy something small every half-hour. Not that this was truly necessary, but it made Dan livid, and thus was a cheap form of entertainment.

The nights that Dan left early became a happy occurrence. Customers were fewer in the dire weather, and it felt like the store belonged to them. They had magazines, drinks, food, smokes, even scratch-off lottery tickets. One week Jace spent almost his entire paycheck on items from the store, but he didn't care. He'd already saved up enough money for Christmas, and these little indulgences were worth the boost they gave Victor's spirit.

That was the new challenge. As happy as Jace was by these forced circumstances, Victor became increasingly glum as the snow and ice refused to melt. Even Star couldn't come to his rescue, since the roads were so slick. So Jace did everything he could to cheer up Victor, loving every moment. One night he bought a bottle of whiskey. If Bernard noticed, Jace would say it was a Christmas present for his father. This wasn't the only lie he had planned. He told his parents he was staying at Greg's, but spent the night in Victor's basement bedroom. They drank so much that Jace blacked out, but what he could remember had been heaven; Victor's smile, the sound of his laughter—they were more intoxicating than the liquor.

And then there were snow days when school was canceled because so many cars couldn't leave their driveways and the school buses were stranded in their barn. Jace had bundled up and made the walk downtown, often sliding and falling on his way, but any struggle was worth his destination.

When Christmas rolled around, Jace woke up early like he did every year. He met his sister in the hallway, and together they woke up their parents. Then they raced down the stairs to the tree, waiting impatiently for their mom and dad to arrive so they could begin opening presents. Not that they were waiting in suspense.

"Do you think I should go for the stereo first?" his sister whispered. "Or is that too obvious?"

"Maybe open one of the CDs," Jace suggested. "Act all confused about not having a CD player before going for the big box."

Michelle laughed. "Okay."

He and his sister knew every place their mother hid presents.

What they were getting hadn't been a mystery since Jace was eight. These days Serena had the items gift wrapped at the store, but there were ways around this too. The nice glossy paper made it possible to carefully peel back the tape. Otherwise, using a box cutter, they could make small incisions on the bottom of the present to see what they were dealing with.

This year was different because Jace could actually buy presents for his family. He bought his father a bottle of whisky after all, and for his mother, her favorite perfume. Michelle got a nice pair of headphones for her new stereo, which only left a small envelope under the tree. That was for Victor. Jace tore through his presents as quickly as possible, then raced upstairs to take a shower and get ready. The sun had barely risen when he hopped in the car and drove to Victor's house.

Thankfully, Victor didn't have any philosophical misgivings about Christmas. A warm light was on in the front window, and when Mrs. Hemingway answered the door, her hand was pressed against the necklace Jace had helped Victor pick out. And paid for, but hey, all part of the holiday spirit!

"Is that new?" Jace asked, drawing attention to it. "Wow! Gorgeous!"

"Yes, Victor gave it to me!"

"How sweet!"

Mrs. Hemingway gave a coy little smile. "I think he has something for you too."

Jace paused. He wasn't really expecting that, and the prospect made him oddly nervous. "Uh, these are from my mom."

He handed Mrs. Hemingway a tin full of homemade cookies. After a little more small talk, he went downstairs to Victor's room. Jace found him lying in his bed, wearing an old Misfits T-shirt and a pair of flannel pajama bottoms. Maybe Victor planned on giving him the sort of present Jace was in the mood for.

But these thoughts were chased away when he saw what his boyfriend was doing.

"Are you reading?"

Victor lowered the book. "Believe it or not, I do know how."

Jace chuckled nervously, hopped into bed next to him, and checked out the title. "*The Survivalist's Handbook.* A present from your mom?"

"Yup! There's a whole section on surviving freezing temperatures."

"Great, I'll never see you again!"

Victor grinned. "Sure you will. I'll have you over for hot chocolate once my new igloo is built."

"Better make it milkshakes if you don't want the walls to melt." Jace licked his lips nervously and dug in his pocket for the envelope. It was smaller than a greeting card, no bigger than a business card because that's all it was. "Merry Christmas."

Victor took it, flipping it over a few times. "You first," he said, rising from bed to fetch a present on the nightstand. He tossed it to Jace, who managed to catch it.

Whatever it was had more weight than he expected. The wrapping job was rough, like a kid had crumpled paper around a rock. He could detect all sorts of edges beneath the surface. Feeling apprehensive, he tore off the paper. Jace smelled the wood before he saw it, and after turning the object over, he saw a small hand-carved lion looking him in the eye. There was no mistaking it. Four legs, a tail, and a mane, but unlike the way most lions were depicted, this one wasn't roaring. Instead it appeared calm.

"Did you make this?" Jace asked, throat tight.

"I sure hope so!" Victor said. "I can't imagine anyone paying money for it."

Jace disagreed. The carving was good. Really good! "I love it," he said truthfully.

"I'm glad. I feel like it's a part of your home, since it's from the woods by your place."

Jace looked up. "You carved this there?"

"Whittled," Victor said, getting back into bed. "And yeah. I sat out there thinking about you, and that's what came to mind."

"A lion?" Jace balked. "How am I a lion?"

"Well—" Victor reached over to muss his hair. "You've got the mane. You know I love your hair. But more than that, you have a sort of nobility, like a king who rules with kindness instead of brute strength. That's what I see when I look at you. A noble lion."

That's not what Jace saw, or what he imagined Victor saw when they locked eyes. He caressed the deep lines in the wood, feeling moved. The idea that Victor had been thinking of him back then... Jace could still remember being stuck in his bedroom, grounded, his thoughts obsessively fixed on one person. He had never expected that Victor had felt the same way. And now they were together. Jace the lion, Victor the fox.

Then he realized how well their two presents fit together. "Open yours!" he said.

Victor did, pulling a business card from the envelope. He saw the back of it first, the crude drawing of a fox running along a black line. Then he turned the card over and read out loud. "*Tint and Tone Tattoos*. Hey, this is Mike's store!"

"You know him?" Jace asked.

"Well, I was in there once when I was fourteen. I tried to get a free tat out of him. I said he could experiment on me with new inks or dangerous needles. I even offered to sweep up or something." Victor laughed at the memory, before looking puzzled. "Did you get me a job there?"

"No, stupid. I'm getting you a tattoo. The one you've always wanted."

"You don't have to do that," Victor said. "By which I really mean 'oh my fucking god, I hope you don't change your mind!'"

"There's no time to," Jace said. "Your appointment is in a few hours."

Victor's jaw dropped. "No shit? On Christmas Day?"

"Mike said it wasn't that unusual a request. He's done at least one tattoo every Christmas since he opened." Of course it had cost extra, but Jace didn't care. The grin on Victor's face was worth every penny.

"Does it hurt?"

"I told you to stop asking me that," Victor said.

"I know, but that's when you were actually getting the tattoo. I want to know if it hurts now."

"Terribly," Victor said, but he smiled.

They sat together on the couch in the family room. Upstairs Jace's mom was getting something ready to eat. Next door, they could hear Michelle's stereo blaring, as it had been all day. Jace's father had retreated to the upper floor, trying to escape her Queensrÿche marathon.

"It looks like it hurts," Jace said, poking the bandage.

"Ow! It does when you do that!"

"Sorry."

Victor turned his glare to the gauze covering. It resembled

the kind packed with meat to sop up the excess blood. "It sucks not being able to see it. I'm taking it off."

"It hasn't been six hours," Jace said

"I'm taking it off," Victor repeated.

Jace didn't stop him. He wanted to see it too. Victor slowly peeled back the first two pieces of tape, as if his skin were made of delicate paper. The bandage flopped open, revealing a masterpiece. Mike wasn't just good with a needle. He was an artist! A fox ran along a thick black band, its head turned to the side, as if it had just spotted the viewer. The fox's eyes were multicolored, one green, one brown. Jace thought that an especially nice touch. On the inside of his arm, above the black band, Victor had made his own contribution by requesting two little words. *No limits.*

"That's sexy," Jace said.

"Yeah?" Victor eyed the raised skin proudly. "I like it too. I guess I'm supposed to wash it now."

"Wait here." Jace hopped up and ran upstairs. When he returned he had a bowl from the kitchen, filled with warm sudsy water and a washcloth. Victor had removed the bandage completely, so Jace got the cloth wet and gently dabbed at the tattoo. When he looked up, he found Victor watching him instead of his actions.

"Feel okay?" Jace asked.

"Yeah." Victor smiled. "I'm happy. Not just with the tattoo, but with you. With us. I really like being around you."

Jace dabbed at the tattoo. "So what you're saying is that you lll—" He acted like his tongue wouldn't work right. "That you lll—llo—"

Victor shoved him playfully, water slopping onto the couch. "Come upstairs with me and I'll show you how I feel."

Jace didn't need any more prompting than that.

Chapter Eleven

Star lived in a maisonette apartment in downtown Kansas City, just off the illustrious Country Club Plaza. Jace didn't know what a maisonette was, but as they toured the apartment and were led up the spiral staircase, he figured the second floor was what made the difference. The entire apartment was gorgeous, more spacious than where Victor's mother lived, and decorated with furniture expensive enough to be considered tasteful, no matter how much of it went against common sense. Nestled in the top corner of the building, the apartment's every window offered a breathtaking view.

The first floor housed a kitchen, separate dining room, bathroom, and balcony. The upper floor featured two bedrooms, a spacious master bath and—because one is never enough—another balcony. Star led them out onto this, which was high enough to see over the treetops. The Plaza lights twinkled at them, trying to lure them into the maze of upscale shopping and dining.

"Must be hard living in the slums," Jace said, leaning over the iron rail and watching the traffic below zoom by.

Star laughed, her breath visible in the cold night air. "Every day is a struggle," she said.

"How'd you manage to escape from Warrensburg to this?" he asked with envy.

"Bank robber," Victor said, lighting a cigarette.

"Boyfriend," Star countered. "One with more money than time, which is just how I like them. He keeps me here, and just over there—" She pointed to houses in the distance. "—he keeps his wife and children."

"He's married?" Jace said, not hiding his shock. Star giggled and Victor shook his head, making him feel out of his element.

Which he was. Trips to the city were normally with his family, around Michelle's birthday when she wanted a special shopping trip. Or with Greg, when they went to the haunted houses in the rundown industrial district. The level of freedom Star had was unprecedented to him. Is that why Victor liked her, because she was living on her own terms, like he did? Then again, Victor hadn't seemed impressed during the tour, but maybe just because he'd seen it all before.

Star shivered, grabbed Jace's arm, and led him back inside. Victor remained smoking on the balcony.

"So how are things with you and Victor?" she asked.

"Great!" Jace said. "Unbelievably good. He's been around a lot more. We even went on a double date!"

"Victor," Star deadpanned. "On a date."

"Yeah, I know. My best friend, Greg, he's really supportive so, uh, he arranged everything. I don't think his girlfriend knew what to make of us, so that was awkward. Then, halfway through the movie, Victor dragged me off to the bathroom to smoke a joint. I ended up feeling paranoid, which sucked, and Angie never stopped staring at us. But Greg and Victor seemed to have fun together."

"Maybe they should be dating instead," Star teased. "So aside from an awkward date, you two are—"

"Hot." Jace laughed nervously. "I think that sums it up."

Star nodded in approval, but her eyebrows were raised kind of funny. Was it surprise over Victor's behavior or something more?

"Do you always get paranoid when you're high?" she asked.

"No. Just that once. I guess because we were in public."

"That's good. Tonight won't be pretty if that happens a lot."

"Oh." Jace wasn't as into drugs as Victor seemed to be, but weed could help take the edge off. Except it wasn't that simple. Once Victor was back inside, they all gathered in the kitchen.

"Mushrooms," Star said.

That was stating the obvious. On a decorative dinner plate were a handful of dried mushrooms that looked like they'd fallen behind the refrigerator a few months back.

"I thought you were getting acid," Victor said.

"So did I," Star replied. "This was all the guy had. Any idea how we eat them?"

Victor shrugged, grabbed one, and popped it in his mouth.

"How do they taste?" Jace asked.

"Mushroomy."

"I'm putting sauce on mine," Star said, turning to the fridge. "I have got the best thing in the world in here."

Behind her back, Victor mouthed the words "honey mustard."

"Honey mustard," Star said. "Oh, shut up," she added when Victor started laughing.

"You put that on *everything*," he said.

"Now I'm putting it on magic mushrooms, and if you want to eat anymore, they'll be slathered in sauce."

Jace grinned along with them, but really he felt apprehensive. Smoking pot was one thing, but tripping sounded scary. He pictured himself prancing through swirls of multicolored clouds until flying off one of the balconies to his death. Then again, the anti-drug films shown in school were hardly reliable. He'd seen one where a stoned girl went into a fit, screaming at her family, when in reality, she'd probably just calmly ask them to pass the Doritos.

"Oh, that came for you," Star said, nodding toward an envelope while dribbling honey mustard over the mushrooms.

Victor picked it up with disinterest, Jace casually craning his neck to see who it was from. He only saw that it was addressed to Victor Hemmingway. Why would he get his mail sent to Star's place? Did he live here sometimes?

"What is it?" Jace asked.

"Identification," Victor said with distaste.

"It's more than that," Star said. "Besides, it's about time you become a real boy."

"I can't believe you talked me into this." Victor shook his head and shoved the envelope into his front pocket. "I'll never use it."

"Then I'm so glad I paid for it," Star muttered under her breath. She lifted up the plate of mushrooms, presenting it to them. "Anyway, dinner is served!"

Jace gobbled down his share of the shrooms, bracing himself to be transported to a magical cartoon world. Instead, nothing much happened. Star mentioned a leaky pipe in the downstairs bathroom, Victor doing his best to tighten the connection without a wrench. Thrilling. It wasn't until they were outside smoking that Jace noticed the tracers left by Victor's cigarette. Every time he moved his arm to take another drag, the orange light from the embers would remain in the air as a solid line that faded slowly.

And Jace found he was cool with it. The effect wasn't terrifying. He wasn't losing his mind.

That came later.

Jace stared at the open dictionary with something nearing

devout affection. Never before had he realized how beautifully the words were arranged, how they blended together in progressive measurements. *Mute, muted, mutilate, mutinous.* Perfection! Each word faded into the next—like shades of colors in the spectrum. In a way, letters were just as orderly as numbers. Jace read each word aloud, savoring it before moving on to the next. *Mutter, mutton, mutual, muzzle.*

Farther away, Star was sitting on the couch, rubbing her hands on the cushions to each side of her and nearly drooling. Victor was on his back, head near one of the stereo speakers. The music made him smile, but to Jace, the lyrics were all gibberish. Were the vocals in English? Was the singer male or female? He couldn't tell.

There were a lot of things he couldn't understand anymore, and that tiny little kernel inside that represented the sober Jace from before had one message for him: *You've gone insane.* And he had! Jace paused from his recital to laugh. He'd gone completely, irreversibly insane. This was his world from now on. Miniscule details had become overwhelmingly important. The fabric of reality had unraveled, allowing him to examine the threads. The experience was terrifying and wonderful, and he might have freaked out, but anytime he came close, he sought out Victor's eyes. Green and brown, like the colors in a forest. Earthy. Grounding. And so huge Jace felt they could swallow him up.

"Come feel this," Star said, reaching out a hand to him. "When I bought this couch, I had no idea. How could I not know?"

Jace went to her, plopping down on the soft cushion. Star took his hand, placing his palm flat on the fabric.

"Rub," she said, with a crooked smile.

Jace did so. What was this material? Suede? Frosting? "Oh! It gets warm! My hand is warm!"

Star burst out laughing, Jace joining her. They laughed so hard they clutched at their stomachs, tears in their eyes. Insane, but not alone.

"Look at you!" Victor stood over them, beaming until exaggerated worry marred his features. "Timberrrrrr!"

Jace and Star shrieked and giggled as Victor tumbled down on top of them. Jace began rubbing the recently buzzed sides of Victor's dark hair. One look at Star encouraged her to do the same.

"Stop it!" Victor said, pushing their hands away. His grin was impossibly wide as he looked back and forth between them. "Look at you two," he said again, shaking his head. "Right here, together. You're both so beautiful."

Jace snorted and Star tittered.

"Seriously," Victor said. "I love you guys so much."

Love. That distant sane part of Jace reacted to this word. He'd wanted to hear it, of course, even considered saying it, but he thought it might scare Victor away. Now Victor had said it first, but not in the way Jace had sometimes imagined. Not solely to him.

"We love you too," Star said, sighing like she was in a dream.

"So beautiful," Victor repeated. "I want to see you kiss."

"What?" Star shrieked, giggling like a child, but when her head stopped shaking back and forth, it was facing Jace.

She *was* beautiful. Victor was right. Women had always been mysterious to Jace, like an alien species, but not in a monstrous way. They were almost angelic, too good, a miracle that shouldn't be touched by mere mortal hands. He admired them, found their appearance alluring, their strange ways fascinating. They just weren't meant for him.

Victor came nearer, kissed Star on the forehead, pulled Jace over to do the same. Now he and Star were even closer. Her eyes were innocent, the pink gloss on her lips like candy. Jace wanted to taste it. He leaned forward and closed his eyes.

The kiss was soft, gentle, but not entirely innocent. He wasn't sure if it lasted a long time, or who decided that tongues were acceptable, but he didn't mind. Only when he pulled away and saw that Star's eyes had changed, were looking at him in a new light—reassessing him—did he feel uncomfortable.

"I love you guys so much," Victor repeated.

Star kept her gaze fixed on Jace a moment longer. Then she turned to Victor with a smile. "Yeah, yeah. We know. Now put on some better music."

Later, when the sky began to grow light, and the insanity seemed more like pretend than an effect of the mushrooms, they were forced to admit that the party was over. Jace struggled to remember much of the night, such as how they escaped the strangeness of the couch and ended up coloring pictures on the downstairs balcony—but he vividly remembered that kiss.

"Do you want to crash here?" Victor asked him.

"No. Michelle needs the car. I promised her I'd be back in the morning."

"Okay. Think you can drive?"

"Yeah." Jace nodded. "I feel pretty normal now. Are you coming with me?"

Victor shrugged. "Do you want me to?"

"Yes. Please."

"Okay."

Star seemed sleepy as she saw them to the door, but nothing felt awkward. Only when they were saying goodbye did Jace notice her curious gaze return. He had the slightly uncomfortable impression that, for the first time, Star now took him seriously.

Victor was in high spirits on the drive home. Cruising down a rural road, they raced to meet the sun as it rose, farmland and forests glowing tangerine in the early light. Jace was a twisted mess of emotions inside, but Victor chatted happily, as if nothing had happened.

"Star is a good girl, but she lies through her teeth. She doesn't have a boyfriend. At least not one who pays for her apartment. It's her father who keeps her in a gilded cage. When we first met she flaunted me in front of him just to piss him off, but when it comes down to it, she never pushes hard enough to lose his support."

Jace tightened his grip on the wheel. "Why are you friends if she uses you like that?"

Victor looked sidelong at him, picking up on Jace's tone. "Because we're the same. We both find ourselves running in hamster wheels, and we both want to break free. We just haven't figured out how yet."

Jace didn't think they were the same. Victor went to extremes to buck the system, while Star was living in the lap of luxury. Maybe she didn't want to be her father's little princess, but she still intended to inherit the kingdom. Jace bit his lip, tasting lip gloss even though he had scrubbed it off in the bathroom. Maybe it was all in his head or some after-effect of the mushrooms. Regardless, he wished it would stop because he wanted to forget that kiss, erase what it meant and the potential it had to ruin everything.

"I'm sorry," he blurted out. "Star and I— We shouldn't have—" Jace wiped at his eyes. The car swerved, causing Victor to grab the wheel.

"Pull over," he said.

Jace did—not due to a few tears, but because his heart was pounding with panic, his mind swarming with questions, implications, and fears. "I shouldn't have kissed her," he said. "I only want you. Maybe it was the drugs or something, I don't know, but I swear to God that I only want to be with you!"

Victor studied him a moment, then reached for the door handle. "Let's get some fresh air."

Jace checked the road, deserted this early on a Sunday morning, before leaving the car and joining Victor on the hood. Ahead of them, on a stretch of farmland soggy with melted snow, was an old barn. Next to it sat a church—little more than a rectangle of weather-worn boards hammered together—topped by a steeple shaped like an outhouse. Considering the broken windows and sunken roof, a Sunday service was extremely unlikely.

"I feel like I cheated on you," Jace said.

Next to him, Victor shrugged. "You can't break a commitment that hasn't been made."

Jace felt his face flush. "But I have. Maybe you don't like titles, or the idea of us being special to each other, but in my mind, we're all of those things. In my mind, we're committed!"

Victor sighed. "You *are* special to me. I can still feel, you know. I'm not scared of emotion. But this is exactly why I despise the modern concept of a relationship."

"Don't!" Jace said. "Don't make this one of your political lectures. This is about you and me and nobody else!"

"It's about Star too!" Victor shot back. "In case you're forgetting, I'm the one who suggested you two kiss. And before you fly off the handle about that, answer me one thing, but think about it first. Set aside any point you want to make right now and tell me, honestly, just one thing."

Jace looked up. "What?"

"Did you want to kiss her?"

Jace remembered the sparkle in her eyes, how it felt like kids playing a game. Harmless. Innocent. Only afterwards, when he saw her strange expression, had he considered the implications and let it become a problem. "I'm gay," Jace said, voice strained. "I fought and fought to accept that. What the hell does this mean? Why would I want to kiss her?"

"Because we're not gay or straight, good or bad, single or married. We're human, and that means we're all sorts of things, and I know you don't want to hear one of my stupid ideas right now, but think about how often we're told to choose. Our whole lives we're asked to. Which side are you on? What are you? Which team, which army, which political party? Even when that choice is hard, goes against what the majority considers acceptable, we still fail ourselves by letting it define us."

"It's not a choice," Jace said. A car zoomed past them, blowing his hair into his eyes. "If it *was* a choice, I would have taken the easy road and let Greg hook me up with some girl."

"Fine. So you like guys. But in the right circumstances, you're open to more. Maybe it's not what you usually want or look for, but it's possible. Why limit yourself? What if I had done the same? Do you think I would be with you now? What if I started falling in love with you and refused to acknowledge it, just because I tell myself 'No, no! I'm straight! That's not what I do!'"

"I would hate that," Jace whispered.

"What if I wasn't around and you fell in love with a woman?"

"I wouldn't."

"But what if you did? Seriously! This world is one crazy-ass place. Anything is possible and that's fucking wonderful. Why go through life and limit what you can experience and what you can feel?" Victor shrugged off his jacket, pulled up his T-shirt sleeve to reveal his tattoo and pointed to the words. "No limits. That's what I told myself, and yeah, I know it's scary as hell to let go of our titles because we start asking who we are without them. But I didn't let fear take me for a ride, and look what I got out of it."

Jace brushed the hair out of his face, saw Victor's eyes wide and pleading.

"Does love cease to exist the second you kiss another person? Is love that fickle?"

"No," Jace answered, refusing to believe his feelings were so weak.

"Kissing Star, did it change what you feel for me? Did wanting her, no matter how briefly, stop you from still wanting me?"

"No," Jace said. "It didn't."

"Good. No one can change how we feel for each other except us. There was a kiss I wanted to see, and that you wanted to feel. We can either embrace that or let it tear us apart. And it won't just be Star, because having feelings for one person doesn't mean not feeling anymore. Maybe it won't be a girl next time. Hell, maybe it'll be Greg or some other guy, and that's okay. It doesn't matter who you kiss, who I sleep with, or who either of us loves, because it won't change what we feel for each other. Not if we don't let it."

"I just thought—" But Jace couldn't find the words to match the images in his mind: his parent's marriage, the idea of belonging solely to someone, of someone being only for him— the commitment he'd always dreamt of. Maybe these ideas were selfish and hollow. Maybe they were outdated. But they were what he wanted. "You wouldn't understand," he finished lamely.

Victor's mismatched eyes searched his. "You still need a commitment."

Jace nodded, ready for Victor to shake his head in disappointment, but instead he hopped off the car and grabbed Jace's hand. Shoes squelching in the mud, they made their way across the field. At first it seemed the barn would be their destination, but Victor took them to the church. Jace's imagination went wild. First he pictured Victor dropping to one knee, proposing to him on sacred ground, but this seemed extremely unlikely. Then he worried Victor would make a mockery of what he wanted—busting down the church door, dragging him down the aisle, and heartlessly rattling off the usual words to show Jace they held no special meaning. But being cruel wasn't like Victor either.

They reached the church door, which hung ajar on one rusty hinge. Still holding onto him, Victor pushed open the door with his free hand. Inside were three rows of pews, separated down the middle by an aisle. Water leaked from the roof in multiple places, accounting for the musty smell. Victor didn't let this dissuade him. He walked with Jace down the aisle. Somewhere above them, they heard a bird flapping its wings.

When they reached the wooden podium at the end, Victor turned and took Jace's other hand as well. For awhile he just stood there, locking eyes. Behind Jace, light flooded in through a broken window, the orange glow of the sun vibrant now. Jace could feel it warming his face.

Victor squeezed his hands tight. "You want something that belongs only to us, that no one else can touch. I can give that to you. A relationship, a marriage, is nothing without a promise. Only the promise matters, because once it's broken, nothing is left. I promise you, Jace, that I love you. I love you now, and I will love you forever and ever. Nothing can change that."

Before Jace could answer, Victor's lips were on his. *This* was what he needed. Not a title he could flaunt or a ring made of gold. Jace needed Victor's love. As he squeezed his eyes tight against the sun, hands clutching the back of Victor's shirt, he felt certain this promise would be enough.

"You're quiet," Jace said. "I hate it when you're quiet."

Next to him on the bed, Michelle exhaled slowly. Together they stared up at the posters on her ceiling. These days, in addition to being too young, Corey Haim seemed bitter instead of vulnerable, as if he knew that Jace had moved on.

"I'm not sure I understand," Michelle said. "I mean, it's romantic, but I would have had so many questions. After he said that, did you talk about it?"

"No. We, uh—"

"Oh. In the church?"

"Yeah." Jace sighed. "Later, on the drive home, I was happy. And it wouldn't be very romantic to hit him with a bunch of questions."

"I guess not." Michelle rolled over to face him. "So are you in an open relationship? Or did that promise mean that it's just you and him from now on?"

Jace shook his head. "I'm pretty sure it doesn't."

"Are you okay with that?"

"I don't know." Jace turned his head, saw how concerned his sister appeared. "I have to try. If it's the only way I can have him, then I'll deal." Jace looked back at the ceiling. "What he says makes sense. People don't stop wanting other people. Why should kissing someone else or whatever be a big deal? It's only wrong because we say it's wrong. Logically, if we all agreed to get over it, then it wouldn't be a problem."

"There's nothing logical about love," Michelle said. "If there was, Valentine's Day cards would be covered in brains instead of hearts."

Jace chuckled.

"I'm serious," Michelle continued. "There's a reason we talk about our hearts like they're something real. Besides the actual organ, I mean. We have this imaginary part just to describe where all these feelings come from that don't make sense. *Love* doesn't make sense."

"No," Jace said, "it doesn't."

"So what are you going to do?" Michelle asked.

Jace grinned. "Try to make him see nonsense."

"You're not taking this seriously. How are you going to feel the next time he sleeps with Star?"

Jace squirmed. "What do you want me to do? Break up with him? How is that going to make me feel any better?"

"It always hurts in the beginning." Michelle exhaled. "But then you get over it and meet someone else. You have to keep playing the field until you find the right person for you."

"Where?" Jace pushed himself up on his elbows. "Where am I going to meet someone else? You know what, it doesn't matter, because it's Victor I want to be with. You said it yourself. Love doesn't make sense, so it's not fair for you to approach it logically."

Michelle narrowed her eyes but then sighed. "I just don't want to see you get hurt."

"I know," Jace said. "I don't want to see me get hurt either, but I think Victor's right. We love each other. That's untouchable, no matter what happens."

Michelle was quiet for a moment. They could hear their mom cleaning up after dinner, the garbage disposal running as she worked, their father carrying on a conversation by shouting over the noise rather than waiting until she was finished. "Did you tell Victor that you love him? Did you say it back?"

Jace shook his head. "After everything that happened in that church, it felt too obvious. He knows most of what I think before I say it, anyway." He hesitated. "And I don't want to scare him away, or make him feel trapped by my expectations. I already pressed him hard on those issues, and instead of pushing back, he opened his arms to me. That's a good sign, right?"

"Yes," Michelle answered after a beat. "Although I don't think you should have to worry about anything like that. It's not normal."

"*I'm* not normal, so that's fine by me. I can at least try to see the world his way." Jace nudged his sister playfully. "As much as I love you, Michelle, I'm going to prove you wrong. Victor and I are going to make this work."

His sister smiled. "You do that."

As winter melted into spring, Jace found it easy to trust Victor's promise. When they were together, Jace felt loved. The times when Star whisked Victor away to Kansas City were harder. She no longer invited Jace to come along. He suspected that she saw him as competition now, a theory proven correct after one particularly trying week.

Victor disappearing on the weekend wasn't so unusual. Of course Jace preferred having him around when he didn't have school or work, but they still managed to spend a lot of time together. Victor hung out at the store so much that even Bernard was getting to know him. The gas station felt like a second home for them both, which made it all the more shocking when Star walked in. Jace was already on edge because Victor had been gone an entire week this time. Considering how long she had kept him away, Jace expected Star to appear smug. Instead, she was a mess, eyes red as if she had been crying.

She pushed her way past waiting customers. "We're both stupid. You know that?"

Jace handed a middle-aged woman her change and turned his attention to the next customer in line, which meant looking around Star as if she wasn't there.

"Seriously?" she snapped.

"Can't this wait?" Jace said.

"Sure, why not?" Star stomped toward the door. "That's all I do anymore is wait!"

An old trucker chuckled as he slid cash across the counter. "You know they love you when they get that upset."

"Right," Jace said, forcing a smile. "Lucky me."

In truth, they loved the same man. Jace kept glancing out the window as he worked. Star paced back and forth, smoking a cigarette. Once the store was empty, he went out to join her.

"He's back home now," Star said. She seemed to have calmed down. Somewhat. "He's all yours."

"I'm glad," Jace said.

"*I'm glad,*" Star parroted with a snide expression. Then she rubbed one of her temples. "I'm sorry. That was mean. It's just— you're like me. Like I used to be. In the beginning, I was willing to do anything for Victor. No wait was too long, no rule too twisted. His love is enough, right? That's what you keep telling yourself?"

Jace's only response was to clench his jaw.

"Yeah, that's what I thought." Star tossed her cigarette butt to the ground and stomped on it. "Believe me, it's not enough. You'll want more, and you might think playing along will get more from him, but it won't. You should quit while you still can."

"Gee, okay," Jace said. "I'll do that right away. I'm glad you're looking out for me, and not trying to cut me out of the picture."

Star glared. "Of course I want you gone! Put yourself in my shoes. Imagine you and Victor, three years from now. Three years! And then some other person saunters along, and suddenly that's all he talks about. Suddenly you're sharing him and wondering how long you can hang on before you lose him entirely. At first I thought you were just one more taboo he wanted to break, but—" Star shook her head. "You just wait until the next one comes."

"How will that be any different than now?" Jace snarled. "I've been sharing Victor with you since day one. You can stand here and bitch all you want, but at least you had those three years alone with him. Maybe you're the one who should stop seeing him, because I know what I want and I've been getting it all this time!" That wasn't exactly true, but it infuriated Star, which made him feel better.

Star scoffed. "You think I've had him to myself? Are you kidding? If you haven't figured out who the real third wheel is, then I feel sorry for you! She's been around way longer than either of us."

Jace's chest clenched with fear until he realized who she was talking about. "His mother? You're jealous of her too? That's pathetic."

Star looked ready to pounce, but then her shoulders slumped. "Maybe it is. We're both stupid for loving him, but unlike you, I know the truth and still stick around." Star started walking to her car, but then she turned. "Does he give you those wonderful lectures about how it's all love, and how it's only wrong if we let it be?"

Jace nodded grudgingly.

"That's what I thought. He doesn't see what it does to us. When he's not there, he doesn't know how we suffer. It's only wrong if it feels wrong, and this sure as hell doesn't feel right to me."

"Maybe you should tell him that," Jace said.

Star's smile was ironic. "You first. Ever get the feeling that Victor is playing us, feeding us both the same lines? 'People don't stop wanting other people.'"

Jace's stomach sank. Had all the words they shared simply been practiced speeches? "No limits," he murmured.

Star's eyes narrowed. "What does that mean? It's on his tattoo, but he won't talk about it."

Hope exploded in his chest like a bursting balloon, and yet somehow he kept his expression neutral. "No idea," he lied. "He won't tell me either."

As Star got into her car and drove away, Jace wondered briefly if she was right. Her being in the picture didn't feel right. Jace's brain said it shouldn't matter, but his heart... How long could he continue to walk the thin line between logic and emotion? As he returned to work and began watching the door for a familiar punky hair-do, he told himself it didn't matter. Victor was back, which meant they would be together again.

No limits.

Chapter Twelve

Jace was sitting up in bed reading when a polite knock sounded on his door. That couldn't be anyone in his family, since they didn't respect his privacy, nor Greg or Victor, since they were too familiar to knock. Who then?

"Come in," Jace said, probably for the first time in his life.

When the door opened, the creases in his brow deepened. It *was* family. His father, in fact, carrying what looked to be multiple boxes of condoms.

"Okie dokie," his father said, not making eye contact. Instead he walked to the bed and dropped the load in his arms onto the comforter. Aside from condoms, there were pamphlets, a banana, and a bottle that said something about lubricant on it. Bob sat on the edge of the bed, looking uncomfortable. Jace had no trouble matching his expression.

"Your mother and I saw a news story about AIDS the other night. No, I'm sorry—" His father grabbed a pamphlet. "HIV. That's the virus. AIDS can come later. Uh, let's see. This page here has some questions. Okay. Ready?"

"No?" Jace tried.

"Number one. Is your child sexually active?"

"I don't have a child."

His father glanced at the front of the pamphlet. "Oh, right. This is how to talk to your child about safe sex. In that case, they could have phrased the questions better."

"Next one," Jace said.

"Does your child—er, do you know how to use a condom?" His father put down the pamphlet, picked up the banana, and pointed it at him. "This was your mother's idea. Which sort of condom should we try? There are three varieties here. The magnums made me chuckle, since they are for big boys. Would you say a banana is above average?"

"Okay, let's stop right there." Jace put his hand on the banana and lowered it, like he was dealing with a loaded gun. "I promise to read through all this material, very *very* carefully, if you promise never to discuss my sex life with me ever again."

"This is very serious," his father said. "A matter of life and death."

"I know. You're right, and it's super cool of you guys to

worry. I think I can handle the rest on my own."

"Okay. You know if there are any questions, you can ask me."

"I know." Jace grabbed the condoms and shoved them into the nightstand drawer. Then he picked up the bottle, pausing to read the label. *Water soluble personal lubricant.* What the hell was that for? It made it sound like people sometimes needed an oil change.

"Any question is fine," Bob said, looking hopeful. "That's why I'm here."

"Okay, what's this for?"

"HIV is transmitted by blood, and to help reduce the likelihood of any cuts or tears..." His father blanched. "Well, you see, when a man loves a woman—or another man—sometimes he puts his... You remember when you were a kid and you got your head stuck in the banister? Your head was really jammed in there between two poles, so your mother took butter and—"

"Got it!" Jace said, tossing the bottle into the drawer with the condoms. He and Victor had found plenty to do together, but nothing requiring lubrication. His father's speech didn't have Jace eager to try, either.

"Are you sure, because we can lube up the banana, and there's a melon in the kitchen we can carve a hole in."

"No need!" Jace said, trying to banish the image from his mind. "I'll read through the pamphlets, I swear. You can keep the banana."

"Thanks!" To Jace's horror, his father peeled it and took a bite. Chewing thoughtfully, he said, "You know, that went smoother than I thought it would!"

"Yeah. Good talk, Dad."

Jace hoped that would be the end of it, but beneath the pamphlets he found a handful of envelopes, bundled together with a rubber band.

His father handed the stack to him. "Before you look through these, I want you to know that your mother and I support any decision you make. *But,* if it were up to us, we'd really like to have you close. I know four more years of living here seems like a long time, but it'll go by in the blink of an eye. You have your whole life to see more of the world. Your mother and I won't be around forever." After another bite of the banana, he added, "Your mother told me to say that last bit."

Jace thanked his father as he took his leave, turning his attention to the envelopes. Each had been opened already, meaning all were a viable option. Jace read the return labels. Colleges, from all over the country. Colleges that were inviting him to join them.

"We have it narrowed down to three," Jace said, adjusting the envelopes on the bedspread so the corners lined up. "Four if you count CMSU, but I sure as hell don't."

Victor considered the envelopes from where he sat next to them. Jace knelt on the floor in front of his makeshift desk, waiting for some sort of response. Victor didn't show much enthusiasm. Maybe all of this was too foreign for someone who hadn't finished high school, but Jace meant to include him exactly for that reason. This choice affected Victor's life just as much as it did Jace's.

"Why doesn't CMSU count?"

"Because there's no way I'm staying in this shit town." Jace took the envelope and tossed it aside. "That leaves Albuquerque, which could be amazing. I've always wanted to see the desert. Or Sacramento. California says it all, really. I'm sure life there is incredible. Houston wouldn't be bad either. I bet the weather is great. Besides, I've always wanted a cowboy hat."

Victor watched him, looking less than impressed. "You sound like you're planning a vacation, not choosing a college."

Jace shrugged. "I don't know what I want to do. I *was* thinking about nursing. I love the idea of helping someone feel better, but I still get squeamish about medical stuff. I don't know. College will buy me time while I figure that out, and unless I choose a specialized field, any college will do."

"Then why not CMSU?"

Jace stammered, overwhelmed by all the different ways Warrensburg was lacking, but in the end, none of them mattered right now. "I want more than this," he said, gesturing around. "I thought you would too. Maybe California is a dumb choice, since it's expensive," Jace tossed aside that envelope. "But Albuquerque is supposed to be really alternative. There are probably tons of people like you there, trying to live life in a different way. You'd like that, right?"

Victor looked away. "What makes you think I'm coming along?"

Jace stared. "Why wouldn't you? You're not tied down by anything. I know college life doesn't appeal to you, but I'm looking into off-campus housing. I'll need a job to help pay for that, but it won't be any different than now."

Victor stood and walked to the window. "It's not that simple."

"Why not?"

"What if something happens to my mom?"

Okay, fair enough. Jace had his own reservations about leaving his family behind, but at least they had each other. If it was just his mom, all on her own, he'd worry too. "Houston is closest," Jace said. "It's only twelve-hours from here. We could drive up once a month, maybe more. If there's an emergency, we could be back the same day."

Victor still had his back to him. "And your friends? What about Greg? Or your sister? You don't want them in your life?"

"Of course I do, but—"

"Twelve hours is a long time. What if your mom's car breaks down somewhere? Or your sister ends up in the hospital? Half a day can mean the difference between being able to say goodbye and never seeing someone again."

"That's a little morbid."

Victor shrugged. "That's reality. If you love people, you should keep them close to you." He turned and smiled. "I'm flattered you want to take me with you, but I'm not sure I can let go like that."

Jace wondered how much this had to do with Star and not just his mother, but didn't broach the subject. Instead he gathered up the envelopes with a sigh. "I thought you would be excited."

"The idea *is* exciting, but it comes at a price."

Jace turned to face him. "You mean us?"

Victor shook his head. "I made a promise. I'll keep it no matter what you do."

Jace considered the envelopes, feeling more uncertain than ever.

"Besides," Victor continued, "isn't out-of-state tuition way more expensive? If your parents are paying for this, that's a lot to ask of them."

"I have a partial scholarship," Jace mumbled, feeling guilty regardless. "And I've been saving money."

"Okay." Victor went to him, wrapping his arms around Jace's

waist. "I'll support whatever decision you make. If you do leave, I'll still be around when you visit. I'm sure you'll find me."

Jace doubted that. He pictured Victor withdrawing even more from society, or spending more time with Star. The sad thing was, Jace wasn't sure which would be worse.

"There are a lot of people here who love you," Victor said.

Jace sighed. "Maybe you're right."

Victor rewarded him with a kiss, tangling his fingers through Jace's hair.

"Cut it off!"

"Just give me a second! Geez!" Greg walked around the chair where Jace sat, crouching over to be eye level with him. "It's one thing to want a haircut, but you're approaching this with a vengeance."

Jace glowered. All around him was beautiful scenery. From the patio of Greg's house, he could see trees fresh with newly unfurled leaves, wildflowers blooming farther down in the valley. Beyond, blue sky reflected off the lake. The weather had been ideal all month, which only made Jace's pain harder to deal with.

"There's something you aren't telling me," Greg said, shaking the electric clippers at him.

"If I wanted questions, I would have asked my sister to do this."

"Fine, fine." Greg sighed, walked around to the back of the chair, and placed a hand on Jace's bare shoulder. The physical contact made Jace yearn inside, but not for Greg. That's not who he wanted. "Last chance. Once I start, there's no turning back. I can only do one hairstyle, and that's a buzz."

"Do it."

Jace closed his eyes. He thought of how Victor would toy with a lock of his hair, murmuring that Jace was his noble lion while running his fingers through his mane. But now it was the buzz of a vibrating razor that tickled his scalp. With every clump of hair that fell around him, Jace felt more and more vindicated. When the electric clippers stopped humming, Greg faced him and took a step back, as if in shock.

"That bad?" Jace asked.

"The hair looks good. It's your face that's scary."

Jace tried to scowl, but found he already was. "Oh."

Greg brushed some of the loose hair off his shoulders. "It's Victor, isn't it? You haven't mentioned him in the last couple of weeks. I take it he's been gone that long?"

"A month," Jace spat. "Since March 18th. At least that's when I last saw him. One month ago today."

Greg scrunched up his face. "On your birthday, you said you were meeting him that night."

"I lied." Jace looked away. His birthday had been a few weeks ago, April 2nd. Back then he hadn't yet given up hope. "I was too embarrassed to admit that my own boyfriend had ditched me on my birthday."

"You have nothing to be embarrassed about," Greg said. Now *he* was starting to scowl. "Did he call you? Leave you a note? Anything?"

"Nothing. The last time I saw him, everything was fine. We went for a night drive and had a good time." Jace clenched his jaw. "If we had argued, I might understand. I'm used to him being gone for a week, but a whole month?"

Greg nodded. "That's shitty. What's the point of being with someone if you never see them?"

Exactly. Why should he ache and long and worry without end? For all he knew, Victor could be dead, or starting a new life somewhere, or just hanging out with Star in Kansas City. Jace had tried calling her. At first he hung up whenever the answering machine picked up, but then he started leaving messages, pleading with her just to let him know that Victor was all right. Doing so had been humiliating, but would have been worth it just to know that Victor was okay.

"You can do better." Greg put both hands on Jace's shoulders to get his attention. "You know I like Victor. He's cool—or at least I thought he was—but he's crazy to treat you this way. He doesn't realize how lucky he is."

Greg's face wasn't far away. His warm hands felt good on Jace's skin. More than that, Jace saw nothing but sincerity in his eyes. Greg really believed that Victor was the lucky one.

"This is the part where you kiss me," Jace said. "Then I forget all about Victor and we live happily ever after."

"Believe me," Greg said with a grin, "if I could be that guy for you, I would."

"My chest is the problem, isn't it? I'd have to get boobs."

"Sorry, buddy. I'm superficial like that." Greg rubbed Jace's freshly buzzed head. "When Victor does come back to you—and he will—don't let him get away with this. I think you should dump his ass, but I know it's not that easy."

"No." Jace swallowed. "It's definitely not."

"Honey? Should I let him in?"

Jace's mother stood at the door to his bedroom, her face knotted up, just like Jace's stomach was. Funny how he hadn't said a word about Victor's disappearance, or all the despair this caused him, but still she understood. Otherwise she would have let Victor come up to Jace's room, as she usually did. Instead, Victor was standing outside, waiting for Jace to appear. He should keep on waiting for five weeks, like Jace had, but one last shred of hope remained. Maybe Victor had a good reason for being gone so long—something understandable, anything at all that would exorcise this anger and allow Jace to hold him tight again.

"No. I'll go down and see him."

His mother nodded and made herself scarce. Jace felt jittery walking down the stairs to the front hall, hand shaking as he pulled open the door.

There he was, punk hair gelled—which was unusual—and nose red with sun. He was handsome and different and familiar, but the smile he usually summoned didn't appear on Jace's face.

"Whoa, what happened to my lion?" Victor said.

Jace ran his hand over his short hair. At first he felt it looked too militant, but a week's worth of growth helped a little. Jace pulled the door shut behind him, crossed his arms over his chest and wished it would help calm his heart.

"Where were you?"

"I know," Victor said. "Sorry. Star surprised me with a trip. I had no idea until she—"

"Star," Jace said. "Yeah." Victor looked less certain. "She drove me to the airport and the next thing I know, I'm on a flight to Europe and—"

"Europe?" Jace said. "How?" But he already knew. The mysterious envelope addressed to Victor and delivered to Star's apartment. More than identification, she had said. A passport. She must have been planning something like this for ages, even back when she was still pretending to be Jace's friend.

"Star paid for everything. Or her father, I should say. It was amazing, Jace. We saw Italy, France, Germany, but my favorite was England. I never wanted to leave—"

"But there are so many people who love you here," Jace said, not hiding the sarcasm in his voice.

"Exactly." Victor's smile faded. "I missed you. Of course I did. I thought of you all the time. Look." From the plastic bag he was carrying, Victor pulled out a T-shirt and handed it to him. "The mane may be gone, but you're still my noble lion."

It almost worked, Victor calling on Jace's good heart, but the T-shirt ruined it all. Not that it wasn't nice. Above the word "England" was a lion, rearing up on its hind legs, but he knew Victor hadn't paid for this. He pictured Star helping Victor pick it out, her knowing that it wouldn't be enough, that no gift would be sufficient to make up for five weeks of absence, and that this one was especially lacking. Jace wanted to tear it to shreds, to set it ablaze so he would never have to see it again. Instead he handed it back.

"You don't like it?" Victor asked.

His expression was so pathetic that it almost broke Jace's heart, but that was impossible, because his heart had slowly been breaking all this time. Jace just hadn't realized it until now. He imagined Star and Victor gallivanting around Europe together, seeing sights he could only imagine. The idea of going out of state for college had made Jace so excited, but what was Sacramento compared to Paris? Houston compared to London? And of course they would have shared a room, and probably a bed, but he couldn't bring himself to ask about that, because he was pretty damn sure it didn't matter anymore.

Star was right. They were both fools. Jace wasn't even angry at her anymore because he could imagine doing the same. Hadn't he wanted to, when asking Victor to move away with him? And poor Star probably thought their European tour would make all the difference, that Victor would forget about Jace and finally love her and only her. But here Victor was, right back at Jace's doorstep again. She would never change him. He saw now that no one could.

"Jace." Victor stepped close to him, enough that he could smell the gel in his hair, see the flecks of gold in his one brown eye. And when Victor moved in for a kiss, Jace meant to stop him, but he gave in, kissing Victor with passion, because part of him was relieved Victor was okay, was happy to see him. Jace breathed in his scent as deep as he could, knowing he wouldn't have another chance.

Then Jace pulled away.

"That was the last time," he said.

Those mismatched eyes searched his, but this time they remained confused. "What?"

"You're my friend," Jace said. "I know you don't like titles, but that's what you are. Nothing more, nothing less."

"I'm sorry," Victor said. "She said it was going to be for a week. I didn't know how long we were staying until we were over there. I should have called."

"Or written a letter or even a fucking postcard!" Jace snarled, but he forced himself to take a deep breath. It wouldn't have made a difference even if Victor had told him in person before leaving. Jace still would have thought about Star's desperate ploy, and of Victor seeing the world, all while he sat miserable and alone in Warrensburg, Missouri. And Victor was right about a lot of things. There was no sense in being angry at someone you couldn't change, so Jace did his best to set aside these emotions.

Steeling himself, he said, "You're my friend, and I want to see you again. I mean that, but today I can't stand the sight of you." He turned around to face the door, opened it, and paused. "Go see your mother. She's probably worried sick."

"I love you," Victor blurted out.

Jace looked over his shoulder, forced himself to smile. "I know." Then he turned and went inside the house. Once he was back in his room, he opened the nightstand drawer and took out three envelopes. Sacramento, Albuquerque, Houston. Anywhere but here.

Jace felt good. Past the tears, the heartache, and the second-guessing, there was summer. Literally and figuratively. By the end of May, he had made his peace with being only Victor's friend. The first couple of times they hung out together were tense, conversation stilted, and when it did flow smoother, hidden insults seemed to be behind everything they said to each other. Eventually, the ice between them thawed. At times Jace even forgot about what they had and what they could have been.

Those were the best days, carefree and full of laughter, but often they would end with Victor growing solemn. Or worse, Victor would look hopeful.

In June, Bernard offered Jace full-time work, which was appreciated since Jace wanted to bulk up his savings before beginning his new life at the University of Houston. He accepted the job on one condition: Jace wanted to be assistant manager. Mostly he just wanted the job description so it would look good on his resume, but he also did it to piss Dan off. Jace didn't really expect the authority that would come with being assistant manager, but Bernard took him under his wing, teaching him how his business was run.

In July, Victor moved in.

Sort of. He returned to the campsite not far from Jace's house. He had stayed there occasionally when the weather was warm, but now he made it his permanent home. Every time Jace sought Victor, he would find him there. His progressively dirtier clothes tipped Jace off that Victor wasn't going home anymore. He looked like he was losing weight too, and he didn't have much to spare.

"How long do you plan on staying here?" Jace asked him one weekend night.

Victor stared at him from across the fire before answering. "Five weeks."

Penance. Or an apology. Jace was moved, but at the same time, it made more work for him. He brought Victor food, usually leftovers from family meals. When Jace's mother learned what he was doing, she started cooking larger portions to ensure there was more than they could finish. Jace did Victor's laundry a few times, despite his protests, and asked Greg to help teach Victor to fish, forage, or anything else that would keep him going.

As touching as Victor's self-imposed exile was, Jace sometimes wished he would go home. He began to fantasize about a boyfriend who took care of himself, worked a steady job, had a phone number and a favorite television show. He couldn't picture Victor like that. Victor as a contributing member of society wouldn't be much like Victor at all.

Sometimes Jace imagined this discontent must be mutual, that Victor wished Jace would chill out, not be so hung up on things like commitment, monogamy, and responsibility. Victor probably felt equally frustrated at falling in love with someone who was so wrong for him. Or maybe, like Jace in his moments of weakness, he thought about how their differences meant they had so much more to offer each other.

In late August, Jace threw a going-away party. He invited Greg and Angie—who were still going strong, Michelle and her latest disposable boyfriend, and Bernard and his wife—a woman who always seemed to be cackling, especially when she was telling dirty jokes. Even Dan was invited, but mostly just to annoy him. He didn't come, of course. Victor didn't either, not that Jace really expected him to. Still, Jace kept listening for the doorbell, and even though he had a good time, the evening didn't feel complete without him there.

After everyone had gone home, Jace walked down into the valley. The night was blistering hot, making him want to strip off his clothes and jump into the lake, so he wasn't surprised to find Victor sitting on the dock, drying off after a swim. All he wore was a pair of cut-off jean shorts, but this didn't unnerve Jace like it normally would. He didn't need to be strong. Not tonight.

"I'm leaving tomorrow," Jace said. "This is my last night here."

Victor nodded. "I know."

"Come home with me."

Victor looked up at him, his hair shaggier than Jace had ever seen it. His own was still kept short. This lion had been tamed. No more running through the jungle.

"Please."

Victor offered his hand, and Jace helped him stand, but he didn't let go. After Victor slipped on his sandals, they walked together through the dark, Jace remembering a colder evening the year before when they had leapt and danced around the fire. A time when everything had seemed possible.

They didn't have much to say to each other. Not anymore. Once in Jace's bedroom, he let Victor kiss him, undress him, lay him out on the bed. When Victor reached for the nightstand drawer, Jace nodded. This was the right time, because it would be the only time. He wasn't scared, even at first when it hurt, because Victor still saw right through him, kept his eyes on Jace the entire time and knew what he needed, even though he couldn't always give it to him. Their bodies moved together slowly, both of them wanting it to last forever. Jace wished they had discovered this sooner, had found this magic that let Victor become part of him. He nearly cried when it was over and they separated again, but he didn't. He was done with tears.

"I'm going to keep my promise," Victor whispered against Jace's skin as he held him. "I'll always love you."

Jace took a deep breath. "I'm still leaving tomorrow."

"I know." Victor kissed his shoulder. "I still have to stay here."

There was no accusation in their voices, no anger or disappointment. Only acceptance. Jace forced himself to stay awake the entire night, not wanting to miss a single touch, the gentle sound of Victor's breathing, or the whispered promises. When the morning came, Victor untangled himself and got out of bed.

Only then did Jace close his eyes, unable to watch him go.

Part Two:
Texas, 1995

Chapter Thirteen

"School's in session," Adrien said, strolling into their dorm room wearing nothing but a towel.

"Uh—" Jace said into the phone pressed against his cheek.

Adrien grabbed the towel around his waist and whipped it off in one smooth motion. "I'm going to teach you how to fold a towel correctly, even if it kills me!"

'Lithe' was probably a fair word to describe Adrien. He didn't have an ounce of fat on his frame, and while he was anything but a beefy slab of manly meat, the aerobics he was so fond of toned what muscles he had. His auburn hair was already blown dry and swept back into a pompadour, a combination of hairspray and mousse holding it in place. Adrien stood there, buck naked, one hand on his hip while the other flipped the towel around impatiently. The door to the hallway was still open.

"Uh—" Jace repeated.

"You okay?" Greg said into his ear.

"Yeah, sorry." Jace pressed the phone between his cheek and shoulder and went to close the door. "So next week?"

"Friday night. Don't forget." Greg chuckled nervously. "You're going to be so surprised!"

"Surprised?"

"Yup! See you then. Peace!"

The line clicked and went dead. Jace glanced at the phone to make sure it was hung up, then looked back at his boyfriend, who was shimmying into a pair of bikini briefs. "Sorry, I was on the phone."

"I kind of pieced that together," Adrien said with a wink. "Your mother?"

"Greg."

"Oh, him."

Adrien said it dismissively, but Jace wasn't buying it for a second. Greg had been cute when they were teenagers, but nearly four years of college had shaped him into something normally found on romance novel covers. Sans the pirate shirt and long flowing hair, thankfully. Angie was ancient history, paving the way for tons of women who threw themselves at Greg. Tons of women—and Adrien.

"Get over here," Adrien said, standing by the bed. But this

request wasn't of the amorous variety. "I'm not walking down that hall one more time with a poorly-folded towel under my arm."

"God forbid!" Jace said sarcastically, which Adrien failed to recognize. This was a very serious issue! To him, at least.

As Adrien showed him the "proper" way to fold a towel, Jace zoned out like he always did, thinking about what a curious creature Adrien was. He was delightfully girly, absolutely lispy, and on bad days, terribly queeny. Jace practically felt straight dating someone so feminine, but that was the appeal. Adrien was unapologetically gay. When first arriving at the University of Houston, Jace had gotten involved with just about any LGBT group he could find, visiting each with one goal in mind: love.

Or at least a relationship. He dated a few closet cases, and while they were nice enough, he found the secrecy and paranoia tiresome. He had already moved on from that stage, and soon discovered that pushing someone to come out before they were ready was impossible. Rather than try, Jace focused on his studies instead. At the end of his sophomore year, he allowed a friend to drag him along to a gay book club. Adrien had been there, dominating the discussion with an hour-long rant about how terrible the book had been, and even though Jace hadn't read it, he spent most of the hour laughing.

These days Jace knew that Adrien's sarcasm and dark humor were just who he was. Adrien didn't realize that he was being funny, like now, when he asked Jace to follow his instructions and fold the towel. Jace made a mess of it, and Adrien pressed his hands to his cheeks in horror, like he was witnessing a botched heart surgery.

"You weren't paying attention!" he accused.

"You're in your underwear," Jace said, playfully slapping Adrien's ass. "Can you really blame me for being distracted?"

"I suppose not." Adrien looked pleased. "It's a good thing you have me. Otherwise your towels would be a mess."

"That's why I asked you to move in," Jace said.

"That was my idea! I'm the one who arranged the room transfer. *And* I had to put up with that bitch from admissions." Adrien pressed fingers to his temples. "I had to jump through so many hoops that—"

Jace smiled as Adrien rambled on. He could be grating at

---

times, but Jace liked Adrien's energy. And his pride. Not only was Adrien gay, but his entire world was as well. Everything was rainbow flags, gay books, homoerotic movies, nightclubs full of lip-synching drag queens and sweaty men gyrating their hips together. Adrien often said he wanted to get married on a parade float. Jace believed him. Adrien treated heterosexuality like an urban legend. He could scarcely believe that straight people existed. In a state where being gay could feel like trying not to drown, Adrien managed to twirl through life like it was water ballet.

That meant there was no confusion. No lectures about how there shouldn't be limits to what someone experienced. And no room for someone like Star.

"Oh my gosh!" Adrien moved to the dresser, picked up an envelope, and shook it excitedly. "You didn't see what came in the mail yesterday."

Jace recognized the handwriting. The contents were always the same, but he pretended not to know. "Who's that from?"

"My grandma, and yes, she sent me a very handsome photo of Ulysses S. Grant."

"Fifty bucks? Nice!"

"Very nice," Adrien said, coming toward him with a seductive gleam in his eye. "Which means I'm taking you out to dinner tonight. There's a little French place I've been dying to try."

"Frog legs?" Jace said. "Snails? Baguettes?"

Adrien playfully whacked the envelope against Jace's chest. "There's more to French cuisine than that. You'll see. I want you to wear the forest-green dress shirt I gave you for Christmas. It matches your eyes."

"My eyes are blue," Jace replied.

"Then it compliments them." Adrien moved in for a kiss.

"Wait," Jace said with a chuckle. "Nine months together and you don't know what color my eyes are?"

"I commit other parts of you to memory."

"Yeah, well the memory is all you'll get right now," Jace said, backing away. "Maybe you can seduce me when I'm stuffed full of snails and groggy from wine."

"Have it your way," Adrien said. "I didn't want to muss my hair anyway. So what did Greg want?"

"Oh yeah! He's coming to visit."

"Next week?" Adrien raised an eyebrow and returned to the dresser to choose an outfit. "Will he be snoring away on our couch again?"

"No, that's the weird thing. He's getting a hotel."

Adrien turned around, fingers buttoning up a pearl-colored shirt. "Really? Can he afford that?"

His boyfriend looked surprised. As much as Adrien liked to put on airs and play the cultural sophisticate, he was still a poor college student. The way Adrien had managed to transform their little dorm room was the perfect example. He and Jace shared a bed every night, cramming onto a full-sized mattress so short that Jace's feet always hung off the edge, but this left enough space for a small couch and a tiny coffee table. The dorm room looked like a living room in miniature, and Adrien had done it all on a budget, raiding thrift stores and bargain bins for every decorative vase or mood-enhancing light fixture. Adrien had created a little kingdom for them both, even if it was built from matchsticks. He understood that money was tight.

"I said he could crash on the couch, but he wanted to get a hotel."

"Maybe some girl finally managed to tie him down." Adrien frowned, tugging on a pair of slacks. Then his face lit up. "Or maybe some lucky guy finally got him in bed!"

"Keep dreaming," Jace said. "Anyway, it'll be good to see him again."

It always was. Jace only made it home for the Christmas holiday and occasionally summer break. This wasn't enough for Greg. He came to visit as often as he could, and every time he did, it felt like he brought a little piece of home with him. Jace shook his head. To think that he would ever miss Warrensburg!

"So what are we going to do with this gloriously free Saturday?" Jace asked.

"Shopping," Adrien answered instantly.

"Ah, you mean window shopping?"

Adrien shot him a wink. "Honey, we're so broke we can't afford shops fancy enough to have windows!"

Jace grinned. "Then it's off to the mall we go!"

The French restaurant felt more like a café, the tables small and rustic. There were no tablecloths or mysterious little forks and knives that served very specific purposes. Jace was glad. Some of the restaurants Adrien liked made Jace uncomfortable, although he had become good at pretending otherwise.

"Let's order a bottle of wine," Adrien said, nearly licking his lips in anticipation.

"Can we afford that?"

"If you mean do we have enough cash to pay the bill at the end, then yes." Adrien's eyes sparkled. "If you're asking if we should waste money on something as nonessential as wine, then of course not."

Jace shrugged and smiled. "As long as we can afford to pay."

"Will you be having chicken or fish?"

Jace glanced at the menu. "I was thinking about the beef. Uh… The beef borg…"

"*Boeuf bourguignon*," Adrien said with a perfect accent. "I'll never understand why you took Italian instead of French."

"Well, if we ever went out for pizza, maybe I'd have a chance to impress you."

Adrien didn't crack a smile. Instead his attention was focused on the wine menu. "And if I also choose beef, which I will, what sort of wine will I order?"

"Red," Jace said. "So, a Merlot?"

"Very good," Adrien said approvingly, "but I think we'll opt for a Pinot Noir instead."

The waiter arrived to take their orders. He was the same age as they were, probably went to the same school. For once it felt good to be served, instead of serving. Jace had waited tables since his first year in Houston, as had Adrien until he landed a job at the university library a few months back.

"I'm excited," Adrien said. "Are you excited?"

"About the food?" Jace glanced around to make sure no one was listening. "They had frog legs on the menu."

Adrien waved a hand dismissively. "Only because people expect them to. Maybe you could get a job here instead. Bring me home cold snails every night."

Jace couldn't tell if he was kidding or not and didn't want to ask. When the waiter returned, he had a basket of sliced baguette and their bottle of wine. He went through the uncorking ritual that Jace always found hard to take seriously. After pouring a little in their glasses, the waiter invited them to try the wine. Jace took a sip. It tasted like wine. What a shock!

"No," Adrien said, his face sour. "Definitely not. This wine has been corked."

The waiter stared, mouth open. "Corked?"

"*Tainted,*" Adrien said, voice rising. "Try it."

"I don't have a glass," the waiter spluttered.

"You might as well drink from the bottle. We certainly won't be drinking that!"

"Adrien," Jace said softly.

"Look," Adrien snapped, his attention still on the waiter. "Just bring us another bottle. A Merlot this time."

Jace was quiet until the waiter had disappeared into the back room. "Was that necessary?"

Adrien looked surprised, as if he couldn't find anything wrong with his behavior. "What do you mean? The wine was corked. You're getting your Merlot now, so you should be happy."

"Thrilled," Jace said. He would have been just as happy with water. "It's just... You know how hard this job can be, and it looks like he's the only one working tonight."

"*I* wouldn't have argued," Adrien shot back. "I would have tried the damn wine when the customer asked me to, and I sure as hell would have known what 'corked' means."

Jace clenched his jaw, but forced himself to take a deep breath. "Then you would have come home and complained about that customer."

Adrien shrugged. "He's more than welcome to bitch to his mother or whoever when he's off work." He poked at a slice of bread. "I want us to have a nice night. It's so rare we get to do this. I just want everything to be perfect."

"I know," Jace said.

When the waiter returned with another bottle, Jace assured him the wine was fine, even before they had taken a sip. Adrien glared at him from over the wine glass as he drank.

Jace met his gaze. "It's fine, right?"

"Yes. It's fine." Adrien filled their glasses higher while frowning. "So was the first bottle."

"What? Then why—"

"You saw the look he gave us when we came in. Or did you miss it?"

Jace *had* seen it. Although not when they first came in. But when the waiter asked them the obvious, if there were two of them, and Adrien had answered—that's when it happened. The waiter's eyebrows had risen, and he had looked between them, putting the pieces together. Not that anyone needed to be a detective. When Adrien spoke, people heard a lisp and judgment was cast. Jace had seen it happen to Adrien before. The woman in housing who Adrien had referred to as a bitch earlier in the day had snidely suggested he transfer to the dorms for women. Just because Adrien was feminine. Sure, maybe he could be rude at times, but not entirely without reason.

"I saw the look," Jace answered. "But maybe he's gay and was excited to see two guys together."

"No." Adrien shook his head. "I've been putting up with this my whole life. Believe me, I can tell."

"But maybe—and I'm just throwing this out there—it isn't worth reacting to people like that. Who cares what he thinks about us?"

Adrien was uncharacteristically quiet, toying with the edge of the burgundy cloth napkin. "I tried to change," he said eventually. "When I was younger. I kept getting picked on at school, and I asked my parents what I could do about..." Adrien gestured at himself. "They took me to a speech therapist. I was excited too. Finally I would sound normal! The speech therapist encouraged me to avoid words with an 's' in them, which is fucking impossible, and then he gave me these screaming exercises."

"Screaming?"

Adrien's smile was bitter. "I was supposed to scream into a pillow for a certain amount of time each day to tear my vocal cords or something and make my voice deeper. Honestly, I think the doctor was a quack."

Jace was almost scared to ask, but he did anyway. "Did you try?"

"Of course I tried," Adrien said softly. "It felt kind of good, helped get all the frustration out. But that's all it did. Eventually I decided I didn't care." He shook his head. "That's not true. I still cared, but I decided not to put up with anyone's shit again. Perhaps that's horrible, but it was a turning point for me. I was still me and people still hated me for it, but I became defiant." Adrien locked eyes with him. "I like that word. *Defiant.*"

"I'm sorry," Jace said. "I wish I had known you then. Sounds like you needed a friend."

Adrien smirked. "You would have been more than my friend. And it's not a big deal anymore. I like who I am. Besides, all this seething anger will come in handy in the courtroom. That's when I'll have my revenge on the world."

Adrien's dream was to become a prosecuting attorney. Jace could just imagine the cocky expression on a criminal's face when a gay lawyer swished into the courtroom, and how it would change to fear when Adrien's vicious side emerged.

Their food arrived, and to Jace's relief, it tasted fine. Great, in fact. Warm food in their bellies, and a glass of wine or two later, and their evening out together felt a lot more relaxed.

"I have some good news," Adrien said. "Potentially. A friend of a friend tipped me off about a condo that's opening up soon."

Jace saw where this was going. Adrien was always searching for a scheme to get them off campus. "Did this friend of a friend tell you where to find buried treasure as well?"

"I know, but trust me, this thing is cheap. I say 'condo' when really it's a miserable one-bedroom apartment."

"Sounds charming."

"*With* a nice little balcony," Adrien continued unabashed, "that overlooks a pedestrian zone on some little shopping street. I have no idea where, but I love the idea of sitting on the balcony, sipping martinis and lording over all the little people below."

"It would have to be ridiculously cheap," Jace said.

"I know. Money will be tight, but you'll have graduated by then and be working full-time."

Jace snorted. "And you'll be in law school. So I'm supposed to support your ass for three years?"

"I've always wanted to be a kept boy," Adrien said, motioning for the check. "Besides, I'll return the favor when I'm a filthy rich lawyer."

"Maybe," Jace said.

"We can at least look at the place."

"Maybe," Jace repeated, but he couldn't help smiling at the idea. Sure, they already lived together, but having a home of their own, no matter how small, could be nice.

After they paid, they walked back to campus. Adrien was in high spirits, grabbing Jace's hand and holding on to him. Every time Jace glanced over, he saw bedroom eyes. That they made it back to the dorm instead of finding bushes to hide in was a small miracle. Adrien was always like this after a few glasses of wine. As soon as the door to their room was closed, Jace was accosted. Adrien's lips smashed into his, nimble fingers working at the buttons on his shirt and pants.

"I love you," Adrien breathed.

Jace responded, like he always did, by kissing him harder. That was enough.

Usually.

Adrien pulled away. "Why don't you ever say it back?"

Because— Jace's chest felt tight. Because of many reasons. Or just one. He had never said it before. Not like that, at least. But this wasn't the problem. The real issue was that Jace had never said it to Victor. All the time they'd shared, and despite Victor never holding back with these words, Jace had never dared to utter them in response. That alone attested to how messed up their relationship had been, but in the present... Well, if he'd never said those three little words to Victor, he sure as hell wasn't going to say them to Adrien. Because—

He didn't want to think about it. Instead he dragged Adrien into bed. "Words can be hollow," Jace murmured. "Actions are not."

"What sort of actions?" Adrien asked, hormones silencing any doubts. As Jace worked his magic, all either of them could do was moan. Maybe it was the wine, but as Jace closed his eyes, thrusting above Adrien, he thought he could hear the wind blowing through the trees, the crackle of a fire, and the splashing of water as two boys jumped into a lake together.

A series of raps on the door—one, two, three!—and then it swung open. Jace turned around, the breath catching in his throat. Sometimes—rarely—he saw Greg with a fresh perspective. Especially after being apart months at a time. He saw the amber eyes, the brown hair that complimented his tanned skin, or the easy smile that was as loose as Greg's muscles were tight. Then history would catch up with Jace, bringing visions of an eight-year-old boy hunkered down so low on his bike that his head was nearly between the handlebars. Or the teenager who wore a Band-Aid over his first pimple until it healed and went away.

Greg was his friend—practically his brother. To others, he was gorgeous. To Jace, he was family.

"Come here, you!" Greg threw his arms open wide, but only long enough to trap Jace between them and squeeze. Somehow he managed to swing Jace around, even though he was a few inches shorter than him. "How are you, you son of a bitch?"

"Fine," Jace said, and then added, "you fucker."

"Nuh-uh. Don't try to sound straight." Greg pushed him playfully. "I like you just the way you are, you big homo."

"Thanks, you miserable breeder."

"That's more like it." Greg flopped down on the couch, still grinning. "Haven't managed to reproduce yet. I keep trying, but…"

"Practice makes perfect." Jace sat on the bed across from him. "To what do I owe this pleasure?"

"A guy can't visit his best friend on a whim?" Greg surveyed the room, which didn't take long, considering its size. "Where's Adrien?"

"Working," Jace said.

Greg sat up. "Really? That's a relief!" He managed to appear sheepish. "I mean, it's nice to have you all to myself."

"I know exactly what you meant," Jace said, but he let it slide. "Is that why you're staying in a hotel? I know Adrien can be a handful, but—"

Greg waved a hand dismissively. "Nah. I just needed the extra space. You'll see. Hey, you want to go for a walk?"

Jace smiled knowingly. "You brought a girl along, didn't you?" He stood and went to the window. "Which one is it? The blonde?"

Greg joined him at the window. "Nope, but it might be if we get down there in time. Let's go."

"If you insist." Jace said, opting to leave his jacket behind. Winter had retreated and the trees were in bloom. Maybe he'd even get a light tan.

"Wait up," Greg said as Jace headed for the door. "Do you always wear your hair like that? No gel or anything? I don't remember it being so poofy."

"It's the humidity here," Jace said, reaching up to ruffle it. "Adrien says it looks good."

"Yeah, it does. I guess. What do I know, right?"

170

"Right." Jace raised an eyebrow. "As long as you aren't embarrassed to be seen with me."

Greg winced. "I don't mean it like that. I just want to make sure you're looking your best. And you are. Have you been working out?"

"No," Jace said, trying not to squirm as Greg looked him over. "Uh, you're freaking me out."

"Sorry. It was a long drive." Greg waved a finger in circles around one of his ears. "Makes me feel a little crazy. Or maybe I'm just hungry. Can we eat at Grumpy Towers like last time?"

"Moody Towers," Jace corrected, although he had to admit the residence hall was oddly named. He led the way down the stairs and outside to gloriously warm weather. The afternoon sun was still high, as if unwilling to set—the sky still blue and hinting of the summer to come.

"Man, that's nice," Greg said. "We had snow last week."

"Really?"

"Yup. It didn't stick, but we won't be seeing green any time soon." Greg nudged him. "Mind if we cut through that park? I want to enjoy this while I can."

"Sure." Jace's every step felt light, and it wasn't just the weather. Being around Greg when he visited always felt good, the best of both worlds: Jace was far away from Warrensburg but had his best friend here with him. "I suppose, seeing as it's our last semester of college, that there's no point in talking you into transferring down here?"

Greg chuckled. "Not unless we both go for our master's degrees."

"Don't tempt me," Jace said. "I still don't know what I want to do."

"You want to move back to Warrensburg," Greg said, "and be my partner in the business I'm starting."

Jace stopped in his tracks. "You've decided?"

Greg nodded. "You're going to laugh, but I'm going into land development."

"I could see that being viable," Jace said, keeping a straight face. "Where will you be moving to?"

Greg feigned a punch at him. "I'll never understand what you have against Warrensburg. It's a college town! We have a state university. It's only a matter of time before the city—"

"Town," Jace corrected.

"Until *it* explodes."

"Sounds good to me. I'll help you blow it up."

Greg shook his head, walking in a different direction. "You'll see. Warrensburg has potential, and I'll be there to cash in on it."

"If you can turn that town around, you'll be doing me a favor as well." Jace considered the gently swaying trees above. "Until then, I think I'll settle down here."

"Bummer," Greg said. "Your family misses you."

Jace nodded. "I miss them too."

They walked a little further before Greg stopped again. "Not just your family. A lot of people back home miss you."

Jace felt moved. "Trust me, there isn't a day that goes by that I don't feel the same way. But I like it here. It took time, but it's starting to feel like home." He gazed across the park at the students sitting on the grass, textbooks open but forgotten as they chatted with friends. The two young women tossing a Frisbee back and forth. The guy leaning up against a tree and smoking. "Maybe I'll teach here," Jace murmured, almost to himself.

Funny, he thought, how sometimes you see a person who looks familiar, and despite knowing that it couldn't possibly be them, part of you still entertains the idea. In Jace's economics class was a girl who reminded him so much of Michelle that it always made him homesick. Or sometimes he would see the kind of guy who—despite being dead-set against wars and the politics behind them—still bought clothes at an Army surplus store. Like the guy under the tree smoking.

From beneath long dark bangs, the glimmer of eyes watched him. For the first time, Jace wondered if he looked familiar too, his appearance calling up the ghost of a person he'd never known and never would.

"About that surprise," Greg said.

Jace tore his attention away. "What?"

Greg smiled. "Look again."

Jace did, this time his eyes wide with shock. The guy under the tree was the right size, had the right build. And that jacket. Was it *the* jacket from all those years ago? The guy's hair was long, shoulder-length, and along with the shade of the tree, conspired to hide any facial features. But the way his hand stayed cupped over his mouth as the cigarette burned orange, the casual manner in which he then flicked it away in a fiery arc—

"I'm going to kill you," Jace said.

"No, you won't," Greg said. "I'll give you guys some space. Meet me at the cafeteria when you're ready."

"Wait!" Jace grabbed Greg's arm, but his best friend slipped out of his grip, laughing as he walked away. Jace knew that laugh. There was nothing malicious about it. Instead, it was the mad sort of chuckle reserved for when Greg did something really nice for him, like the time he tracked down an expensive out-of-print copy of Marlene Dietrich's biography for Jace's birthday.

As he turned around, Jace wondered if that's what this was supposed to be—a present. In Greg's mind, maybe plopping Victor down in the middle of Jace's new life seemed like doing him a favor, old friends reunited. Except they'd never gotten the hang of being friends. Not entirely.

From beneath the tree, Victor shook his hair from his eyes. Then he smiled, gave a little nod, and started strolling toward Jace as casually as if they always met there. But then, why should either of them make a big deal out of this? They had met plenty of times since that last night together. When home for a visit, Jace usually tracked Victor down, or Greg would tip off Victor ahead of time and he'd show up at the front door. Sometimes they didn't meet at all, such as the recent Christmas holiday. When had the last time been?

His thoughts scattered as Victor drew near. The mismatched eyes had him pinned in place, Jace staring at the silky dark hair framing a face that was both older and unmistakably familiar. Victor's stubble grew in thicker now, which only made him seem more masculine and untamed, a stark contrast to Adrien's pristine skin. Cigarette smoke instead of a waft of designer cologne, a worn T-shirt with a frayed collar instead of a pressed dress shirt, a five o'clock shadow instead of powder and base. They couldn't be more different, Victor and Adrien, which was no accident.

"You look like you've seen a ghost," Victor said, lips resisting a smirk. "Or a monster that used to hide under your bed at night."

"In the morning," Jace corrected, smiling at the memory. "As if my parents did room inspections or something. You could have just slept in."

"Better safe than sorry, I guess."

They eyed each other in the way old lovers did, their eyes still having permissions that their bodies were denied. Jace took a deep breath and shook his head. "What are you doing here?"

Now the smirk came out in full force. "Isn't that obvious?"

No. Not in the slightest, but part of him still wanted to please Victor, to pretend he could keep up with whatever his strange worldview was at the moment, so he didn't ask. Instead he committed an even bigger transgression and attempted small talk.

"How was your trip down? Long drive, isn't it?"

They were the sort of words they never shared before, which is probably why Victor didn't respond to them.

"This place suits you," he said, still sizing Jace up. "There's an energy here. A buzz. You always had that about you, even in Warrensburg, like you had it all figured out but were in the wrong place and time. Or maybe the wrong story. Now you fit in."

"It's not about fitting in," Jace said. "I'm not here to conform."

Victor shook his head. "That's not what I'm trying to say. It's like you were out of synch before. The world wasn't keeping up with you. Now it's finally at the right speed."

"Thanks," he said lamely. The handful of sentences just traded were already more meaningful than any conversation he'd shared with Adrien, which made Jace suspicious that his best friend was doing him more than a favor. If that was the case, Greg hadn't thought this through. There was a reason it hadn't worked before. There was a reason it couldn't now. Unless... "Move down here," he tried. "You'll love it."

Victor looked away, his expression neutral. "No."

Jace nearly sighed in relief. Instead he placed an arm around Victor's shoulder, gave a platonic squeeze, and led the way through the park. "I'm glad you finally decided to visit."

"Greg can be very insistent," Victor said. "I didn't really have a choice. But I'm glad. It's been a while."

"Half a year," he guessed.

"Over a year," Victor stated with certainty. "Nearly two."

"Really? No!" Jace struggled to remember the last time. How could he have gone an entire summer without seeing Victor? Then again, Jace had stayed in Texas for most of it to work full-time. The Christmas before was a blur of wrapping paper and too much food.

"Time flies when you have a life," Victor said with a chuckle.

"Or so I would imagine."

"I don't feel like I have one," Jace said. "School and work take up most of my time. What little remains goes to…" He trailed off, wondering if it would be cruel to mention Adrien.

"Greg told me about your boyfriend," Victor said without menace. "Adrien, right? You don't have to hold back. In case you've forgotten, I'm not the jealous type."

"Of course, how silly of me," Jace said, hiding a smile. "Did Greg also tell you how hung Adrien is?"

"Uh…"

Jace held his hands apart, like he was describing a fish. "This big," he lied. "At least."

Victor's eyes widened. "Wow. What is that, twelve inches?"

"Fourteen. And he's a trained survivalist. Adrien can walk through the snow barefoot, living off roots he digs up with his bare hands. He's so in-tune with the wilderness that a pack of wild pigs once invited him to stay the night."

"They never invite me," Victor complained. "Okay, so maybe I'm a little envious… but still not jealous."

"Is it wrong that I wish you were?" Jace said, tone growing more serious.

Victor shrugged. "You're asking the wrong guy." They walked in silence for a moment, leaving the park behind and getting caught up in the rush of students on campus. "So what's Adrien really like?"

"Organized," Jace said immediately. It was an odd word to describe a romantic partner, but it fit. "You could meet him." The thought alone made his stomach churn with nerves. "If you want. I mean, I don't know what the plan is."

"It's probably better that you don't," Victor said, as they entered the cafeteria.

Before Jace could ask what this meant, Greg was waving them over to where he waited in line. "We don't have this problem at CMSU," he complained. "I'll starve before I even order."

Greg's presence helped Jace relax again. Not that he wasn't comfortable being alone with Victor. He just felt like every conversation danced around what he really wanted to say: *I know why it didn't work, but why couldn't it have worked?* There was no logic to this statement, but rather a compulsive need to shout it over and over again, just to rob it of power. He wouldn't though.

They never discussed it during previous reunions, and Jace knew the compulsion would fade when he and Victor parted again.

Instead, conversation turned to the past. Greg dredged up his favorite embarrassing stories about Jace, or told him about camping out with Victor over the summer. That took Jace aback. He vaguely remembered Greg mentioning it during a phone call and purposefully not asking questions. Now he felt desperate for details, even though Greg was more interested in talking about changes to the shelter he'd made, or natural techniques for purifying water.

"Where to now?" Jace asked when they were leaving the cafeteria.

"You said Adrien was off work soon?" Greg asked.

"Should be by now," Jace said, checking his watch. "Let's head back to the dorm and see."

"Hold up," Greg said, placing a hand on Jace's shoulder. "Why don't I go hang out with Adrien? We always get along, right?"

Adrien tended to alternate between drooling over Greg and wincing, but Jace supposed that was a camaraderie of sorts.

Greg grabbed Victor's shoulder too. "That'll give you guys some private time. Go out to dinner or something."

"We just ate," Victor pointed out.

"Drinks then," Greg said.

"How about we all go out for a drink?" Jace suggested. He couldn't imagine Victor hanging out in a bar. At least not the kind filled with dance music and flashing lights, but what else was Jace going to do with him? The dorm room was awfully small for four people, and they couldn't all go squat in the woods somewhere. Nine times out of ten, that was the environment Jace pictured Victor being.

"Drinks sound good," Victor said. "Let's go get Adrien and show him a good time."

A good time? A high school sweetheart, a prima donna boyfriend, and a best friend with the most hell-paved of good intentions... Of all the potential the night held, Jace wondered if a good time was even remotely possible.

Chapter Fourteen

The bass of the music matched pace with Jace's heart. *Boom boom boom bu-dah boom boom boom!* His pulse was racing too quickly, but it wasn't passion or lust that had his blood pumping. Instead, Jace suspected he was experiencing his first anxiety attack. Or maybe this was the normal feeling that preceded committing murder.

"I've often wondered why homeless people sleep on the streets," Adrien was shouting over the music. "Why huddle under a filthy cardboard box when you could live in the woods? Much prettier!"

Adrien's face was scrunched up, as it had been since meeting Victor, struggling with an unsolvable conundrum. Adrien assumed most people were gay, but Victor didn't fit any stereotype or archetype he could dig up. Twink, bear, queen, or sugar daddy? None of the above. Jace could see him struggling to work it out, the strain playing out on his face. At one point, Adrien even seemed to mouth, "Art fag?"

"I don't really consider myself homeless," Victor said. "I just stay in a variety of places. Although really we're all homeless. You don't own the dorm you live in, or the apartment you'll inevitably rent next. If the owner of the property wants you out, you'll have to go, one way or another. Even if you own a home and land, you'll find yourself moving if the government wants to build a highway or airport there. Or you never know when the next natural disaster will hit. So really, we're all just guests at the mercy of more powerful forces."

Adrien blinked. "So you really eat out of trash cans?"

Jace tightened the grip on his beer bottle. "He doesn't eat out of the trash!"

"Sure I do," Victor said, calm as can be. "Grocery stores are always throwing out perfectly good food just because of a trivial expiration date. I've done my share of dumpster diving."

"That's disgusting!" Adrien cried.

"Oh, come on!" Greg looked ready to pounce. "You've never found and eaten something in your cupboard that was past the expiration date? Cookies? Or milk that still smelled fine?"

Adrien rolled his eyes. "Digging around in the trash is completely different."

Victor seemed amused. "We're talking dumpsters full of products still in their packaging. It's like one messy cupboard. I'll show you tonight. We'll hit the local grocery store and dig up something for breakfast."

"Bathing must be a bitch," Adrien continued unabashed. "What do you do, roll around in the dirt?"

"Care to dance?" Jace snarled, standing up from the table.

Adrien looked surprised, but only for a moment. "Gladly," he said.

Jace offered his hand, mostly to keep it from doing something violent, but he wasn't gentle in yanking Adrien toward the dance floor. When he swung around, he expected to see Adrien wearing amusement, or maybe anger. Instead his eyes were downcast, his feet finding the rhythm. When he looked up, there was hurt in his eyes.

"Did you know he was coming?" Adrien shouted.

Jace could barely hear him, so he moved closer, placing his hands on Adrien's hips and bringing them near to his own. "I had no idea, I swear."

Their bodies swung and swayed as if they were having a grand ol' time, but Jace suspected he looked just as unhappy as his boyfriend did now.

Adrien moved his lips close to Jace's ear.

"You talked to Greg on the phone before he came down," Adrien said. "He didn't mention Victor?"

Jace pulled away, shook his head, tried to show his own puzzlement. Adrien didn't look convinced.

"I didn't know!" Jace shouted. "So stop being a dick to me." Whatever sympathy he was hoping to win was ruined when he added, "And stop being a dick to him."

Adrien broke body contact, spun around, let himself get wrapped up in the music. He danced this way through the next two songs, Jace letting him work out his frustrations. The third song was one they both knew—had danced to before on a night that had been filled with laughter and sweat. Adrien made eye contact again, placed a hand on the back of Jace's neck to draw him near. The glare had disappeared. That was progress.

"I didn't know," Jace repeated.

Adrien nodded, finally believing him. "Are you glad?"

Jace glanced toward the table, or tried to, but the layers of gyrating bodies made it impossible to see. "It's awkward as hell," he shouted. Then he placed his head alongside Adrien's. "Just be civil. For me. They'll be gone Sunday morning."

When he pulled back, Adrien rolled his eyes, but in a jokey "oh fine" sort of way. Good. Crisis averted. That was until the true source of all their problems came sauntering up.

"Yo, Adrien!" a voice boomed, doing a poor impersonation of Sylvester Stallone.

Adrien winced like he did every time Greg made this joke, but his eyes softened as he looked Greg over. In fact, he positively lit up when Greg spoke next.

"Mind if I cut in?"

"Feel free!" Adrien said, but his thrill faded when it became clear Greg intended to dance with Jace. Before Jace could utter a single word, Adrien turned and disappeared into the crowd.

Greg smiled, looking like the king of the frat boys, ready to shake his money maker and see what it attracted. When he started to do just that, thrusting hips in his direction, Jace decided he'd had enough. Grabbing Greg by the arm, he dragged him toward the back of the bar, heading for a glowing red exit sign.

Once they were outside, Jace breathed in the cool air, trying to calm down. He didn't want to yell at Greg, especially after having a few drinks. He knew how ugly alcohol could turn the simplest of disagreements, but they needed to talk. Now.

"What are you doing?" he said.

Greg tried to play innocent, but stopped when he saw Jace's expression. "You needed to see him again."

"Why?" Jace insisted. "What's changed? Not Victor, that's for sure."

"He has a job now," Greg said.

Jace felt like he'd been punched in the stomach. "What?"

Greg nodded. "To help take care of his mom. He didn't tell you?"

Jace shook his head.

"That's why I wanted you guys to have more alone time. You need to give him another chance."

"Need?" Okay, now Jace was getting angry. "I have a boyfriend!"

"Adrien is an asshole," Greg muttered. Then he added, "No offense."

"Can you blame him for acting that way? How would you feel if a girl's ex-boyfriend showed up out of the blue? Brought by the person who was supposed to be your best friend!"

"I'm a naughty boy!" Greg said, but his smile faded when he saw this only made Jace angrier. "You can do better. You know I got along with Adrien on my previous visits. I know he's not always *that* bad, but he isn't... He's not good enough. Not for someone like you."

Jace took a deep breath. "You said the same thing about Victor once."

"I know." Greg kicked at the ground. "But he really has changed."

"He still won't move here. I asked him."

Greg raised his head. "You did?"

Jace snorted. "Almost immediately, because I figured that's what this was about."

"Oh. What did he say?"

"What do you think?"

"The thing is," Greg said, revving back up, "you're graduating soon. We both are. So I mean, you could move back. Maybe not to Warrensburg, but there's always Kansas City. Or maybe St. Louis, although that's pretty far away and the drive would get old, but I'd still make it. If we took turns visiting each other, it wouldn't be so bad."

Jace stared. Then he sighed. "Are you seriously telling me that you've done all this just to get me to move home?"

Greg's shoulders rose and fell. "Well, yeah. That's a big part of it. But I also think Victor is a good guy. We've been hanging out more, and I figured maybe he's finally ready for you. He sure talks about you a lot."

"He's always loved me," Jace said. "That wasn't the issue."

"Yeah, I know," Greg said reluctantly. "But—"

"I'm staying." Jace said it firmly. "I like Texas. And I know Adrien can be a pain in the ass, but he wants to be with me and only me."

Greg scowled. "I bet if I—eh, forget it."

"What, you're going to seduce him just to prove me wrong?" Jace chuckled. "By all means, go ahead! But you'll have to go all the way to prove it to me. *All* the way."

Greg pretended to mull it over "Would I get to be the guy?"

Jace smirked. "Trust me, Adrien wouldn't have it any other way."

"Nah, I'd rather seduce you."

"You're not my type," Jace lied. Greg was nearly everyone's type. "But you can help me salvage the night by dancing with Adrien. That should cheer him up."

"Yeah, all right." Greg flexed a muscle casually. "A guy like me is used to being treated like a piece of meat."

"And no more trying to force Victor and me together," Jace said. "We had our shot already. Once was enough."

"Yeah, yeah." Greg looked like a chastised puppy. "That's what he kept saying on the drive down. Although he didn't say once was enough. Do you want to know what he said?"

"No." Jace told himself to go back in the club, to forget about it. He even made it to the door. Then he sighed. "Okay, what?"

"Victor said that nothing had ended. Not for him. He still loves you." Greg let that sink in a moment. "Then he started rattling on about how, since it was never a relationship in his mind, that there wasn't anything to end. Or something. That part wasn't as romantic. Forget I mentioned it."

Jace laughed, shook his head ruefully, and opened the door, reentering a world of superficial beats. Later, when the bar had mostly cleared out and Adrien still gleefully held Greg prisoner on the dance floor, Jace caught Victor's eye and they both smiled in amusement. Victor was right. Relationships come and go, but the feelings that power them, those stay forever.

Jace had a simple fantasy, one that was fairly innocent, especially for a guy strolling into a hotel without his boyfriend. Of course it helped that the sun was shining, the air still early-morning fresh. This made it feel less sultry. Besides, he knew he wouldn't find Victor. Or if he did, Victor wouldn't be alone.

Jace tried the breakfast buffet first.

"Room number?" a young lady asked, clipboard in hand.

"Six oh two," Jace murmured, distracted by who he saw sipping coffee by a window.

"Go ahead, Mr. Trout," the lady said, gesturing toward the food.

"Thanks," Jace said, stifling a laugh when the conversation caught up with him. He'd be eating Greg's breakfast for him.

His stomach rumbled, his body craving something greasy like it always did the morning after he drank. He wasn't hungover, exactly. He'd stopped drinking after his conversation with Greg outside the club, wanting to be in full control of his actions. Jace loaded up on hash browns and eggs, grabbing an orange juice on the way to the table.

He sat down without announcing himself, reveling in Victor's surprise since it happened so rarely.

"Greg sleeping it off?" Jace asked.

Victor nodded. "And where's your date?" he asked without looking around for Adrien.

"The same."

"Ah."

Jace felt his face flush. Just the idea of them being together, alone, despite being surrounded by feasting travelers, felt so... Ugh. This was silly.

"Interesting smile," Victor said.

Jace didn't realize he had been. The smile didn't go away, even when he willed it to. "It's just odd seeing you here. This isn't the sort of environment I ever pictured you in."

"Odder than seeing me at a gay bar, like last night?" Victor picked at a half-eaten bagel. "Besides, you know how I feel about free food. I'm loading up my pockets on the way out."

"That'll be interesting when it comes to the scrambled eggs."

"Those I'll hide like a hamster does," Victor said, blowing up his cheeks with air. "I figure I can get two handfuls in."

"Or you can come live with me and I'll cook you all the eggs you can eat, every single morning." Jace focused suddenly on dousing his hash browns with ketchup. "Uh, can we rewind that real quick and make it an internal monologue?"

"I still would have heard you thinking it," Victor said, winking at him. "I'm psychic, remember?"

"So what am I thinking now?" Jace said, locking eyes with him, but for once his thoughts were fairly quiet. Instead he felt a mix of emotions. Desire, mostly, with a tinge of sorrow. The balance started to shift the more he examined Victor's face and realized that he would soon be out of his life again.

Victor was the first to break eye contact, looking down at his coffee. "We're not going to give Greg the satisfaction of winning, are we?"

"No." Jace's food had lost its appeal. He forced a few bites anyway, mostly just to keep himself from saying something stupid.

Victor filled the silence for him. "I like Adrien."

Jace snorted, then stared when Victor appeared serious.

"Really, I do. It's refreshing to meet someone with so few filters." Victor scratched at his chin. "You remember Star? She's his opposite. Everything that girl says is calculated and rolled in three layers of bullshit. With Adrien, you know what you're getting up front because he'll make sure to tell you."

"He does make an impression," Jace admitted. "You weren't offended?"

Victor smiled. "I'm also not going to let him win, so no."

Jace felt like apologizing for Adrien, or at least explaining where he was coming from, but mostly he wanted his name to be banished from the table. He wanted to talk about them, which was frustrating because there was nothing new to be said. Nothing had changed. Well, nearly nothing.

"Greg said you got a job."

Victor looked embarrassed, something even rarer than him being surprised.

"That bad?" Jace asked. "Fast food industry?"

"No. It's just that there aren't many people willing to give someone like me a shot. I never really worked before, so—"

Jace shook his head, still not understanding.

Victor seemed amused. "I'm not copying you or anything creepy like that."

"Bernie's?" Jace said, slapping the table. "No way! Bernard gave you a job?"

"Yeah."

"He didn't say anything about it to me when I saw him on Christmas break."

"It's a fairly new development." Victor looked defiant. "*And I hate it.*"

"You love it," Jace teased. "And look at your hair. You've got your own lion's mane now. I bet you figured if you couldn't have me, you'd try to *be* me."

"You're cruel," Victor said, grinning. "And I still have you. In my own way."

Jace wouldn't deny that. Part of him would always belong to

Victor. But he was still too shocked by this news to ponder that
now. "So what made you get your own hamster wheel? Trying
out something new? Or is it somehow ironic?"

"No, no," Victor shook his head, attention on the salt shaker
he was twirling between two fingers. "It's my mom. She's uh—"
His hands went still and he stared into the glass vial like it was
a crystal ball. Half a minute passed before he spoke again. "It's
harder for her to work these days, so I thought I'd help out."

"Is she okay? Nothing serious, is it?"

"She's fine," Victor said dismissively. "It's just my turn to
take care of her."

Why'd he have to go and do something noble like that? Now
if the issue of Victor not wanting to move came up again... Jace
mentally backpedaled. There had always been more issues than
that. Otherwise he would have stayed. If Jace thought it could
have worked, he would have gone to college in Warrensburg
instead.

"I think that's awesome," he said, the wind having left his
sails. "Tell her I said hello."

Victor nodded. "Yeah. I will."

Jace excused himself and went to get a bowl of cereal, even
though he wasn't hungry anymore. The funny thing about four
years of not getting what you want, he thought, is how time made
that forgivable. Maybe it didn't matter anymore that Victor would
never be exactly what he wanted or needed.

Maybe Victor was worth another shot, even if it wouldn't be
perfect.

Jace left the cereal bowl on the counter without pouring
milk, went upstairs without telling Victor what he was doing.
He always seemed to understand anyway. Then he found room
602 and knocked on the door. He needed Greg to be there with
them—needed a chaperone, as stupid as that might sound.
Otherwise he saw himself happily making the same mistakes
all over again.

"Goodbye."

The words didn't come easy. Jace felt three pairs of eyes
watching him. Standing next to the driver-side door, Greg was
entertaining one last hope. Waiting farther away, Adrien had
an eyebrow cocked. He had done well on Saturday, remaining

civil and not taking any more potshots at Victor. Bowling was fun and had given them all something to do. Victor was a terrible bowler, Jace not much better. Greg and Adrien had owned the lanes, which kept them both in high sprits, and more important, distracted from their two very different crusades. They also remained near enough to stop Jace from saying anything awkward to Victor. Now was his last chance, something all of them seemed to sense.

Two eyes, one green, the other brown, watched him with amusement. Jace had said goodbye, which should have banished Victor from his life once more. Instead Victor just stood there, watching him, before he turned to Adrien.

"He has the heart of a lion, you know." Victor jerked a thumb in Jace's direction. "And he's the most beautiful man you'll ever meet."

Adrien's eyes widened. Clearly he didn't know what to make of this. "I know," he managed.

"Take care of him for me." Victor opened the passenger-side door, not looking at Jace again until he was seated. A green eye considered him briefly before winking. Then his profile was lost to his long dark hair. Jace stared anyway, resisting the urge to chase after the car when it started moving. When it disappeared around the corner, he turned to find Adrien watching him. He gave a tentative smile.

"Okay, so maybe I can see why you were so crazy about him." Adrien offered his hand, like they were going to shake on a business deal. "Come back inside with me. The bed is still warm."

Chest tight with feelings he could barely comprehend, Jace reached out and took Adrien's hand.

Chapter Fifteen

"The balcony is nice, but it makes this room cold in the winter."

Jace watched with detached interest as the young woman opened the double doors. He'd already forgotten her name, despite the recent introduction. Adrien had the situation in hand. He sprang like a ballerina out onto the balcony, gasping in delight. Jace joined him, staring down at the street, the people shopping in the warm evening air, the lone green tree surrounded by brick and concrete.

"It's small, but you can grill out here in the summer," the current tenant said. "Just don't let the police catch you."

"Oh, they won't care," Adrien said dismissively. "I'll bribe them with burgers. Right, baby?"

Jace grinned on cue. "Of course."

"We could probably get a Christmas tree out here in the winter. How classy would that be?"

"Good idea," the young woman said, filling in for Jace. She seemed happy to chat, which made the rest of the tour easy for him. There wasn't much to see. The apartment was a small living room with a kitchenette in one corner, an even smaller bedroom, and a bathroom with a toilet and shower stall. Adrien seemed thrilled enough. Four years in a dorm could make even the smallest apartment feel like paradise.

"What do you think?" the young woman said, leading them back to the living room.

"We're definitely interested!" Adrien said.

The tenant was transparently relieved. "Great! My lease runs out the end of summer, but I want to move home after graduating."

"Where's home?" Jace said, feeling he should make an effort.

"San Antonio. Um, I guess you'll need to talk to the landlord. You'll probably need your parents to cosign since he acts like anyone in college is still a child."

Adrien turned to him with a pleading expression. He didn't have the best relationship with his parents, so it would be up to Jace's.

"No problem."

"Okay. I'll get you his info. I think I have it in the bedroom."

Jace zoned out while Adrien circled the room, naming off improvements.

"We can put a divider there to section off the kitchen, like a dressing screen. Or maybe some sort of shelving. I want an antique divan against the wall here. Anything but a boring old couch. I know you like the one we have in the dorm, but I never could get the drool stains out from when Greg stayed the night. I pity the woman who lands him. What do you think about the bedroom? I actually like the light fixture in there. We could build a color scheme off it: ivory and gold. Jace?"

He blinked, trying to piece together the words he'd barely been listening to. "The couch is fine. I like the drool stains."

"Fine." Adrien sighed. "It's not like we'll be able to afford new furniture right away, but I was asking about the bedroom."

Jace grimaced. His head hurt. What he really wanted right now was to step back out onto the balcony, alone, just for some space.

"Are you okay?" Adrien asked. "You've been so out of it ever since—"

This got Jace's attention. He raised his head, waiting for one of them to finally say it, to set the truth free so it could be dealt with. Things hadn't been the same for the past month, and they both knew why. He just needed one of them to verbalize it.

"—well, for a while now," Adrien finished. "I'm worried about you."

"I have a headache, that's all." He glanced around the apartment, trying to show interest. "It's going to be great, but let's not start planning until after we get it."

Adrien bit his bottom lip. "You think your parents won't cosign?"

"They'll be fine. It's the landlord who sounds like a jerk."

"He can be," the young woman said, returning with a scrap of paper in hand. "But as long as you pay rent on time, you'll never have to deal with him again. It's a very affordable apartment for the area."

"Don't worry." Jace said. "I'm used to dealing with jerks. I live with one."

"Oh, you're so funny," Adrien said, slapping his arm. Then he smiled, took hold of Jace's arm affectionately, and addressed the current tenant. "He'll have the landlord eating out of his hand in no time. I speak from experience."

This cheered Jace up somewhat. Adrien totally got his sense of humor, and they did have fun together. The best way to forget the past was to make something of the future. Moving into this apartment would change everything. Jace would have his degree, find a job, and finally make something of himself. Adrien would continue to study, and from the way he had rocked their dorm, this dingy little apartment would soon be transformed into a classy and comfortable home. *Their* home.

Jace liked the sound of that.

Laws that regulate the benefits and working conditions of employees, when imposed by government—

"Oh, tell me about it!"

Jace furrowed his brow at the text. *Laws that regulate the benefits and working conditions of employees—*

"Sorry, hon. Do you remember where I put the cocktail napkins?"

Jace refused to be discouraged. *—when imposed by the government can lead to decreased expenses for—*

"Never mind, found them. Do you want a martini? Jace?"

"I'm trying to study!" he snarled. His face remained red, from embarrassment more than anger because they weren't alone in their dorm room.

Across from him on the couch were two students. Caleb was new to Adrien's circle. A chubby Asian freshman, he looked even younger because of his wide-eyed approach to the world. Most freshmen had gotten comfortable by now, mere weeks away from the end of their second semester, but the first-day jitters never seemed to have left Caleb. The way he followed Adrien around like a duckling was adorable. Normally. Today Jace wanted to tell him to stop staring and get his shit together.

And of course Tanner was watching him, like he always did. Tanner didn't talk much. Not until someone else said something incorrect. Then he was happy to smugly educate them. He fancied himself an intellectual, his elitist attitude the common bond he and Adrien shared. Tanner was the one who talked Adrien into working at the library with him instead of waiting tables. Fewer hours and no tips, meaning less pay. But it fueled their image, so no doubt they both felt the sacrifice was worth it.

"Less talking, more drinking," Adrien said, bustling over with a tray of martinis. "Hubby needs to study!"

Jace clenched his jaw. He hated when Adrien called him that. Lately, everything Adrien did set his teeth on edge, but now was especially irritating. Ten in the morning on a Saturday with finals looming straight ahead, and they were drinking? Adrien assured him they also intended to study, but Jace didn't think Tanner shared any of his classes.

The next time Adrien spoke, he did so in a whisper, the others taking a cue from him. Jace turned his attention back to the book, skipping ahead a page because he couldn't stand to read the same lines over again. The whispers took some getting used to, but eventually he managed to start absorbing information. That is, until the martini shaker started rattling for a second round of drinks.

"Shaken, not stirred!" Adrien said with an apologetic look. "Sure you don't want one?"

"Sure you want another?" Jace countered. "Why don't you guys go find a bar?"

"I'm not twenty-one," Caleb whispered. At least he intended to stay quiet.

"But Adrien *is*. In Texas, if you're old enough, you can buy liquor for a minor."

Tanner scoffed. "In Texas, only a minor's parent, guardian, or spouse can buy them alcohol, and must remain present when the alcohol is consumed."

"Fine," Jace said. "Why don't you marry Adrien and then you two can adopt Caleb? That way you can drink away the weekends all you like."

"That's hardly legal," Tanner said, unperturbed.

"Just one more drink and we'll head out," Adrien promised. After he distributed the second round, he sat on the bed next to Jace. "We were talking about our first times."

Jace grunted, turning his attention back to the book.

"Caleb slept with the school janitor!" Adrien said, still addressing him.

"He just jacked off in front of me," Caleb said shyly.

Jace lowered the book and raised an eyebrow. Then he tried reading again.

"Of course Jace's story takes the cake, since it was with a homeless guy."

"See, Caleb," Tanner said in helpful tones. "That's a notch lower than your first time."

"The janitor was young," Caleb said defensively. "Barely out of high school, so we were practically the same age."

"I'm sure it was very romantic," Adrien said. "At least yours had a job. And somewhere to sleep at night."

Jace shut the textbook with a snap and set it aside. "Victor wasn't homeless. He had a room at his mother's house, just like anyone else his age. He just didn't like staying there."

"Every homeless person has parents," Adrien said. He took a sip of his drink thoughtfully. "It's when people would rather starve on the street than go home that makes them homeless."

"He wasn't homeless," Jace said through gritted teeth.

Tanner raised an authoritative finger. "Technically, a teenager who refuses to return home can be defined as homeless."

"There you go," Adrien said, looking pleased. "You slept with a homeless person."

"Fine," Jace said. "That's what you want to hear? No problem. I first met Victor when he was begging for change on the street. I tossed some coins into the old cup he was rattling around, and he stole my heart by barfing on my shoes. Later, after I'd seduced him with a bottle of vodka—which he downed in one gulp—we retired to his cardboard box. I fucked him once he blacked out. That's my story. Happy?"

"No," Tanner said. "The stereotypes you are perpetuating do a disservice to—"

"Shut up," Jace said. "Unless you want to tell us how your first time was screwing a hole you cut out of a textbook."

Caleb giggled with glee, which made Jace feel a little better.

"You're being very rude," Adrien said.

"Me?" Jace said. "I'm trying to study. You're the one dredging up my past, something you wouldn't do if you ever bothered to learn how much Victor means to me. But you never bothered to ask, did you?"

"I don't care," Adrien said candidly. "If he was so important, he would still be in your life."

Jace was on his feet. "Oh, wait. You *did* ask me something when he came to visit. Let's see. You were drunk, and we were in bed. What was it you wanted to know?"

"Shut up," Adrien said.

"That's right! You wanted to know if his dick is bigger than yours. I didn't answer you then, but since he's not important, it won't bother you to learn the he is in fact bigger than you. In every way possible."

Adrien shouted something in return, but the blood thumping in Jace's ears made him deaf. Jace stormed out of the room, slamming the door behind him. He took a deep breath. Then another. When that didn't work he turned around and punched the wall. Unfortunately for him, it was solidly built. The only thing damaged was his fist, which hurt like hell. No, that wasn't true. More of him was damaged than that, and had been since he'd last seen Victor. The pain in his hand was nothing compared to the ache in his chest that never seemed to cease.

Maybe there was only one cure. Jace felt his pockets. Thank goodness he had his wallet and keys. His pulse switched gears, his heart working harder, his breath coming even shorter, but it wasn't anger that propelled him toward the parking lot, into his car, and onto the highway. Twelve hours north and he would be home again. Twelve hours until Victor.

The problem with a long trip is how much time it allows for thought. The problem with thinking so much is how it inevitably leads to doubt. The drive out of Texas was easy, Jace spurred on by a curious mixture of anger and love. The empty horizons of Oklahoma were harder. He had finals next week, was supposed to be at work in a matter of hours. If he turned around now, he would be late to start his shift, but he wouldn't get fired. And Adrien...

Well, Jace was still pissed at him, but he knew their problems hadn't been one-sided. Jace had been ignoring him a lot lately, and when he did give Adrien his attention, he'd been irritable and moody. Try as he might, Jace couldn't seem to break the cycle. Looking past Adrien's imperfections used to be easy. Ever since Greg's stupid stunt, it was like Adrien wasn't good enough anymore—a horrible feeling. Arrogant too. Maybe he should turn around, drive back to Houston, and apologize to him.

Or maybe he should keep driving and tell Greg off for ruining everything. That's what he would do!

This idea propelled Jace to the Kansas state line. Then he admitted to himself that it was an excuse. He knew what he was doing, who he was rushing to see. As the sun set, he gave into certainty. He would see Victor. Tonight. Even if he had to plow the car through every forest in Missouri, he would find where Victor was staying.

And then?

Jace grinned, feeling happier than he had in months, and pressed harder on the accelerator.

The car pulled up to the pump running on fumes, the engine spluttering to a halt when Jace killed the ignition. After all these years, it wasn't sounding too healthy. He'd have to check the oil while he was there, but first—

Jace glanced toward the windows of Bernie's to make sure he hadn't been mistaken when pulling into the parking lot. There he was, stripped of his Army jacket and standing motionless behind the counter. Jace got out of the car, struggling with mixed feelings. On one hand he was glad Victor had changed. If he kept changing, no matter how long it took, maybe there was hope for them yet. On the other hand, Victor was his wild boy in the woods. That was who Jace had fallen in love with. He didn't want to see Victor here, think of him night after night, bathed in cold fluorescent lights. Not for the first time, Jace felt the urge to rescue him, to save him from all of this. But he didn't know how.

By the time Jace reached the door, he could see puzzlement on Victor's face, and when he stepped into the store to the familiar scent of microwaved hotdogs and the humming of refrigerators, that puzzlement turned into joy.

"If I'm high, never let me come down," Victor said. He was around the counter, intent on giving Jace a hug, but restrained himself at the last moment.

Jace wasn't having that. He pulled Victor to him, roped his arms around him like his life depended on it, and felt relief when Victor's hands slid up his back. He could have stayed there all night, breathing in the faint smell of smoke in Victor's hair. Let the customers come, witnessing what true love looked like before leaving empty-handed. No bottles of soda or cartons of cigarettes tonight!

"Are you okay?" Victor said, breaking their embrace.

Jace let it all show on his face, knowing he wouldn't have to explain in words. He almost felt hurt when Victor still didn't understand.

"What are you doing here?"

"I'm here to see you," Jace said.

"Well, yeah." Victor chuckled. "I mean, what are you doing in Warrensburg?"

"I just told you."

Realization dawned on Victor's face. "Oh!"

Jace suddenly felt sheepish. "Is that okay?"

"Yeah. Are you kidding?"

They grinned at each other. Now what? Lock the doors, turn off the lights, and make paradise out of a gas station?

"My shift ends in an hour," Victor said. "Unless you want me to pull a Dan."

"No," Jace said reluctantly. If the store belonged to anyone but Bernard... "Whatever happened to him, anyway?"

"Fired," Victor said. "Bernard finally got tired of his shit. Last time I saw him, he was working the McDonald's drive-thru."

"Over one billion customers sneered at," Jace quipped. "Man, it feels good to be here."

Like home! His first job, the place he met Victor, and the setting for countless other memories. A customer came in to pay for gas, so Jace wandered the store and the back rooms, eventually sitting at Bernard's desk. Aside from the dates on the calendar, nothing seemed to have changed. For once, that felt reassuring rather than suffocating.

When he returned up front, he and Victor whiled away the hour recounting memories made there. This helped Jace relax, get used to being in Victor's presence again. By the time an older man came to relieve Victor, it felt like no time had passed at all. After fueling up the car, Jace asked where they were headed.

"Home," Victor said.

Jace smiled. "Where is that this week?"

"I mean my mom's house."

"Oh. Okay."

That took him aback. He imagined them driving to Jace's old neighborhood, sneaking down into the valley, and rekindling more than one old fire. After all, it was nearly summer. Victor never stayed home in nice weather.

They were parked in front of Victor's house in no time. Unlike Bernie's Stop and Shop, it had changed, needing maintenance more than ever. He wondered if he should volunteer to help fix it up over the summer, or if that would be insulting.

"Can you stay in the car for a minute?" Victor asked. "Let me run in first and take care of some things."

"Uh, yeah. Of course."

"Thanks." Victor stepped out of the car, then bent over before shutting the door. "It might be more like ten minutes."

"That's okay," Jace said.

What was going on? Maybe Victor's room was messy or something. All Jace knew was that he was sick of being in the car. Funny how a drive could be so taxing to the body when it mostly involved sitting still. He leaned the seat back and rested his eyes.

—*knock knock knock!*—

Jace's body jerked, his eyes shooting open. Victor was at the driver-side window, his face somewhat drawn, but he grinned regardless. Jace glanced at the clock. More than half an hour had gone by.

Victor opened the door, offering Jace a hand. "Come inside. Be quiet though. Mom's in bed."

"So was I," Jace said, feeling embarrassed.

Together they entered the house and crept down the stairs. In the dim light, Jace thought the house appeared less organized. Maybe Mrs. Hemingway was having back problems and couldn't do as much as before. His concern for her was forgotten when he entered Victor's room.

Here things had changed. All remnants of a child's room had been removed. No more old toys or stuffed animals. In fact, the room didn't hold anything decorative at all, no posters or art. The walls were empty. Except for a lamp and a bed, there was nothing.

"Blank space," Victor said, tapping the side of his head. "No distractions."

"Fine by me," Jace said. All he wanted to focus on was right in front of him.

Victor opened the high-set window. The sound of trees waving in the wind preceded a gust of warm air. Victor kicked off his shoes, eyes on Jace. Then he flopped on the bed and patted the spot next to him.

"Come tell me everything."

Jace took off his shoes, placing his keys and wallet in them since there wasn't even a nightstand now. As he climbed into bed, he found the last thing he wanted to talk about was Adrien. He didn't even want to remember he existed.

"Must have been a bad fight," Victor said. "You two break up?"

"No." Jace shook his head, gobbling up every detail of Victor. Seeing him felt too good. "You still have that tattoo I got you?"

"No, I sold it at a garage sale." Victor smirked, starting to lift the sleeve of his shirt before he thought twice and took off the shirt completely. "It's getting a little faded. Like me, ha ha."

Jace was glad for the excuse to get near him, his index finger stroking the dark line the fox was running along. He could feel Victor watching him and hoped his thoughts were more transparent then ever.

They were.

Victor pulled on one of Jace's arms, forcing him to stretch across his body and lay partially across his chest. The heat from Victor's skin, the familiar scent, the wiry chest hair—Jace felt like his senses were on overload. He shifted, bringing himself closer to Victor's face.

"Are we going to do this?"

Jace wished that Victor hadn't asked. "I don't want to cheat on him," he admitted, but his mind was racing to find a way. A hug wasn't cheating, so neither was the current nearness of their bodies. And surely if a slap was okay, then the way Jace stroked the hair away from Victor's cheek was too. He let his fingers brush against Victor's lips, substitute for the kiss he couldn't give. How could he justify that? Would he have to? Maybe, if he never returned to Houston, none of this would matter. Could he do that?

"You aren't going to sleep in your jeans and shirt, are you?" Victor asked.

Of course not. Jace stood and undressed with his back turned. Everything but his underwear. He turned off the light before returning to bed, letting himself be clumsy as he got under the sheets, his bare leg brushing against Victor's to discover his jeans were off too.

"Roll over," Victor said. "Your back must be tense from that drive."

Of course! A massage was safe. People did that for a living, a respectable occupation, so it couldn't be cheating. Hell, maybe they could find some sort of chiropractic technique that would casually allow them to get each other off. He was about to suggest they stop playing games when Victor kneaded his back muscles, causing him to moan with relief.

"How come you never did that in the old days?" Jace managed to say.

"Because we were both more interested in other parts."

That hadn't changed, but now they were forced to explore other options. There wasn't much they could do. The massage simmered down to Victor tracing a finger along his back. Then Victor scooted near, one arm resting across Jace, his nose pressed against his shoulder. Only an inch or two of space separated them. Not quite cuddling, but not quite safe either.

"If you were going to be completely selfish right now," Jace murmured. "What would you do?"

Victor didn't hesitate. "I'd ask you to stay here permanently."

Not the answer he expected. Not at all. Victor closed the gap between them, their bodies pressed together now, but he was tactful enough to keep his crotch away from Jace. Had they crossed a line? Friends spooning wasn't unheard of. Hell, it was a lot more platonic than what Jace wanted to do. He tried to silence those urges by distracting himself. Instead of thinking of tasting and touching Victor's body, he posed questions to himself. *Can I? Can I move back here? Can we be together again? Can I live this life again?* The two words were still on his lips as he finally found sleep.

Can I?

Chapter Sixteen

Jace awoke to an empty bed, even reaching over to grope the vacant spot just like they did in the movies. Why did they always do that? In case the other person had turned invisible? Flopping over onto his back, he considered the events of the night before. For a moment, Jace thought they had given in to temptation. His dreams had been sex-fueled, never concluding in release. He still felt frustrated, even now, which meant that he hadn't betrayed Adrien.

Just thinking of his estranged boyfriend helped deflate Jace's erection. Driving here hadn't solved anything. He wanted to be with Victor so much that there didn't seem to be room for anyone else. Jace was stuck, unable to act on any of his desires. Unless he called Adrien and broke up with him over the phone. That would free him and Victor to—

Jace swung out of bed rather than chase the thought down another dead end. After getting dressed, he made his way upstairs, the smell of sizzling eggs drawing him into the kitchen. He pictured Mrs. Hemingway at the stove, wearing a comfortable old nightgown while Victor yawned at the table, awaiting his meal.

Jace was nearly right, but the people were in the wrong places. Mrs. Hemingway sat at the table, flipping through a magazine while Victor attacked a frying pan with a spatula.

"Oh! Jace!" Mrs. Hemingway hopped to her feet. She still seemed spry. Wasn't she supposed to be struggling somehow? "It's been so long since I've seen you. Oh, you look so grown up!"

Jace let himself be hugged, matching Mrs. Hemingway's grin when she pulled away.

"It *has* been a long time, hasn't it?" she asked.

"Yeah. Well over a year. I was surprised too."

"Oh good!" She put a hand over her mouth. "I mean, not good that we haven't seen each other. Good that I got it right!"

"Sit down, you two," Victor said. "Breakfast is ready."

Jace took a seat, not hiding his puzzlement. Since when did Victor cook? Jace stifled a grin, wondering if all of this was to show him how much had changed.

"Scrambled eggs and toast," Victor said, sounding apologetic as he set a plate down in front of him.

"It smells great!" he said truthfully. "Why are they pink?"

"That's the barbeque sauce," Mrs. Hemingway said. "I always use that."

"You always use cheese," Victor said. "I'm the one who started using barbeque sauce."

Victor's mother waved a hand like he was being silly. Then they all tucked in. Besides a gas station burger on the drive up, Jace hadn't eaten much lately. Once his stomach realized this, it couldn't get enough. Jace shoveled in the food, accepting Victor's offer of more toast. Then he swigged it all down with coffee.

"That's how a growing boy eats," Mrs. Hemingway said approvingly.

Victor snorted. "Let's hope he doesn't get any bigger. His feet were hanging off the bed this morning."

Jace pictured Victor standing over the bed, watching him while he still slept. Jace would have done the same and had in the past. They felt the same way. There was no denying it. Why hadn't he broken up with Adrien before coming here?

"How is your family?" Mrs. Hemingway asked.

"Fine," Jace said, wiping his mouth with a napkin. "Actually, I haven't seen them yet, but I'm sure everything is fine. They don't even know I'm here."

"Won't they be surprised? I love it when my Victor shows up unexpectedly."

"Yeah." Jace nodded. "I should probably head over there now. You want to come with me, Victor?"

"He can't," Mrs. Hemingway said. "Victor has to go to school."

"Mom," Victor said warningly.

"What?" Jace asked looking between them. "You're taking classes somewhere? College or vocational?"

Mrs. Hemingway tittered like a little girl. "Victor can't go to college. He's just a little boy!"

Jace's stomach sank. He watched with increasing trepidation as Mrs. Hemingway's expression became distant. Then she got up from the table to fetch the coffee pot. Victor's eyes remained fixed on the table.

"More coffee?" Mrs. Hemingway offered, the pot poised above Jace's cup.

"Thank you."

He studied her as she poured, seeing no mischief in her eyes. This was for real. She smiled pleasantly at him as she refilled Victor's cup next.

"I'm going to take a shower now. You boys enjoy yourselves today."

"Thanks, Mom." Victor was quiet until the sound of water running could be heard elsewhere in the house. Then he met Jace's gaze. "Sorry about that."

Jace felt strangely frightened. "What's going on?"

"She gets a little confused these days," Victor said. Then he rolled his eyes, as if disgusted with himself. "It's worse than that. She has Alzheimer's."

Jace didn't know how to respond, at least when it came to words, so he got up from the table and went to Victor. He wanted to hug him, comfort him somehow, but when he reached out Victor brushed his hands away.

"Don't," he said. "I'm sorry, but I don't want a hug because my mom's going crazy. That's not going to make it all better."

"I'm sorry," Jace said lamely. "That was stupid of me."

"It wasn't." Victor exhaled. "I'm not used to talking about this, that's all. Who would I tell? It's just me and her."

Jace slid into the chair next to his. "So what does this mean? This is probably a dumb question, but is she going to be all right? I mean, they have treatments for this sort of thing, don't they?"

"She's on medication," Victor said. "But she needs someone to make sure she takes it. Mornings are always like this. Or nights, when I get back from work. You know that trip I took with Greg? I came home and she was sitting in the bathtub, fully dressed. The water was stone cold. I have no idea how long she'd been sitting there."

A mad chuckle escaped Victor's lips. He put his hands over his face, as if to quell the muffled noises that sounded more like crying. His eyes were red and moist when he moved his hands away. "That's when we went to see the doctor. Before then, I just figured she was getting old. Who doesn't forget where they put something, or struggle to remember a name? That's not so weird, right?"

Jace thought of his own mother, suddenly feeling a need to see her, to make sure she was okay. "Does the medicine help?"

"Yes," Victor said. "She does pretty well on her own.

Sometimes it's easy to pretend there's nothing wrong. Then she'll make an oddball comment and— Well, you saw for yourself. She just needs extra help sometimes. It's early onset Alzheimer's, that's all."

"I wish I could help," Jace said.

"Nah." Victor put on a brave face. "I've got it under control. So how long are you going to be in town?"

Thoughts of Texas made Jace's stomach turn. Did he still have a job? "I'm not sure. I need to swing by my parents' place, make a few calls."

"Go do that," Victor said. "Then come see me again, okay? I'll be here all day. I don't have to work."

"Okay." Jace didn't move. He didn't want to leave after Victor had dropped a bombshell like that, but he could also tell that Victor wanted to be alone. Jace supposed he could understand that. They would talk more about this when he returned. First, he wanted very much to give his own mom and dad a very big hug.

"I'm sorry honey," Jace's mother said, leaning back in the patio chair. "It sounds to me like the symptoms are already quite serious."

"Definitely advanced Alzheimer's," his father added from next to her. "My aunt, your great aunt, had it. Stuffed a turkey one year and left it in a cold oven for hours. Served it that way too. Worst Thanksgiving ever." Bob sniffed, not an ounce of amusement in his voice. "She was so old we thought it was just age. Didn't have many years left in her, which was a mercy."

"Dad!" Michelle said. She was stretched out on the wooden deck, jeans rolled up to expose her legs to the sun. "We don't want Mrs. Hemingway to die!"

"I didn't mean it that way. I mean it was a mercy she was already so old before it got bad. That was a long time ago too. I'm sure treatment options are better now."

Jace sighed. Sitting cross-legged on the patio, he held one of his mother's purring cats in the basket his lap made. He never could keep track of their names. "She seemed okay in general. A little absentminded, maybe. Mrs. Hemingway was always a little flaky, but I figured it was just her personality."

"Regardless," Serena said, pursing her lips. "It can't be easy for Victor. I wish there was something we could do."

"Me too," Jace said.

"Then move home," Michelle said.

"Stop that," their mother chastised. "Jace has his own life to worry about." She looked moderately hopeful. "Unless you want to, of course. We wouldn't mind."

"He's not doing anything until he graduates from college," Bob said. "And then he's getting a job to pay us back for all that tuition."

"I already have a job, Dad."

"Then go buy me some whisky, you no-good bum!"

Jace smiled and shrugged. "I will. You coming with, Michelle?"

"Sure, but we're taking my car."

Maybe it was a perk of being the youngest, or perhaps a benefit of staying home, but Michelle had a brand new car bought by their parents. They called it a high school graduation present. All Jace had gotten was the old car they used to share. Oh, and the out-of-state tuition. Still, it was nice to ride in a car that didn't have a crack in the windshield or a radio that stopped working if the air conditioning was turned on.

"You're really leaving again tonight?" Michelle asked as they cruised out of the neighborhood.

"Yeah. I called work and told them there was a family emergency. That saved my ass, but they expect me back on Monday. Plus I have a final tomorrow that I haven't even studied for."

"Tell me about it," Michelle said. "I thought college was going to be all parties and pretty boys."

Jace grinned. "The boys *are* very pretty."

"True. How's Adrien?"

Jace sighed.

Michelle sat upright and smiled. "Did you two break up?"

"You don't have to look so excited about it. And no, we didn't. But things aren't looking good."

"Sorry. It's just that he's kind of a jerk."

"Funny, Greg said nearly the same thing." Jace glanced out the window. Four years away from Warrensburg and nothing seemed to have changed. "Maybe Adrien isn't the right one for me."

"You might want to consider your options," Michelle said

with slightly more tact.

"What about you? What's his name?"

Michelle was silent.

Jace glanced over at her. "Nobody?"

She shook her head.

"That's unusual for you. You're awfully young to be calling it quits."

"Awfully young to be settling down," she corrected. "Anyway, shame about Victor."

Jace slumped down in his seat. "Yeah."

"Maybe after you graduate, you could come back. Give him a hand. Greg says that you two are still hot for each other."

"Greg seems to know more about my love life than I do," Jace grumbled.

"Is he wrong?"

Jace stared out the windshield, unseeing. "No. He's not wrong." Then he blinked. "Since when are you so friendly with Greg?"

"Small town," Michelle said dismissively. "And he lives within shouting distance. It's worth considering, isn't it? Coming back, I mean. Are you really going to stay in Texas forever?"

"I don't know."

"I'm not trying to pressure you," Michelle said.

Jace snorted.

"I'm not! I'll lend Victor a hand. Mom and Dad too. If things get worse, we can check in on Mrs. Hemingway when he can't be there. I'm sure Greg will help. He's always liked Victor and helped him out in lots of ways. Hell, even Bernie chipped in by giving Victor a job. I want you here, but not because you feel obligated. Small communities have their good side too. We'll watch out for him."

Jace looked at his sister. She was getting awfully mature these days. No more crazy little sister, letting boys sneak into her window. Michelle was a woman now.

"Maybe," Jace said. "I want to graduate. After that, I'm not sure what's left for me in Houston anymore."

Michelle smiled. "You know how they say you can never go home again?"

"Yeah."

"They're full of it. The truth is, you can never leave home.

Not completely."

Jace thought about it. "Sage advice. You're so grown-up."

Michelle nodded. "Totally. Hey, once we're home again, let's drink half of Dad's whisky and fill it back up with water."

Jace grinned. "Why settle for half?"

Victor's arms were looped around the chains of the swing. Hunched over and with a cigarette hanging out of his mouth, he listened impassively, never interrupting as Jace rambled on about his unhappy relationship with Adrien.

Jace, twisting back and forth on his own swing, had never intended to talk to Victor about any of this. He preferred to focus on the moment. Or the distant past. An hour ago, they had walked to a nearby park. While not as nostalgic as sitting in the woods together, this more natural environment caused a stirring in Jace's chest, a longing for a different time. So when Victor asked how he and Adrien were doing, Jace starting talking, mostly to keep himself in check.

"I flew off the handle. Really bad. Rather than stick around and make things worse, I hopped in the car and drove up here."

"To see me?" Victor said with a smile. "In that case, I'm surprised last night went the way it did."

"Yeah." Jace swallowed. "I should have broken up with him before leaving."

Cigarette burnt down to the filter, Victor flicked it away. "You make it sound like a done deal."

"Isn't it?"

Victor shrugged. "This is exactly why I don't like relationships. You and Adrien could go on being friends, sleeping together, getting all lovey when the mood strikes you. Instead it's like this job position that gets put under review occasionally. If the other person isn't performing to your satisfaction—" Victor swiped a finger across his neck.

Jace rolled his eyes. "It's perfectly normal that people outgrow each other."

"Maybe," Victor said. "But then again, here we are, all grown up and desperate to revisit the past. We never had to stop, Jace. Even if you needed to leave, to get away from me, from Warrensburg, or whatever—that doesn't mean we had to call it quits. Why does it have to be all or nothing?"

"I don't know," Jace said. "Maybe it doesn't have to be."

"For either of us."

Jace did a double take. "You mean Adrien?"

"Why not?"

"Because of the way he acted!"

"He's human," Victor said.

"So am I, but I don't act that way."

"Still not a good enough reason to kick him out of your life." Victor reached for another cigarette but then changed his mind. "Tell you what, the next time things get ugly with Adrien, just walk away. Every time he acts like that, leave. Eventually he'll get the point. If he wants to be around you, he'll have to be civil. You keep telling me he has a good side. Be there for that part of him, but turn your back when he gets mean."

Jace shook his head. "Thanks for the reminder. I'd nearly convinced myself that you wanted me all to yourself."

"Love knows no boundaries," Victor said. Then he smirked. "And neither do I."

"You're hopeless," Jace moaned, but he couldn't help smiling. "There's another reason I think Adrien and I are over."

"What now? He brushes his teeth too loud?"

"No," Jace said. "Because, after I graduate, I'm moving back here."

Victor's brow crinkled. "Why?"

"A lot of reasons. Well, mostly just one. I want to be there for you. I know what you're going through with your mom is hard, and I want to help out. And you're right about other things. You and me, for instance. Maybe I was wrong. Maybe I won't be so jealous or…" Jace's throat felt too dry to continue. Of course it didn't help that Victor was looking less and less happy.

"No."

"No?"

Victor shook his head. "You're not giving up on your dreams for me. Especially because my mom is sick. You think that's going to make me feel good, watching you wither away in Warrensburg again, just because I can't bring myself to leave?"

"It's not just your—"

"I meant what I said." Victor stood, one hand clenching the swing's chain. "Texas suits you. Being away from here, that's what's right for you. Taking care of my mother, that's my burden to bear, and you know what? I'm happy to bear it. All those years she struggled to keep us both fed, all the things I ended up putting her though—now's my time to make it up to her. I wish that she wasn't sick, but at least now I can finally do the right thing. I don't need your help."

Jace clenched his jaw. "I think you do! And if you'd listen, I'm talking about more than just your mother. I'm talking about us!"

"Star's moving in with me," Victor said. "Next week. She's going to help me."

Jace felt the blood drain from his face. "Really?"

Victor sighed. "No. But your expression tells me all I need to know. Just the idea of someone else being there hurts you. I can't be the person you want me to be, Jace. Not in the long run. If you want to come to me for a night, that's one thing. But you're kidding yourself if you think you'll be any more happy with me now than when we were younger."

"Don't tell me what I feel!" Jace said through gritted teeth, but he wasn't angry. He felt like crying, and he'd promised himself a long time ago not to cry over Victor anymore. That he was tempted to now spoke volumes. Victor was right. Jace nearly hated him for it, but Victor was so damn right.

"Then again," Victor said, looking mischievous. "Bernard would probably give you a raise for having a college degree. Maybe a whole dollar!"

"Forget it," Jace said. "You had your chance. I'm going back to Texas to become an oil tycoon."

"Good," Victor said. "Do something amazing with your life so I can take credit for your formative years."

"I will."

"And the next time you're single—if things don't work out with Adrien that is—be sure to look me up. But only if you're really single. I can't stand another night of blue balls." Victor stood and offered his hand. "Come on. I'll walk you to your car."

Jace took a deep breath. Then he exhaled, grabbed Victor's hand, and clung to it until he had no choice but to let go again. Once he was in his car, sealed away from the rest of the world, he kept his promise and didn't cry. Instead he looked to the future, and tried to decide what he would make of himself.

Chapter Seventeen

"Where were you?"

Those were the exact words Jace had expected. The entire drive back to Houston, he kept hearing them, except they sounded at lot more accusatory in his imagination. In reality, Adrien sounded more concerned than anything.

"I went home," Jace said.

"To Warrensburg?" Adrien asked, sitting on the edge of their dorm room bed.

When Jace nodded, Adrien's reaction was pained, like his worst fear had come to pass.

"You went to see Victor, didn't you?"

"I went to see everyone," Jace said, tossing his car keys on the desk. He moved to the couch, sitting so he could take off his shoes. "I saw my family, and yes, I saw Victor."

Adrien bit his lip. "Did you—"

"No." Jace looked him in the eyes. "Nothing happened between us. I didn't cheat on you."

Adrien didn't seem too relieved. "I messed up," he said. "I shouldn't have been drinking like that, but the stress lately is horrible. I ended up making it worse for myself. And for you. I'm sorry."

Jace hadn't expected this. He'd been braced for an argument. From one side, at least. He'd planned on taking Victor's advice and turning his back rather than feeding into the anger. Never had he considered that Adrien would be feeling remorse. Still, this didn't change anything. Jace had thought about other things on the drive down. Things that had to happen.

"You're right," he said. "The stress is rough. And it's only going to get harder next week. That's why I think we should take a break."

"What?" Adrien looked like he'd been slapped. "No!"

Jace raised a hand. "Not like that. I'm not breaking up with you. I just think we should focus on what needs to get done. Then we can look at our relationship with clear heads. Until then, I'll sleep on the couch and try to stay out of your way. That shouldn't be hard, considering how much there is to do."

Adrien stared at him with mouth agape. Then he moved to the couch, placing thin fingers over Jace's hand. "Please don't do this! I know I was being a bitch, but I've been… I'm jealous of him. Ever since Victor came to visit, you've been different. Distant."

"I know." Jace closed his eyes briefly, feeling guilty. "I had some unresolved issues to take care of. And I did."

"That's why I was acting so crazy," Adrien said. "Well, that and everything else. I know you probably can't understand it. Someone like you never needs to feel jealous, but I'm lucky to have you. Just imagine if you were me, and one day some other guy comes along. Suddenly you feel like you have to share, like you'll never have the person you love all to yourself again."

Jace thought briefly of Star. He knew the feeling all too well. He hadn't realized he was doing the same thing to Adrien. Or something similar. Adrien was shrewd enough to know the source of Jace's mood changes. Of course he had known, and had been struggling with the same feelings Victor had once put Jace through.

"I don't want a break," Adrien said. "I want you!"

His delicate hand moved up Jace's arm, over his shoulder, to the back of his neck. Then Adrien's lips were on his. All the pent-up hormones inside Jace responded, eager to finally find release. He kissed back, did much more than that, but he did so with his eyes closed, another face haunting his fantasies. Later, when Adrien was sleeping tangled up in his arms, he told himself he would make this work.

In his heart, he already knew this was a promise he couldn't keep.

Jace was searching. The right time, the right excuse, the right words. Adrien wasn't making it easy. Suddenly he was everything a perfect boyfriend should be. He was quiet when Jace studied, wordlessly placing snacks or drinks next to him to keep him going. In the rare moments they weren't busy, Adrien was pleasant. Too pleasant. The cheerfulness felt forced from someone normally sarcastic. Jace found himself wishing for the old Adrien, but mostly in the hopes they would argue and he could break it off.

Soon finals were all they could concentrate on. Even if Jace wasn't busy, he'd be pretty low to break up with someone in the middle of so much stress. When Jace returned from the last of his finals, he found the room lit by candles, Adrien waiting with a bottle of wine. In the mood to celebrate, Jace set aside his uncertainties. Only later when Adrien started to kiss him did Jace feel empty inside, going through the motions without feeling much of anything.

That was the real problem. Regardless of how horrible or wonderful Adrien could be, Jace just didn't feel the same toward him anymore. Without those emotions, he didn't even feel like being his friend. What he wanted was to graduate and move on—another stage of his life completed, another chapter closed. Adrien seemed to feel the opposite. All he could talk about was the apartment and how wonderful it would be. Jace wished he had never signed the lease, hadn't asked his parents to cosign. He felt like he was marching toward a cage—one he would pay for the privilege of being trapped in.

As the days went by, he began to resent Adrien, no matter how nice he was being. Why couldn't he have given Jace his break? Some nights Jace felt like he couldn't breathe. He needed out. Right now. Well, not *right* now. At the moment he was waiting tables. It wouldn't be a good night for tips, since Jace was lost in his thoughts instead of charming customers. He was so distracted that he didn't even recognize a very familiar patron.

"What can I get you?" he said, already focusing on the pad of paper in his hand.

"A smile would be nice."

Jace looked up, shoulders tensing. Why did *he* have to be here? Why now?

"Are you all right?" Adrien asked.

No! How could he not recognize that? But instead Jace nodded, because he realized that maybe this was his chance. Right here. Even Adrien wouldn't make a scene in public. Would he?

"Can you sit down for a second?" Adrien asked. "I need to talk to you about something."

Jace glanced around. "Okay, but make it quick."

Adrien raised an eyebrow, a hint of his real self. "I called my parents today."

"You did?" Jace's surprise distracted him from the other issues. To say that Adrien and his parents didn't get along was putting it mildly.

"I actually invited them to the graduation ceremony."

"Wow! What did they say?"

"Oh, that they needed a new roof and the car was acting up, so they couldn't make the drive or afford the trip." Adrien rolled his eyes. "It's all bullshit."

"I'm sorry," Jace said.

"Thanks." Adrien bit his lip. "I know you wanted some private time with your parents when they come down, but do you think I could tag along? Caleb is busy with his family. Tanner too. *Everyone* is. Except for me."

Jace clenched his jaw. He couldn't help it. The only reason he wanted private time with his parents was to get away from Adrien. He was always at the dorm when Jace was off work, occupying every free moment. But now obviously wasn't the time, nor would it be until after graduation. Of course then they would be busy packing to move into their new apartment. Jace could hear the door clicking shut, the thud of locks and the jingle of chains sealing him in forever. This had to stop.

"Adrien—"

A hand fell on his shoulder. "Are you on break?"

Jace looked up into the eyes of his manager. She didn't look happy.

"Two of your tables have their food drying out under the heat lamps!"

"Sorry!" Jace hurried to his feet, but turned back before he got far. "Don't go away!"

Once back in the kitchen, he ordered Adrien's favorite meal and headed out to his tables. For the rest of his shift, he was nearly manic with glee, partially because he felt panicked, but also because he felt hope. He could do this. He *would* do this! When Adrien was finished eating, Jace brought him a glass of wine. Oil for the machine. At least he hoped it would make things go smoother. Finally his shift was at an end. He was free. Well, almost.

Taking a deep breath, he invited Adrien to walk home with him.

"You're fucking kidding yourself if you think you're moving into that apartment. *My* apartment!"

Bless every star in the sky, angry Adrien was back! Jace was so happy he felt like kissing him, which of course would defeat the purpose of this moment. They had been walking across the park to their dorm room when Jace finally said it. *We're not working out. I don't think it's going to. At least, I'm not willing to try anymore.* Adrien hadn't pleaded like the week before. Instead he flipped out, and was continuing to do so.

They were near the tree where not long ago Victor had been standing and smoking. Jace could imagine him there now, smirking and shaking his head, his opinions on relationships confirmed yet again.

"I'd give you the apartment in a heartbeat if I could," Jace said, so far managing to keep his cool. "But it's my name on the lease. The landlord wouldn't accept you as a tenant without a cosigner."

Adrien scowled. "Then sign the lease over to me!"

"With my parents' names still on it?"

Adrien growled in frustration. "I don't know why you're doing this! You can't afford the place on your own."

"Neither can you. Be happy you aren't stuck with it."

"I am," Adrien said. "It's not good enough for me. Two more years, and I'm going to be rich. What are you going to do with a degree in English Lit? What's that even good for?"

Jace shrugged.

Adrien wasn't finished. "You'll be poor your whole life and wish you'd been smart enough to stay with me."

"Could be," Jace said evenly. "Time will tell."

Adrien seemed to search his face for some way to make him angry, exhaling when he came up empty-handed. "It's *him*, isn't it? That's what this is about."

"No," Jace said. "I think it's about me. It'll never work with Victor, and it'll never work with you. I'm the common denominator in both situations, so as clichéd as it might sound, it's me, not you."

"Well then, that makes it okay. You're just going to live alone the rest of your life until you croak. I'm so happy for you!"

Jace's skin crawled. Adrien couldn't know. Jace had never told him, but that old fear rearing its ugly head now was unexpected. And unwelcome. Although even it couldn't dissuade him. He and Adrien were finished.

"You never loved me," Adrien said with a huff. "You never

said it. Not once. Do you know how fucked up and worthless that made me feel?"

Jace sighed. "I'm sorry. I really am. I hope you do end up rich. And I hope you find a guy who never makes you feel jealous or unloved, because I never wanted you to feel either of those things. I'm honestly sorry I couldn't be that person. The only thing I can do is let you go so you can find him."

Adrien glared. "So I should thank you?"

"No, you should say goodbye."

Adrien's mask slipped, and for a moment he appeared vulnerable. Then his jaw set, which was never a good sign. "Better find yourself somewhere to sleep, because you're not coming home with me!" Then he spun around and marched off.

Jace watched him go, waiting for a pang of regret somewhere deep inside, but it never manifested. Instead, he felt positively liberated. This was the right thing to do. Reaching into his pocket, he counted up his tip money for the night and wondered he could find a hotel room for thirty-two dollars.

When Jace's parents said they were bringing someone with them to his graduation, he knew better than to expect Victor. He wouldn't play with Jace's emotions like that—not after the last conversation they'd had. Jace knew it wasn't his sister, so he figured it would be Greg. As he watched from the dorm room window, standing next to the packed boxes of his possessions, Jace smiled when he saw not one, but two white-haired, balding heads get out of the car. Jace raced down the stairs to meet them, slighting his parents by hugging Bernard first.

The graduation ceremony went by in a blur. Jace's heart raced until his name was called, but slowed to a crawl while he waited for all the other graduates to receive their diplomas. After tossing his hat in the air, he left it behind to meet his family. Bernard certainly counted among them. Jace loved him too much for Bernard to simply be his friend.

Now they were gathered around a table in a restaurant packed with other parents and happy graduates. The wait staff seemed exhausted already, Jace glad not to be among them today.

"You know," Bernard said over a celebratory mug of beer, "maybe I should open up a second Bernie's down here, start competing with the big boys."

Jace laughed. "You'd look great in a cowboy hat!"

"Or you would, since you'd be running the place." Bernard shot Jace a wink.

"No, my gas station days are behind me. Thanks anyway!"

Not that he thought Bernard was really serious. Of course this begged a certain question, which his father voiced.

"What exactly *are* you going to do? You kept saying you'd figure it out after you graduated. Well, now you have."

"Bob," Jace's mother said warningly. Her voice was softer when she addressed Jace. "You can always move home."

Bernard perked up at the idea. "That would be easier than opening a new location. Come home and I'll put you in charge of the place. It's about time I retire."

Now *that* was a serious offer. Probably. Not that it mattered. "I'm still moving into that apartment," Jace said. "Even without Adrien. I'll work extra hours at the restaurant until I can find something. Maybe I'll teach or find some celebrity who wants me to pen their biography."

"You can write mine," Bob offered. *"The Secret Diary of a Dry Cleaner.* How's that for a title?"

"I can hear Hollywood calling already." Jace smiled. "Let me see how I do on my own. If I fail miserably, I promise to come home and mooch off you guys."

"You've got a good safety net in us," Bernard said. "Just remember that if things get overwhelming."

"You'll always have a home to return to," Serena said in agreement.

"Speaking of home," Jace said. "What was Michelle's excuse for not wanting to see her big brother graduate?"

Bob snorted. "Probably because she wants to—"

"Space," Serena said, cutting off her husband. "Your sister was eager to have the house to herself. When we cosigned your apartment, she practically threw a fit about needing her own place."

Jace could understand that. Living in a college town meant not needing a dorm room. Or a job to pay for expenses, so there was a trade-off. Michelle could focus on her studies, while he had to— Jace beamed suddenly. No longer would he have to juggle a job and his studies. The nightmare was over.

"A little something to help you get started," Bernard said,

sliding an envelope across the table.

"And one from us too," his mother said, handing him a greeting card.

The card was a little too heavy to be empty, and a casual squeeze of the envelope revealed the familiar outline of cash. Later, when Bernard excused himself to use the restroom, Jace allowed himself a peek. Green, green, and more green. Yes indeed, the nightmare was officially over. Let the dream begin!

In Jace's dreams, he wasn't quite so broke. The first thing he realized when moving into the apartment was how few things he owned. He didn't have a dining room table. Just as well because he didn't own any dishes. Likewise, a couch didn't have much purpose without a television across from it. The worst was not having a bed. Or shelves to house the many books he owned. At first he thought about using them to build some furniture. A stack to sit on and a few rows of books as a table. That idea lasted about half a day.

Bernard and his parents had given him a ridiculous amount of cash, probably knowing what he'd be facing. Jace made buying a bed his top priority, then very unhappily learned how much a new mattress cost. After that purchase, the budget he'd written out looked ridiculous. He skipped a bed frame. The mattress could go on the floor. No more new things, either. Jace hit a few thrift stores and charity shops, slowly covering the basics and trying to be clever. A table for eating could also serve as a desk. One of the chairs at the table could be pulled into the living room too. He couldn't justify a television, but he did find an old stereo, so he'd have some form of entertainment besides reading. The books he lined up against the walls as orderly as possible. After asking around at work, he managed to find a cheap dresser to keep his clothes in.

The rest of his money went to all the small things that added up quickly: dishes, towels, sheets, a shower curtain, pots and pans. He stocked up his kitchen with the very finest foods from the Orient (ramen noodles), Italy's most delicate cuisine (macaroni and cheese), and a selection of drinks in the event guests should stop by (Kool-Aid, lemon-lime and black cherry flavors). Luckily he got a free meal at work, which meant he wouldn't die of malnutrition.

Once he was settled, Jace had planned to drive to Missouri for a little fun with Victor. While he no longer expected them to give love a second chance, he was eager to make up for the previous visit's frustration. Unfortunately, he couldn't afford the gas. Or the time off. Jace began working more shifts that filled up his nights, leaving his days free for job-hunting. After all, having a college degree meant no longer having to wait tables. Or so he thought. Most of the jobs he applied for required experience in that particular field, which was frustrating since apparently he couldn't get experience without having previous experience.

Eventually, after a month of circling classifieds by day and hoisting trays at night, he found his first real job.

No more food industry. Jace was now working in an office as a personal assistant. The job title sounded glamorous. When he applied, he pictured following some flustered CEO around, calling the boss's wife to make excuses before arranging front-row seats at whatever the big game was that night. Instead, Jace was a secretary who was also expected to run annoying errands, like fetching takeout orders for the rest of the office. Welcome back to the food industry! At least the pay increase was substantial. And yet, his first paycheck was a few dollars less than what he could bring in working tables. Those tips on weekend nights added up quickly. Without the daily free meal, Jace calculated he was actually earning less now.

Still, the experience had to be worth something. The overworked office jockey of today was the task-delegating manager of tomorrow. Jace worked through the summer, pinching every penny he earned and mastering coupon-clipping. Eventually he upgraded his life with a microwave and coffee machine, and rarely was his refrigerator ever empty. Still, one part of him was left hungry. Except for some harmless flirting with an older guy at the office, his love life was seriously lacking. Jace had saved enough money to buy a used television, but he opted instead for a different form of entertainment. Filling the tank of his car, he headed north.

Twelve hours later, he pulled into the parking lot of Bernie's, but left again when he didn't recognize the worker behind the counter. Then he drove to a small run-down house, parked his car, and knocked on the door. The man who answered looked tired, but there was still something wild in his eyes. And his grin, when he heard what Jace had to say.

"I'm single."

"Not expecting me to change that, are you?" Victor said.

Jace shook his head. "I just mean that there's nothing we can't do." Then he added, "No limits."

Chapter Eighteen

Jace breathed in, the cold air making his lungs feel small and tight. Flurries of snow circled his head, carried on a biting wind before the flakes recovered and swayed lazily downward again. The sun's reflection off the blankets of snow nearly blinded him. He missed this. All those long winters, wishing for spring to return, and here he was enjoying weather that had everyone else in Warrensburg grumbling. Of course Jace had another reason for feeling so cheerful as he walked to his car. Soon he would see Victor again.

This time Jace had promised himself to see his family first. It hadn't been easy considering how long it had been since his last visit, since he'd kissed or touched or held anyone. Jace could have gone to bars. Occasionally he browsed personal ads, but why go to the trouble when the best lover he'd had was a drive away? Jace had planned on these visits occurring monthly, but real life had gotten in the way. Money was always tight, time always short. There were weekends he could afford a trip but opted instead to improve the home he returned to every night, or make much-needed repairs on his car. He hadn't meant to let nearly half a year slip by, but the separation would make tonight all the more delicious.

He drove first to Bernie's, not seeing Victor at the counter but still going inside when he saw an older man checking off items on a clipboard.

"If you're here for your present," Bernard said after hugging him, "you'll have to come back tomorrow."

"You're dressing up as Santa again, aren't you?" Jace said, not hiding his amusement.

"You may be too grown up to have any fun, but the kids love it."

"Not half as much as you do," Jace teased. "I'll stop by tomorrow."

"Good!" Bernard beamed at him. "You can wear the elf costume I had made."

"Please tell me you're kidding."

Bernard looked crestfallen. "It's a very nice costume. Hey, you need to tank up while you're here? It's on the house."

Jace shook his head. "Actually, I was looking for Victor."

"Oh." Bernard's jovial mood disappeared. "He doesn't come in very often."

"He quit?"

"No, he still has a job here. He tends to show up when he really needs money and asks to be paid in cash."

An uncomfortable feeling stirred in Jace's stomach. "That doesn't sound like him. Well, maybe it does, but it doesn't sound good."

Bernard mirrored his concern. "No, it doesn't. I'm worried about him too, but he doesn't open up to me anymore. Not like he used to. I was hoping you'd be able to get through to him."

"Yeah, of course." Jace was halfway to the door before realizing he hadn't even said goodbye. When he turned around, Bernard nodded in understanding and waved him away.

The drive to Victor's didn't take long but was enough time to imagine all sorts of nightmare scenarios. Maybe Victor's mother had died. Or maybe Star had introduced him to something much worse than acid and he'd find Victor's arms riddled with needle marks. When Jace pulled up to the house, he knew something was wrong. None of the Christmas lights Mrs. Hemingway enjoyed so much had been hung this year. She always relied on Victor to put them up. What if he was—

The thought was too much to bear. Jace pounded on the front door, noticing all the curtains were drawn shut. When he got no answer, he pounded again and again until the door swung open.

"What?"

Jace didn't care that Victor was scowling, or mind the black circles under his eyes. He was too glad that Victor was alive and... Unfortunately, he wasn't well. His cheeks were too gaunt and bloodless, at least from what Jace could see. Most of Victor's face was hidden beneath a full beard.

Victor sighed. "Don't look at me like that. In fact, it's probably best you don't see me at all."

The door was swinging shut when Jace snapped out of it, putting a shoulder against it to stop its progress. "Victor! What's going on?"

The resistance on the door let up. Victor gestured for him to come in. Jace did so with increasing unease. The interior was dark, only slivers of light coming from between the curtains. And it was cold. Was the heat even on? Mrs. Hemingway would have never allowed this. When Jace had seen her last, she was struggling, but she still maintained herself and her home.

The door clicked shut. Jace turned to find Victor watching him, arms crossed over his chest.

"Where's your mother. Is she okay?"

Victor's eyes narrowed. "She's great."

"I'm sorry," Jace said, his voice wavering. "You're freaking me out. Just talk to me. Did something happen? Did she pass away?"

Victor exhaled, his arms dropping to his sides. "She's still alive. If you're going to stay, come downstairs to my room. I can't stand being up here anymore."

Jace followed him down. Victor's door was closed. The second it opened, he heard a few high-pitched meows.

"Hurry up," Victor said, squeezing into the room. "Don't let him get out."

Jace followed, expecting a disaster beyond, but the room was still organized. One of the comfy chairs from upstairs was here now, as was a side table. The bed was covered in quilts and a few books. The basement window was unobscured, allowing natural daylight in. Best of all was the big-eyed kitten that stumbled over to greet them. Jace's worry was momentarily forgotten as he stooped to pet gray fur, the kitten's orange eyes brimming with so much innocence that the poor thing looked like it had just received a lobotomy.

"You're so tiny!" Jace said to it before laughing. When he looked up, even Victor had a subtle smile on his face.

"That's Samson. Cute little thing, isn't he?"

"He's so adorable that it's overwhelming. You should make him wear a grotesque mask or something."

"Now there's an idea. Whatever happened to that werewolf mask of mine?"

Stowed away in a dresser drawer at Jace's Houston apartment, but he wasn't about to admit that. "I pictured you as more of a dog person," he teased. "Cats are so domestic."

Victor grimaced. "He was supposed to be for my mom. I thought having something to focus on would help her."

Jace turned his attention away from the cat. "What happened?"

Victor sat on the edge of the bed, head hung, long hair obscuring his face. "She kept getting worse—forgetting where she'd put things right after setting them down, or acting confused about where she was. Sometimes she would get paranoid, like I was trying to trick her. It was a nightmare, but I was taking care of her. She was never hungry or dirty."

Victor raised his head, brushing the hair from his angry eyes. "I took care of her better than any stupid nurse in a crappy state-run home! I love her! What can they possibly do for her that I can't?"

Jace sat next to Victor on the bed, putting an arm around him and mumbling how sorry he was. The words were insufficient, but all he could think to say.

"She was wandering the neighborhood in her nightgown," Victor said. "First snow of the year. Someone out walking their dog spotted Mom. When they tried talking to her, she wasn't making any sense, so they called the police. If I hadn't been working that night—" His voice ended in a squeak. Jace pulled him close, letting him cry while his mind raced, trying to find a way he could make this right.

"We can get her back," he said. "Have you tried?"

"Of course I've tried," Victor said, pulling away. "They say she needs twenty-four hour supervision."

It killed Jace to say it, but he had to. "Maybe she does. I mean, you can't always watch her. You have to work or go out for groceries sometime."

Victor tensed, his lips pulled back to retort, but then he shook his head. "Maybe you're right."

"Can we go visit her? I'd like to see her again."

"It's a long walk, but yeah."

"I can drive you," Jace said. He eyed Victor. Mrs. Hemingway probably wouldn't like seeing her son in this condition. When was the last time he'd taken a shower or eaten a decent meal? "I wanna grab something to eat first," he suggested casually.

Victor shrugged his indifference.

Jace took his hand, noticing how cold it was. "Is the heat turned on?"

"Got shut off a few weeks ago."

"Can they do that in winter?"

Victor shrugged again.

Okay. Enough was enough. As much as Jace didn't want to hurt Victor's feelings, he also didn't like seeing him in such a pathetic state. After nagging and briefly arguing, he got Victor to hand over the utility bills to the house. "Maybe we can bring her home for Christmas," he said, knowing he was being manipulative. "Do you want her coming home to a cold house?"

Once he had the information he needed, he made a few calls, then headed into town alone to take care of business. He had a very stupid discussion with a man at the gas company who insisted Jace couldn't have the gas turned back on because the service wasn't in his name. He argued that he only wanted to pay the debt, which would then mean they could resume service. In the end, he spoke with the man's manager, who was much more sensible. She helped Jace and assured him that the gas would be back on within the hour.

Looking at the other bills, Jace saw the electricity was on the verge of being turned off, so he went to pay it too. So much for his savings account! Then he went to the grocery store, picking up the same cheap staples he lived on, along with some food for Samson. By the time he got back to Victor's house, the heater was blowing much-needed warmth through the vents. He walked through the house, opening curtains before dragging Victor upstairs.

"I'm hungry and need to cook something," Jace said, not leaving him a choice. "I can't afford to eat out."

Victor came along reluctantly, Samson happy to follow and gleeful when a can of gooey cat food was slopped onto a plate for him. Victor watched the cat gobble it all up, chuckling at his scoffing noises. "He's only had dry kibble before."

Jace smiled. "Well then, Merry Christmas, Samson. There's more where that came from."

A couple of frozen pizzas and generic-brand soda filled their stomachs. After eating, Victor looked better. Not great, but halfway human. He was acting less morose too. "Visiting hours are only until six p.m.," he said, looking hopeful.

"Then you still have time to get cleaned up," Jace said pointedly. "Do me a favor and lose the beard."

"Why?" Victor asked. "You don't like it?"

"It's fine, but I'm not sure I can find your lips in there. Make it easy on me and shave it off."

"What do you need to find my lips for?" Victor asked, but he headed toward the bathroom without further prompting.

When he heard the shower running, Jace exhaled. They'd been on the brink of disaster, but things were going to be okay. Samson wobbled across the table to him, plopped down on the placemat, belly swollen with food, and stared at Jace with big eyes.

"Don't worry, little guy," Jace said. "I'm going to make it all better."

Closing his eyes contentedly, Samson began to purr.

The nursing home wasn't quite what Jace had expected. In his mind, he had pictured more flowers, sunlight streaming through every lace-curtained window. Or nurses chatting happily as they slowly rolled a wheelchair-bound patient through gardens. Heaven before actually getting to Heaven. Faced with reality, Jace realized just how naïve this vision was.

His first impression after being buzzed inside was that they'd reached a waiting room full of elderly patients. A television blared in one corner of the room, wrinkled faces gathered around to absorb the latest daytime soap opera. Random clusters of tables were filled with elderly crossword enthusiasts, chairs occupied by magazine readers. Everywhere else they looked, old people sat and observed their surroundings with weary eyes. Waiting. Jace thought they would have to sit among them and wait too, until he realized this was it. This was their destination.

He glanced over at Victor, who didn't show any surprise, even when an old woman walked up to them. She was muttering under her breath, touching her ear, then her shoulder. Ear. Shoulder. Over and over again.

"Hello," Jace tried.

The old woman didn't stop her stream of incoherent mumbling, or her strange touching ritual, even as she wandered away again.

"Mom's room is this way," Victor said, nodding toward the right.

Ahead of them was a nurses station, hallways branching out on either side of it. Victor seemed eager to skirt this, but one of the nurses spotted them.

"Excuse me? Mr. Hemingway?"

Victor stopped, shoulders tense as he turned. "What?"

The nurse, heavyset with tightly curled hair, narrowed her

eyes. "You know you have to sign in and out."

Victor stomped over to the station and grabbed a clipboard from the counter. The nurse turned her attention to Jace, regarding him with the same suspicion, but relaxing a little when he smiled. He read her name tag. Sandra Bennett.

"Visiting hours end at six," she said.

Victor tossed down the pen, having finished signing in. "No one can forbid me from seeing my mother," he said before turning and walking down the hall.

The nurse watched him go, her face turning red with anger.

"The holidays are rough on him," Jace explained.

"That's understandable," she said grudgingly. "Then again, they're rough on us all." Something over Jace's shoulder caught her eye. "Marcy, you put your robe back on!" Sighing, the nurse rushed off. Jace stared after her, his eyes unwillingly taking in more wrinkled flesh than he ever wanted to see before he hurried after Victor.

His stomach felt tight with dread. Being here wasn't quite the same as being in a mental hospital, but it was disturbingly close. He could already see why Victor wanted his mother at home, no matter how difficult taking care of her might be. Jace braced himself for anything when entering the room Victor led them to. Maybe Mrs. Hemingway would be restrained to the bed, or raving like a lunatic.

He exhaled with relief when they found her sitting in a chair by the window, watching the light snow flurries with a pleasant smile. She looked good. Not older or more haggard. She was clean and had a rosy glow to her cheeks. Jace could almost imagine that her being here was some terrible mistake.

The room itself wasn't impressive. Two single beds with rails that could be lowered and raised. They navigated around these, Victor taking the lead and stopping two feet away from his mother.

"Hello," he said.

"Oh, hello!" she replied.

Why weren't they hugging? Why didn't she look more excited to see her son?

"How are you doing?" Victor asked.

"Fine. Did you come to tell me it's time for lunch?"

"No," Victor replied. "Lunch is over. Didn't you eat?"

"Oh, that's right! I did eat. Thank you." Mrs. Hemingway turned back to the window, as if this concluded their business.

"Jace is here," Victor said.

Stepping closer and feeling awkward, Jace said hello.

Mrs. Hemingway smiled and nodded cordially. "Hello."

Dread settled at the bottom of Jace's stomach. She seemed distant, if not downright cold. Victor didn't seem perturbed. He sat on the edge of the nearest bed. Mrs. Hemingway seemed a little put off by this behavior, but he soon distracted her with conversation.

"I used to love building snowmen," he said, nodding at the window. "I always thought they should have a beard. You told me once that Santa has a beard to help keep him warm in cold weather, so I figured snowmen needed one too."

Mrs. Hemingway laughed. "You can use a mop," she said. "Or cut a beard out of felt."

"That's exactly what you did," Victor said. "Every year you'd come up with something different. Remember the year we used straw?"

Mrs. Hemingway's smile faltered. "How do you know all that? Who are you?"

Jace felt like crying, or maybe running to the nurses station to tell them something had gone horribly wrong. How could she not remember her own son? The worst was that Victor didn't seem fazed by this, which meant he had lived through it before.

"Look at my face," he said, brushing the hair from it. "Look carefully."

Mrs. Hemingway shifted in her seat. She was trying. Her eyes narrowed in concentration, then puzzlement, and finally joy. "Richard! Oh, I'm so sorry." She stood, placed her hands on Victor's cheeks. "How silly of me. Oh, you look handsome. When did your hair get so long?"

Victor smiled, gently moving away her hands. "I keep meaning to get it cut," he said. "Sit down, Rachel. Please."

Jace tried to keep up. Who was Richard? For the next fifteen minutes, he listened as Victor repeatedly guided the conversation back to his childhood. A few times Mrs. Hemingway acted confused about who either of them were. She mentioned Richard again too. Eventually, Victor seemed exhausted and gestured that they should go.

"You need to sign out," Sandra said from the nurses station.

"I'm just going out for a smoke," Victor snapped. "I'm not leaving my mother alone so quickly."

Jace followed him outside, but kept his mouth shut until Victor had a cigarette lit and had inhaled a few times. Then Jace started slowly. "It's hard seeing her like that," he said. "I'm sorry."

Victor nodded. "Today was a good day. Sometimes she's angry. Or scared. Mom will react to me like I'm a stranger breaking into her home. She can give the nurses hell too. That one in there, Sandra, she gets on my nerves. I saw my mother tear into her once, screaming up a storm about how she was going to call the police and have her shot, but Sandra kept her cool." Victor scowled at the concrete walkway, jaw clenching. "I wish I could do that. You know I think it's pointless to get angry about things that can't be changed. I can't help it though. Part of me wants to knock this place to the ground, brick by brick, just so I can take her home again. No, fuck that. I want to destroy it just for the satisfaction. I want to break the world for being the sort of place where this can happen."

Jace remained quiet, letting Victor smoke his cigarette and not commenting when he finished and lit another. Only when his face had returned to its normal color did he dare to ask. "Does she ever remember you?"

"Yes," Victor said. "Less and less, but if I'm persistent, I can get through to her. Or she'll think I'm Richard. That's my father. I guess I look like him or something. When that happens, I try to play along, hoping it'll be a bridge back to me." Victor closed his eyes and shook his head. "I don't know what I'm doing."

"I wish I could help."

Victor shook his head again, but then looked up. "When we go back in, let me try by myself. I think it's confusing for her that there are two of us. Maybe you can talk to the nurse about us bringing her home."

"Okay," Jace said. "No problem."

Except Victor's attitude made the atmosphere at the nurses station tense. Jace sidled up, tried a smile that Sandra didn't return. Instead she continued rolling up cutlery into cloth napkins.

"Any way I can help?" Jace asked.

"With your friend or in general?" she huffed.

"Sorry," Jace said. "He doesn't mean to act that way. He even said what a good job you're doing."

"Ha!"

Okay, maybe Jace was laying it on thick. "Fine. He said he wished he could keep his cool, like he saw you do with his mother."

Sandra seemed somewhat placated by this. "It's normal what he's going through," she said. "Adults tend to cry. The young ones, they get angry. Usually it's a grandparent. When it happens to your parent…" She shook her head. "That's rough."

"She's all Victor has," Jace said. "It's just him and his mother."

Sandra seemed taken aback by this. "No other family?"

"No one."

She looked up from her task, hands still working. "Wife or girlfriend?"

"Nobody. Just me." And Star, he supposed. Jace wondered what she thought of all this.

"You seem like a good friend," Sandra said. After a moment, she added. "I'm sorry he's on his own. I didn't know that."

"I think he'll be all right, once he adjusts. I mean, people get used to it, right?"

"Their parents slowly forgetting who they are?" Sandra finished rolling the last napkin and set it on the pile. "You want the fairy tale answer or the truth?"

"The truth," Jace said.

"We all lose our parents. One way or another, we watch them go, and it's never easy. Every single one of us goes through that trial, and I can't say you come out stronger, but you sure as hell appreciate your parents more when they're gone. With a slow death, at least you learn that lesson soon enough to tell them."

"I should have asked for the fairy tale version," Jace said.

Sandra laughed. "Yes, you should have."

Now seemed like a good time to try, while he had her laughing. "Listen, do you think we can take Mrs. Hemingway home tomorrow for the holiday? Just for the day."

"I don't recommend it," she said. "I understand wanting to bring a loved one home for Christmas, but at her stage of Alzheimer's, you're in for a struggle. Getting her settled into her routine here was the best thing for her."

"Regardless," Jace said. "If we wanted to try, just to see how she does, would we be allowed?"

Sandra looked offended. "Of course! This isn't a prison. Mr. Hemingway has DPOA."

"DPOA?"

"Durable power of attorney. If your friend wants to take his mother out of here forever, he can. I've told him that myself, but I've also chewed his head off for even suggesting it. I can't divulge what's in her file. You'll have to ask him how she came to be here, but I keep telling him that taking care of someone in her condition is a twenty-four hour job. Now that I know he's alone, things make a lot more sense, but I'm even more determined that she stay."

"But it's not up to you," Jace repeated.

"No it's not," Sandra said, crossing meaty arms over her chest.

Jace would hate to tangle with her. Not that he intended to. "Sorry. I just wanted to be sure I understood. He acts like this is all against his will."

Sandra let her arms drop. "Honey, nobody wants this for their parents, even if it's best for them. Like I said, the young ones are angry. You want my advice?"

Jace nodded.

"Bring Christmas to her. Decorate the room, put up a small tree and do it all here. Taking her home again isn't going to bring her back, but a little home here can do wonders. Not a miracle, but I think she'd enjoy it."

"Okay," Jace said. "Thanks."

Duty called Sandra away after that. Jace sat in the main room and waited, thinking over what he had learned and trying to imagine what he would do in a similar situation. He and his sister had always been braced for their parents to die earlier than they were ready for. That fear came with having older parents, but he hadn't seriously considered one of them slowly forgetting who they were.

Soon an old woman sat next to Jace and chatted to him about her grandkids. She seemed happy enough, if not a little desperate for conversation, which helped improve his opinion of the place. He talked with her until Victor reappeared.

"Ready to go?"

"Yeah," Jace said, standing and saying goodbye to the old woman. On the way out the door, he braced himself and asked, "How did it go?"

"I was Richard for the rest of the visit, but at least she thought she knew me. Better than being a stranger. Come on."

During the drive home, Jace told him what Sandra had said. At least about Christmas plans. Victor didn't take it well.

"She doesn't know. None of them do! My mom loved Christmas. Maybe it will help her remember."

"Maybe it won't," Jace said carefully. "When she still lived at home, was she forgetting who you were?"

"Yes," Victor hissed. "But that could have been a bad phase."

"I don't think it works that way."

"Suddenly you're an expert?"

Jace could feel the heat of Victor's glare. "No, but that nurse deals with this sort of thing every day. I can't say I like that place, but your mom seems cared for. And safe. Can you honestly offer her that at home?"

"Do I have a choice?" Victor shot back.

Jace swallowed, unsure if he wanted to go there, but he and Victor had never shied away from the truth. Not with each other. "She also said you have power of attorney, so yes, you do have a choice."

Victor was quiet. They were parking in front of the house when he spoke again, his voice terse. "I don't have a choice because you're right. I know I can't take care of her the way she needs me to. They can, and I resent them for it because it should be me. I'm just a fuck-up. It should be me, but I know I can't do it."

"You're not a fuck-up," Jace said, reaching over to take his hand. "And you're still there for her. Maybe deep down she still recognizes you. She would want you to keep visiting and would be proud of your bravery."

"Jace—" Victor said, sounding like he wanted him to stop.

But he wasn't quite done. "Tomorrow is Christmas. We'll go there in the morning, decorate her room, and count how many times we make her smile, no matter who she thinks we are."

Victor sighed, looked out the window at the house. Dusk was approaching, and no windows were lit. A house was an empty shell without a family inside.

"Deal?" Jace pressed.

Victor nodded. "Deal."

"You're glad I'm here, aren't you?" Jace breathed, touching the tips of their noses together.

From beneath him, Victor smiled, reaching up to toy with one of his ears. "I never said I wasn't."

"But you never said you were," Jace prompted.

"Okay. I'm glad you're here."

Jace kissed him and grinned. "I knew it!"

"And yet, you still needed me to say it."

"Yeah."

Victor's hands found his hips and ran up the sides of his torso, bunching up his shirt the higher they went. "Take it off."

Jace pushed himself up to a sitting position, Victor's hard bulge beneath his rump. He stripped off his shirt and tossed it to the bedroom floor. From the side table, a little gray kitten had its huge eyes fixated on them.

"Uh, what's Samson staring at?" Jace asked.

"He probably thinks we're fighting for dominance," Victor said. "He's waiting to see who wins."

"Well I *am* on top."

Victor smirked. "We both know that's not how things will play out."

Jace glared at him, forcefully pulling Victor's shirt up and over his head. Then Jace stretched out on his side next to him so he could run fingers from his chest to his stomach and back again. "So if Samson's never seen anything like this before, that means you haven't gotten much action."

"At home, at least," Victor said. After a humble expression, he added. "Or anywhere. Not since your last visit."

"Really?" Jace said a little too hopefully.

"Don't take it as a sign of commitment," Victor said.

"I wasn't."

"You were."

Jace shrugged. "Okay, so maybe the thought crossed my mind."

Victor gave him a knowing look, then rolled over on top of him. Bracing himself with his arms, he pressed down with his hips, rubbing their crotches together in a steady rhythm. "You still like it slow?" he asked.

"I guess."

"You guess?"

Jace bit his lip, thought about drawing blood just to distract from the question. And the emotions filling him. "I don't do this with anyone but you."

"You mean—"

"I'm a top," Jace said.

Victor chuckled, but then his face grew serious. "Really?"

"Yeah."

"We don't have to—"

"No!" Jace said. "I like it. But only with you."

Victor's eyes searched his. "Should I take that as a sign of commitment?"

"No, but only because I don't want to scare you away." Jace laughed at Victor's glare. "Commitment or not, when is this going to end? Are we going to be ninety years old and still playing this game?"

"I hope so," Victor said, but then shook his head and rolled off to the side. Propped up on one elbow, he considered Jace. "No, eventually you're going to meet someone worthy of you and wander off."

"Will he be pretty?"

"Breathtaking."

"And he'll want a commitment?"

Victor thought about it briefly. "He'll propose on the first date and expect the wedding to happen on the second."

"And on the third date?"

"Matching tattoos."

Jace sat up. "And if I tire of this gorgeous, clingy man?"

"Then you'll come back here to discover that I've kept my promise."

Love. Victor still had it for him after all this time. And if they wanted, they could keep making it together for the rest of their lives. In fact, Jace was up for making some right now. But first he gently picked up the kitten, set him outside the room, and closed the door.

Chapter Nineteen

On Christmas morning, Jace showered at Victor's and then drove to his parents' house. Gone were the days anyone woke up at five to celebrate. When Jace arrived at nine, his sister had just crawled out of bed. He went through rituals that once thrilled him but now left him bored. Not that the presents weren't nice, or that he was too grown-up for such things, but this year he had more on his mind. When his mother expressed frustration at how withdrawn he seemed, Jace apologized and told them about the nursing home.

"That explains a lot," Michelle said. "Greg mentioned that he hadn't seen Victor around lately."

"I don't know who I feel more sorry for," his mother said, pressing a hand to her cheek. "What Victor is going through is terrible, but to forget your own children…"

The festive mood became somber until Jace mentioned their plans to give Mrs. Hemingway a good Christmas. That sent his family into action. They repurposed a few presents, such as scented candles and a coffee table book of wildlife photos, Jace's dad wrapping them while Serena gathered food they could take along. Once his car was packed with these things, Jace headed over to Victor's.

Meeting him at the door, Victor seemed somewhat pensive. Jace asked him to help load the Christmas decorations they had sorted out the night before. That got him moving and more optimistic. At the nursing home, Jace was surprised to see Sandra on duty again.

"Don't you ever go home?" he teased.

"No," she grumped. "Even if I got time off, I probably wouldn't know where home is."

Jace slipped her a frosted Christmas cookie for her troubles. Then came the moment of truth: carrying boxes into Mrs. Hemingway's room. He worried she might find it upsetting or confusing and send them away. She appeared uncertain at first, clearly not recognizing either of them, but when the first decoration came out of the box, she was hooked. Jace had pictured her sitting in her chair and watching them work, but she wanted to help. The part of her that loved the holidays remained intact.

Mrs. Hemingway's roommate, an elderly black woman who repeatedly smacked her lips over her toothless gums, also seemed to enjoy it. Jace hooked her up with some cookies as well, and she treated them to very whistley versions of a few Christmas carols.

They stayed until the very last minute of visiting hours, and as evening approached, Jace could feel Victor getting impatient for the breakthrough he was dreaming of. Jace hoped for it too—anything small, even just Mrs. Hemingway getting Victor's name right. In the end, their Christmas miracle didn't happen. After dinner, they left his mother smiling at the door to her room.

"You're such wonderful people," she said. "Truly wonderful!"

Victor hesitated. Jace imagined he was probably hoping for a hug. Victor's mother shook his hand and patted them both on the shoulder when she said goodbye. That would have to do.

"I'm sorry," Jace said when they were back out in the crisp night air.

"Nah," Victor said with a hollow smile. "You showed me she can still be happy. That's all that matters. I want her to feel good."

Jace knew much more than that mattered, but he felt relieved when Victor's fingers intertwined with his own before pulling him close.

"And she's right," Victor said. "You are truly wonderful."

"So are you," Jace said, giving Victor the hug his mother no longer could. "Merry Christmas."

Staying wasn't an option. As the holidays wound down, Victor made sure to drive this point home, but he didn't need to push much. Jace had expected this, understood how things would be. But he promised to return a couple of weeks later.

Life back in Texas returned to normal: answering phones, typing letters, and running errands by day. His free time was spent clipping coupons and finding free things to do, like exploring the city by foot or hitting the library for something new to read. He wanted every spare penny going toward his next trip to Missouri.

On the Friday he planned to start the drive north, he was leaving work to run an errand when his car's engine wouldn't start. There was no indication as to why. No grinding or chugging. Jace turned the key and nothing happened. Suspecting his battery was dead, he got a jump-start from a coworker, but even that didn't help. After staring at the engine and not knowing what to do, he called a tow truck. Hours later at the shop, he was given the bad news. He didn't understand half of it, but he took the list of needed repairs to a payphone and called his dad.

"Do you think I should even bother?" he asked. "Wouldn't it make more sense to get a new car?"

"It's twelve years old," his father said, "and they sure as hell don't build them like they used to. My Thunderbird went through—"

"Dad," Jace said impatiently.

"No, you're right. At this point, you either need to plan on fixing things as they break down, or you need to finance a new car. Do you think you can handle a car payment every month?"

Jace could barely handle groceries. "No."

"I see. Have them make the repairs for now and start saving. Maybe your mother and I can help a little bit when you have enough for a down payment."

Not the news Jace wanted to hear. He didn't expect his parents to buy him a new car, but he had hoped his dad knew some clever way out of the situation he hadn't considered. The worst, of course, was the money he'd saved for his trip being eaten up by the repairs. Those would take a few days, so Jace was trapped no matter what.

Once back at his apartment, he tried calling Victor, not surprised that the number had been disconnected. Then he called Greg, who said he hadn't seen Victor lately. Jace left a message with him anyway. After thinking it over, he called Bernie's in the hopes Bernard was there. He was in luck.

"Victor was coming in regular at the start of the year," Bernard said. "The last few days he's been missing in action again. I always have to schedule someone else to be here, because I never know if he'll show."

"You don't have to put up with that," Jace said, quickly adding, "but I'm glad you do."

"Yeah, I wouldn't be able to sleep at night either. He'll show up again. When he does, I'll give him your message. Sorry to hear about your car. You need a loan?"

"Jesus, Bernard! You're too nice! How is it that you're not broke?"

Bernard's laugh crackled over the receiver. "I'd be a whole

lot richer if I was mean, wouldn't I?"

"Yes. And thanks, but I'll be all right."

"Okay. When you do make it up here, you stop in and see me. Maybe I can take a look at your car and avert the next crisis."

Jace wished he could push the piece of junk up there right now. Or push it into a lake. After thanking Bernard, he hung up, mentally tightened his belt, and went to the classifieds to look for a second job.

Three more weeks passed before Jace was able to make the trip. In the interim, he called Bernard and Greg a few times as a way of checking up on Victor. Greg still hadn't seen him. Bernard had, but it was becoming less and less common. Jace tried to put a positive spin on this. Maybe Victor was spending too much time with his mother, or had cooked up some new scheme for his life. Maybe Star was wining and dining him, still trying to win his heart completely.

When Jace cruised into Warrensburg, he felt relieved that he wouldn't have to wonder anymore. Parking in front of Victor's house and trotting up to the door, he felt a race of nervousness, excitement, and need. No doubt about it. He'd fallen for Victor again, heavier and harder than ever before. When he saw the envelope taped to the front door, his nervousness edged ahead of his other feelings.

'Hemingway' was written across the white paper, so Jace ignored it and knocked on the door. He continued to stare at the envelope while he waited for an answer. When it didn't come, curiosity got the better of him. The envelope was only folded shut, not glued, allowing him to read the letter inside. He scanned it once, then read it again more carefully. He returned the letter to the envelope and sighed.

Rent was long overdue. Jace always assumed Mrs. Hemingway owned this house. That obviously wasn't the case. If rent wasn't paid in a couple more weeks, Victor would be evicted. Jace knocked again and then tried the doorknob. It turned under his hand.

Letting himself in, he breathed in stale air tainted with cigarette smoke. The house was dark, the curtains pulled. He didn't know Victor was there until he spoke.

"Well, well. Look what the cat dragged in."

Jace flinched. When Victor came toward him, he felt oddly threatened. Even in the dark he could see that Victor's beard had returned. Jace moved away to open the curtains and let in the dwindling light. Then he turned to consider Victor again.

He looked like shit. The assessment was harsh but accurate. The beard didn't hide the sunken cheeks or the pale clammy skin, or that the shine had gone from his long dark hair. "Are you okay?" Jace asked. "You look... sick."

"I'm fine," Victor said, waving a hand.

Jace couldn't pull his eyes away, the feeling of unease still not having left him. Luckily, Samson came bounding into the room. Already he was bigger. Jace reached down to pet him. Even the cat looked malnourished.

"Hungry?" Jace said to him, but then looked up to Victor, who shrugged.

"I've been fasting," he said.

"Right, well, time to break that fast."

Jace moved toward the kitchen, opening curtains and blinds on the way, or switching on lamps. He found food in the cupboard, only a partial relief since most were things he had bought last time. From the backpack he had slung over one shoulder, he took out the presents he had brought with him—cans of food for Samson and a six-pack of beer for him and Victor to share.

"Oh, nice." Victor said, coming up next to him at the counter. He didn't smell very good. When's the last time he'd taken a shower?

"Feed the cat first," Jace snapped when Victor reached for a beer.

Then he busied himself with boiling water, staring at the macaroni and cheese instructions when he didn't have anything else to do. He felt... angry? Disappointed? Disgusted? He found he couldn't settle on just one thing. When Jace had found Victor like this last time, it had felt good bringing him back from the edge. Not that he'd been happy to see Victor down in the dumps, but at least it allowed Jace a way to show his affection by helping. By the time he'd left, Victor had been smiling again. Now, in barely more than a month, Victor had reverted to that same miserable condition. Maybe worse.

Still, what could he do? Sighing, Jace turned around to face the kitchen. Samson was licking a plate clean. Victor leaned against the refrigerator, watching him.

"How's your mother doing?" Jace asked.

Victor considered the question. "I'm sure she's fine."

"You haven't been going to see her?"

Victor went to the beer, taking one but then raising his eyebrows, as if seeking permission. Jace nodded.

Victor cracked open the can and took a swig. "There's no point in going to see her if she doesn't know who I am."

Anger rose in Jace's chest again, so he turned away to finish making the meal. When the food was done, he served most of it on one plate. Jace had left his appetite at the door.

"I'm not hungry," Victor said.

"Eat," Jace insisted.

They sat on opposite ends of the table, like monarchs trapped in a cold marriage. While Victor ate, Jace studied him. He felt like shouting, but kept reminding himself that it wouldn't make a difference. Not with Victor. But he couldn't just sit there and pretend like nothing was wrong.

"What are you doing?" he asked. "Bernard said you haven't been showing up at work much. Did you see the letter taped to your door?"

"Another one?" Victor asked with disinterest.

"You've gotten this notice before?"

Victor gave a single nod. "This makes three."

"That's serious!" Jace said. He wasn't sure, but he thought there was some law about three notices. Regardless, it was clear from the most recent letter that they wanted money soon or else. "I can't afford to pay this."

Victor snorted. "I didn't ask you to. Do you think I want to live here?"

"No," Jace said with a huff. "No doubt you'd like to be out in the woods somewhere, but it's still winter. You need somewhere to stay, at least until then."

"I'll be fine," Victor said with his typical self-assurance.

"You don't look fine," Jace mumbled.

Samson hopped up on the table, sniffing Victor's plate before padding to Jace. Petting him, Jace felt the pronounced ribs on his side. From the cats his mother had over the years, he knew this wasn't normal.

"Look," Jace said, his temper rising, "it's one thing if you don't want to take care of yourself, but at least feed the goddamn cat!"

"I've been trying to."

"How? By doing what?"

Instead of replying, Victor crossed his arms over his chest and leaned back in the chair.

Jace couldn't do this. Not again. "I have to go see my family," he said. "I'll come back tomorrow. If you love me, please get your shit together before then."

Before Victor could respond, Jace was on his feet and heading for the door. Once he was in his car he felt like screaming. Instead he looked back at Victor's house, hoping to see him standing at the door and showing remorse. But he wasn't there, nor was his silhouette in any of the windows.

Jace found his mother cooking in the kitchen. The house was clean, if a little chaotic, but at least it was full of light and noise and life. He felt a pang of regret for snapping at Victor, imagining how dark and dingy this house would become without his parents in it. Then again, he'd still try to make them proud by living the best life he could.

After giving his mother a desperate hug that made her giggle, he asked where the rest of his family was.

"Your father is out running an errand. The other two are downstairs."

Other two? Jace went down to the family room to find Michelle and Greg watching a movie together. As usual, Greg was talking over the explosions and car chases. When they saw Jace, they stood up and turned off the TV.

"What are you doing here?" Jace asked.

"I heard you'd be in town today." Greg looked bashful as he said this. Jace didn't even know he was capable of that.

"So you're forcing my sister to watch one of your horrible movies?" He turned to Michelle. "Or are you trying to steal away my best friend?"

Michelle and Greg laughed. A lot. This gave Jace pause, but his mind kept returning to Victor. Just thinking of him so disheveled and unhealthy made Jace's heart ache and his head hurt.

"Listen," he said. "I don't think I'm going to be good company tonight. Why don't you guys watch your movie? I think I'll go lie down."

"Okay," Greg said. "Are you sure? We don't have to watch the flick."

"It's not the movie," Michelle said, studying him. "Are you okay?"

"Don't psychoanalyze me," Jace said. His sister was majoring in psychology, which would suit her well, but he didn't want to be part of her studies. "I'll be fine. I just need some quiet."

Jace left them looking puzzled and went to his room. Once there, he shut the door. Little remained of his previous life. The bed and the rest of the furniture were still there. The desk was now covered with his father's papers. The posters and childish things had been cleared away, but the room still gave shape to memories. Victor, sleeping next to him in bed. Or standing at the open window, sneaking a cigarette in the middle of the night by exhaling through the screen. He had been so amazing then, so impossible and unguessable. Now…

Jace couldn't bear to think of it. Past or present, he didn't want any part of it. His sister and his best friend were a few floors down, and he was ignoring them just because his ex-boyfriend was a mess? Forget that! He wasn't going to mope around his room, doing an imitation of Victor. Returning downstairs again, Jace found Greg and Michelle talking quietly on the couch, the television still turned off.

"Maybe we should talk," Greg said.

"Or maybe we should go out for some drinks," Jace said, smiling at them. "Come on. Let's set this town on fire!"

"Sports bar!" Greg said, punching the air.

Michelle rolled her eyes. "I want to actually talk to my brother, not shout over some stupid game. Besides, you promised me a real meal."

Jace raised an eyebrow. "He did?"

"I owe her money," Greg said. "Real food and drinks it is. On me. Come on, I'll even drive."

Greg took them to a Chinese restaurant, but Jace barely noticed. He'd begun ranting about Victor in the car, and continued to complain after they were seated in a booth backed by ornate wooden carvings. His sister ordered for him when he realized he hadn't looked at the menu, and his food was cold by the time he finally wound down.

"He has to do something with his life, right?" Jace said. "I mean, he can't just keep rotting away in that house until they throw him out on the street."

"First of all," Michelle said, pointing at his plate, "eat. Second, maybe that's what it will take for Victor to finally grow up. I know you've always loved that he's a complete weirdo, but he'll have to face reality eventually. Sometimes you have to let a person hit bottom so they can bounce back."

"But—" Jace said with a mouth full of Peking duck.

"But nothing," Michelle said. "I know what he's going through with his mother is hard, but he's not the only one this has happened to. Other people don't let themselves fall apart. The problem started way before she got sick. Victor has always struggled. He used his mother as a crutch, and he used you as one too. Now he finally needs to learn to walk on his own."

"We've all tried to help him," Greg said. "Michelle is right. If we coddle him any more, he'll never change. Bernard's the only one that's doing it right by offering him a job. Victor will choose to work rather than starve. I promise."

"You can't promise that," Michelle countered. "People end up on the street for all sorts of reasons. Maybe it's alcoholism or mental illness, or maybe some people just can't cope with life's demands. Victor might be one of those people."

Greg looked concerned. "You think he'll end up on the street?"

"He might," Michelle said with all the authority of her would-be degree.

Jace let the horror show on his face. "You guys aren't making me feel better."

"Sorry, big brother, but you've got to face the facts. Victor's life is his own responsibility. You can't save him without giving up your own, and he won't thank you for it. As selfish as he can be, he's always wanted the best for you."

Greg nodded. "She speaks the truth. I can't tell you how often I've heard him say he's proud of you for doing your own thing. After all, that's what Victor is all about. He respects the decisions you've made."

"So what do I do?" Jace said. "Turn my back completely and let him crash?"

"He'll crash anyway," Michelle said. "There's only so much you can do. Like you said, you can't pay his rent and bills. You can't make him be more responsible. But you're still my wonderful big brother, so I know you'll try to save him anyway. I just don't want you to be totally shocked when you realize that you can't. None of us can."

"I think I need that drink now."

They agreed to move to a bar. When the waitress brought their bill, three fortune cookies rested on the plastic tray. Without having to ask, all three were shoved in Jace's direction. He felt a surge of affection for them both.

"You don't have to give them to me."

"Everyone knows what a whore you are for them," Michelle said with a grin. "Just don't forget to give us our fortunes."

Jace felt a little embarrassed, sitting there and eating all three cookies while they watched, but damn if he didn't love how they tasted! Why were people always going on about chocolate chip cookies or whatever when they could be eating something so wonderfully crisp? Mixing up the three fortunes, he passed them out randomly.

Michelle read hers first. "'Ignorance is the greatest cause of arrogance, and knowledge the best cure for both.'" She thought about this for a moment. "Well fuck you, fortune cookie!"

Greg laughed and then read his. "'One doesn't need to travel to find love, not if one is already home.'"

"What's that supposed to mean?" Jace asked.

Greg's cheeks looked a little flushed. "I guess I'm staying in Warrensburg. What else could it mean?"

Jace eyed him, shook his head, and turned his attention to his own fortune. "'Never loose your sense of humor.'"

"Loose?" Michelle asked.

Jace double checked. "Loose."

"Think that's intentional?" Greg asked.

Regardless, they all started laughing.

Jace woke the next day feeling invigorated. And a little hungover. After a nice greasy breakfast of hash browns and eggs, he showered and stocked up on cat food from his mother's pantry. Maybe Victor needed to finally survive on his own, but that didn't mean Samson should starve. Then he said goodbye, because after spending the day with Victor, he would drive back to Houston again.

He felt apprehensive when knocking on the door, but less so when Victor answered cleanly shaven and freshly washed. There was still tension between them, but they both knew the cure for this. Jace willingly went downstairs to Victor's bedroom, where they spent an hour in bliss. Nearly. Despite how distracted his body was, Jace's mind remained filled with concern. Even when they lay cuddling together, enjoying the fading euphoria, his thoughts would not be silent.

"How are you going to pay the rent?" he asked softly. "I don't want you living on the street."

"Let me worry about that," Victor said patiently.

"Okay." Jace sat up, his back against the headboard. "It's just that I don't think you're going to pay it. If you are, just tell me so I can stop worrying about it."

Victor rolled over to face him, considering him before he too sat upright. He reached for the cigarettes on the side table. "I'll be fine," he repeated.

Michelle's advice sprang to mind. Jace knew she was right. He couldn't keep doing this. But— "I was thinking. My old bedroom at my parents' house isn't really used for anything, and it's close to the woods you like, so maybe I can talk to them. That way you'd have a place in winter and—"

"That's enough," Victor said. He got up to open the basement window before returning to bed. He looked so damn skinny. The way he pulled the blankets up to his armpits made Jace think of how exposed he would be to the elements.

"Or maybe you could sell what's in the house." Jace said. "Get a cheap RV or something to park on their property."

"I said that's enough," Victor repeated.

But it wasn't. That was only the tip of the iceberg when it came to Jace's worries. "Or Star. She'd love to have you live with her. I know she would."

Victor snorted. "I haven't seen Star for years."

"What?"

Victor flicked his ash into a coffee cup next to the bed. "She finally found someone rich enough to replace her father. Ran off with him pretty quick. I got a wedding invitation in the mail from Pasadena or somewhere like that. She knew I wouldn't come."

Or she thought it was worth one last chance, just in case Victor wanted to storm the wedding with dramatic timing. If so, she was kidding herself. And yet, Jace wished she was still around, one more person looking out for Victor, no matter how bad it hurt. The news that she was gone only increased his panic.

"What about Houston? My place is small, but—"

"Come on, Jace. Not again. Please."

"Then what are you doing here? Before it was your mother, but you don't visit her anymore."

"I didn't say that," Victor said. "I said there was no point. She doesn't remember me. At all. I'm a complete stranger. I'm not even Richard anymore. When I do visit, I can't go to her room because she doesn't understand why I'm there. When I talk to her in the living area, she seems puzzled, like I'm a salesman who can't bring himself to mention what he's selling. But I'm not leaving, because maybe that will change."

"I don't think it will," Jace said gently. "If it does, they can call us in Houston and we'll drive right back up here."

Victor stubbed out his cigarette and considered Jace's pleading eyes. Then he shook his head. "That won't make me who you need. I still won't feel the way you do about relationships, and you'll keep hanging on, hoping I will. Then when you do find the right guy, I'll be a burden."

"I don't care," Jace said, throat aching.

"Yeah, you do. That's the problem."

"Then what are you going to do?" Jace pressed. "How long are you going to play this game? Until it kills you?"

Victor smirked. "Life is fatal. It does us all in eventually."

"I'm serious! Eventually you'll have to get a job. Or hell, start working the one you already have. It's not a big deal. Everyone else does it! Why can't you grow the fuck up and take care of yourself?" Jace was yelling now, and no matter how much Victor's face told him it wouldn't matter, he couldn't help it. "I'm so sick and tired of worrying about you! I never stopped. Not one fucking day has gone by since I left for college that I didn't wonder if you're okay, and you're not making it any easier now. It hurts me. Do you get that? When I come back here and see you withering away, it kills me inside."

"I get that," Victor said. "How do you think I feel every time I see my mother?"

Jace wouldn't let this dissuade him. "But you have a choice! She doesn't. You can be a real human being for once. You used to say that all that out there was the dream. Well, if sitting around a dark house choking on cigarettes is reality, I don't want to wake up."

"I never said you have to."

"I can't!" Jace yelled. "Not while you're still here. I can't move on until I know you're okay."

Victor looked away, toward the window. Jace watched him, chest heaving, waiting for a response. He sat there for what felt like an eternity. "Answer me," Jace said. "Say anything. Tell me you'll come live with me, or tell me to fuck off, but don't just sit there doing nothing. You have to do *something!*"

But Victor still wouldn't look at him, even when Jace tossed a pillow at him. He felt like lashing out, punching him just to get his attention, and that's when he knew he had to go. When anger outpaces love, it's time to leave. Jace only wished he wouldn't have gotten sucked back into this trap. Hell, even Adrien was better than this.

After getting dressed and gathering his things, he opened the bedroom door. He stopped there and turned around, hoping that Victor was watching him. He wasn't. His head was still turned. Maybe this was his way of cutting Jace loose. If so, it only pissed him off more. Jace eyed the increasingly faded tattoo on Victor's arm. The fox was still running along the black line, but only now did Jace realize that it was a circle. Just like them, the fox was running in circles.

Turning his back, he went upstairs. After saying goodbye to Samson, he left the house, knowing this time that he would never set foot in it again.

Chapter Twenty

"We're flying you home."

Jace switched the phone to his right ear, as if that would help him hear better. "What?"

"We're flying you home," Michelle repeated. "Today."

Jace laughed. "That's short notice!"

"You weren't answering your phone last night."

Because he'd been out dancing, part of his "get over Victor" plan. So far, over the last two weeks, it hadn't helped much, although he did score a phone number last night. The guy wasn't his type, but Jace's ego had moved up a notch.

"Your flight leaves at 10:43 a.m. from George Bush International."

"Wait," Jace said, backpedaling. "What's going on? We talked about me flying up for your graduation later this year."

"I guess Mom and Dad can't wait because they want to see you now. Whenever you drive here, it takes up all your time. Listen, we can squabble about this in person. You have less than two hours to catch your flight."

Jace swung into action. He drank his coffee in the shower and had his breakfast while packing. By the time he arrived at the airport, he didn't have any waiting to do. The plane was already boarding at the gate, so in a very short period of time, he found himself landing in Kansas City International Airport. He had to admit, a couple of hours among the clouds was a lot better than half a day on the road.

He was at the baggage claim when someone tackled him with a hug.

"Hey!" Jace said, laughing and untangling himself from his sister. "Where are Mom and Dad?"

"Waiting at home," Michelle said. "I wanted time alone with you. How was the flight? Any hot flight attendants?"

"Fine, and no."

They made small talk until his luggage came around. Once back in the car, Michelle chatted nonstop. She talked about school, classmates he'd never heard of, and friends he'd never met. They were halfway home and still she talked. A new road in Warrensburg. A coffee shop that had come and gone. The neighbor's son across the street who had been throwing loud parties. She was talking so much that Jace didn't know how she could breathe. That's when he knew something was wrong.

"Michelle!" he snapped.

"What?"

"Why am I here? Why the rushed flight? I was just here a few weeks ago!"

Michelle kept her eyes on the road.

Jace's stomach sank. "You called me, not Mom. And Dad *loves* the airport. There's no way he wouldn't come, so what is it? Is one of them in the hospital? Did one of them—"

"No!" Michelle exhaled. "No. I promise you, they're fine. And yes, there are things all of us need to talk about, but let's just get home."

Jace shook his head. "I don't like this."

Michelle sped up. "Ten minutes, okay? We're almost there."

Jace looked out the window at the alternating farm land and forests. That's when he saw the dilapidated old church, the roof having finally caved in. And then he knew. "Tell me," he said. Quietly at first. Then he shouted it. "Goddamn it Michelle, just tell me!"

Michelle hit the breaks, swerving to the side of the road. When she faced him, there were tears in her eyes. "I'm sorry," she said.

"Victor." His name came out as a croak. When Michelle nodded, the ache travelled from Jace's heart up to his throat, manifesting as a moan of despair.

"Mom and Dad wanted you home before you found out," Michelle said. "We didn't want to tell you over the phone."

Jace tried to control his tears so he could speak, but his body was wracked with sorrow, convulsing with the pain of it all. "How?" was all he managed.

"Jace," his sister pleaded. She tried to hug him, but he shoved her away.

"How?"

"Suicide. He shot himself."

Jace couldn't breathe, literally couldn't find any air to force into his lungs. He didn't want this, couldn't face it. He scrabbled at the door handle and stumbled out into fresh air. Then he remembered the church. It couldn't be too far away. Finally his lungs worked. He sucked in air, then took off at a run. He heard Michelle call after him, but it didn't matter. Nothing mattered anymore, except reaching the place where Victor had made his promise.

I promise you, Jace, that I love you. I love you now, and I will love you forever and ever.

Victor had said that, sworn to him. He couldn't have taken his own life. That would be breaking the promise. His sister had lied to him. Victor would be there, waiting for him at the church, his green and brown eyes twinkling with amusement at Jace's needless panic. Then he would smirk, and take Jace into his arms.

Jace burst into the church, the smell of rot filling his nose. The podium was gone, crushed beneath the fallen roof. He considered clawing through the debris to unearth it, to bring the past back to life. Instead he fell to his knees and sobbed.

Victor was gone. Victor had died.

His cheek was pressed against the wet earth when he felt a hand on his shoulder.

"Jace."

The voice wasn't Victor's, but it did belong to someone who loved him.

"Jace, you're scaring me."

He sat up, let his sister wrap her arms around his neck. There was something frantic about that hug, like she hoped to keep him from running away again. And he wouldn't. He was still her big brother and tried to make himself behave that way.

"I'm okay," he lied, getting to his feet. "Let's go home."

Michelle led the way, glancing back as if afraid he'd try to make another break for it.

"I'm fine," he assured her as she stepped outside.

He didn't follow. Not right away. At the door to the church, Jace turned and looked back at a room that belonged only to ghosts now.

Forever and ever...

"The police had come to evict him," his mother said at the kitchen table. She had that conflicted look on her face, the kind normally reserved for when she had to take him to the dentist, or drop him off on the first day of school. She hated what she was doing, but she had to for his own good. "That's when they found the body," she continued. "Victor had shot himself in a way that would have been quick and painless."

"How?" Jace asked. He needed to know, because otherwise he would never stop imagining all the different possibilities.

Serena looked pale. "He, uh… Bob."

His father cleared his throat. "He got hold of a shotgun, son. Put it in his mouth. There's nothing slow about dying that way, I promise you. He couldn't have felt a thing."

Jace put his head down on the table and cried. He would give anything to undo this, to turn back time and be there when Victor had felt so desperate. He would sell his soul just to take that gun away from him and tell him, *"Not this. Anything but this."*

His mother stroked his hair until he had calmed down again. "We took care of everything. We told his mother. I don't know if she understood really, but we told her. Victor's body is taken care of too. He was cremated, but we didn't want him ending up in a common grave, and Mrs. Hemingway is in no condition to make decisions."

"Where are his ashes?"

"Here," Bob said. Then, with discomfort he added, "In your room. You can decide what to do with them, but the public administrator wants to know so he can make a note and inform Mrs. Hemingway. He knows the situation with her and was very understanding. We just need to keep them informed."

Jace shook his head. He didn't have a clue what to do with the remains. He wanted Victor, not a pile of ashes. Part of him still couldn't believe any of this was real. Victor was much too clever to take his own life. Jace couldn't picture him with a gun. Even when he'd considered robbing Jace at the store, Victor had been empty-handed. "The shotgun!" he said with painful realization.

"That's something else," his father said. "Once you've had a few days, maybe you could go see Bernard. He's taken all of this very hard."

Jace winced. That this had happened to Bernard of all people was devastating. But he couldn't think about that now. Jace already felt like his head was going to split in two, that he would go insane from the constant ache and pain inside.

"I think I need to lie down," he said.

"Okay," his mother said. "You take all the time you need. We're here, though, okay?"

Jace nodded despondently, trudging up to his room. He didn't want to see the ashes, didn't like that they were in there, but he didn't blame his parents. Where else would they keep them, on the entertainment center? Maybe that's why the door to his bedroom was closed, so they wouldn't have to see them when walking past.

When he opened the door to his room, he pictured the urn laying on the bed, the spot his mother would always leave something new for him. A jacket, a toy, his favorite candy, and now, his cremated boyfriend. He was right. There was something waiting on the bed for him. From its center, a small gray head lifted and blinked sleepily at him before meowing. Jace cried again. He wasn't sure if it was sorrow or if it was joy. Possibly it was neither. All he knew, when he crawled into bed and Samson pressed a dry nose against his tear-stained face, is that he wouldn't have to get through this alone.

Between bouts of crying, Jace tried to understand. He searched for any reason to make sense of this madness. Victor had always been unpredictable, but Jace had never seen this coming. Even as he watched Victor slowly crumble, the worst Jace had expected was for him to wander off into the woods and never be seen again. Of course Victor dying had been part of that nightmare scenario, but never like this.

And yet, Victor had always struggled with the world, always fought against it, suffering each time he was forced to compromise and play the game. Jace found himself wishing Victor *had* disappeared into the woods, turned his back on them all. Instead, his mother had forgotten who he was, and Jace—

He swallowed against another wave of tears. The last thing Jace had done was yell at Victor, telling him to do something. And he had. Were Jace's words what pushed him over the edge? He regretted them, wished more than anything he could take them back. His only comfort was that Victor had never listened to him before, had always done what he wanted, despite what Jace or anyone else thought. Victor had always forged his own path and made his own choices. Jace could only hope this was what he truly wanted. If Victor still existed in some form, maybe he was happy now.

Between fits of sorrow, guilt, and even anger, Jace dozed off. He dreamt he felt arms around him, strong and reassuring. He heard the sound of crying too. That's what woke him completely. The tears weren't his own, but they were real. As were the arms around him. Jace was curled up on his side, another body spooned against him from behind. He lifted his head to see who.

"I'm sorry, man," Greg said.

"Are you okay?" Jace asked, puzzled by the situation. "Why are you crying?"

"Because I know how bad this must hurt you." Greg shifted, as if to move away, but Jace clung to his arm, craving the comfort he gave.

"Stay here," Jace said, throat constricting. "Please."

"I will," Greg said. "Just promise me you won't do something stupid. Don't follow him, okay? I still need you."

Jace wanted to smile, maybe even laugh that Greg could think of something as romantic as Jace chasing after Victor. But in truth, it hurt that he hadn't considered it, hurt more that he wouldn't be able to. What Victor had done was forever. Jace struggled with this unavoidable truth, but there was no denying it. Victor was gone, and there was nothing any of them could do except hold on to each other and ache.

"Life has a funny way of teaching you a lesson," Bernard said.

They were sitting at the small kitchen table in his RV, the very same one that Jace had stepped into soaking wet so many years ago. Together they huddled around a bottle of something terrible and two shot glasses. Jace didn't know what he was drinking, but he didn't think it would kill the pain. The last few days had done nothing to ease his sorrow.

"Or maybe life is just cruel sometimes," Jace said.

Bernard nodded. "Yup. That too."

"I'm sorry," Jace said. "You wouldn't have tried to help Victor if it wasn't for me, and he wouldn't have stolen your shotgun and—"

Bernard waved him into silence. "Maybe I wouldn't have known him. Maybe I would have met him on my own. I still would have tried to help him."

Of course he would have because Bernard was a good person. And because he had lost his son to suicide, and had done everything he could not to make the same mistakes. Life was fucking mean to do this to him, to put Bernard through it again even when he'd done everything right.

"You don't get to be my age without losing people you love," Bernard continued. "You don't get used to death, by any means, but it becomes more familiar and less shocking. Suicide is something completely different. Losing someone to age is natural. Illness you can get angry at. You can rage at the conditions that cause an accident, and in war you can hate the enemy for taking a life. But when it comes to suicide, only the person who committed it is responsible. Who in their right mind would put the blame on them? Maybe that's why those left behind end up blaming themselves instead."

Jace nodded, understanding all too well. "I could have done more. If I had moved back here, stayed with him, then maybe he wouldn't have—"

"Maybe," Bernard said. "Hard to say what was going through Victor's mind at the time. Did he leave a note?"

Jace shook his head.

Bernard grunted. "Don't blame yourself. You did plenty for Victor, all you could at the time. In retrospect, it's always easy to find more. Maybe we all could have done more, but none of us can really say what might have happened. That's not a game worth playing. Trust me."

"Then what do we do?" Jace asked. "How can life ever make sense again after something like this?"

"Learn from it."

"What's the lesson?" Jace asked.

Bernard exhaled. "The lesson is you can't always save someone, even if you love them. As strange as it sounds, it gives me some relief. I always thought if I'd been a better father, that my son wouldn't have taken his own life. I'll never know, but I tried to do right by Victor, and it wasn't enough. Some people are too haunted by their own demons. Maybe my son would have been the same way. I can't say, but I'm done blaming myself."

"You saved me," Jace said. "You know that?"

"How could I forget?" Bernard's face twitched with something close to a smile. "Thank you for saying so, but the truth is I helped you save yourself. At the end of the day, decisions like these are up to the individual. You can't save someone who doesn't want to be saved. But that doesn't mean I'll ever stop trying." He raised a glass. "Here's to not giving up."

Jace understood. Bernard was still looking out for him after all these years, making sure he wanted to be saved. Jace raised his glass. "I'm not giving up. Cheers, old man."

Now Bernard really did smile. "Cheers, you little brat."

Clinking glasses, they sent fire chasing down to their bellies.

Jace didn't need time to let go of Victor's ashes. He held no attachment to them. They weren't Victor at all, merely the husk that was left behind. Cardboard box held between both hands, he walked down into the valley, feeling like a solitary pallbearer. How strange that a person could fit inside a space smaller than a shoebox, and how insignificant it made the body seem compared to all the thoughts a person had, all the deeds they had done, and all the lives they had touched. Seeing a body so condensed only further convinced Jace that a person was much more than the physical form.

He reached the lake, walking past it without stopping. He had considered scattering Victor's ashes across the half-frozen water where they had once swam naked together, but there was another place that seemed more appropriate. Jace hadn't been to the clearing in years. What remained didn't match his memories. The shelter wasn't where it had once been. Greg had moved it to the other side of the clearing, probably taking wind direction into consideration. Or maybe he'd torn it down and started from scratch, because what stood was much sturdier and more solid than what Jace remembered.

He let himself stare for a moment before getting to work. Jace set the box of ashes in the shelter and began gathering firewood. Snow still covered most of the ground, so wetness and cold quickly soaked through his gloves. Eventually he took them off and tossed them aside, still gathering wood. When he had a pile big enough, his frozen fingers struggled with getting the wet wood to light.

Jace knew it didn't really matter, that he could simply scatter the ashes here and go, but he wanted a fire burning first. He didn't want to leave Victor in the cold. That didn't make sense, but he didn't need it to.

In desperation, he fetched the cardboard box. He'd already peeked once. He knew Victor's ashes were in a plastic bag inside. He removed this and tore the box to shreds, using it to kindle the fire. After more work and frustration, he finally managed a steady blaze.

For a while he just knelt in front of the fire, holding his hands out to defrost while he considered all the memories they'd made here. Coming out to Greg, his first kiss, or even later, when Victor had exiled himself here the summer before Jace had moved to Houston. This clearing had been the setting for so many conversations. Some good, some bad, but all precious now that there wouldn't be any more.

Jace stood, and without looking down, tore open the plastic bag. He walked to the edge of the clearing, numbly at first, as his fingers dug into what was once Victor's body and scattered him across the snow and ground. Then he began crying, moving faster, spinning around as he tossed away a fistful of ashes. He anointed the shelter with them, sprinkled them into the fire, tossed them into the air and watched them fly. By the time he was finished they were everywhere, the ground, the trees, his hair, his lips. This place was Victor now.

No, not now. That wasn't quite right because in Jace's mind, this place had *always* been Victor, was always the setting Jace pictured him in. At least, that was the dream. He couldn't begin to imagine where the real Victor was, but Jace was certain of one thing: Victor was free. Now, after all this time, they were both free.

"I have to go back," Jace said, preempting any begging.

Michelle and Greg sat on the family room couch with pleading eyes. Jace stood in front of them, determined not to give in. More than ever, he wanted to get away from this town. He didn't even want to be in Houston again. What he wanted was to run, to not look back until he was far away from everything he knew. Only then did he feel he could begin to heal. This last week of being home had done little more than dredge up more memories for him to ache over.

"I'm not staying," he insisted.

"It's not about that," Greg said. Then he bit his lip and looked to Michelle.

"I thought you were going to tell him?" she said.

"You're his sister."

"You're his best friend!"

Jace was having a heart attack. He was sure of it. The poor organ had been strained enough recently, but even the idea of more bad news made him feel like it would burst.

"Tell me!" Jace shouted.

Michelle looked at him, shock on her face when she realized what this must remind him of. "You're going to be an uncle," she blurted out.

"What? What do you mean?"

Michelle rolled her eyes. "When a man loves a woman—"

"I know all that," Jace said. Then he laughed. "Are you serious?"

Michelle smiled. "Very. Almost two months serious, as it turns out."

Jace's heartbeat took on a much happier rhythm. "Oh my god! That's incredible. Who's the father?"

Greg raised his hand sheepishly. "Sorry, man. I got your sister pregnant."

Michelle sighed, palm of her hand to her face. "Don't say it like that. You make it sound sleazy."

"Sorry, honey."

"Honey?" Jace repeated.

"Yeah," Greg said. "That's the other thing. I've kind of been dating your sister. For a while now. Please don't be mad."

"Mad?" Jace said. "Why would I be mad?"

"I told you so," Michelle murmured, studying her nails.

"I don't know," Greg said defensively. "I mean, it's not exactly kosher when your best friend goes after your little sister."

"That does seem kind of weird," Jace said, pretending to mull it over. "Maybe I *should* be angry."

"But it's not like that," Greg said quickly. "I love her. I really do, and I'm going to be there for her. Uh, just a second." He stood, placed an arm around Jace's shoulder, and guided him away. "I haven't asked her yet," he whispered, "but I'm going to pop to the question."

"You better!" Jace whispered back.

"You know what this means?" Greg grinned. "This'll make you my brother-in-law. We're going to be brothers!"

Jace laughed. He couldn't help himself. "Please tell me that's not the only reason you've done all this."

"No, man." Greg turned to Michelle, who waited on the

couch innocently, as if she didn't know what was going on. Jace had no doubt that all of this was completely transparent to her. "I love her. We're starting a family—and you and me, we're going to be family!"

Jace might have cried if he wasn't so damn sick of doing so. Instead he nodded. "All right. But this means I'll have to find a new best friend. I can't be best friends with my brother. That's just sad."

"That would be sad," Greg agreed. "But I wouldn't mind."

"Yeah, me neither. Now let's head to the store and buy some champagne. I can't wait to see Michelle's face when she realizes she can't drink any."

The cabin pressure changed, meaning the plane was beginning its descent. Jace flexed his jaw to pop his ears and bent over to check on Samson. He was doing well. Jace didn't imagine many cats were fond of being stuffed in a carrier and shoved under a seat, but so far, Samson was a trooper. Jace stuck his finger in the carrier and wiggled until he felt a nose bump against it.

"How's he doing?"

Jace looked up to see a flight attendant with short blonde hair. She'd moved Jace up to first class so he'd have more room for Samson, which was exceedingly kind.

"He's good," Jace said.

"How'd you get him to stop meowing?"

"I promised him a can of tuna all to himself when we land."

The flight attendant smiled. "I'll have to remember that. Think caviar would work?"

"No idea," Jace said. "I'm a new dad. I haven't had him for long."

"Oh. Don't worry. You seem like a natural to me!" The flight attendant moved away to check on the other passengers.

Jace watched her with interest. Seemed like a good job, really, despite being customer service. He worked in the same industry, albeit in a boring office. The flight attendant had it made. If there was anyone she didn't like, all she had to do was wait a few hours until the flight was over.

When she did her final seatbelt check, Jace asked her if she liked her job.

"Love it," she said. "Although it's not for everyone. Some people like to stay home, have the comfort of the familiar around them. And others—" She cocked her head. "Ever feel like you never want to stop traveling? Like you could run circles around the globe and it still wouldn't be enough?"

Jace chuckled. "Yes. Especially as of late."

"Well, in that case, we're hiring."

"Seriously?"

She nodded. "I'll get you the info before we land."

After she walked away, Jace bent over again. "What do you think, Samson? Should your dad become an astronaut?"

There was a rather cranky meow.

Jace wasn't sure if that was a yes or a no, but as he leaned back and considered the possibility, he felt he already had his answer. Like Icarus he would take to the skies, but fortunately, Jace had already learned not to fly too close to the sun.

Part Three:
Houston, 1999

Chapter Twenty-one

Nearly four years. Jace leaned against the galley cabinets, listening to the monotone hum of the aircraft. This time of year was always a countdown for him as his mind ticked off the events of the past. Driving down to see Victor in the fall with the news that he was single. Their first night together again after an eternity. The coming of winter, Victor's breakdown, Christmas Day with Mrs. Hemmingway in the nursing home, and then...

But the calendar hadn't gotten that far, not yet; Christmas was still approaching. The airline paid double for working on holidays. Ironic since Jace would have paid them triple just for the privilege of missing out. That's why he had volunteered for the dreaded Christmas shift, just as he always did. His family complained that he wouldn't be home for the holidays, Jace matching their frustrated tones when in truth he felt nothing but relief. He couldn't stand Christmas. Not any more.

Funny that he'd lived through twenty-five of them, but one was enough to spoil the rest. Well, not spoil exactly, but to cast a shadow over them. Even the good ones. Getting Victor's tattoo, feeling the carved lion's mane beneath his fingertips... Jace wished they all could have been like that. Every single one. Or maybe he wished he could forget the good ones, be free of the memories that came unbidden, like ghosts rising from the grave.

Ghosts? Graves? Too Halloween-ish. If his thoughts were going to take a melodramatic turn, they should at least be seasonal. Jace checked his watch. Three minutes until midnight. Three minutes until Christmas.

The call-attendant light went off. Jace didn't need to look to see who needed his attention. A mere twenty-eight passengers occupied the economy section tonight, and most were dozing. Only a middle-aged woman in the center of the plane seemed intent on getting as tanked as possible. She'd already blown through two glasses of Merlot halfway through a three-hour flight. No doubt she had family waiting for her in Houston that she wasn't looking forward to seeing.

Jace felt a pang of guilt as he fetched another bottle of wine. He wanted to see his family and loved them just as he always had. He just wished they didn't live in Warrensburg. Rather than be poor company during "the most wonderful time of the year," he chose to keep his distance.

"Keep 'em coming!" the woman joked.

Jace smiled, collecting the small empty bottles on her tray. There was a policy about not allowing passengers to get too drunk, but damned if he was going to enforce it today of all days. Besides, the woman hardly seemed like a lightweight.

On the way back to the front of the plane, he checked on the passengers in his care. Older man—sleeping. Teenager—head nodding to the tinny sound coming from his headphones. Young couple—cuddled up and sleeping. Woman with the curly red hair—nose deep in a romance novel. Cute guy with the haunted expression—stretched out across three seats. Sleeping.

After confirming that he wasn't being watched, Jace allowed himself to linger. He could fetch one of the thin blankets from the overhead compartment, drape it over the slender form. Of course the guy would wonder who had tucked him in. Awkward. Then again, Jace's job was to take care of his passengers and ensure their safety. In the end he made sure the three air nozzles above the seat were all closed shut so there wasn't a draft. That would have to do.

Jace returned to the galley, which was just a few steps away, and made himself look busy. His eyes kept returning to that first row of seats. The passenger had caught his eye when boarding. He was shorter—like Victor. Jace seemed to prefer smaller guys, maybe because of those formative years. His frame was thin, his hair long enough to cover his ears—also like Victor during those final days. Mercifully, the similarities stopped there. This person had dark-blond hair that Jace imagined would turn golden in the summer sun. His eyes were brown and perpetually out of focus. Whereas Victor had seen everything at first glance, this person seemed oblivious to the world around him.

The passenger had stared out the window until Jace gave his safety demonstration. Then his head faced in his direction, but Jace had the impression this was only out of politeness. Rather than demonstrate how the seatbelts worked, Jace could have barked and done backflips and still gone unnoticed. Soon he was drawn in by the mystery. Maybe the passenger had a phobia of flying and was on tranquilizers.

If so, they were good pills, since he didn't react as the plane took to the air. The passenger didn't browse the airline magazine, or entertain himself in any way. Unlike the woman chugging wine, he didn't seem to dread his destination or miss his point of departure. He seemed completely lost in thought until he lay down to sleep. Over the next hour, even though the passenger did nothing but lie there, Jace's attention kept returning to him. He had a strange urge to brush the hair from his face to see him better.

The plane tilted, banking to begin its descent. Jace walked the aisles, making sure everyone was buckled in and sitting upright. When he returned to the first row, his blond mystery was stirring. Jace quickly flipped down the jump seat across from him and tried to affect casual disinterest.

Stretching as he sat up, the passenger fastened his seatbelt and considered the city lights outside the window. He stared and stared—always with that same haunted expression. Jace figured it out. A death in the family. Maybe not someone close, since he didn't see any tears. An aunt or cousin, maybe. Distant enough not to be upsetting, but close enough to make a person ponder mortality. That had to be it. Jace tapped a beat on his legs, hoping to attract his attention, but still the passenger was oblivious. In fifteen minutes or so, this person would stroll off the plane and disappear from his life, and Jace would never know if he was right.

Oh, what the hell.

"Funeral, huh?"

The passenger turned to regard him, as if Jace had appeared out of thin air. He didn't just take in Jace's features, but looked him up and down as well. Fair enough, since Jace had done the same countless times while he slept. Jace had good reason to, being a hopeless homosexual. This guy... Well, anything was possible.

"Sorry?"

"You're flying because of a funeral," Jace said, pleased when the passenger looked surprised.

"Well, yeah. How did you know?"

Jace adopted a pose he thought suited to Sherlock Holmes, one hand on his chin as he tapped the side of his face with his index finger. "Your face was sad. People never look sad when they fly, unless there is a funeral involved."

There it was—a shadow crossing his features. But there was conflict as well, as if that wasn't the entire story. A funeral was much too simple.

"Of course," Jace pressed on, "we also get sad faces when people leave their partners behind, although passengers usually recover from that by the time we land."

"Well, if you must know," the young man said with transparent agitation, "not only is there a funeral, but my boyfriend robbed me yesterday, thus becoming my ex."

"That would explain it. A double whammy." Jace felt almost overwhelmed. Usually his fantasies ended at the word *straight*. Not only was this guy gay, but he was single as well. Jace dug two tiny bottles of vodka from his uniform pocket and held them up. "Here, on the house." He tossed them to the passenger, who looked at them only long enough to catch them before his eyes returned to Jace's again. No doubt about it. If booze was less interesting than he was, then he stood a chance. Time to get personal. "My name's Jace, by the way."

"Your name tag says Jason."

"I know." Jace considered the tag with disdain. "Isn't that mean? I told them I wanted one that says Jace, but that's not my legal name. Where do they get these things, anyway? Is there a store that sells them somewhere? That would be cool. Then I could buy my own."

This earned him a laugh, and upon hearing it, Jace knew that once wouldn't be enough. He wanted to hear that happy sound again.

"Do you happen to have a name of your own?" he asked.

The passenger nodded. "Yup. But I'm afraid I left my name tag at home."

"So I have to guess?"

"Go for it."

Jace rubbed his chin, scrutinizing the passenger like he had X-ray vision. "You look like a… Yeah, no doubt about it. Your name has to be Stephanie. Am I right?"

The passenger laughed again. "Right, but you can call me Ben."

"That can't be your legal name either," Jace replied. "It must be Benjamin?"

The smile faded, the answer tense. "Just Ben."

Feeling like he was losing ground, Jace played the fool. "Well, it's very economical at least. Only three letters."

Ben considered the tiny bottle in his hand, still somber. Then he looked up and held one out. "Care to join me?"

"Nope. Not allowed to drink on duty." Jace waved a hand dismissively. "I don't really drink anyway. I only take them because they make such nice stocking stuffers."

"Are there flights on Christmas?" Ben asked.

"Oh, yes," Jace replied with same exasperated expression he used on his family. "There isn't a day of the year the airlines don't serve."

"That must suck."

Au contraire! "It can, but this year I finagled it so I have Christmas off." Jace felt another pang of guilt. He'd told his parents he was working on Christmas day, and while this shift was late enough to be technically true, he still could have made it up there tomorrow. Or the next day or the next, because Jace had an entire week of vacation. But Warrensburg wasn't where he went to unwind. Texas was his sanctuary now. "It'll be nice to be home again," he said, mostly to himself.

"So you live in Houston?"

Jace blinked and returned to the present. "Yeah. You?"

Ben shook his head. "Chicago."

"Too bad," Jace said, and he meant it. Work took him to Chicago enough to have an affair, but nothing more. The idea of casual encounters didn't appeal to him.

"I'll probably be in town a few weeks," Ben said, cheeks suddenly flushed.

Of course, life was short, and a few weeks could be a very long time. Jace smiled encouragingly, waiting for Ben to take things further. When that didn't happen, he decided to be more direct. "You know, there is a strict company policy against asking passengers out on dates."

Ben looked crestfallen. "Oh."

"That's not to say that you can't ask me."

"Oh!" Ben grinned.

Jace joined him. "Are you staying with family? Or do you have a vacation home here?"

"A vacation home? Of course!" Ben said playfully. "But I allow my parents to stay there. In return, they do maintenance and keep my affairs in order."

"How generous of you," Jace said. "And are there set hours that you receive visitors to your estate?"

Ben's amusement faded. "That might be complicated, actually. Tomorrow's the big day, and after that... I'll have my hands full. It's my best friend's father who died."

"I'm sorry," Jace said quickly. "I totally disregarded the reason for your flight."

"No, don't worry," Ben said reassuringly. "I never really liked the guy. I just want to be there for my friend, you know? Give her a shoulder to cry on."

"Of course," Jace said. "Look, why don't I give you my number, and if you find any free time, call me. If you don't, I'll try not to take it personally. I know firsthand how complicated these things can be."

"Oh yeah?" Ben looked concerned for him, which was sweet since they'd known each other all of five minutes.

"Yes."

"Any advice?"

"You've got the right idea already. Be a sympathetic ear. Don't tell her it will get better or that time heals all wounds."

"Doesn't it?" Ben asked, but then he seemed to reconsider. "Never mind. You're right."

The plane touched down, meaning Jace had work to do. With an apologetic expression, he rose, walked through first class and deactivated the emergency slides on the doors. While waiting for the telescopic corridor to connect, he found a pen and scribbled down his number on a cocktail napkin. Then he waited as the passengers disembarked, relieved to see that Ben had waited to let the others go first. He approached Jace a little awkwardly, face expectant.

"My number," Jace said, brandishing the napkin.

"Thanks." Ben accepted it.

From his bashful demeanor, Jace probably didn't need to say anything. The guy wasn't swaggering at getting a phone number. Still, he wanted to be sure. "I'm interested in hanging out. Maybe dinner or something."

Ben nodded. "That would be fine."

"Good. I, uh. I just want you to know that I'm an old-fashioned girl. I'm not looking for anything casual."

"Understood," Ben said. "I'll ask my mother to play chaperone on our first date."

"First date implies more than one," Jace replied.

Ben nodded again. "I know." After a dopey grin, he turned and walked down the gangway. Jace seriously considered abandoning the airplane just to join him.

Jace awoke late on Christmas morning. Samson was already alert, curled up in the curve of his arm. When their eyes met, the cat stood excitedly and starting doing "happy paws" by kneading the sheets.

"It's Christmas, Sam," Jace said. "Were you a good boy this year?"

Samson meowed, but mostly just because he was still excited about Jace being home again. Jace's job kept him on the road—well, in the air—more nights than he would prefer. While he was gone, Samson relied on the little old lady in the first-floor apartment to take care of him. Soon that wouldn't be an option, since she was moving in with her daughter.

That meant having to find someone new to take care of him. Situations like these made him wish he had a roommate. Not that his current home would be suitable. Sitting up in the loft bed, he had a good view of the apartment below. The walls were raw brick, the floors well-maintained wood. Jace had fallen in love with the studio on first sight. After the tiny rooms of the apartment he and Adrien had once chosen together, having one large room felt like a luxury.

His job had been good to him too. The small kitchen in the corner had everything necessary to cook—which he rarely did—and enough remaining space for a dining room table. A couch, chair, and coffee table—all set on an old carpet—formed the living room. Unlike his previous apartment, this one had room enough to entertain. Not that he had as of late. Ever since Mark, his ex-boyfriend who loved to host dinners for anyone from close friends to people he met on the street, Jace had come to appreciate solitude.

Enjoying his privacy was the day's agenda. Climbing down the bed's ladder, he turned to watch Samson make his usual daredevil jump, flying through the air and landing on the couch. Then they walked to the fridge, where Jace had moved a small wrapped package from the freezer the night before.

"Look what Santa Claws left you!" he said.

Just as well that Mark had found someone new. Jace was steadily becoming one of *those* people. Like a proud father, he talked about Sam to his coworkers, even carrying a photo of the cat in his wallet. He fretted if his flights were late, delaying his return, and always called once a day to make sure everything was fine back home.

Grabbing the wrapped package, he shut the refrigerator, eyeing for a moment the child's drawing on the door: a cat, wearing a red suit and surrounded by blue crisscross snowflakes. Below were two illegible words, beneath which his sister's handwriting clarified their meaning. *Santa Claws*. Great. Not only was he becoming a crazy cat guy, but his madness was spreading. Still, he loved that his niece had thought of him, especially since he wasn't around much.

"Sorry, Emma," Jace said to himself. "Your uncle is busy pitying himself."

But he wasn't feeling sad. Not here, so far away from it all. Unwrapping the package with Samson revealed the two salmon steaks Jace had bought for this occasion. Samson didn't seem impressed until Jace started pan-searing them. Taking Samson's steak out while it was still raw in the center, he added whisked eggs to the pan. Soon he and Samson were enjoying breakfast together.

Afterwards, he sat on the floor and emptied the stocking he'd stuffed for Samson. Once the living area was littered with toy mice and treats, Jace allowed himself a long lazy soak in the bathtub. He passed the rest of the day in a similar manner, taking everything slow, wasting every single minute on luxury. The dishes could wait until tomorrow. Even the presents sent from home could be opened some other time. All Jace wanted to do was play with Samson and read. And find some takeout later if anything was open.

The afternoon had come to an end, Jace dozing on the couch, when the buzzer sounded. Curious... Who could be at the door? His friends all had plans, and he didn't think Mark was ever coming back. Maybe it was the old woman downstairs, checking up on him. If so, why would she be ringing the bell outside the building? The door buzzed again. Sighing, Jace stood and walked to the door, pushing the button for the intercom.

"Hello?"

There was no answer, but he thought he heard a giggle.

"Hello?" he tried again.

Nothing. Maybe the intercom was on the blink. Jace pushed the button to unlock the front door, listening to the cage elevator as it rumbled down. When it was on its way back up, his jaw dropped when he saw was who was inside. A woman. And a very young lady. The woman was glaring, the young lady beaming with delight.

"Busy flying the friendly skies?" Michelle asked as she hobbled out of the elevator.

"I worked this morning," Jace said, grinning despite the accusation. "What are you doing here?"

Emma latched herself onto his legs. "Merry Chrissmiss, Uncah Jace!" She was still young enough that she constantly slurred her speech, sounding like a toddler who'd had one too many.

"Merry Christmas," he replied. "Did you drink too much eggnog?"

"She does not sound drunk," Michelle scolded, but she smiled as Jace ushered them in. "Wait until you hear Preston. All he does is scream. I swear he's a crack baby."

"You're a terrible mother," Jace teased.

"Says the horrible uncle."

They hugged, Jace being careful not to squeeze against her swollen belly. "I had no idea that Number Three was so big already!"

"Tell me about it," Michelle said. "Two more months, and then I'm shutting down this baby factory."

Jace kept an arm around her as she wobbled to the couch and plopped down, sighing with relief. "How did you get here? Where are the others?"

"Greg has Preston. He wanted to drive around the neighborhood a few times before he came in. You know how he is these days. It's all about real estate."

Greg's land development plans had never come to fruition, but he had fostered a successful career in real estate. That Greg oozed charm when he wanted certainly helped, as did the television commercials that caught the attention of wives and single women alike. The last time Jace had driven through Warrensburg, numerous signs were stuck in front yards, advertising homes for sale, a photo of Greg's smiling face in the corner of each.

"Does he still have the mustache?"

"Oh my god!" Michelle looked exasperated. "Not only does he still have it, but he's gone full handlebar. He's been into cop movies lately. He looks like one of the Village People."

Jace grinned. "Hot!"

"It's so not," his sister replied. "If you want to give me one thing for Christmas, talk him into shaving it off."

"I'll see what I can do," Jace said. He glanced over at Emma, who was chasing Samson around the apartment. "So you guys came all this way to see me?"

"Of course. That's what the holidays are about."

Jace frowned.

"That wasn't meant to make you feel guilty," Michelle said. "I get why Warrensburg is hard for you this time of year. Greg understands too. He's the one who pointed out that we could visit you."

"So you drove down?"

His sister nodded. "Had Christmas with the kids early in the morning and then loaded them up. My sisterly instincts told me you might be home."

Jace was moved. As much as he'd been enjoying his solitude, having family here made it feel like a real holiday.

"Of course there is one other reason," Michelle said.

Before Jace could ask what she meant, the doorbell rang again. He went to buzz Greg in, grinning as the elevator brought both his best friend and his nephew to him. Greg looked great, as always. Jace saw plenty of parents during flights who seemed in a constant state of exhaustion. Greg positively glowed. An early morning spent opening presents and a long drive to Texas, and Greg looked like he could still run a marathon. Even now, burdened down by diaper bags and lord only knew what else, he carried his son like he was a trophy.

"Howdy, partner!" Greg said in an exaggerated accent. Or maybe he was channeling John Wayne.

"I keep telling you," Jace said, taking Preston from him, "nobody talks like that here."

"Nah, they must," Greg said dismissively.

Once they were inside, he slung the bags down. Emma, still

chasing Samson, tripped and hit the floor. Then she started to cry. Preston, having spotted the cat, began to scream with joy—one long high-pitched wail that seemed endless. Already Jace felt one of his headaches coming on.

Greg beamed at Jace. "Did Michelle tell you yet? We're moving in!"

They were kidding. Almost.

After a couple hours of using outdoor voices, stomping around, and spilling glasses of orange juice, the kids had finally crashed. Greg carried Emma and Preston up to the loft bed where they now slept. Since then, the adults had been conversing in whispers around the coffee table.

"You're really moving to Houston?" Jace repeated.

"Yes," Greg said.

"Maybe," Michelle countered.

"I was at a conference in October," Greg said, "and met an agent who works down here. We had some drinks at the bar that night, which loosened his tongue about the kind of money he's making. You know I love Warrensburg, but I'm lucky to move a house for anywhere near $200,000."

"You sold that one on Hillary Street," Michelle said proudly.

Greg smiled at her before addressing Jace. "There are homes here worth millions. Moving down would be a risk, since I'd be starting from scratch again, but—"

"You'll do great," Jace interrupted. "That's not flattery. I want you guys here, but I also don't want your kids to starve. If I didn't think you'd be successful, I'd tell you not to risk it."

"It'll be a risk either way." Greg shook his head as if he was no longer sure. "I'm a big fish in a small pond right now."

"More like a small puddle," Jace interjected.

"Regardless, I'll have to work hard to get myself established."

"You can start by ditching the hokey accent," Jace said. "Oh, and there's one other thing."

Greg sat upright with concern. "What?"

"It'll be a major sacrifice for you."

"What is it? Tell me."

Jace did his best to look reluctant. "The mustache will have to go. They're not in style here at all. The Texans say you can tell how dishonest a man is by how much he hides his face."

Greg looked to Michelle.

"I'd understand," she said. "You'd be doing it for the family."

"All right," Greg said. "But I'm getting a cowboy hat. And one of those big belt buckles."

Michelle winced.

Jace laughed. "You'll fit right in."

Chapter Twenty-two

Jace found himself playing tour guide the next day, a task easier than he expected. Greg was most interested in driving through areas he'd researched, stopping at homes for sale to gather brochures or talk to the owners. When the kids became impatient, the adults would do anything to prevent more screaming, be it an emergency trip to a playground or a visit to McDonald's for a Happy Meal. In the evening, Michelle requested what she called mommy time, which had little to do with actually being a mother. Instead, Greg took the kids back to the hotel with him.

Jace was glad for the one-on-one time. Greg was family now, but there were some things he still felt more comfortable discussing only with her.

They settled down on the couch together. Samson was curled up on Jace's stomach, perhaps feeling the need to compete with the baby inside Michelle.

"How are they?" he asked.

"Fine," Michelle said, understanding immediately. "Mom and Dad will outlive us both, I swear. I don't worry anymore. You should see them. It's like they're teenagers again."

"Really?"

Michelle nodded. "Did you know Dad is selling the stores? He's finally retiring. All he and Mom talk about are their travel plans. I think they're trying to say it's all right."

"You moving here?"

"Yeah. Not that I think they're faking. They're total love birds lately. It's repulsive." Michelle rubbed her belly affectionately before considering him. "What about you?"

"Love?" Jace laughed nervously. "No."

"What's it been, a year since the last one?"

"Not that long," Jace said, doing some mental calculations. "More like eleven months."

Michelle snorted. "Big difference, although I can understand why you've been counting the days. Mark was weird. Can a person be too friendly? Because I think he was."

"Mark was a little needy, yeah."

"Anyway, isn't it time to try again? You can't tell me no one wants my handsome big brother."

Jace broke eye contact, a smile coming unwilled.

"I knew it!" Michelle said, trying in vain to sit up. "What's his name?"

"Ben," Jace said. "And he's just some guy I gave my phone number to. He'll probably never call."

"Just some guy," Michelle said, nudging him. "They're all 'just some guy' until you take them home with you. Oh, those were the days!"

"My sister the player, brought down by children."

"No regrets here," Michelle said. "I'd do it all again. Still, this one really is the last. I didn't get that degree in psychology to play shrink to my family, handy as it may be."

"So what do you want to do?"

"Once the kids are all in school?" She paused thoughtfully. "I think I'd like to work with children."

Jace laughed. "That's like a fisherman retiring so he has more time to go fishing."

"True. But I want to help, you know what I mean? Not everyone's so lucky."

"Not everyone has Greg," Jace agreed. "Or a wonderful mother like you."

Michelle smiled at the compliment. "Or such an awesome uncle. Preston loves the stuffed tiger you sent."

"And Emma?"

"She wanted a Power Ranger, not a Barbie."

"Ah. Well, the stores are open again tomorrow. Think she'll forgive me?"

"If you deliver the goods."

Jace moved Samson onto a cushion and excused himself so he could use the restroom. While he was in there, he couldn't help but feel envious about everything his sister and Greg had together. That he would soon share a bigger role in their lives made him happy. Family in Houston! Maybe his parents would eventually move down here too.

The phone rang while he was checking himself in the mirror. He heard his sister say that she would get it, so he didn't feel rushed. Until he considered who could be calling. Jace hurried out of the bathroom. His sister had the phone pressed to her ear, wearing *the look* on her face. The one that said "Ha ha! I'm making my brother's life hell and having so much fun in the process!"

"Who is this?" she demanded sternly, sounding like a suspicious wife.

Jace rushed her. If she wasn't pregnant, he would have tackled her to the ground. Michelle cackled like a witch, giving up the phone without too much struggle.

"Idiot!" he scolded before bringing the receiver to his ear. "Sorry, this is Jace."

"Hey, it's Ben. Look, did I call at a bad time?"

"Ben! Hey!" Why did the room suddenly feel like there wasn't enough oxygen? "No, not a bad time at all. That was just my sister. She enjoys destroying my social life."

"I know what you mean," Ben said sympathetically. "I have one of those too."

"Yeah, they're a pain." Jace watched Michelle make a face as she put on her coat. "She was just leaving anyway. Hold on." He covered the phone. "Are you sure you can drive? It's late!"

"Aside from barely fitting behind the wheel, I do fine."

"I should at least walk you to the car."

Michelle waved away the offer. "I'm fine. Really. I can't remember what it's like not to be pregnant."

"Okay. Love you."

"Love you too. Good luck!"

When his sister closed the door behind her, he took a deep breath and raised the phone. "So, what did Santa bring you for Christmas?" he asked.

Ben laughed. "What?"

"For Christmas. What did you get?"

"Uh, actually I haven't even opened my presents yet. I've been with my friend almost the whole time since landing. My parents are probably dying to see me, actually."

"They'll have to wait," Jace said. "Do you want to meet tonight?"

"It's almost midnight!"

"Is it already?" Jace checked the clock. He'd been talking to Michelle for hours. "You see what flying so much does to you? I have no concept of time anymore."

"Tomorrow would be good," Ben said.

That was a promising sign. No small talk to decide if they should actually meet or not. Now they just needed a place. "Can you ice skate?"

"No."

"Excellent! Why don't we meet at the Galleria Ice Rink? Do you know where that is?"

The line was quiet a moment. "Of course."

"Next to the skate rental booth. Around dinner time?" This time the pause was even longer. Maybe Jace was moving too fast. "I'm not a serial killer or anything. It's just that I would prefer to stare into those lovely brown eyes of yours when we talk."

"My eyes are green," Ben said.

Jace checked his memory and smiled. "No, they aren't. I'll prove it to you tomorrow. Seven o'clock?"

"Yeah, all right." Ben sounded upbeat again. "Central time zone. Don't forget."

"I won't, promise." Then for good measure, Jace added, "Go see your parents tomorrow!"

"All right, all right! Geez. You'd think we were married already."

"Now who's rushing things? Goodnight, Ben."

"Goodnight."

Jace hung up the phone and in his excitement, spun around to face the apartment. He wanted to tell someone the good news, but as usual, only one living soul was there.

"Hey, Samson," he said. "I've got a date! Want to give me a makeover?"

Still exhausted from the onslaught of children earlier, Samson buried his face beneath one paw and continued sleeping.

Shoppers swarmed around Jace, hungry for bargains or driven to exchange unwanted gifts. This never failed to surprise him. The buildup to Christmas was filled with stressful shopping. Most people were glad when it was over, but only a few days later, the mall corridors were again stuffed with eager consumers. To seek out more stress after the holidays seemed like madness. Of course, trying to start a new relationship wasn't exactly relaxing either.

Waiting by the skate rental booth, he kept his eye on the elevator, the most likely place Ben would appear. He quelled any nervousness by telling himself nothing would come of this. Spontaneous flirtation was one thing. Trying to sustain the mood was wholly different. On a rare night out at a gay bar, Jace had met a hot guy on the dance floor. Together they had spun and sweat and smiled for an hour. Before the dancer's friends dragged him away, they had exchanged numbers and agreed to meet. When they did, the chemistry they felt on the dance floor was nowhere to be found. The guy had been shy in public and didn't have anything of interest to say. The night had been awkward and unsatisfying, probably like this evening would be.

And yet, every time the elevator dinged and the doors slid open, Jace stood on his toes to get a better look. When a guy with medium-length blond hair stumbled out, uncertainty crinkling his forehead, Jace doubted the night would be boring. At the very least, he'd be doing his best to impress, because there was something about Ben that made him hopeful. Maybe it was the way he assessed Jace, sizing him up instead of undressing him with his eyes. Ben wasn't easy, and that made him instantly more appealing.

Jace waved, not that he needed to, and smiled as Ben walked to him. Slowly the look of concern became more optimistic. That was good. The dim lights of a nighttime flight could be flattering, so he hoped Ben wasn't disappointed with what he saw.

"Hey," Jace said. "Fancy meeting you here."

Ben returned his smile. "Yeah, what were the odds?"

Were they supposed to shake hands? Or hug? Jace opted for putting a hand on Ben's back to guide him toward the line for renting skates. Not exactly the most stimulating of situations.

"So how are you?" Jace asked. "How's your friend?"

"I'm fine. She's a mess. Uh, how's your sister?"

Jace chuckled. "Oh, you know. Same ol' same ol'."

"Right, of course." Ben took a deep breath. "So…"

"So." Was it over already? God, why hadn't Jace suggested they meet somewhere more exciting, like in the middle of a hurricane? He had to say something. Anything! "I'm just throwing this out there, but what if we end up spending years and years together? People will ask us about our first date, and we'll have to tell them how we shuffled our feet awkwardly while waiting for ice skates."

Ben blinked at him.

"That was supposed to be funny," Jace said.

"Oh! Yeah, it was." Ben managed a pitiful laugh.

Jace was bombing, and hard. Luckily they were next in line.

"What's your shoe size?" he asked.

Ben did an imitation of a fish out of water before closing his mouth. "I can't remember."

Then it became clear that maybe they were both feeling a little nervous. Unless Ben didn't actually know his own shoe size. Funny thing, first dates. The other person could be crazy, stupid, brilliant, or any number of possibilities. All anyone could do is talk, send out signals, and see how the other person reacted.

Jace stepped close, putting his shoe next to Ben's. "I'm a size eleven, so I'm guessing you're... nine? Does that sound right?"

"Yes," Ben said, sounding relieved. "Nine and a half."

They were finally at the window. Jace rattled off their shoe sizes and paid, winking at Ben during the brief wait. As soon as they were on the rink, he'd be in his element again. Moving a little farther away, they sat to put on their skates. He glanced over to see how Ben was doing and their eyes met.

"Are you any good at this?" Ben asked.

"Oh, I do all right." Jace yanked his laces tight, then noticed Ben's skates. "Wait. You missed a rung and the tongue is stuffed in. Here."

He got on one knee, flashing Ben a smile before he undid the laces and wove them up again. Ben's cheeks flushed. Closet case, shyness, or maybe he wasn't interested anymore? There was so much Jace didn't know. Including Ben's age. Helping him with his shoes was giving Jace a little-brother vibe. Surely he was legal. Right? The skates laced and tied, he stood and offered his hand.

Ben accepted it, letting Jace pull him to his feet. Once he was up, Jace loosened his grip enough that Ben could pull his hand away if he wanted. But he didn't. Together they wobbled to the edge of the rink.

Ben eyed the ice with transparent apprehension. "I really can't ice skate at all. I did once when I was eight, and all I remember is falling on my ass until I finally gave up."

"You didn't have me then." Jace saw interest in Ben's smile. Feeling encouraged, he stepped out onto the ice. "Ready?"

Ben followed experimentally, releasing his hand to grab the side of the rink. "Uh," he said.

Jace laughed. "Hold on to me. I won't let you fall."

This time Ben took his elbow. They made it a few feet before Ben started to slip. Jace placed a helpful arm around him, hoping this didn't seem like an excuse to grope Ben. Not that it couldn't be. Rather than let his mind go there, Jace focused on coaching. Regardless of how much he demonstrated the right way, or tried to get him to relax, Ben's feet kept slipping out from under him. So maybe he wasn't the athletic type, but Ben laughed at himself every time he messed up, his eyes lighting up with joy. Jace liked that.

Eventually, Ben relaxed enough to release Jace's arm. Taking his hand instead, their fingers interlocked. Jace set a slow steady rhythm so Ben wouldn't have trouble keeping up.

"This is nice," Ben said. "Anywhere else and people would be staring at us, but here we have a reason to hold on to each other."

Busted. "I have to admit that was part of the plan, but I don't need a pretense to hold another guy's hand in public. Let people stare if they want."

Ben glanced at him. "Where were you when I was in high school?"

"I was wondering that myself. You look much younger now that you aren't suffering through a late flight."

"Oh. I just turned twenty. You?"

Legal, thank goodness, but twenty seemed a long time ago to Jace. "A little bit older than that."

"Thirty?"

"Hey!" Jace shook his hand free from Ben, skating away from him. Thirty? Seriously? He let Ben struggle, punishment for his insolence, only coming to his rescue again when Ben's arms started pinwheeling. "I'm only twenty-six!"

"Well, you were the one acting dramatic about it," Ben teased. "What do you like better anyway? Younger or older?"

"Doesn't matter. It's the personality that counts. Mind if I do a couple of rounds on my own?"

"Sure."

Jace took Ben to the rail again before skating into the lane of traffic. After going slow, breaking free without restrictions felt good. Jace glided past more cautious skaters and considered what he'd learned. Six years was a big age difference. Seven years come April. He tried to imagine being twenty again, college age. Would he have liked being with someone so much older? In his mind, he aged Adrien. No more dorm room. Adrien would have his own apartment and full-time work. That would have been nice.

They'd been so tight on space and money. Instead of them both freaking out when finals came around, only one of them would have been stressed. Also nice. But he wondered if Ben liked to party, if he was truly interested in finding the right person to settle down with. Did anyone really expect to meet the love of their life while in college?

Jace knew he wouldn't have minded. As for Ben... Well, skating solo wouldn't answer any of his questions. He found Ben bravely trying to make a round on his own. Ben smiled at him proudly, Jace nodding his approval before leading the way to the exit. Time to see how they would do without this distraction.

"Hungry?" Jace asked.

"Starving," Ben replied.

Yup. Definitely a college boy. This was the first question Jace asked when they were seated at a seafood restaurant not far away. The ride over in Jace's car had been a little quiet, but the awkward edge was definitely gone now.

"So I take it you're still in college?" Jace asked.

"Yeah, up at Columbia College in Chicago."

"How do you like it?"

Ben shrugged. "It's all right."

"I couldn't wait to get out," Jace said. "The only good thing about college was having four extra years to figure out what I wanted to do."

"I didn't know flight attendants went to college," Ben said, a foot-in-mouth expression following shortly.

"It's not a requirement. It's just that— Well, what do you want to be when you grow up? What's your major?"

"I have no idea." Ben chuckled. "It changes on a daily basis."

"There you go. Paying tuition is just an expensive way of buying time."

Ben chatted him up about his job, which most people did out of politeness, but he seemed genuinely interested. Jace was happy to talk about his career, since he was proud of it. Eventually, he became tired of the sound of his own voice. He wanted to know more about Ben.

"So what's it like growing up in Chicago?"

"No idea," Ben said. "I'm an imposter. I'm actually from here."

"Oh, that's right," Jace said. "You mentioned your parents

lived in the area. Columbia must be a good college, then. Out-of-state tuition is a bitch."

"Don't remind me," Ben said. "And yeah, it's a good school, but mostly I just wanted to get away."

Jace fought down a grin. Sounds like they had something in common. "What exactly were you trying to escape?"

Ben exhaled. "More like a who."

"What was his name?"

Ben shook his head. "Doesn't matter. And it wasn't really him, anyway. I was sick of being *the* gay guy, you know? I came out when I was in junior high—"

"Seriously?"

Ben nodded. "I was fourteen and some of my friends were… experimental."

"Ah."

Ben's cheeks flushed. "Yeah. I thought what we were doing was normal, and I was the first to put a name to it. I was young and naïve enough to think they'd be happy I figured it out for us, but *us* soon became just me. That dividing line remained all through high school, and by the end of it, I was desperate to get out of there."

Jace frowned. "So you're not open in your new school?"

Ben snorted. "Are you kidding? I go to an art school. Being gay is practically a requirement for admission."

Jace chuckled appreciatively.

"No, I'm definitely open," Ben said. "I never regretted coming out. I just got sick of feeling like I was the only one who had gotten over it, you know. To everyone else, it was a big deal. To me, being gay is just part of who I am. So when I could move on, I did."

"I can relate," Jace said. "I'm also an imposter."

Ben raised an eyebrow. "Oh?"

"Yup. Born and raised in Missouri." He said it with a country twang, pronouncing the state's name like the natives sometimes did: *Miz-zur-ruh*.

Ben grinned, brushing a lock of hair behind one ear. "So what were you running away from?"

"A boy. Of course I ended up running back to him a few times. How about you?"

Ben shook his head, seeming uncomfortable with the subject, so Jace changed it.

"So if you're enrolled in art school, what's your secret talent?"

"Finger-painting," Ben said with a straight face. Then he smiled and softly sang, *"You'll find out when I sing for my supper."*

"Wow." Jace leaned back. "That was nice. Sing some more."

Ben opened his mouth just as the waitress approached with their food. He shrugged apologetically. "Eating and singing don't go together well. Not unless you have a protective tarp handy."

While they ate, Jace asked more about Ben's school, and his life in Chicago. Jace had been there for work, allowing them to compare notes. When they were finished with their meal, he brought the conversation back to Houston again.

"Do you get along with your family?" he asked.

Ben nodded happily. "Yeah, my parents are great. They've always been supportive. Barely blinked an eye when I came out. They helped get me through the hard times. Allison too. That's my friend who lost her father. You'll have to meet her." Ben narrowed his eyes playfully. "If you make the cut."

"How am I doing so far?"

"Well, you haven't asked me what I'm into. That's good."

Jace groaned. "I know exactly what you mean. The first time a guy asked me that, I rattled off my hobbies. Then he started talking about... uh, well things you'd have to wear a glove to do."

Ben grimaced. "That's taking the question literally. He was *into* you. Or wanted to be."

Jace laughed. "I left him wanting. Anyway, that's why I made sure before this date that we were on the same page."

Ben looked shocked. "Wait, this is a date?"

"Yes. Whether you like it or not."

"Good," Ben said. "On both accounts. I like taking it slow. Part of me doesn't, but the rest of me knows it's better that way. I should at least know the guy's last name, right?"

There was an awkward pause.

"Holden," Jace said at the same time Ben said "Bentley." Then they both laughed. Jace signaled the waitress and ordered dessert. He was already stuffed but didn't want the meal to end just yet. They talked more about their families and friends, describing their lives through the people around them rather than trying to do the impossible and explain who they were. Hopefully they would find that out as they went along. When the waitress asked for the third time if there was anything else they needed, Jace gave up trying to prolong the inevitable and paid. The night was too late for a movie, and they were both driving so drinks were out. There wasn't anything left to do besides take Ben back to the mall.

Once there, they chatted a little longer next to Ben's car, both of them distracted by what should happen next. Taking it slow was one thing, but no successful date ended without a goodnight kiss. The only problem was trying to segue into an appropriately romantic moment. Standing in an empty parking lot certainly didn't help.

"This is no place for a first kiss," Jace said in frustration. "You could come home with me, meet the cat."

Ben smiled. "Not on the first date."

"Nothing has to happen," he said, not wanting the night to end.

"Trust me, if I get you somewhere private, something *will* happen."

Jace's pulse kicked into high gear. "Well, well! I guess that means I get to see you again?"

"How about Thursday?"

Three days away? Jace was hoping for something sooner, but then again, he still had to entertain Michelle and her family. "It's a deal. Look, I'm kissing you tonight, but I refuse to do it here. Just follow me in your car for a minute, and I promise I'll let you go home afterwards."

Ben grew somber and nodded. "Okay."

Both in their cars, they drove a few blocks, Jace racking his brain for an environment even remotely romantic. A river glistening with reflected stars, or a garden filled with roses. In the end, he settled for a public park. Ben's car parked behind his. Jace could only imagine what Ben was thinking, but at least he got out of his car instead of driving away.

Ben definitely didn't seem convinced. "Are you sure about this?" he asked.

"No," Jace said, glancing around. "I'm improvising. Over there."

Taking Ben's hand, they strolled together toward a baseball diamond. Also not an arena known for romantic potential. There was the pitcher's mound, which seemed tasteless, or home base, which was kind of funny. This gave him an idea. Jace led them to one point of the diamond outline.

"First base?" Ben asked. "You've got to be kidding."

"I assure you," Jace said, pulling Ben close, "I'm quite serious."

Before he could second-guess himself, or worry if this was too fast for Ben, Jace brought their lips together. The world shrank down to this moment, distant sounds and distracting thoughts going mute. Jace pressed his body close to Ben's, kissing him deeper and tasting a hint of the lemon sherbet he'd had for dessert. Or maybe Ben always tasted like that—citrus fresh and candy sweet. Jace was only sure of one thing: Ending the kiss was difficult indeed!

"Second base is just over there," Ben said with a wry smile.

"Not on the first date." Jace took one step back as if to avoid an explosion. He stroked his thumb against Ben's cheek before gesturing toward the cars with his head. Together they slowly strolled back.

"I was just kidding about the taking it slow stuff," Ben said.

"You weren't."

"No, I wasn't. But that was before we kissed. You can tell how compatible you are with someone by kissing, don't you think?"

Jace thought about it. "Depends what you mean by compatible."

"You can tell if you have potential," Ben explained. "For love or a relationship or whatever."

"What's the whatever?" Jace asked.

"I don't know." Ben laughed nervously, taking hold of his arm. "My last boyfriend had a lip piercing, which was distracting, and he tasted like smoke the first time we kissed. That didn't work out. Another guy I was with for a long time, kissing him was almost electric."

"So it's like palm reading but with your lips?"

"Yeah," Ben said. "Exactly."

"Then why aren't you and the electric kisser still together?"

Ben considered this, brightening up when he found the answer. "Like I said, it only reveals potential. That doesn't mean things will work out."

"I see. And how did I do? How much potential do we have?"

"Hm." Ben's brow came together thoughtfully. "You know, I can't seem to remember."

Jace smirked. "Then let me remind you." He kissed Ben again, putting all of himself into it. When they pulled away—Ben with a slight gasp—he grinned and said:

"Fire. Kissing you is like catching fire."

Jace nodded in satisfaction. "Then I'll say goodnight before you get burned."

Ben looked as though he had something else in mind, but then he smiled dreamily and backed away toward his car. "You'll call me, right?"

"I still don't have your number," Jace said.

"Then I'll call you. Maybe. Probably."

"I'll sit by the phone and weep jilted tears until I hear from you."

"Good." Ben waited by the driver-side door with a hopeful expression.

Jace shook his head. "Go home."

"I don't want you to think I'm easy," Ben said, opening the door, "but I hope that's the last time you ever say that to me."

As Jace got in his car and pulled away, he felt certain it would be.

Chapter Twenty-three

That Jace didn't bring Ben home turned out to be a blessing, since he returned to find Greg on the couch. His best friend and brother-in-law was slowly working his way through the miniature bottles of booze Jace pilfered from work. At least someone was getting use out of them.

"Daddy time," Greg said, kicking back another bottle.

Jace tossed his jacket over the arm of the couch. "Everything okay with you and Michelle?"

"Yeah, we're great! She figured we could use some guy time, and you gave us a spare key, so..." Greg suddenly seemed uncertain about the idea.

"It's cool," Jace said, and it was.

"Besides, I have some news." Greg leaned back, stretching his arms wide on the back of the couch. "I met with a realtor today to look at some houses. Really, I just wanted to get the inside scoop on the scene here. Anyway, we got to talking and he has more clients than he can handle—"

Jace sat on the edge of the coffee table. "So you're really moving down here?"

"Yeah!"

"That's awesome!"

"I know!" Greg demanded a high five.

Jace humored him. "You know what this means, right?" he said after they'd slapped palms. Then he tapped his upper lip meaningfully.

Greg covered his mustache protectively. "No!"

"Yup!"

"Fine." Greg grabbed another bottle. "Let me work up my courage first."

"Okay, but you're not leaving here with that thing on."

Greg rolled his eyes. "So how was work?"

"Oh. About that." Jace had told Michelle he had to work a shift at one of the airport counters. Lying wasn't usually his style, but he figured she'd make a fuss about his date. Not knowing how the evening would play out, Jace had decided to keep it a secret. Now he felt like raving about it.

Greg was a captive audience as Jace filled him in on the

details. He was still talking about Ben when he guided Greg to the bathroom, parked him in front of the mirror, and put a shaving razor in his hand.

"Did you guys do it?" Greg asked.

"Stop stalling," Jace said. "I already told you—a few kisses and then we parted ways."

"So you've got a major case of blue balls?"

Jace shook his head at Greg's reflection in the mirror. "We're not discussing my balls."

Greg smiled like a naughty eight-year-old. "Should we discuss mine?"

"Only if you want to talk about getting a vasectomy."

Greg shrugged. "We Trouts are a fertile people." He tossed the razor in the sink, not having shaved a hair, and turned to face Jace. "So what do you think? Is this Ben guy marriage material?"

"He's a little young for that," Jace said. "Actually, he's a little young in general. We're six, maybe seven years apart."

"Doesn't matter," Greg said. "Not if you're the guy in the relationship. It's normal for chicks to dig older guys, and Ben sounds like the girl to me."

Jace stared at him and shook his head. "You know, sometimes it blows me away how sensitive you can be, and then you go and spout crap like that."

"Ah ha!" Greg waggled his eyebrows. "So *you* are the girl."

Jace crossed his arms over his chest. "You're not goading me into talking about this."

"Come on," Greg pleaded. "Just once. Guys are supposed to spill their guts to each other. Brothers too. You're doubly obligated to talk about these things with me."

"Fine, but there is no 'girl' in the relationship. I don't even think it works that way for heterosexuals. Are you telling me Michelle is never in charge of you?"

This gave Greg pause. "You know, she does joke that she wears the pants in our relationship. Oh god! Am I the girl?"

Jace laughed. "Either way, it's too late to back out now."

"Funny, that's what I keep telling her. So anyway, do you think the age difference is a problem?"

Jace thought about it and shook his head. "No. It felt kind of nice being a few steps ahead of him. He asked about life after college and got this deer-in-the-headlights look. Being able to reassure him felt good. I could take care of him, keep him safe. You know?"

"That's really sweet," Greg said. "So this means you're the top, right?"

Jace raised an eyebrow. "How about you turn around so we can get down to business."

Greg looked momentarily concerned until he remembered their original goal. Reluctantly, he turned and picked up the razor. "Do I have to?"

"Yes," Jace said. "Once you've made your name down here and have millions in the bank, you can grow all the eccentric facial hair you want. But for now, the mustache has to go."

"But I love it," Greg whined. "My mustache is practically my best friend. We go everywhere together. I call him Little Greg."

Jace stepped forward, picked up the shaving cream, and squeezed some into his hand. Then he smeared it all over Greg's mustache. "I love you, but I don't love Little Greg. It's time for him to die."

Greg gazed somberly at his own reflection. "I guess I do look like a wimpy version of Hulk Hogan."

Jace slapped him on the rump. "The Hulkster's got nothing on you." Then for good measure, he added, "But shave the damn thing off anyway."

The phone rang the next morning. Jace poked his head over the loft bed, squinting against the morning light. Greg was sitting up on the couch, rubbing his eyes.

"Should I get it?" he asked.

Jace nodded and flopped back into bed. He figured it was Michelle, wanting to know where her husband was. Or maybe Ben was eager to hear his voice again. When Greg tossed the phone up to him, Jace wished they hadn't answered it. Work. Too many people had called in sick. On the holidays. Go figure. So much for his vacation. Of course this would mean more money for him, which was great. Greg was driving his family back home today anyway, and Ben wasn't free until Thursday, so why not?

What Jace discovered when he got to the airport was that he wouldn't be home again until Friday. He stressed about this the whole day, feeling even worse when he called his answering machine that night to hear Ben's nervously excited message. At least he left his number so Jace would be able to explain.

As it turned out, he had little to worry about. Ben was understanding—a hopeful sign. Abrupt changes in his schedule happened all the time, something any boyfriend of his would have to cope with. They made plans instead for New Year's Eve. It wasn't until Jace hung up the phone that he realized, this year, he'd have someone to kiss as the new century came rushing in.

They met at a party thrown by one of Jace's coworkers. Like ice skating, he thought this would provide enough distraction to get them past any initial jitters or awkwardness. He regretted the decision the moment Ben arrived. Seeing him justified the countless thoughts and fantasies that had run through Jace's mind the last couple of days. What he wanted, more than anything, was to be alone with him. After some frustrating attempts at conversation that were interrupted by others, Jace suggested they leave, encouraged by Ben's relieved expression.

This gave him enough courage to suggest they head back to his place. Jace didn't intend for them to get there and hop into bed. As appealing as that sounded, he'd rather talk to Ben, get to know him better. The drive across town was trying, since they were in separate cars. Jace swore that once they arrived, he wouldn't let Ben get away from him again. Even if that meant giving Ben the bed while he slept on the couch, Jace was determined to spend all of his delayed vacation with him.

Except when he parked and stepped out of the car, Ben seemed uncomfortable. "You all right?" he asked.

"Yeah." Ben's eyes betrayed him, darting around the neighborhood.

So maybe it wasn't the prettiest part of town. In the past the area had been an industrial district, and attempts to make it a residential zone hadn't been completely convincing. But it wasn't like there were body outlines chalked on the street or hobos warming their hands over flaming barrels.

"Where did you say you were from again?" he asked.

"The Woodlands," Ben answered. "Why?"

Jace nodded. That made sense. The Woodlands was a good half-hour north of Houston and well known for its wealthy communities built around golf courses. Jace felt much more at home in an environment like this one. "It might not be the prettiest neighborhood, but I've never had any trouble here."

"It's fine," Ben insisted. "You should see my place in Chicago."

Regardless, he seemed apprehensive when they stepped into the cage elevator. Maybe he was thinking how little he really knew about Jace. Ben laughed nervously as they rattled their way to the top floor. Perhaps the boy had good instincts, since Jace didn't plan on letting him escape from here. It would be a kidnapping, but one of the most loving variety.

Jace was still tickled by this thought when they entered the apartment. Like a dog, Samson always greeted him at the door. Sure enough, he came strolling over, keeping a wary eye on the stranger.

"Samson!" Jace said, picking him up. "We have a visitor."

After Samson marked him by rubbing a cheek against his chin, they both turned to consider Ben. Please let him be a cat person! At the very least, don't let him be allergic. That would ruin everything. To his relief, Ben reached a hand out to pet him, but Samson was only interested in sniffing it.

"Security scan initiated," Jace said in a mechanical voice, nodding when Samson didn't hiss or put his ears back. "Mm-hm. I think you've passed. Let's see about getting you something to eat."

Jace set about feeding Samson, pretending to be distracted so Ben could survey his apartment. Not that Ben seemed to have any hesitation about openly snooping. After inspecting the corner kitchen, Ben walked through the living room, taking it all in. Jace only wished he had straightened up more, but he really hadn't expected them to end up here tonight.

Once Samson was fed, Jace opened two single-serving bottles of champagne, and poured them into flute glasses. Then he joined Ben, who was examining his extensive collection of biographies. Funny how possessions could speak for an individual. That was never Jace's intent. He didn't decorate to impress. He simply surrounded himself with what he loved. Now he wondered what conclusions Ben was drawing from these things. That he was celebrity-obsessed?

"I love reading about people's lives," Jace said from behind. "Do you read?"

"Yeah, but mostly fiction."

"That's what some of these are," Jace said. "If you were writing an autobiography, would you really be able to resist the temptation to doctor the past? Who wants to write about crapping their pants in grade school when it's more fun to exaggerate success and talk trash on old flames?"

Ben chuckled. "Good point."

"Biographies are even worse since they are mostly speculation written by adoring fans, spoon-fed false information from the celebrity's agent. Regardless, I can't help but read them. It's a guilty pleasure of mine."

Ben pulled his attention away from the books and noticed the glasses of champagne. "Oh, wow! I didn't hear the bottle pop!"

"It didn't," Jace said. "More freebies from the airlines. They only have the single-serving bottles with the screw top."

"It's cool that you get stuff like that for free."

"Not exactly free." Jace grimaced. "At least, it's not supposed to be, but who doesn't pilfer from their job?"

Ben carefully took a glass from him. "Just promise me you have something better in bed than those dinky airline pillows."

Hint taken! "Wait and see," Jace said, raising his glass. "Here's to new millenniums and new friendships. Assuming the Y2K bug doesn't destroy us all, that is."

They clinked their glasses together and drank, Jace's eyes never leaving Ben's. When he noticed this, Ben managed to look a little bashful, but Jace couldn't help wondering if it was an act. Either that, or Ben's mouth was a lot braver than the rest of him. Right now it was asking how much time remained in the year.

"About an hour."

Jace motioned for them to sit. Once on the couch together—Samson hopping up on his lap as always—Ben had to make room on the table for his glass. Greg had gotten the munchies and raided his fortune cookie stash, strips of prophetic paper everywhere.

"You sure like Chinese food!"

"Not really." Jace felt embarrassed at having to explain this quirk. "I just really like fortune cookies. There's a restaurant down the road that sells me full shipping boxes. I know it sounds insane, but they're my absolute favorite treat."

Ben seemed amused, eyes shining as he considered Jace. "So explain to me how it is that you're still single."

Definitely a brave mouth. Jace just hoped Ben wasn't all talk. "I could ask you the same question."

"Well, I wasn't until a week ago." Ben washed down the bitterness with some champagne.

"Right, right. The burgling boyfriend." The word 'rebound' sprang to mind. "Have you heard from him since?"

"Nope, and don't change the subject. Are you the kind of guy who can't settle down?"

Jace winced. "Quite the opposite. I've had my share of boyfriends. It's just the job that gets in the way."

"What do you mean?"

Might as well tell him the truth. "The hours suck. I'm gone for days at a time, and until I have more seniority, my schedule is constantly shifting. So I can't promise anyone when I'll be home, or if I'll even be there at all. Something about sleeping in a hotel every night gives people ideas, so if it isn't the hours, it's the jealousy."

Ben nibbled his bottom lip, mulling this over. "I don't know. It doesn't sound all that bad to me. Being apart and not seeing each other every day would keep things fresh. I think I could deal with that."

"That's what they all say at the beginning. Not that I'm trying to discourage you. I'd love for you to prove me wrong. Speaking of which, I fly to Chicago all the time."

Ben smiled. "What are you suggesting?"

Jace took a deep breath. He might as well lay all his cards out on the table. "That I like you and that I want more than to just sleep with you. I know we're moving fast, that we don't know each other very well, but what I've seen so far is a charming, considerate, and surprisingly mature college student who is on his way to becoming someone great."

Ben appeared appropriately flattered. "Thanks. I think you're the bee's knees too."

Jace laughed in relief. So far so good. Just one little concern left. "What I'd like to know is how serious you and your prince of thieves were. Are you coming out of a relationship of years? How long before things turned sour?"

"Just a few weeks. He was nothing. Really." Ben held his gaze long enough that Jace believed him. "What about you? Any emotional baggage I need to know about?"

Loads, and all of it overweight. "There was, but the airline lost it all. Typical really."

Ben didn't laugh, but Jace was feeling pretty serious himself. There was nothing standing in their way now. That they both liked each other was obvious, and that they wanted more than just casual sex was good. Jace had to admit, though, that he wouldn't mind some committed sex right about now, but pushing it seemed—

Ben glanced up at the loft bed longingly, and Jace couldn't help but chuckle. He stood, Samson leaping off his lap just before with eerie cat instinct. Jace slid an arm under Ben's legs, another behind his back, and picked him up off the couch. Ben didn't resist in the slightest. Instead he threw an arm around Jace's neck and giggled like a kid as Jace carried him toward the bed. He paused when reaching the ladder, Ben's expression of amusement turning to concern when he saw Jace was still determined. With a heave, he tossed Ben over his shoulders, gripping one of his arms to make sure he didn't slip loose. Then he stepped onto the first rung.

"Put me down!" Ben cried in protest.

"This is like a hot, gay version of *King Kong*," Jace grunted, pulling himself up rung by rung with his free hand. When they reached the top, he bent over, Ben rolling into bed before Jace clambered in after him.

Ben was still laughing, his hair messed up as he looked around. "Airline pillows!" he said in mock disgust. He grabbed a couple and tossed them at Jace.

"You won't be sleeping much tonight," Jace said, crawling over to where Ben was.

Ben lay back so Jace could get on top of him. Greg would probably be smug as hell if he could see them now, because it was obvious that Ben was very comfortable with Jace taking the lead. Not that he was passive. Ben was already fumbling at Jace's shirt buttons.

Moving his hands gently away, Jace kissed him. This is where he wanted to start. He'd promised himself to take things slow, and while he'd done a miserable job so far, now he meant to do just that. They had the whole night to explore each other.

Running a hand through Ben's hair, Jace lifted his head to bring it closer, his tongue slipping inside Ben's mouth. Last night their cold noses had bumped together, lips a little dry from the winter weather, but now they were both warm, mouths increasingly wet as they caressed each other.

Ben's hands kept going for his shirt, or the waist of his jeans, but Jace kept moving those hands away, eventually pinning them. He laughed at Ben's frustration, and admired his stubbornness when Ben wrapped his legs around Jace's waist, drawing him close and rubbing the hardness in their pants together.

That motivated him to take it further. Rolling over so Ben was sitting on top of him, Jace stripped off Ben's shirt, admiring the thin frame, the gentle lines of ribs—little rolling hills made of pale skin instead of grass. He allowed his fingers to brush against these, summoning goose bumps. Ben's back arched when Jace toyed with his nipples. A moan escaped from his throat as Jace slid the tips of his fingers into the waistline of Ben's jeans before pulling them out again.

Ben gave him a look that was both pleading and half-mad with pleasure. Jace sat up for a kiss, stroking Ben's back as their tongues reunited. Again Ben's hands began to wander, but Jace caught them just before they could reach anything particularly interesting. Finally Ben had enough and pushed Jace down on the bed, hands flat on his chest.

"I'm about to suffocate you with one of these airline pillows," he threatened.

"Is that a fetish?" Jace asked.

"No," Ben growled, "but at least then I could do what I want to you!"

Jace laughed. "In that case, I surrender."

He let his arms flop to the sides, amused by the kid-in-a-candy-store expression that came over Ben's face. He allowed his shirt to be unbuttoned first, enjoying the way Ben's eyes travelled over him before his hands traced the same path. Then Ben carefully unbuttoned and unzipped Jace's jeans, grinning victoriously as he yanked them off his hips.

"Seriously?" he said. "Speedos?"

Jace responded by flexing one muscle in particular. That shut him up. Well, almost. Ben squeezed Jace's cock through his underwear. "Size doesn't matter," he said, "but it sure is nice when you've got it."

Jace grinned his agreement, then moaned as Ben began to

pump. He closed his eyes and bit his lip, nearly drawing blood when Ben pulled his underwear down and enveloped him in wet warmth. That mouth was brave, that mouth could sing and—holy shit!—that mouth had other talents as well. Jace's mind produced a list of the guys he'd slept with and swiftly crossed their names out one by one. None of them were as skilled as Ben. What the hell did they teach people at that college of his?

Eventually he recovered from this bliss enough to pull Ben up by the arm pits. Ben held himself above Jace as they kissed so that Jace could get at his jeans. As soon as the top button was undone, Jace thrust in a hand, feeling a drop of excitement on Ben's dick as he took hold of it. Ben had nothing to be ashamed of either, but Jace took satisfaction in being bigger. Ben toppled over on his side, eager to remove his jeans. Jace did the same, also shrugging his shirt the rest of the way off.

Finally, they were both completely naked together. After eyeing each other like hungry sharks, they came out of the situation enough to laugh. Jace didn't think he'd ever get tired of that sound. He planned on sticking around a dozen decades or more just to have his fill. Lying next to Ben, Jace kissed him gently, stroking his skin again, but this time he didn't hold back. He brushed his fingers down Ben's arms, up his thighs, across his chest, down the center of his cock to his balls. Everywhere he could reach, he wanted to caress. Jace watched Ben's face the whole time he did this, seeing a need that was much more than physical. Had anyone ever given Ben what he needed emotionally? Ever?

Jace's lips took over for his hands as he kissed and licked, bit and nibbled. Sometimes Ben laughed, sometimes he moaned. When Jace finally went down on him, he sighed, as if in relief. Ben's hands clutched at his hair, and when Jace felt him getting close, he pulled away, sitting up on his knees and offering himself. They took turns in this way until Jace almost couldn't hold back any longer, but he did, just long enough to bring Ben to the brink once more. He had Ben's cock in his mouth, his hips thrusting against the grip Ben had on him, and in a series of groans and hisses, they came together in a way that Jace could only describe as spiritual.

Outside, fireworks exploded as drunk voices called out to each other. Not wanting to miss the moment, he placed his forehead against Ben's. "Happy New Year," he said before kissing him.

Afterwards, he pulled the covers over them both, cradling Ben to him. If kissing could reveal the potential they had together, what they'd done just now promised unlimited possibility. He remembered the oath he'd made as a teenager, the night Bernard had dragged him from the river. Jace had sworn then that he'd find the person he was meant to be with, no matter how long it took. This person sharing his bed with him now... Maybe.

Chapter Twenty-four

Jace watched Ben sleep, thinking about how he'd first done so at forty thousand feet above Texas. Now Ben had dropped from the heavens and landed in his bed. Blond hair a disaster and a steady stream of drool leaking from his mouth, Ben couldn't have looked more adorable if he tried. Of course most guys didn't mess up their hair and drool when they wanted to impress, but perhaps it would become trendy one day.

The intensity of Jace's stare stirred Ben from his sleep. He wiped his mouth on his arm and furrowed his brow, perhaps not yet remembering where he was.

"I want to get to know you better." The words had been on Jace's lips for the last ten minutes. It felt good to finally speak them.

Ben smiled. "You didn't get to know me last night?"

"That was very educational," Jace said, "but I want more. Tell me about your life. Better yet, show me. Is it too early to meet the parents?"

"Yes," Ben replied. "I want you to be madly in love with me before you realize how nuts they are."

"That bad?"

Ben shook his head. "Not really. Well, my sister isn't easy to get along with." After rubbing his eyes he peered at the clock. "You could meet Allison."

"Your best friend?" Jace asked, feeling proud for remembering this detail.

"Yeah. I could show you around The Woodlands too, since that's where I grew up."

They'd slept in long enough that they agreed to skip breakfast. Instead they hit the shower together, which was fun and allowed Jace to check out Ben's body in daylight. Ben wasn't shy about looking him over either, which led to a prolonged shower. When the hot water ran out, they shut it off, ending up on the bathroom floor together.

Eventually they managed to keep their clothes on long enough to rejoin civilization. Sadly, this meant getting in their separate cars again. Now that they were serious, in the future Jace would rather make the half-hour drive to pick Ben up. Not that things would stay this way for long. Ben would return to

Chicago in a couple weeks, making the opportunity to see where he grew up more imperative.

Jace wasn't completely unfamiliar with The Woodlands. The area had a reputation for being a wealthy community, which had caught Adrien's attention. They'd visited together on one of their "splurge nights" they used to save up for. After putting on their best clothes, he and Adrien would go off to a fancy restaurant, pretending to be anything but broke college boys. One such night had them visiting The Woodlands. Jace enjoyed the way that trees hid the suburban landscape, but he hadn't been terribly impressed otherwise. Despite its reputation, the city seemed much like any other, which was fine. Money had a way of making Jace uncomfortable, especially in extremes. Too much money felt decadent, while too little had its own discomforts.

The neighborhood Ben led them to was somewhere in the middle. After some signaling, Jace parked in a driveway next to a beat-up Ford Escort that had seen better days but probably couldn't remember them anymore. Ben parked behind him, the engine still running when he got out.

"I need to bring the car back to my parents," he explained. "They live a few blocks over."

"Oh," Jace said, not hiding his puzzlement. Couldn't they have done that first?

Ben grinned. "Have fun with Allison. I'll catch up with you guys soon."

Jace put on his best poker face, waving at Ben as he drove away, when really he felt apprehensive. Should he knock on the door and introduce himself? He supposed it would be weirder to stand out front and wait for Ben to return. Besides, he was pretty sure this was a test. Standing there like an idiot was a surefire way of failing it. Jace strolled up to the door and rang the bell.

A pretty black woman answered. This had to be Allison. Not only did she seem to be the same age as Ben, but she had a shadow hanging over her, the kind that stuck around long after someone close had passed away.

Allison looked him over. "Can I help you?"

"There's an old proverb that goes 'the enemy of my enemy is my friend,'" Jace said. "That always struck me as a huge assumption, since my enemy's enemy could be the kind of person who kicks puppies."

"And you're selling…" Allison asked.

"Now then," Jace continued, "the friend of my friend is also my friend makes a lot more sense, even though it's harder to say. I figure your best friend, let's call him Ben, has plenty of good reasons for liking you. If I like Ben, and he likes you, then it stands to reason that I probably like you too. Hopefully that also works in reverse."

"Depends," Allison said. "Did Ben put you up to this, or are you a creepy stalker?"

"A little of both?" He held out his hand. "I'm Jace. Ben's taking his car back to his parents, and I imagine he thinks it's funny putting me in this awkward position."

Allison considered his hand before taking it and squeezing gently. "Or maybe I'm supposed to appraise you, decide if you make the grade."

"How I am doing so far?"

"Well, you're handsome, but the crazy ones usually are." Allison looked him over once more. Then she nodded toward the interior. "Come on in."

Jace wasn't sure what to expect. Vases full of condolence flowers, or furniture draped in black cloth, maybe. Instead the house seemed fairly normal. The curtains were all open, letting in the sunshine, and Jace could hear a Top 40 radio station in another room. Allison led them toward this sound, which grew louder and louder until they entered the kitchen. She went to a counter and shut off the radio before turning around to face him.

"Want something to drink? Whisky? Beer?"

Jace shook his head. "I don't drink during the day."

"Oh, first test passed!" Allison said with some humor. "How about an iced tea?"

"That would be fine."

She took two large plastic tumblers from the cabinet, then a pitcher from the fridge that she used to fill them. After handing one to Jace, she raised her glass in toast. He did the same, laughing nervously. While they drank, they considered each other. Okay, so this was a little uncomfortable. Allison spoke first.

"I'd invite you to sit down, but—" She nodded at the table, which was covered in cardboard boxes and paperwork. "We could go to the living room."

Jace considered the mess on the table. He knew what had

caused it. There had been boxes when Victor had died. Jace's parents had worked with the public administrator, moving as many of Mrs. Hemingway's possessions to her room at the nursing home as they could. He didn't know what happened to the rest, but his parents had boxed up some things from Victor's room, thinking Jace might want them. He'd barely recognized anything, which had only upset him further. He hadn't kept any of it, except the beat-up Zippo. Besides the lighter, all he had from those days were a few photos, an old werewolf mask, and a carving of a lion.

"I'm sorry," Jace said. "I didn't know your father, and I don't really know you, but I know what it's like to lose someone."

"Thank you," Allison said.

"If there's anything I can do to help..."

"Not unless you know how to dissolve an estate." Allison sighed, walking toward the stacks of paper and considering them. "I stayed up half the night trying to make a plan. Should I keep the house? I don't know how much Ben has told you, but it's just me, really. My mother died a long time ago, and my dad and I didn't get along so well." She looked up at him. "I don't want this house, but I don't feel like I have the right to sell it either. I mean, it's his. Not mine."

Jace understood that too. The little box of Victor's possessions had made him equally as uncomfortable. Disposing of it had seemed treacherous, and it had been many months before Jace had been able to do so. "Don't rush anything," he said. "That is... Do you mind if I get personal?"

Allison shrugged. "The friend of my friend is also my friend."

Jace smiled. "Is the house paid off? If not, are you able to make the payments?"

"It's nearly paid off," Allison said. "There's an insurance policy that will do more than cover the rest."

"Then you have time," Jace said. "Losing your father is hard enough. Let the house stay as it is for now and focus on dealing with your loss. When you're back on your feet, you can decide what this house means to you, if anything."

Allison exhaled, as if relieved. "Yeah. Maybe you're right. You know what's funny? If I do sell the house, the idea of having all that money terrifies me. Isn't that stupid?"

"Nope." Jace shook his head. "It just means you're too smart to do anything foolish with it. I have a suggestion though."

Allison took another sip of her tea. "An investment tip?"

"Sort of. Buy yourself a new car. That's your Ford Escort outside, isn't it?"

Allison raised an eyebrow. "And what if it is?"

"Just looking at it gives me chills," Jace said. "If cars could become zombies, yours would be one. It probably lurches through the streets at night, devouring the engines of other vehicles instead of brains."

Allison pretended to be offended. "Next to Ben, that car is the most loyal friend I have."

"Really?"

Allison snorted. "No. I can't wait to get rid of it. Speaking of which, my father's car. I don't know if it's paid off or…"

Looking panicked, she set down her tea and started rifling through the papers. Jace asked if he could help. She accepted. By the time Ben entered the kitchen a few minutes later, they were seated at the table together, Allison on the phone with the dealership where her father had purchased his car, holding a list of questions that Jace had helped her compile. Jace fixed Ben with a stern expression and put a finger to his lips, as if his intrusion was unwelcome.

After the call, Allison beamed at Ben, the first real smile Jace had seen. "I'm so glad you sent him to me," she said.

"You can't keep him," Ben said. "He's mine."

God, how Jace loved the sound of that! This called for a celebration. "Let's grab lunch," he said. "We'll go somewhere nice. My treat."

They agreed, but first Allison went upstairs to change her clothes. Ben went with her. When they returned, his hair was nicely styled. Allison wore makeup, subtle perfume, and a smart black top.

"Should I run home for something dressy?" Ben asked, tugging at the flannel shirt he wore.

Jace considered him thoughtfully. "No, I think they'll let you in like that."

"Is it that fancy?" Ben asked, intimidated.

"Yes," Jace said. "Although festive is probably a better word. Shall we?"

They piled into his car, and after a short drive, they pulled into a parking lot. "Ready, kids?" Jace said, unbuckling his seat belt. He turned in his seat to face his passengers. Ben looked as apprehensive as Allison did excited.

"Chuck E. Cheese's!" she squealed.

"Not fancy enough for you?" Jace asked when Ben didn't respond.

"He's scared of the robots," Allison said, playfully shoving her friend. "Come on, you big wimp. We'll protect you!"

The calm atmosphere of the parking lot gave way to one of complete chaos when they entered the restaurant. Kids screamed with delight as bright lights flashed from all directions, the bangs and roars of video games accompanying them. If Jace closed his eyes, he suspected it would sound like a war waged by children, their army spreading across the nation as they conquered every toy store in their path. They wandered through this paradise, Jace grinning at it all. Was this the right time to ask if Ben wanted kids? Probably not. They made their way to the dining area, Ben gripping Jace's arm as if they were in a haunted house. On stage, a giant animatronic rat and his friends were telling terrible jokes and singing outdated songs.

Once they had ordered their pizza, he couldn't resist asking, "Why are you scared of the robots?"

Ben just shook his head, but Allison was happy to fill him in on the details.

"He had a birthday party here when he was little," she said. "Ben was standing in front of the stage, shaking his thing and singing along with Chucky when the power cut out."

"It was a thunderstorm," Ben said. "Like the kind from hell with big boomers and tons of lightning."

"Hurricane season," Allison said. "Anyway, all the lights go out, so of course the robots stop singing—"

"—*and* moving," Ben said defensively. "So I turn to look at them, and let me tell you, a seven-foot-tall rat is a lot scarier in the dark. As I'm staring into the dim reflection of his dead eyes, Chuck hisses and bends over to kill me."

"Or," Allison said, "the hydraulics started draining of air, making the robot slump over slightly."

"Like a kid understands that," Ben said. "For weeks I had nightmares about him grabbing me and turning me into one of his singing robots."

"Oh, I'd like to see that," Allison said. "What animal would you be?" Before he could answer, she started snapping her fingers as a new song started. Soon she was singing along with the worst version of Wham's *Jitterbug* that Jace had ever heard. Only Allison's voice made it tolerable, since she could really sing. After the first verse, Ben joined in. They sang together like lovers did in musicals, making cute faces at each other and pointing to signal when one should take the lead. The pun that popped into Jace's mind was terrible, but their music revealed the harmony they shared. This wasn't a casual friendship. They loved each other. Jace thought of Greg, happy Ben had someone like that in his life.

When finished eating they hit the game room, competing in such time-honored sports as Whac-A-Mole and skee-ball. They earned enough tickets to get Allison a cheap and tawdry tiara from the prize counter, which she wore like the Queen of Texas. Allison and Ben remained in high spirits on the drive home, chatting in the backseat like a couple of teenagers. This made Jace feel like the adult chaperone, but every time he glanced in the rearview mirror and saw Ben's smile, he couldn't help but do the same.

"You guys go do something romantic," Allison said when they pulled into her driveway. "I have things I need to take care of."

"Need any help?" Jace offered.

"I'm good," Allison said. "Thanks for lunch. I had a nice time."

"Me too," Jace said. "Just remember the free pizza when you write your report on me."

"Will do." Allison nudged Ben. "Speaking of which, call me later if you're not busy."

Ben smiled sheepishly as she hugged him and got out of the car. Once Allison was safely inside, Jace looked again to the rearview mirror. "Where to?"

"This is my old neighborhood," Ben said. "We could go for a walk. Leave the car here."

"Okay."

Jace liked Allison—a lot—but was glad to have more time alone with Ben. Once they were on the sidewalk he offered his hand, Ben taking it and smiling up at him.

"That was a cool idea," he said. "I didn't think I'd see Allison that happy any time soon."

"It's impossible to be sad at Chuck E. Cheese's," Jace said. "They should stop catering to kids and start doing funerals."

Ben laughed. "You might be on to something. They could program the robots to give eulogies and sing hymns."

"I'm putting that in my will," Jace said. He considered the neighborhood houses, which weren't so different from Warrensburg. "So you lived around here?"

"Yeah," Ben said. "I'll show you."

A quarter of the way around the block, a sidewalk lined with trees wound between houses. Jace had read about the bike paths, or maybe Adrien had told him. He knew they ran all through the community, allowing residents to walk, jog, or bike just about anywhere. Ben led them a couple of blocks over to an innocuous two-story house. The car he had been driving was parked in the driveway.

"There it is," Ben said. "Pretty thrilling, huh?"

"It's hard to tell much from the outside," Jace said.

"I guess we could go in."

"Nah. I want you all to myself."

Ben nodded his agreement. "Anyway, that's where I grew up. It seems small now. In my memory, it felt like my entire world at times. Now when I come home, it's like the house isn't big enough for me, like I couldn't stay there long without feeling cramped."

"I know what you mean," Jace said as they continued walking. "My whole hometown feels that way. When I go back now, I nearly suffocate. I used to have a friend—my first boyfriend, actually—who never wanted to be indoors. I couldn't really understand why until recently. He must have felt something similar."

"How old were you?" Ben asked.

"When I had my first boyfriend? Seventeen."

Ben nudged him. "Got you beat! I was sixteen!"

Jace chuckled. "Lucky you. On second thought, lucky him."

Ben's smile faded. They entered another bike path, one that branched off in a couple of different directions. They turned right, and Jace could see a small lake and park ahead. Ben stopped. Jace glanced over at him, but Ben's attention was focused on the lake.

"You all right?"

"Yeah," Ben said. "Let's go a different way."

"Okay." They backtracked in silence a few moments. Ben was clearly lost in thought, or the past, which is exactly where Jace wanted to go. He wanted to know more about him, but knew he couldn't force matters. "If it's hard for you to be here, we can go somewhere else."

"It's not hard," Ben said. Then he smiled ironically. "But it's not easy."

"Ah." Rather than walk in silence, Jace decided to pry. "The reason you moved to Chicago?"

"Kind of," Ben admitted. Then he squeezed Jace's hand tighter. "His name is Tim. Did you ever have a crush on a straight guy?"

Jace shook his head. "Honestly, no."

"Oh. Well, it's not important."

Feeling the lifeline slipping away, Jace quickly added, "Then again, my boyfriend couldn't admit he was anything, straight or gay."

Ben glanced over at him. "How does that work?"

"Don't ask. Victor was a very strange person. Anyway, I know what it's like to love someone who can't love you back in the way you need."

"Exactly." Ben looked relieved. "That sums it up perfectly."

"So did Tim live around here too?"

"Yeah," Ben said. "Not too far away. I used to sneak over to his house at night. Everything was a big secret with him. That's the kind of guy Tim was. Get him to take off one mask and there'd be another beneath it. Over the course of a year, I got past them all. Or at least I thought I did."

"And what happened?"

"I loved him," Ben said. "That's what happened. He seemed okay with that, so we kept on doing what we did. I thought he would eventually see that us being together was okay, that it wouldn't be the end of the world if anyone found out. Instead, he kept getting increasingly wound up about it all, like more and more was on the line. Looking back, I think he was falling for me. That's what did it in the end. Despite all the crap that happened to us, I think the real problem is that Tim realized he loved me."

"And that forced him to face who he was," Jace finished.

"That would have been nice." Ben stopped and turned to him, eyes vulnerable. "I hate secrets. I know this is probably asking a lot, but— If you have any secrets, or any hang-ups about who you are, either tell me now or walk away. I like you, Jace. I like you more than anyone I've met in a very long time, but I don't want to go through that again."

"I won't hurt you," Jace said.

Ben shrugged. "You know what? I don't even care about that. Love is worth the pain, but I hate losing people. Maybe I'm crazy, but I'd rather be miserable with you than be miserable without you."

Jace laughed. "Can't you be happy *and* with me?"

"Of course." Ben's arms went slack. "This is why I hate talking about Tim. It's like one big head-trip all over again."

"I don't have any secrets," Jace said gently. "What you see is what you get. I'm not ashamed of who I am, and if being with you feels as good as the last couple of days have, then I don't see why I would ever leave you."

Ben smiled in relief. "Would it be creepy to kiss right after talking about our exes?"

Jace shook his head, coming close. "Consider it revenge. Tim's loss is my gain."

Ben's features softened as he tilted his head upward. As Jace kissed him, he made a promise to himself. No more trying to be someone he wasn't, like he had for Victor. And no more unfair comparisons or holding back his emotions like he'd done with Adrien. This time he would get it right.

"I like him," Jace said.

Greg tossed luggage into the trunk of his car before turning to face him. "Oh no!" he deadpanned.

"I'm serious."

"I know you are. I just don't understand why you sound so upset."

"Because I *really* like him." Jace tried handing the diaper bag to Greg, who signaled that it needed to go up front. "I do this every time. I meet a great guy, things are perfect for days, weeks, even months, and then— Remember Mark?"

"Mr. Chatterbox?" Greg slammed the trunk shut. "Yeah, I remember. He and I went to pick up beer, and he ended up talking to everyone in the store. *Every single person.*"

"Yeah, he was weird. Anyway, the longer we were together, the more I would start to panic."

Greg snorted. "Gosh, you must be the first guy to ever feel that way."

Jace shook his head. "I don't mean a fear of commitment. That doesn't bother me in the slightest."

"Then what?"

"Victor."

"Oh." Greg thought for a moment, then nodded in understanding. "Still freaked out that it could happen again?"

Jace exhaled. "Yeah. It's not like I think Mark, Ben, or anyone else is going to kill themselves. You never know, but it took me years to get over what happened. Not that I am. Not completely. Anyway, if things between Ben and me continue getting serious and something happens to him, what then?"

"You survived it once." Greg leaned against his car. "Listen, I get what you're saying. I feel the same way about your sister, and man, don't even get me started on the kids. That's my worst fear. Easily. If something happened to them…" Greg shook his head. "That's life. We can't keep everyone we love safe, no matter how much we want to. Simple as that. You can either let it drive you crazy, or you can try to put it out of your mind."

Jace sighed. "So you think I'm crazy for worrying?"

"Hell no! Listen, as much as I loved Victor, the guy wasn't stable. He had his demons. We just didn't recognize them in time. Now you will. If you see something like that in Ben, bail before things become too serious. Until then, get to know the guy. Give him a chance. You're smarter for having gone through it before. This time you'll see it coming before it's too late."

"You think so?"

"Yeah."

Jace smiled. "You're good at this. Maybe you should have been a relationship counselor."

"Nothing is more important to me than family," Greg said. "Now go tell your sister to get her ass down here or she's walking back to Missouri. If she has to leave the kids behind, that's fine with me. You'll take care of them, right?"

Jace shook his head. "You wouldn't make it an hour without any of them."

Greg winked. "Sure I would."

"Okay. I'll tell her what you said."

Greg looked terrified. "Don't! I was only kidding!"

"Too late!" Jace said, running toward the apartment building, laughing as Greg chased after him.

Jace wobbled out of the restaurant, wondering if this was how Michelle felt every day. An Italian buffet! The prospect had sounded so delectable at the time. Now, after stuffing himself on one of the world's heaviest cuisines, Jace was questioning the wisdom of his choice.

"I sort of feel like I need to burp," Ben said from beside him, "but am scared if I try, that I might barf instead."

Jace laughed, then winced as he rubbed his belly. "I think we overdid it."

"Just a little," Ben said. "They should have ambulances parked outside this place."

As they neared the car, the idea of sitting down again sounded dreadful. "We could go for a walk," he suggested. "Burn off some of these carbs."

Ben wanted to respond, but then he covered his mouth and simply nodded. Yes, they had both definitely overdone it.

They weren't in the most scenic part of downtown Houston. The United States—especially Texas—was very much a car culture, something Houston embraced fully. They walked along crumbling sidewalks, having to hustle past gas station driveways or talk loudly over the traffic on the street. Still, being on their feet did seem to help.

"It was good though," Ben said. "Very tasty."

"Yes," Jace said. "A real treat." He snuck a glance over at Ben to find his boyfriend doing the same. Were they both trying to be polite? Only one way to find out. "Actually, it was disgusting."

"Oh, man!" Ben said with relief. "I didn't want to say anything, but it was horrible!"

"Pasta and buffets don't mix. The noodles were so soggy!"

"And the sauces were either greasy or super salty."

Jace nodded. "Were your breadsticks cooked? Mine had raw dough in the middle."

Ben made a face. "Stop. I can't think about it. Seriously! Otherwise the whole buffet is going to come up again."

They laughed over this as they stumbled down the sidewalk.

"If you thought it was gross," Jace said, "then why did you eat so much?"

Ben shrugged. "It was your treat, and I didn't want your money going to waste. Besides, we're supposed to be celebrating the end of your vacation. I didn't want to ruin the grand finale by being picky. Why did *you* eat so much?"

Jace snickered. "I was trying to keep pace with you."

"Why?"

"I didn't want you to be the only one hogging out. I was worried you'd be embarrassed."

"I am now!" Ben said, laughing about it. "Let's make honesty our sacred policy from now on."

"Agreed. I can't stomach the alternative."

Ben groaned at his joke, eyes on the path ahead of them. "Whatever he's eating, I bet it tastes way better than what we ate."

Jace followed his gaze. At the end of the block, a large dog had his nose in something messy next to the sidewalk. The owner, who looked like he spent most of his time at the gym, was tugging on the leash, his muscles ineffective against the dog's eager appetite. Jace started to smile at the scene until the man's frustration peaked and he kicked the dog in the side.

Jace's jaw dropped as a yelp rang out, his stomach clenching tightly. He was so shocked that he didn't notice Ben let go of his hand.

Before he could react, Ben was at the end of the block, shouting up at a man nearly twice his size. Jace raced to catch up to him, catching the tail end of the man's rebuttal.

" —and I'll do what I want! Understand?"

"How would you like it if someone treated you that way?" Ben shouted back.

"Go ahead and try it, if you think you're big enough!"

Ben definitely wasn't. Even Jace felt intimidated. The man was his equal in height, but had enough muscle to make Greg look scrawny. That made what Ben did next all the more unlikely. Swinging around, one fist extended like Superman taking to the air, Ben decked the man. Or might have if he'd aimed high enough. Ben's fist thunked the man in the chest. Jace wondered if the blow could even be felt through those steely pecs.

The man found this assault just as unexpected, which might

be why he didn't lay Ben flat out on the sidewalk. Instead it was his dog who attacked, snapping and snarling at Ben. Jace's body unfroze. Grabbing Ben around the waist, he picked him up, scurrying backward to get him out of the dog's reach. The leash went taut, the dog barking on his hind legs as it strained to get at Ben.

The man laughed, shaking his head at them. "You're lucky I don't let him off his leash!"

Jace glared, but when it became clear that the man didn't intend to attack them, he gave all his attention to Ben. "Are you okay?"

"Fine," Ben said, glowering at the pair as they turned and walked away.

"Your hand," Jace said.

Ben was holding his wrist, a red line marring his palm. "It's just a scratch," he said.

"A scratch that's bleeding," Jace pointed out.

Ben sucked on the wound, then considered it again. "Just a surface scratch, really. I'm fine. I must have pulled my hand away before he could sink his teeth in."

"The man or the dog?" Jace murmured.

His joke went unheard. Ben was still staring after them. "He can't treat his dog that way," he said. Then he marched in the direction the man was going.

"Ben, wait!" Jace grabbed his arm. "Let it go!"

Ben turned, locking eyes with him. "Not until I have my say."

"I'm no good in a fight," Jace said. "I can't save you."

"You won't have to." Ben slipped out of Jace's grip, yelling after the man, who turned to face him.

Jace stayed on Ben's heels, thankful when he stopped a safe distance away.

"You can't treat your dog like that," Ben said.

The man's response was to lean down and place a hand where the leash was connected to the dog's collar.

"Actually, I guess you can," Ben said. "Dogs are like that, aren't they? You can abuse them, but they'll still adore you. And protect you." Ben held up his hand, showing the wound. "You kicked your dog, but he still went after me for trying to help. The stupid thing loves you. Remember that the next time you feel like hurting it."

The man glared at Ben, but then he straightened up. As he

turned away, he was looking down at the dog, hopefully in a new light. As for Ben, he shook his head, still not satisfied. Then he spun around, frowning. "Let's go back to the car," he said.

Jace put an arm around him, guiding him away. "That was incredible."

"That was pointless," Ben said.

"I don't think so. You got through to him. I really think you did."

"For the dog's sake, I hope you're right. I grew up with one. Wilford was the best. We never treated him like that. I hate the idea of any dog being hurt. They're too stupid to run away from bad owners. Too stupid, or too good."

Jace squeezed him. "You did what you could. Honestly, I didn't know you had it in you."

Ben managed a smile. "I'm a lover *and* a fighter."

He was kidding, but Jace realized it was true. School had been hell for Ben—years of feeling alienated and getting picked on—and he still didn't regret coming out so young. And now, even after the very creature Ben was trying to protect had attacked him, he'd still rallied and gone back to speak his mind. Ben really was a fighter.

One of the hardest things about losing Victor was that he had quit. Despite all his convictions and ideas, Victor had thrown in the towel. After the events of the evening, Jace doubted he'd ever have to worry about Ben doing something like that. Ben would stand his ground, and even if he got knocked down, Ben would keep on fighting.

"Do you ever fly to Austin?" Ben asked. He was sitting up in bed cross-legged, the morning light softly illuminating his hair. He looked hopeful, like a little boy waiting for a birthday present.

Jace sipped at the orange juice Ben had handed him just a moment ago. Not a bad way to wake up, but now he wondered what inspired this bribe. "Austin? No. Why?"

Ben took a deep breath. "I'm thinking about changing schools. Well, not thinking, really. I am. Allison asked me. Now that her father is gone, she's more on her own than ever. And frankly, I'm sick of Chicago. I loved it at first, and I still do in a way, but I think I'd rather visit than live there. Plus my family is down here, tuition is cheaper, and I'll no longer freeze my ass off most of the year."

"I would miss your ass if that happened," Jace said. "Why not Houston? You'd still be able to drive up and see Allison."

"My feelings about returning here still haven't changed," Ben said. "Well, I guess they have, since you're here. But I'd still like to see something new. Austin is supposed to be really cool, and tuition will be cheaper. Of course, if you never fly out there..."

"It would be strange," Jace said. "Arranging my schedule to overnight in Chicago makes sense, but getting a hotel an hour away from my apartment?"

Ben shook his head. "It's farther than that."

"Not by plane, it isn't."

Ben frowned. "So you don't want to?"

"It's not that." He rubbed his eyes, wondering how he could explain. "I just think the airline will find the hotel expense superfluous."

"You won't need a hotel," Ben said.

That was a fair point. Really, it didn't matter what Jace's schedule was. He used to drive to Warrensburg just to see Victor. In comparison, finding his way to Austin was nothing. Jace reached out and took Ben's hand. "Look, no matter what, I'll find a way to see you. I can fly for free, and Austin is only an hour away. You go wherever you feel like you need to be. We'll work something out."

"Really?"

And now the little boy looked like he'd gotten the present he wanted most. Jace laughed. The description wasn't fair. Ben might be younger, but he had crossed over into manhood long ago. "Really. Now, is it going to be breakfast or are you getting in the shower with me?"

Ben grinned, scurried down the ladder, and headed for the bathroom. Jace finished his orange juice, listening to the shower hiss into life. This could be good. He could pop over to Austin when he had time off instead of trying to squeeze in his relationship on weeknights. Of course that would mean more time away from Samson, but maybe he could work something out with his sister when she moved down. Yawning, Jace flopped onto his back and closed his eyes. A few minutes later, a very needy voice called out.

"Jaaaaaaaaace!"

College boys. They could be such a handful. In more than one way.

Chapter Twenty-five

The honeymoon lasted four glorious weeks. The first few times Jace flew to Austin, Ben had been overwhelmed.

"Why did I think switching colleges would be easy?" he moaned.

Jace couldn't offer much advice in that department, but he was happy to ease Ben's woes by taking him out on dates. Jace learned that Ben hadn't been treated this way before. Tim had been too closeted, Ben confided, and money was tight in Chicago, so simple pleasures like dinners or concert tickets were out of his price range. Jace reveled in being able to pamper him. Other times he flew Ben to Houston, especially when Jace wanted them to have more privacy. Not that Allison was invasive. She and Ben lived together in a duplex they rented, and she had her own love life, so there was plenty of opportunity for alone time. But sometimes, Jace simply wanted Ben entirely to himself.

Sadly, that was becoming more and more difficult. The airline was struggling, which meant restructuring. Some lost their jobs, others took pay cuts. Jace did neither, but he found himself working longer hours, his schedule shifting unpredictably as the dust settled. He had to cancel one trip to Austin, then another when his job kept him away from home for two weeks. Samson would have packed up and left had Michelle not been there. Her moving to Houston was a godsend.

Still, she and Greg were in transition too, moving their lives to Houston piece by piece. When Jace finally made it home, she arrived the next morning wearing transparent agitation.

"You're on your own this weekend," she said, "Greg and I are driving up to Warrensburg to get the last of our stuff. Mom and Dad gave us a new stroller for Christmas, and Bernard says he has an old lawnmower he wants to get rid of."

"Domestic life sounds so thrilling," Jace said.

"About as fun as taking care of your cat is for me," his sister retorted.

That left him in a pinch. The little old lady downstairs was gone, and besides, Jace missed being home. From the way Samson sat firmly on his lap, the cat clearly didn't want him leaving either. Hopefully Ben would be willing to fly out. Jace was desperate to see him, not just for the usual reasons, but because he had cooked up something extra special for spring break. He couldn't wait to see Ben's reaction when he heard the news. After calling the airline for possible flight times, he dialed Austin. Ben answered, sounding short of breath.

"Hello?"

"Hey, bucko," Jace said, trying to sound upbeat.

"You aren't coming."

Jace sighed. "I wanted to call you yesterday, but it was the night from hell. I didn't get in until three a.m."

When Ben replied, his voice sounded tense. "So do you have to work this weekend?"

"No, but my sister is out of town, and someone has to take care of Samson."

"Oh, come on! This is the third time you've canceled! I haven't seen you once this month!"

Jace moved the receiver away from his ear slightly. "The other two times were because of work. This is the first time because of Samson."

"He's a cat! Load up his food bowl, and he'll be fine overnight."

"I haven't been home for over a week," Jace countered. "He needs to see me sometime. Anyway, I can get you on an afternoon flight and we can—"

"Forget it."

Jace's stomach dropped. "What?"

"Forget it," Ben repeated. "You have fun with your cat. I'm going to do my own thing."

"Ben, I'm not trying to—"

"I just need my space," Ben interrupted. "I'll see you next weekend."

The line went dead. Jace stared at the phone in disbelief and sighed. This had happened before. Not with Ben, but with guys before him. Jace's schedule sucked. He couldn't always be there when he wanted to. Sometimes he envied people who knew what time they would be home every day. There must be a lot of comfort in having a routine, especially for their partner, but usually Jace enjoyed the variety. He thought Ben understood that.

Not willing to give up, he hit redial. The phone picked up and hung up again in one second flat. Jace's pulse quickened, worried he'd screwed up everything already. He didn't want to lose Ben. Steeling himself, he called again. When the line clicked, he spoke quickly.

"Just let me —"

"I'll call you later," Ben said before hanging up.

Now Jace was getting angry. Maybe he had canceled two previous trips to Austin, but he hadn't done so for fun. Jace was working, not brushing off Ben to go drinking with his buddies. If Ben enjoyed their dinners and dates so much, he needed to realize where the money came from. Jace expected someone in college to appreciate that already. Maybe Ben still believed that graduating meant instantly getting a fat paycheck, when in reality, Jace still scrounged every penny he could. Some of the extra hours he'd taken were for the trip...

Jace sighed, the special plans seeming like an idealistic dream now. Maybe they were, but he wasn't ready to give up. Flexing his jaw, he called Ben again. This time when he answered, at least there was a degree of humility in his voice.

"Hello?"

"Italy," Jace said.

"What?"

"I'm taking you to Italy, you spoiled shit!"

After a pause, Ben sounded miserable, and rightly so. "You are?"

"Yes. I wanted to tell you in person, but—"

"I was being a dick, I know," Ben said, sounding sorry. "Are you serious?"

Jace exhaled, calming down somewhat. "Spring break. You up for it?"

"If you still want me." Ben chuckled nervously.

"God knows why, but I do." And he did, very badly. Jace wanted Ben in his arms so they could pave over this ugly pothole. "Now get your ass to the airport and come apologize to me properly."

Jace gave him the flight times, then called the airline to finalize arrangements. Afterwards he straightened the apartment, his mind returning to Ben's tone on the phone. Was Ben right to be so angry? Frustrated, maybe, or unhappy that they couldn't be together, but Jace hadn't deserved to be hung up on like that. The trip to Italy shouldn't have been the crowbar to get back inside his world, either.

Ideally, in a marriage, people get to know each other before the wedding. The honeymoon is the celebration, the big prize for making it that far. In a new relationship, the honeymoon stage is spent with a stranger. Only after the hormone-powered romance settled down did someone discover just who the other person was. Sometimes that person wasn't worth walking down an aisle with.

Jace didn't want to believe that was the case now, that Ben thought only of his own needs. On the drive to the airport to pick him up, he felt apprehensive rather than excited. As Jace stood in front of the gate and waited, he became increasingly insulted. Who else would regularly fly to see someone they barely knew? Not that Jace always felt that way. Until recently, he thought he knew Ben extremely well. He used to think they had a connection. Now...

Ben appeared in the stream of passengers pouring out of the gate. He didn't smile or wave when he saw Jace. Instead, his shoulders were slumped and he had trouble making eye contact. Ben was ashamed. The ice on Jace's heart started to thaw. Maybe they did understand each other.

Taking Ben into his arms, Jace hugged him tightly. When he stepped away, Ben still didn't look happy.

"Was the flight that bad?" he asked.

"I'm sorry," Ben blurted. "You didn't deserve to be treated like that."

Jace laughed. He couldn't help himself. He felt so happy that Ben wasn't a stranger after all, or a spoiled brat. "You got emotional," Jace said. "Big deal. Let's not allow it to ruin our weekend."

Ben seemed somewhat relieved, relaxing enough to smile, but remained uncharacteristically somber on the way home. He responded with single-syllable answers to Jace's small talk and questions. Not until they were parked in front of Jace's apartment did he speak.

"This is the furthest I've made it." Ben glanced over at him and licked his lips. "Since Tim, I mean. I've dated a lot of guys, and right about now is when I start doing things like this. Sometimes I compare them to Tim, or how strongly I felt about him. Most guys come up short."

"Do I?" Jace said, feeling confident about the answer.

"No. Definitely not. I think that's why I feel like pushing you."

Jace shifted in his seat. "You want to push me away?"

Ben shook his head. "More like I want to push you to see if you'll stay. There was this one guy I was with, and I liked him okay. Things were going really well, but then I asked him to go camping with me. I knew he hated camping because of some traumatizing childhood experience. Nothing too serious, but reason enough to not want to go camping again. Anyway, I kept insisting he go camping with me and he kept refusing. We broke up over it. Can you believe that? The thing is, I hate camping too."

Jace laughed, and after a moment, Ben did too.

"I'll go camping with you, Ben," he said. "I'll even leave the bug spray at home, just to prove how serious I am."

"That won't be necessary," Ben said. His smile faded as he grew serious again. "Tim wasn't there for me. Things got really bad, and that's when he decided to leave. I guess I'm worried that you'll do the same and—"

"I'm not Tim," Jace said. "You don't need to manufacture a situation for me to prove that."

"I know." Ben swallowed. "That's why I feel so bad about acting this way."

"Don't," Jace said. "Just acknowledge it, learn from it, and move on. And when I eventually screw up and do something stupid, just remember how forgiving I was today."

Ben considered him. "You won't. You're too perfect."

"I'm not," Jace said. "I promise you that someday I'll screw up horribly. It'll be embarrassing and terrible and will totally overshadow all the good things I ever did. And then I'll come slinking over to you with sad puppy dog eyes and..."

"And I'll kick you to the curb," Ben said, grinning evilly. "Or maybe I'll keep you. We'll see."

Jace shook his head. "I see that someone needs a spanking before he'll behave."

Ben perked up. "You know, that might be worth a try!"

Italy was chosen very carefully. Rome was romantic, but not overwhelmingly so like Paris. Nor as expensive. The hotel was taken care of by the points Jace built up during his frequent travels. That was a nice perk of his job, as was the greatly reduced airfare. All he really needed to worry about was food and tourism, both of which were affordable with a little careful planning.

He also figured that, for Ben's first international trip, Italy was appropriately exotic. England, Jace knew from experience, was a very different place, but the shared language made it too easy. He wanted Ben to experience the culture shock of not being able to speak with the locals. Plus, it gave Jace an opportunity to show off his language skills.

The trip started rough, he and Ben having gotten into the wrong cab. The unscrupulous driver and his brother thought they could shake gullible tourists down for all the money they had, but Ben—in his typical fashion—fought back. This time, thankfully, he battled using only words. Regardless of his bravery, this experience left Ben shaken.

The next morning brought new optimism and they began having fun. Jace was slightly disturbed to find himself behaving like his father, who would plan out every single hour of a vacation and expect everyone to stick to his schedule. Luckily, Ben was too overwhelmed by it all to protest. They visited the Vatican museum, slighting the Pope by not stopping by to have tea with him. Then they saw the Pantheon, which Jace insisted must have been cooler when dedicated to bizarre pagan gods instead of boring old saints. At the Circus Maximus, they struggled to picture people fighting for their lives in the ancient arena, and in the ruins of the Forum, they fanned themselves in the heat and wished togas were still in style.

Every night they returned, exhausted, to the hotel. The first night, the television remained off. They opened the window to let the warm air drift in and made love Italian-style. Turns out it was just the same as American-style, but they convinced themselves it felt different anyway. The second and third nights the television was turned on and room service was called. Snacking on ice cream, they watched soap operas that neither of them could understand well, although Jace felt free to make up things as he translated.

During one of these nights, Jace realized that no matter what he and Ben did together, it felt good. Having passionate sex, vegging out in front of the boob tube, or soaking their feet in the hotel hot tub—even the most mundane activity was fun when he was with Ben.

For their final day, they visited the Torre Argentina—more

ruins, but these were special. Not only had Julius Caesar met his famous end at this location, but now it was also a shelter for homeless cats who, in contrast to Caesar, didn't have to worry about being murdered. Visiting this location was a selfish wish for Jace. He had a surprise for Ben planned afterwards. Until then, they toured the ruins, but Jace couldn't help focusing on the cats. No doubt about it, crazy cat lady syndrome was genetic and impartial to gender, because Jace had it bad. Not only did being here make him miss Samson, but he felt tempted to take half the cats home with him.

He was squatting to pet a mangy orange one when it jumped on his legs. Laughing, Jace sat down. Two more cats rushed him, apparently desperate for cushioning. The first cat hopped onto his shoulders as the newcomers claimed his lap. Jace was in seventh heaven, so what happened next really broadsided him.

"I love you."

The voice sounded like Ben's. Over the chattering tour group, it was hard to be sure. Regardless, Jace kept his attention on the cats, a thousand thoughts filling his mind. Three months. That's how long they'd been together. Wasn't it too soon? He'd never told Victor, even though he had felt it. How could Jace say it to anyone if he'd never told Victor? Did he even feel it? Making Ben happy made him happy. Jace wanted to provide for him, protect him, do anything possible for him, no matter how big the sacrifice. If that wasn't love, what was? But Victor...

"I love you!"

No doubt about it now. Jace looked up to see Ben at the edge of the tour group. Already a number of heads were turning to see what the commotion was, but Ben was smiling like it was the best news ever. And wasn't it?

But Victor...

For a moment, Jace saw him in his mind, perfectly clear as if it were yesterday. Victor was smirking, like he often did, while shaking his head, and Jace swore he could hear his voice. *Did I ever hesitate to tell you how I felt? Did I ever ask you not to love someone else? If you want to make me proud...*

Victor's ghost disappeared, leaving only Ben. Heart thudding in his chest, Jace stood, the cats abandoning ship by springing away. He rushed to Ben, picked him up in his arms, and swung him around, grinning all the while.

"About time you admitted it," he said coolly. Then he kissed Ben, breathing in the scent of his skin. That's what this feeling was. He had no doubt. Setting Ben down, Jace brushed his nose against his ear and whispered the words that had so often come unbidden, but were finally set free to fly.

"I love you too."

"I'll show you mine if you show me yours," Ben said.

"I've already seen yours," Jace replied.

"That didn't count."

"Are you sure it's a good idea?" Jace said. "Getting them together like that, I mean. The results might be... explosive."

Ben made a lewd face. "Think they'd rub together the wrong way?"

"If we're not careful. Besides, mine's bigger than yours."

"Hm," Ben said thoughtfully. "You know, all the innuendo is getting a little bit creepy."

"Yes," Jace agreed. "It is. Especially since we're talking about our families."

Ben looked surprised. "Really? I thought we were talking about—" Then he grinned. "Seriously though, what do you think? One big family party. Get it all over with."

There were pros and cons to the idea. Jace was dying to meet Ben's family. He'd seen a couple of photos, which didn't reveal much. Now that Ben was on summer break and basically living with him back in Houston, they had plenty of opportunity. And time. This allowed for wonderfully mundane experiences, like now, as they folded shirts and paired socks together at the laundromat. Secretly, Jace cherished domestic moments like these. That Ben was the one to suggest their families meet made him happy too.

"It could be overwhelming," Jace said. "Greg's so excited about meeting you that he giggled when I mentioned the idea."

Ben looked confused. "That buff guy in the photo you showed me?"

"Yup."

"He giggled?"

"Yes, and it was just as disturbing as you imagine."

Ben shrugged. "Still, that won't be nearly as bad as my sister. I've told you that she's going through a divorce, right?"

"So you're saying the timing is bad?"

"No." A pair of jeans flip-flopped in Ben's hands until they were a tidy square. "I'm saying she'll be even more venomous than usual. Of course, flaunting my hot boyfriend while she's got nothing will be satisfying."

"She's your sister," Jace said pointedly.

"That's right."

"Isn't that kind of harsh?"

Ben raised an eyebrow. "Oh, I get it. You're one of those people who's all lovely-dovey with their sibling. Just you wait. You'll stop judging me once you've met Karen."

Jace turned his attention to folding underwear. "So we're doing this?"

"Yes. The only question is how? An awkward dinner? An outing to a park where blood can be spilled freely?"

Jace shook his head. "I know the ideal place."

The great thing about bowling was that it allowed a constant rotation. In a way bowling was like speed dating. Jace would be talking with Ben's mother, a small blonde woman who smiled while she talked. Then she would be called away to take her turn. Then there was Mr. Bentley, who was so easy-going and relaxed that Jace wondered how many of Ben's boyfriends he'd met already. Or maybe he took everything in stride. Their conversation about plasma televisions was cut short when Jace was called to the front.

After sending his first ball hurtling down the lane, he turned to find Greg sitting next to Ben. Chatting happily, Greg had an arm wrapped around Ben's shoulder. To his credit, Jace's boyfriend looked a little overwhelmed rather than giddy, like Adrien used to. Farther away, Mrs. Bentley was holding Sylvester, the latest family member and Jace's second nephew, while chatting with Michelle about topics only mothers understood. Next to them, Emma held Preston to her like a doll, unamused as Mr. Bentley tried the "I've got your nose!" trick.

Jace could get used to this. Family was so wonderf—

"No one else can play if you're going to stand there drooling."

Ah, yes. Karen. Ben's sister who had all the charm of a farting orangutan. Jace winked at her as if she were adorable, even though she reminded him of a Neanderthal wearing sweatpants, and took his ball to finish his turn. Karen was next in line, a small blessing that meant not being around her for a few minutes.

Jace went and sat next to Ben, giving Greg a look. "He's *my* date, you know."

This only made Greg pull Ben closer. "But he's so cute! Can't I borrow him?"

"You wouldn't be interested," Jace said. "He can't make you any more babies."

"That never stopped us from trying," Ben said with an amorous look in Jace's direction.

"Oh, I like this one!" Greg said, squeezing Ben affectionately.

"Me too," Jace said, gently removing Greg's arm from his boyfriend. "Which is why it would be nice if you didn't strangle him to death."

"Sorry," Greg said. When Karen sat next to him—which she kept doing—Greg quickly got to his feet. "I'll grab another pitcher of beer. Be right back!"

Karen watched him go, then turned to her brother and rolled her eyes. "It's your turn."

"Okay." Ben stood but hovered, hesitant to leave them.

"Go on," Jace said.

He watched Ben rush to pick up a ball and toss it carelessly down the lane, just to get his turn over with. Jace was smiling when Karen came up with another gem.

"When I heard you were a flight attendant, I thought you'd be more..." She held her arm out, the wrist limp.

"You thought my wrist would be broken?" Jace asked, continuing before she could respond. "I don't really have to do much heavy lifting. Aside from the passengers who bring aboard a full-sized suitcase stuffed with everything they own. Naturally they block the aisle while trying to shove it into the overhead bin. When it won't fit, they turn to me, like I can magically compress matter or something."

Karen seemed confused, looking between him and Ben, who had already returned. "I mean you don't act like a girl," she clarified. "You don't have a lisp."

"Funny you should mention that," Jace said. "I noticed you don't have a lisp either. Does that mean you're not a girl?"

Karen's brow lowered as she turned to Ben for an explanation. "Is there something wrong with him?"

"No," Ben said, suppressing a smile. "He's perfect."

Later, standing in the parking lot, they waved goodbye to their families as they drove away. Jace felt a swelling in his chest. "I want more of that," he said.

Ben glanced over at him in surprise. "More awkward family get-togethers?"

"Yes," Jace said. "And it wasn't awkward. It was fun. Aside from your sister, who I'm pretty sure is an ape your parents have been shaving for years."

Ben laughed. "I liked yours. Michelle is really sweet."

"Yeah, she's a good kid. I'm glad she moved down here." Being in Houston was beneficial to them, Jace considered as they got into his car. Greg was already established and doing well. He'd provide Michelle and the kids with a good life. Keys dangling unturned in the ignition, he looked over at Ben. "I want a big family. Do you ever think of things like that?"

Ben blinked. "Uh, not really. It's a little early for me. I'm still in college."

"Of course," Jace said, feeling silly. He started the car and pulled out of the parking lot. "Some day when you're an old man, like me. Do you think you'll want kids then?"

"Emma was cute," Ben said. "Can we have her?"

"Don't joke," Jace said. "If Michelle gets pregnant again, we might find a basket on the doorstep. Seriously though."

"Maybe," Ben said. "If I'm with the right guy, I could see it working. Right now, I still feel like a kid myself."

"That won't change. I don't feel my age. A friend of mine, Bernard, he's pretty old and says he doesn't feel grown-up either. How did he put it? 'Some people think ignoring their inner child makes them seem grown-up. When I see someone ignoring a crying child, I think they're an asshole.'"

Ben laughed. "When do I get to meet him?"

"Eventually," Jace said. "He's family now too. Not by blood, or even by marriage, but family is more than that. You find people you love and keep them close to you. That's what a family is." He looked over and caught Ben's eye, seeing understanding there.

When they were back at the apartment, Ben opened the refrigerator and started making them a snack. All summer they had lived together. When Jace returned from work, his home was always full of life, not quiet and empty. Ben picked up around the house, even did the laundry, despite Jace never asking him to.

Samson was also happier. He used to be clingy when Jace returned from traveling, desperate for companionship and love. Not any more. Jace had arrived home late one night to find Ben asleep on the couch, Samson draped across his chest. When Samson stirred and saw him standing there, he simply blinked his eyes and went back to sleep.

The summer had been wonderful. Jace could imagine it always being like this. Ben even worked part-time waiting tables, excited when he got that first paycheck and was able to take Jace out for a night on the town. The last few months had felt like paradise.

Now that time was drawing to a close. Ben would be back in Austin next week, Jace coming to see him when he could, which might be as little as four nights a month. If they were lucky. In a way, it was foolish to dream of having a family when he could barely make time for his relationship.

Ben set a plate in front of him, sandwich cut into eight little triangles like bite-sized appetizers. "Hungry?" he said.

Jace nodded, not thinking of the food. He definitely had an appetite, and a handful of days together every month wouldn't satiate it. A long time ago, he had moved away from the person he loved because it was the only way Jace felt like he could survive. Now, maybe it was time to do the opposite.

Chapter Twenty-six

"I don't know what I did wrong. Actually, I'm pretty damn sure I didn't do anything wrong, so screw you!" Ben's voice sounded huge and angry, even over the tiny cell phone speaker. "If you don't have the guts to face me, that's fine. I thought you were different. I didn't think you were a coward like the rest. At least have the decency to call me if you're going to—" Ben's voice withered to a squeak. "Are we breaking up? I need to know, because I don't see why else you wouldn't even call. I didn't complain when you canceled. I've tried to be understanding, even though I miss you like crazy. What did I do? I thought you— You know how I feel, right? I love you, so why are you avoiding me?"

Then came the sound of fumbling, followed by a muttered "Fuck, how do I delete this?" before the message beeped to an end.

Jace tossed the phone into the passenger seat and sighed. He'd screwed up. Big time. Sadly, all this had come from him trying to be romantic. Had Ben just waited another day or two... Or had Jace not been unexpectedly called into work. Still, maybe it wasn't too late. After all, he had an ace to play. Jace got out of the car and went back into the gas station.

"Forget something?" the clerk asked.

"Yes," Jace said, reaching for the single roses sold next to the cash register. They weren't the best quality, but it was late. He bought all they had, hoping the roses would look good bundled together. Once in his car, he tried to make them presentable before driving to Ben's and Allison's duplex a few minutes away.

Checking his appearance in the rearview mirror, he took a deep breath, put on a smile, and trotted up to the doorway. Allison answered, and from her expression, Jace knew he was in the dog house.

"In the famous words of any guy who's ever been in trouble," he said, "I can explain everything."

"You being here is already good," Allison said. "He's really upset."

"I know, I got the message."

Allison grimaced. "Yeah, about that. We're sort of drunk."

Jace laughed. That was a relief, and went a long way toward

explaining how upset Ben had sounded. Still, those emotions didn't originate from the bottle. Jace told Allison the reason he'd been so busy. This was enough for her to usher him in.

Ben was sitting at the kitchen table, an empty ice cream carton before him. When he saw Jace, he wiped his mouth and patted at his hair, like a sitcom housewife receiving unexpected company. Then he slumped back in his chair and studied the table top.

"I'm sorry," Jace said, holding out the roses. Ben glanced at them, then away again. Jace had the feeling Ben was more embarrassed about the message than anything. "Look, I've been an idiot, but I think you'll forgive me if you come with me."

"I don't know." Ben frowned. "I just don't understand what I did wrong."

"You didn't do anything wrong. I was trying to be romantic and surprise you, but I overdid it."

"Overdid what?" Ben scowled. "Why haven't you called?"

Jace tried not to laugh. With his hair messed up, and his eyes slightly unfocused, Ben was hard to take seriously. Then again, Jace would take him any way he could get him. He offered his hand. "Just come with me, okay? There's something I want to show you."

Ben accepted his hand. As soon as Jace had pulled him to his feet, he was surprised by the sloppiest kiss of his life, one full of high-octane fumes.

"What have you been drinking?" Jace asked once the assault had ended.

"Tequila," Allison said from the doorway. "Sorry."

Jace shook his head, leading Ben toward the door. "It's all right. I'll try to have him back soon."

"No, you won't," Allison said with a knowing expression.

Once they were in the car and traveling, Jace kept looking at his passenger, who seemed a little green under the streetlights. Jace was wishing he'd stolen some barf bags from the airline when he saw realization dawning on Ben's face.

"Wait a minute! This is your car! Did you drive out here?"

Jace nodded. "Yup."

"Why?"

"You'll find out in about two blocks."

The car swung into an apartment complex, and then into an empty space in the parking lot. After shutting off the engine, he turned to see if Ben had figured it out. The tequila wasn't doing him any favors, because he hadn't.

"What are we doing here?" he asked.

"You'll find out soon enough." Jace opened the car door. "Come on."

Ben seemed a little uneasy on his feet, so Jace put an arm around him.

"I drank too much," Ben said, stating the obvious.

Up two flights of stairs, Jace pulled out his keys and unlocked a door.

"You're staying here?" Ben asked.

"You could say that." Jace opened the door and stood aside so Ben could enter. Luckily he did so before Samson could get out.

Ben's jaw dropped when he saw the cat. He crouched to offer his hand. Jace flipped on the hallway light. There wasn't much to see yet, except for some unpacked boxes, but Jace had managed to hang a few things that Ben was sure to recognize.

When Ben stood again, his eyes were wide. "No!" he said in disbelief. "No freaking way! You live here now?"

"Since last week," Jace admitted. "I wanted to have everything set up to surprise you, but then I was called away for work and—"

"You're so stupid!" Ben said, grinning at him. "I can't believe you moved here!"

"After this summer, I realized it would be too hard to be apart from you." Jace put an arm around Ben's waist, bringing them together. "I hope this doesn't freak you out."

"What about your work?"

"Well, you know. It doesn't really matter where I live with my job."

Ben shook his head. "It does if you want to fly international."

That was something Jace wanted very much. International flights had a lot of benefits, but he'd need more experience and seniority to get those routes. Still, he didn't mind that Ben thought he was making a sacrifice. "I'll figure something out," he said coolly.

Ben's eyes were sparkling. "I love you!"

"I love you too. Sorry about being so dense."

"It's all right." Ben took his hand, pulling him down the hallway. "Show me everything!"

Jace had to admit that it lacked the charm of the previous apartment. There was nothing outstanding about it. An entryway, a living room, a couple of bedrooms... Of course having his living space divided into actual rooms was novel, as was the balcony, which Samson adored. He hung out there during the day, eyes on the trees in case any birds were foolish enough to fly close. Jace had sat on the balcony on the first night, imagining it had romantic potential. After showing it to Ben and catching up a little, he led his boyfriend to the kitchen and poured him a large glass of water.

"Got anything stronger?" Ben asked.

"My hand slapping your ass if you don't sober up," Jace said. "Or coffee."

"I'll stick with the water," Ben said. Then, with a mischievous smile, he added, "Don't be mad. You're the one who drove me to drink."

"It's always my fault," Jace moaned, playing along.

Ben nodded happily. "Always. Just think how much more trouble you'll get in with us seeing each other more."

"I can't wait," Jace said, but not sarcastically. This was the next best thing to moving in together. "Think you can take care of Samson when I'm out of town?"

"Of course!" Ben said. "Were Michelle and Greg upset about you moving away?"

Jace shook his head. "They're so busy with the kids lately that they're probably relieved not having to think of Samson. The trade-off was bad for them anyway, since I never babysat."

"Ha! The poor fools." Ben downed his water and went to the refrigerator, examining the photos of their Italian trip, pinned to the door by magnets. When he turned around, he was smiling. "This is big. You moving here, I mean."

Jace nodded, coming close. "Very big. The biggest thing I've done for another guy."

"And what will you do if we break up?" Ben asked.

Jace shook his head. "Stay right here. I'll quit my job, enroll in your school and take all the same classes as you."

"To win me back?"

"Or to creep you out. And to scare away any other guys. You'll never date again. It's me or nothing."

Ben looked thoughtful. "I suppose I'll stick with you. After all, you are kind of cute. Even for an old guy."

"Thanks," Jace said, pretending he was going to bite Ben's nose before kissing him.

This was good. His job would still be crazy, his schedule unpredictable, but when he came home at night, he would find a purring cat, and with any luck, a cuddly college boy. Little by little, Jace was building the family he dreamed of. The world was a very happy place.

Jace ducked into the galley so he could discreetly yawn without the passengers seeing. On an early-morning flight like this, he'd probably cause a chain reaction, a wave of yawns passing from row to row that made the cabin pressure drop. He chuckled at this mental image and checked his watch.

Four more hours until they landed in New York. From there he would try to find a standby flight back to Austin to begin four days of glorious time off. Of course he would still be on reserve, meaning he could be called back into action, but if all went according to plan, the days ahead would be serene bliss.

Barbara, an older flight attendant with so much seniority it made Jace envious, poked her head into the galley. "The captain wants to see us," she said.

Jace straightened his uniform as he followed her down the aisle, wondering what this was about. Maybe to alert them to a company inspection—a rumor that had been circulating lately. If there was an observer from the airline onboard, calling all the flight attendants to the cockpit at once was hardly subtle.

Once they were gathered around the door, the captain faced them, his expression grim. The first officer kept his focus on the controls, but his profile revealed how pale he was. The captain glanced past them to make sure no passengers were within hearing range. Then, in a low voice, he said, "There's been a hijacking."

Jace's stomach sank. A plane being hijacked was one of those fears that seemed terribly unlikely, like being swept up by a tornado or losing your house to a fire. And yet these things happened.

"Multiple hijackings," the captain continued, checking the aisle once more. "Planes have been crashing into New York."

Jace and the other flight attendants all spoke at once, a million half-formed questions on their lips. Jace's thoughts were torn between worrying for the victims of the hijacking and wondering if his own flight was in danger. The captain raised his hand, silencing them.

"Keep calm," he said meaningfully, harking back to their most basic training. "The FAA has executed SCATANA. All air traffic is to be grounded immediately. This flight has been diverted to MEM."

Memphis International Airport. But *all* air traffic? That couldn't be right, could it? Jace glanced over at Barbara. In her twenty years, had she ever seen something like this? From her expression of shock, he doubted she had.

"Right now we're not telling the passengers anything," the captain continued. "I'll make an announcement as we begin our decent. Until then, get back out there and stay vigilant. Keep smiling, but report any suspicious behavior immediately."

There were hushed questions, but if the captain knew anything more, he wasn't telling them. Jace returned to work with adrenaline shooting through his system. Memphis was half an hour away, give or take. No time at all. And yet, suddenly every face in the cabin was suspicious. Why was the woman in the exit row eyeing him so carefully? Jace noticed the muscular young man in the back row. Did he get those biceps from playing sports or military training? The old man who hurried to the bathroom— weak bladder, or a bomb that needed detonating?

Tension rose when the captain announced that they were making an emergency landing due to equipment failure. The captain assured the passengers of their safety, citing regulations more than anything. The passengers groaned their annoyance, but Jace felt electrified. If hijackers were aboard, this deviation would force them to act prematurely.

Jace fielded questions he couldn't answer: layovers, compensation, missed connections. He felt like screaming that people had died—were dying—and that getting to a business meeting on time no longer mattered. But he did his job, making sure his passengers were as safe and calm as possible.

When the airplane landed, Jace glanced out at a runway overrun by taxiing planes. A few of the most astute passengers commented on this, just as the captain made another announcement.

"Ladies and gentlemen, the reason we needed to land this plane wasn't because of equipment failure. Due to a national emergency, the FCC has grounded all air traffic. The United States is under attack."

Jace stood in the airport lobby, shoulder to shoulder with passengers, pilots, and airport staff. Together they watched the footage, looping video of billowing smoke from the top of the first tower of the World Trade Center, a place of business now resembling a monstrous, smoke-belching crematorium. Even knowing what would come—having already seen the footage—many gasped each time the plane smashed into the second tower again.

They stood there for hours, not knowing what to do, or where to go in this strange new world where the impossible could happen. Jace stared at the screen, transfixed, tears running down his face. He wept for the crew members onboard those planes, the passengers who had lost their lives, the families that would never recover from the events of this day. He wondered if anyone ever would. When the first tower collapsed, he cried out. He wasn't alone. They all felt a helpless desperation, an urge to stop the horrible things from happening, but a powerlessness to act. All they could do was look at each other with rapt horror at what was unfolding. Strangers hugged, trying to comfort each other as they cried, but there wasn't anything they could do. Not here.

Throughout all of this, Jace tried calling his family, knowing they would worry. And Ben, who no doubt would check the marker board they had in the kitchen, the one where Jace wrote simplified versions of his schedule. *Denver*, Ben would read, a cartoon airplane flying above an arrow that led to the other side of the board where *New York* was written. Even once Ben learned that the hijacked flights didn't originate in Denver, he would wonder if Jace's schedule had shifted and changed, as it so often did.

Every time he pressed the phone to his ear, all Jace got was a message saying all lines were busy. All lines were busy. All lines were busy. With each failed call, he knew the panic for his safety was increasing. His family would be watching the same footage he was, wondering if Jace's plane had crashed into one of those towers.

Eventually the lobby began to clear as people sought landlines, or fresh air to clear the nightmare images from their minds. The bars were already overflowing. Jace decided he couldn't stand there any longer. There had to be something he could do, some way to help. On his way to find out how, he bumped into Barbara.

"You want my advice," she said, eyes red from crying, "find a hotel while you still can. Before long, there won't be a vacancy for miles around any airport."

"What about us?" Jace said. "Our jobs?"

"Wait for the call," she said, shaking her head. "I feel sorry for you young ones. I have twenty-three years under my belt. After this, I wonder if any of us will ever be flying again." Glancing toward the nearest television screen, she added, "God have mercy on us all."

Jace took her advice, happy for an excuse to flee the airport, if only so he could pretend for a few fleeting seconds that the world still made sense, that all he'd seen was another violent Hollywood blockbuster. But his heart wouldn't stop pounding. He couldn't stop picturing what those last few minutes must have been like for everyone onboard those doomed flights, or the confusing nightmare that must have taken place in the towers.

"Last room," said the flustered woman at the Holiday Inn check-in counter. "It's a double too."

That was good. Jace would call the airline, assuming he could get through, and let them know he had a room. Any crew members who couldn't find a place to stay could share his room. Lord knows they were used to being crammed into small spaces, not only at work, but in the rented apartments and homes used as crash pads during layovers.

Once in his room, he tried the phone. Picturing Ben still standing in front of the kitchen marker board, he called his apartment, thrilled when he heard ringing and nearly wordless when the line clicked and Ben's voice answered.

"Jace?"

"It's me," he said. "I'm okay." But he wasn't. None of them were.

"Where are you?"

"Memphis. Our flight was—"

"Where?"

The line was crackling, the quality so bad that Jace wasn't sure if Ben had heard him. "Memphis. At a Holiday Inn. Listen, I need you to call my family. I don't know if I'll get through again, but if we both try—" A click. "Hello?"

Jace growled in frustration. When he tried calling again, all lines were busy. He tried his family next. Ben knew he was safe. They needed to know next. He tried for another ten minutes, flipping on the television and staring as he hung up and dialed, hung up and dialed. He could only imagine that the same thing was happening all over the country as people franticly tried to confirm that their loved ones were okay.

By evening, two other flight attendants and a pilot were in Jace's room. As midnight came and went, the television remained on, even when one of them tried to sleep. There were no complaints. The same information was being repeated over and over, but the television was their only lifeline to more information, to other developments, and perhaps to an explanation. They all craved it, a reason for what had happened, but it was impossible to imagine any satisfactory answer. There was no logical reason such a thing would occur. Only madness could bring about such chaos.

Jace was sitting on the edge of the bed, staring at the screen, when someone knocked on the door. He glanced at the clock. Two in the morning. Maybe another crew member who couldn't find somewhere to stay. Jace didn't mind. He'd sleep on the floor if need be. He went to answer it, his heart leaping to his throat when he saw Ben's face.

Then they were in each other's arms, Jace squeezing Ben like he was the last sane piece of the world remaining. Since their brief phone call, Jace hadn't been able to reach him, the answering machine picking up every time. Jace had reached his family, but even Allison didn't know where Ben was.

"I love you," Ben was murmuring into his chest. "I love you so much! I'm so glad you're okay."

When Ben pulled away, looking at the other occupants of the room with puzzlement, Jace led him out into the hall so they could have privacy.

"How did you get here?" Jace asked.

"I drove. The second the line went dead, I ran straight for my car." Ben's cheeks were flushed. "Do you know how many damn Holiday Inns there are around Memphis? This is the fifth one I've been to."

On any other occasion, Jace would have laughed. Instead he kissed Ben gently. "I'm glad you're here. It's awful, isn't it?"

Ben nodded, his eyes filling with tears. "Don't fly again," he pleaded. "Ever! Promise me you won't. Please!"

Then he was in Jace's arms once more, his body shuddering as he cried. Jace couldn't make that promise. In truth, there was already talk about the airlines not recovering from this blow, or at the very least, reduced travel meaning fewer flights and less staff needed. Layoffs were inevitable. Chances were, Jace wouldn't have a job at all. But if he did, he'd already promised himself that he would fly again, that he wouldn't let the terrorists win. Now wasn't the time to discuss such things, so he held his boyfriend to him, stroking and kissing Ben's hair as he cried out all of his fears.

Memorial services. Some for coworkers Jace had never known, one for a person who had helped train him. More memorial services, these in memory of everyone affected by the September 11th attacks—those who lost their lives and those who had lost someone. A month later and the world was still a changed place, but it was time. Not time to move on, but time to fight by refusing to give in to fear. Ben drove him to the airport for Jace's first flight since the attacks, Ben crying in despair when it was time to say goodbye, and crying in relief when Jace made it home safely four days later.

Eventually, life became a routine again: work, love, money, stress, sex, bills, television. The illusion of normality returned, but that's all it was—an illusion.

Chapter Twenty-seven

"Have you seen the guy sitting in 22C?" Nancy raised her eyebrows. "His knuckles are as white as his hair. Do you know what he asked me?"

The flight attendant call-button dinged, Jace glancing down the aisle. Seat 22C. He glanced over at Nancy.

"'Can the plane be landed again?' That's what he said." Nancy licked her lips. "Maybe you should…"

Jace nodded. Even four months after 9/11, they all remained on edge, looking for any sign of another attack, thrust into the position of playing detective when it came to human behavior. After some idiot with a bomb in his shoe tried to play terrorist in December and nearly succeeded, suddenly anyone could be a terrorist. So now most flight attendants, Jace included, looked at their passengers with some degree of suspicion. Nancy was more paranoid than most, but considering she'd been on the ground in New York during the attacks, few could blame her.

As Jace walked down the aisle toward 22C, he wondered if Nancy was right for once. The passenger was young. Eighteen, maybe nineteen at the most. His hair was bleached platinum blonde, a style that went out of fashion a few years ago. This guy hadn't gotten the memo, or perhaps he knew how good it looked on him. Combined with his fair skin and pale blue eyes… Well, Jace imagined that if there were such things as angels, they would look something like this. The effect was somewhat ruined by the heavy sweat on his brow and the pupils dilated with fear.

Jace felt a good dose of fear himself. Was this person regretting bringing a bomb onboard, knowing it would cost him his own life? As soon as Jace was close enough, the young man's hand shot out, latching onto Jace's wrist.

"I think I need to get off the plane," he said in a hoarse voice.

Jace glanced around at the other passengers. They too were on edge, so he squatted down and whispered, "Are you sick?"

"I don't know what's wrong with me. I'm freaking out."

"Is something wrong?" asked a gruff male voice from across the aisle.

"Just a little air sickness," Jace said pleasantly. Turning back to the passenger, he said, "What's your name?"

"Kyle."

"Okay, Kyle. Why don't you come with me so we can talk in private?"

Kyle swallowed hard, like his throat was dry. "Can I hold your hand?"

This gave Jace pause, but he nodded. Kyle's hand moved down to take his, the palm slick with sweat. Then Jace stood and led the way down the aisle. He would have felt foolish if he weren't so worried about the source of Kyle's fear.

The galley was the only semi-private place, so Jace took Kyle there. Nancy, who had been watching everything from the other aisle, met them.

"Now," Jace said gently, fixing the baby blue eyes with his own, "tell me what's going on."

"I don't know," Kyle said, trembling lightly. "I think I'm having a panic attack."

"But why?" Nancy asked, an edge to her voice.

Kyle's eyes widened. "I don't know! I don't want to be on this plane! I don't want to be on any plane ever again!"

Jace relaxed slightly. "Have you ever flown before?"

Kyle manically shook his head. "No!"

Jace breathed a sigh of relief. A fear of flying, simple as that. Well, simple for everyone but Kyle. Most people were nervous fliers to some degree, even if it only manifested during rough turbulence. Mankind hadn't evolved to fly, so this was understandable. Shooting through the sky at five hundred miles per hour in a metal tube put most folks on edge. But for others, flying was a serious phobia. Those people didn't get on a plane without heavy medication.

"Are you scared of flying?" Jace asked.

"Yes," Kyle said, his breathing heavy, "but I didn't think it would be *this* bad!"

Jace felt so relieved that he nearly laughed. "You'll have to tough it out. We can't turn the plane around. I wish you were old enough to drink."

Kyle gave a brave smile, but his hand tightened on Jace's. "Will you stay with me? It helps."

Jace glanced over at Nancy, who gave a wide-eyed shrug that said she didn't want to deal with it. After some deliberation, they cleared a row in the front of economy by upgrading a few lucky passengers to first class. Then Jace took a seat next to Kyle, switching sides to give his soaked and cramping hand a break.

"Why are you heading to Boston?" Jace asked, hoping to distract him.

"Boston University invited me up," Kyle said. "I'm going to be an engineer."

"Hopefully not in the aviation industry," Jace teased. "Tell you what, why don't you tell me everything you know about engineering."

After some prompting, Kyle did just that. Focusing on his passion helped him to relax as the flight continued, enough so that Jace was able to conduct his safety checks when the time came. When the plane began descending toward Boston, Kyle panicked again and needed Jace's hand and presence. They made it through. The plane touched down and Kyle stifled a scream. He relaxed considerably when the familiar sensation of rolling over a hard surface returned.

"You might want to take a bus home," Jace said as he stood. "Come on, you'll be the first one off the plane today."

"Thank you," Kyle said when the door opened. "I wouldn't have made it without you."

"All in the line of duty," Jace said with a smile. "Best of luck with your future, Engineer Kyle."

Then he turned and set about doing his job, the angelic face slowly fading from his mind. Until he left the plane with the other flight attendants. To his surprise, Kyle was still standing by the gate, clearly waiting for someone. He smiled when he caught Jace's eye. He really was very pretty, especially now that he no longer resembled a frightened rabbit.

"What hotel are you staying at?" Kyle blurted out.

The other flight attendants giggled, leaving Jace to fend for himself.

"If we happened to be staying at the same hotel," Kyle continued more sheepishly, "I thought we could have dinner together."

"Boston is a big city," Jace said. "The chances of us staying at the same place are low."

Kyle didn't hide his disappointment. "Oh."

"But since I already feel responsible for you, I'll rest easier seeing that you make it to your hotel. For all we know, you might have a fear of taxis."

Kyle brightened. "And then we can have dinner there."

"It's a d—" Jace cleared his throat having almost said date. "It's a deal."

Kyle leaned forward, moving aside the glass of wine that Jace had bought him on the sly. Jace figured the kid had earned it and here, unlike in the air, helping someone underage get tipsy wouldn't cost him his job.

"But a lot of flight attendants are gay, aren't they?" Kyle said.

"Yes," Jace replied. Conversation over their meal had remained fairly neutral until the end, when Jace declined the offer of dessert. Then Kyle had latched onto this subject. Either he was covertly asking about Jace's sexuality, or trying to make a statement about his own. Perhaps both. "Myself included," Jace added, just to find out.

Kyle sat upright. "I'm okay with that," he said quickly.

"Good." Jace had the feeling Kyle was eager to say more, so he gave him an opening. "What about engineers?"

"Yes! I mean, I don't know, but—" Kyle glanced around the dining room, which was nearly empty except for them. Then, in a whisper, he said, "I am."

"Is it a secret?" Jace whispered back.

Kyle laughed nervously. "No. I guess not. Especially not in a city like this. I bet no one here cares."

Jace shrugged. "Who cares if people care anywhere? Try saying that ten times fast!"

Kyle laughed again, fingers fondling the stem of his wine glass, his expression warm. "You're so funny. I really like you."

"I have someone," Jace said, looking away. "A boyfriend. His name is Ben."

"Oh."

Kyle was quiet, so Jace looked back at him, surprised that his eyes were still shining, as if Jace's confession was charming, rather than a cold shower. Maybe Kyle was happy for him. Or maybe he didn't care.

"I should probably get going," Jace said, placing his napkin on the table. "It's been a pleasure."

Now Kyle frowned. "Will you see me to my room? I'm terrified of elevators. Did I mention that?"

Jace smiled at his joke, intending to shake his head.

"Please," Kyle said, blue eyes pleading.

"Okay." Jace stood. "Then it's straight to bed for you, young man."

The ride up to Kyle's floor was quiet. They didn't talk on the way down the hall either. Only when Kyle had swiped his key card and opened the door did he speak, turning around and taking Jace's hand.

"I wouldn't have made it through the day without this," he said, giving the hand a squeeze. "I'd like it to keep me company during the night as well."

"Kyle," Jace said warningly, but part of him was reacting, growing in anticipation, especially when Kyle brought his face near. Thankfully Jace breathed in before their lips could meet, because the mixed scent of wine and an unfamiliar cologne were shockingly different than what he was used to. He longed for the scent of Juicy Fruit gum that Ben was so fond of, or the strawberry tang of Twizzlers that he often snacked on.

Jace's heart, determining that his body had failed in its duty, assumed control. Its first executive decision was to make Jace take a step backward.

"Sorry," Jace said. "The guy I told you about—Ben—I love him. As much as I want to kiss you, it would break his heart."

Kyle clenched his jaw, groaning in frustration, but then gave a smile of resignation. "I hope he knows how lucky he is. Uh, do you want my number? Just in case it doesn't work out between you two?"

Jace knew he'd never have a need for it, but he took it anyway, just to spare Kyle's feelings. Then he said goodbye with a friendly wave and nothing more. When he was in the lobby, he crumpled up Kyle's phone number and threw it in the trash. Once outside and waiting for a taxi, he addressed the sky.

"No need to send any more angels," he said. "I'm more than happy with the one I've got."

The last of the passengers having disembarked, Jace did his final checks before collecting his carry-on luggage and walking down the gangway. Ben was just outside the gate, staring at him with a spooked expression. This took Jace aback momentarily, but the one-year anniversary of the September 11th attacks had been last week, which probably accounted for his worry.

Jace hugged him reassuringly. "I love it when you pick me up at the airport," he said, kissing Ben's neck affectionately. "Are you hungry or should we go straight home?"

"I'm so glad you're back!" Ben said.

Jace frowned. "Is everything okay?"

"Yes," Ben said, his expression still tight. "Everything's fine. Let's go home."

Whatever frustration Ben felt was worked out in the bedroom. He clung to Jace as they made love, pulling their bodies close in desperation. Jace gave as much of himself as he could, concerned there was some bad news Ben wasn't telling him. A medical problem? Or a death in the family? Only afterwards, when Ben's body was curled against his, did Jace get his answer.

"I ran into Tim the other day."

"Ah." Jace's stomach sank, wondering if that was where Ben's passion had stemmed from. "I don't suppose he's horribly overweight? Probably bald and missing a few teeth too, I imagine."

Ben sighed. God what a horrible sign! "He looks pretty much like he always did, just... more."

"Okay," Jace said carefully. "So where did you run into each other?"

"Allison and I were out having coffee, and there he was, simple as that. Turns out he lives in Austin. We go to the same school! Allison knew all along and never told me."

Jace made a mental note to buy her flowers. "So what happened? Awkward conversation before he went on his way?"

"Yes," Ben said, but his body was tense. "At least the first day. We went out a couple of times. One night we went go-kart racing. Then he dragged me off to Six Flags Fiesta, which I felt bad about, since you and I wanted to go there, but it was a surprise and I didn't know until—"

"It's fine," Jace said, cutting him off. Then he sighed. "What else?"

"Oh. Well, I went over to his house too."

Jace refused to ask. There was no point in being with someone without trust cementing the bond. Instead he focused on learning more. "He has his own house?"

"That's the weird part." Ben propped up on his elbow to look at him. "Tim has money. I mean a lot. He had this huge house over in West Lake Hills. You know the area? Anyway, Allison says Tim had a sugar daddy. There were a lot of rumors about it, at least, but the way Tim tells it, they were only friends. It sounds like they loved each other, but it was platonic. When the guy died, he left a lot of his money to Tim."

"And the house," Jace said.

"Yeah." After an awkward moment of silence, Ben bit his lip and added, "It was weird seeing him again. On the one hand, it felt good. He's out of the closet now."

Jace took a deep breath. Over the years, Ben had slowly doled out details about Tim, telling the story of their time together, of their relationship. Ben's feelings for Tim ran deep. He was more than just a high school crush. When Ben loved, he did so with all his heart. Jace knew that firsthand. He also knew that Tim had hurt Ben badly, and his justification for doing so had been his fear of others finding out the terrible terrible truth. Jace couldn't imagine having Ben's love and throwing it away just to stay in the closet. But now Tim was back, openly gay, and rich.

"On the other hand…" Jace said, prompting Ben to continue.

Ben exhaled, "On the other hand, Tim isn't a part of my life anymore. I don't see where he would fit in, if at all. He's being aggressive about it too. He even gave me a cell phone—"

"Gave you one?"

"Yeah."

Jace frowned. "I thought we agreed that would be your birthday present from me."

"I know," Ben said, grimacing. "I didn't ask for it. He shoved it into my hands and walked away. That was after we first bumped into each other. I can give it back."

A tempting offer, but Jace shook his head. He refused to feel intimidated by Ben's past. He believed in the love he and Ben shared, and wasn't about to cast doubt on it by acting panicked about any of this. Instead, he intended to disarm the situation by proving to Ben it wasn't a big deal.

"It's normal to feel excited about running into someone again," Jace said. "Of course you were curious to learn what became of him. You'd do the same even if he had just been a friend, right?"

"Yes," Ben said, already looking relieved. "And the phone?"

"Up to you," Jace said. "Keeping it doesn't mean you're

obligated to answer anytime Tim calls. If you want to, feel free to talk to him. Or not. You're your own man."

"I'm *your* man," Ben said, flopping back down and snuggling up to him.

Jace decided to leave it at that. He had other questions, but left them unasked. Tim wouldn't be a big issue. Not if he could help it. The fewer times his name came up, the better. Ben already seemed more at ease. They shifted, Jace spooning Ben from behind, and perhaps holding him a little tighter than he usually did.

Life was full of temptations. Jace knew that, but he didn't truly understand what Ben was going through until he answered the door late one afternoon. The stranger standing there could be only one person, the facial features vaguely familiar from the tiny yearbook photo Ben had once shown him. That had just been a head shot and didn't reveal the tanned muscled body.

Here he was, Tim Wyman, in the very impressive flesh. Short jet-black hair, silver eyes, and a winner's smile. He looked like a model, *could* be a model, from the way he made a simple T-shirt and shorts appear devastatingly sexy. Of course, Jace had assumed that models only looked this good after their photos had been airbrushed.

Jace took all of this in without his libido responding. Why would it, when he finally saw what a threat this person was?

"Hey!" Tim said with an air of practiced confidence. "Jace, right? I'm Tim."

"Tim, of course." Jace accepted the hand that was offered to him, noticing the lack of calluses. Not a guy whose muscle came from hard work. Jace imagined him grunting away, hour after hour, in front of a gym mirror, driven to achieve some unattainable ideal. Jace supposed that showing up on his doorstep was meant to be shocking, and it was, but he would never reveal that. Instead, Jace behaved as if it was nearly expected. "Ben said he had run into you recently."

"Yeah, it was just like old times. Hey, I was hoping to talk to you both about an idea I had."

"Ben isn't home," Jace said pointedly.

"But he usually is by now, right? I don't mind waiting."

Jace reconsidered him. The confident front hid desperation.

If Tim thought for a second that he had Ben's heart, he wouldn't rely on such tactics. Tim had every reason to be so insecure. After all, Ben had already had his fill. Sure, Tim was handsome and no doubt guys lined up around the block, hoping for their chance to be with him, but Ben already had been. Not only that, but Ben had ample opportunity to mess around behind Jace's back and hadn't. Ben hadn't even accepted Tim's calls since Jace's return, which had surely prompted this new ploy. Tim wasn't a threat. He was old news.

Jace shrugged his indifference and gestured for Tim to enter. He watched impartially as Samson crept up to Tim and sniffed him. Then Jace walked to the living room and sat down in the recliner, petting Samson when he hopped up on his lap.

Tim sprawled out on the couch as if he owned the place, instantly reminding Jace of passengers who thought they could get their way by being pushy. Well, Jace would handle Tim as he would a pushy passenger, disarming him with professional and very detached courtesy. He even let Tim speak first.

"So, Ben tells me you're a stewardess or something."

Jace smiled. Little did Tim know that Ben affectionately teased him sometimes by calling him that. "Yes. That's exactly what I am, although I prefer to think of myself as an astronaut of the stratosphere."

"That's funny," Tim said with a straight face. "Seems like all they talk about on the news lately is airline employees having to take cuts. Must be hard making a living in your line of work."

"I don't live in a mansion," Jace replied, "but I managed to take Ben to London recently. That was nice. Still, I'll be glad when Ben has graduated and is earning money. What are you studying?"

Tim seemed distracted when answering. "Architecture. With a degree under my belt, I'm hoping to put an end to the soulless strip malls plaguing America."

That implied Tim had a brain rattling around somewhere inside his sculpted head. "I don't know much about architecture, although I did see one of Hundertwasser's buildings once, and that was a real eye-opener."

Tim's eyes lit up. "He was amazing! Shows you what's possible if people think outside the box. Buildings can be art."

"True. I suppose it's like poetry. I've never really enjoyed it either, but someone like Dr. Seuss makes it so wacky and fun that it's impossible not to like."

Tim nodded eagerly. "Although it's odd how if you make a painting that's strange and different, most people dismiss it. Everyone scoffs at modern art or art installations, when really that's also being playful within a medium. These days you have to grab people's attention any way you can."

Fascinating. Jace showed just how little of his attention Tim had by checking his watch. "If he's this late, I should probably start dinner."

"No problem." Tim dug in his pocket, pulling out the cell phone that matched the one he'd given Ben. "I'll order us some pizzas. Ben still likes cheese and tomatoes, right? What about you?"

"Surprise me," Jace said, turning his attention to Samson. "No, you can't have anchovies, you silly cat. Tuna? Maybe. Or chicken. But only if you're good."

Tim kept one eye on him as he ordered, probably thinking he was crazy, but Jace didn't care either way. He did wish Ben would show up soon, since he definitely had things he'd rather be doing than hanging out with his boyfriend's ex.

"Should be here soon," Tim said, snapping the phone shut. "Must be nice to travel so much. You visit a lot of other countries?"

For once, Tim's tone was civilized, so Jace answered him equally. "A little, although not while at work. The international routes are highly sought-after. Better pay, nicer perks, such as seeing more of the world. Ben and I take at least one international trip per year."

Tim cocked his head. "I haven't seen much of anything, besides Mexico. Ever been there?"

"No." Jace remembered Ben saying something about Tim being Latino. "When I travel, I try to make sure I get as far away from work as possible. That way they can't call me back in."

Tim nodded as if he understood this, but Jace doubted he did. "Sounds like you have your priorities straight."

"I do." Jace stopped petting Samson and focused on his unwanted guest. "What exactly are you doing here?" he asked, keeping his tone neutral.

"I have a surprise for you both."

"I'm sure you do, but why are you really here, Tim? What do you hope to achieve?"

Tim shrugged, looking away. "Is it so strange that I want to be friends with Ben? He's an important person to me. Even though we haven't seen much of each other these past few years, he's still had a huge impact on my life."

"Such as?"

Tim met his eye again. "Coming out. Slowly learning that it doesn't matter what anyone thinks of me."

"Doesn't it?" Jace asked. "There isn't anyone in your life that doesn't know? Anyone you wouldn't want to find out, because their opinion of your sexuality would have a devastating impact on you?" He agreed that it shouldn't matter. At the end of the day, each person had to answer to themselves, had to deal with the consequences of their actions. But challenging Tim allowed Jace to see something crucially important: doubt. He didn't think Tim had learned much of anything.

The bell rang; Tim took the chance to hop up and answer it. Jace couldn't imagine having the audacity to answer someone else's door, but then he also knew it was too soon to be the pizza delivery and that Ben wouldn't be thrilled with Tim's intrusion. Sure enough, when Jace followed to see for himself, Ben was standing at the door with a shell-shocked expression.

Jace shrugged his helplessness so Ben would know this wasn't his doing. "Look who dropped by," he said in deadpan tones. "Says he has a surprise for us."

"It's nothing, really," Tim said, motioning for Ben to enter.

Jace waited in the hall, happy when Ben gave him their customary kiss in greeting. No doubt about it. Ben wasn't thrilled to see Tim here, and he didn't shy away from showing his affection for Jace.

Shortly after they adjourned to the living room, the bell rang again. This time it really would be the pizza. Tim went to answer it, giving them privacy.

"So, that's the famous Tim?" Jace asked, opening the bag of Thai food Ben had brought with him.

Ben nodded. "How long has he been here?"

"Half an hour or so," Jace dug around in the bag before meeting Ben's eye. "He's a little different than I expected. You didn't tell me that he looked so— Uh..."

"Abercrombie and Fitch?"

"Exactly."

"Well, maybe he's here for a threesome," Ben said it like a joke, but maybe he was testing the waters. After all, most guys would probably be drooling over Tim by now.

"You're more than enough for me," Jace replied. "Anyone else in the bedroom would be an unwelcome distraction."

Ben smiled. Test passed, presumably; not that Jace hadn't been speaking the truth. After all, if Victor hadn't been able to make Jace a swinger, no one could. Jace considered how similar the situations were, how Tim showing up again must be just as confusing for Ben as Victor's surprise appearance had been for him. But what he had with Adrien and what he and Ben shared were completely different. Regardless, he wanted Ben to know that he understood what he was going through.

"Look, Ben—" Whatever else Jace was going to say was cut short by Tim's reappearance in the room, pizza balanced on one palm.

"Ta-da! Dinner is served. Who wants some?"

No one, Jace felt like snapping, but instead he decided to make the best of the meal. Thai and Italian were never meant to go together, and as versatile as pizza could be, there were some combinations that simply clashed. In that regard, the meal suited the situation well.

Eventually, Tim revealed his grand plan. A friend of his was throwing a birthday party and had all of Splash Town reserved for his guests. Splash Town... a waterslide park, which meant they would all be in swimsuits. Jace didn't need to dig to figure out Tim's motivation there. He wanted to flaunt his assets, so to speak.

Ben's eyes lit up at the idea. He could be such a child. For the first time, Jace was forced to recognize that Tim knew Ben too. Maybe not as well, and maybe not the adult version, but they had their history.

Tim excused himself to use the restroom. Jace wouldn't be surprised if he was waiting in the hall, listening to the discussion that followed. He was probably hoping for an argument.

"We don't have to go," Ben said.

"But you want to," Jace replied.

"Well, yeah, it would be fun, but we could always go together some other time."

He recalled the way Adrien had reacted so jealously to Victor, how distasteful that had been. If Jace truly believed in the love he and Ben shared, why should he fear Tim? Why should he fear anyone? "Do you plan on staying friends with Tim?" he asked. "He's going to be in your life from now on?"

Ben glanced toward the hallway, uncertain. "I guess so."

"Then it's a good idea for Tim to see us together as a couple." Jace smiled at the idea. Let him see how strong they were together!

"So what do you think of him?" Ben asked, busying himself by picking up the mess on the table.

"I think he's both insecure and full of himself, and I don't think his intentions are wholly innocent," Jace said. "I also think that he's lonely, and I can see why he'd be the best thing that could happen to an openly gay teenager feeling the same way."

Ben's expression was grateful. "He was really important to me."

Jace nodded his understanding. "I also know that you and I have fun no matter where we are, and I look forward to having you between my legs as we go down the slides together."

If Tim *was* in the hallway, Jace hoped he was peeking around the corner so he could see Ben's gleeful smile.

Chapter Twenty-eight

Tim was... personable. Sure, he made a dreadful first impression, but now that they were splashing around in the water together, the Texas sun burning high in a clear blue sky, Jace was beginning to see that he had his charms.

Like Greg, Tim was a very physical person. Some guys treated their bodies like giant toys, moving with careless ease, leaping, catching, throwing—making even the most skilled feat seem like child's play. Tim grinned all the time, back-flipping into pools, doing handstands underwater, or even falling comically into the water to make them laugh.

And Jace did laugh, even though he never would have imagined Tim could make him feel any sort of joy, but he was such a *guy*, the guyest of the guys, that it was hard not to like him. Of course it helped that he'd stopped being rude to Jace. They sat together in the front seat as Tim drove them down. Allison was along for the ride too, acting as Ben's moral chaperone, or maybe just there to have fun. She and Ben were acting up in the back together, while conversation between Jace and Tim remained civil, if not a little awkward. And interesting at times, because Tim wasn't a dumb jock. He had a strong interest in art, for example, and some surprising insights on human behavior.

This puzzled Jace. Ben had told him, speaking like a lawyer defending his client, that Tim's parents were cold and distant. This made it all the more unlikely that Tim would be such a carefree spirit. Ben also said that Tim had his demons, but as they took a break from swimming to eat cheap hotdogs, Tim wolfing down two effortlessly, it was difficult to see any dark side.

"We need ice cream!" Ben said, rushing off to the restaurant catering to this party.

Jace watched him go, feeling a surge of pride and love. When he looked over at Tim, he saw the same emotions there. That was another thing. Tim obviously loved Ben, or at least cared for him in some way that was anything but superficial.

Tim felt Jace's gaze and turned, looking embarrassed. "Geez, we're like proud parents watching their kid run off to play."

Jace chuckled. "Did you feel that way when you were together? Like you needed to take care of him?"

Tim considered it. "Sort of. I felt like I needed to look out for him, like he didn't understand the dangers of the world. Of course, looking back, I think I was wrong. Mostly. There were definitely times he needed someone watching out for him. He ever tell you how he picked a fight with our high school quarterback?"

Jace shook his head. "No, but it doesn't surprise me."

"Surprised the hell out of me," Tim said with a wry grin. "Anyway, in situations like that, he needed me to look out for him. Usually though, he took care of me."

"He can be very nurturing," Jace said. "Whether you like it or not."

They laughed together, which felt good, but when Tim spoke again, there was an edge to his voice. "You're lucky, you know that?"

Jace nodded. "I do."

Anything further they had to say was cut short when Ben returned with three cones, the ice cream already melting down his fingers. "After this, we'll have to stay out of the water for thirty minutes," he said.

"Urban legend." Jace accepted a cone.

"I'm pretty sure it's true," Tim replied between licks.

"What's supposed to happen, anyway?" Ben asked.

"Remember that part in *Alien*?" Tim said. "When the spider creature launches out of that guy's chest? That's what happens, except it's your food exploding out of your stomach."

Ben was skeptical. "What's the scientific explanation behind that?"

"Pressure," Tim explained, clearly enjoying himself. "An empty stomach is like a submarine full of air. When the hull of a submarine ruptures, it implodes."

"You promised me an outward explosion," Ben complained.

"Besides," Jace chimed in, "wouldn't a full stomach insulate against outward pressure?"

"Like filling a balloon with ground beef," Tim said musingly. "Maybe you're right. We need to stuff ourselves before going swimming."

"Then we would sink," Ben said. "I bet that's why you have to wait half an hour for the food to digest."

"Regardless," Jace said, "after a meal like that, maybe we should take it easy."

"There's the lagoon," Ben suggested.

That's where they headed next. While "lagoon" conjured images of turquoise waters surrounded by lush ferns, the reality was a murky pool with sand at the bottom instead of concrete. An artificial rock formation ringed in half of it, waterfalls cascading down the surface. The lagoon didn't offer the thrills of the waterslides, so they had it all to themselves.

They waded in, eager to cool off. Ben splashed Tim playfully, Tim responding by dragging one muscled arm through the water, creating a wave that drenched Ben. Jace came to his rescue, linking his hands together and making a wave of his own to attack Tim, but there was no malevolence here. They were having fun. Playing.

Eventually Jace craved rest, so he returned to shore to sunbathe. Donning his sunglasses barely helped block out the brightness, so he closed his eyes. And yet, Jace found them opening again and again to check on Ben. And his relative position to Tim. At first, Ben was floating on his back in the water. Tim stood on the rock formation, watching. He had an incredible body. Jace hated to admit it, but Tim's physique was just as handsome as the rest of him. Luckily, growing up around Greg made Jace somewhat immune to this, but he knew Ben didn't have that benefit.

Trust was the key, Jace reminded himself. He believed in the love Ben felt for him. Jace closed his eyes with this in mind, intending to keep them shut. Even when Tim said something about a cave behind the waterfall, followed soon after by an absence of voices, Jace forced himself to relax, the heat and food conspiring to make him tired. Still, he wished Allison hadn't run off with a lifeguard shortly after they had arrived.

When a shadow came between him and the sun, Jace opened his eyes, expecting to see her standing there. It wasn't Allison. Blinking against the brightness, he could scarcely believe who it was: Victor, wearing goofy Hawaiian swim trunks and nothing else. He was young and carefree again, hair punky and shaved on the sides. Victor leaned over Jace, coming close as if for a kiss, a smirk on his lips. And even though Jace couldn't understand how Victor could be in such a ridiculous setting and outfit, his heart skipped a beat. Even though he loved Ben dearly, Jace rose halfway to meet Victor's kiss.

Jace jerked awake with a sharp intake of breath. A shadow had come between him and the sun, but when he opened his eyes, it was only a cloud in the sky. No Victor. Of course not. Sitting up and taking off his sunglasses, Jace found the lagoon empty. His heart was still racing. Just a dream—the mere thought of seeing Victor again, of kissing him—brought all those feelings back. Even though he loved Ben.

He knew then how foolish he'd been, because Tim *was* back, and of course the feelings Ben had for him hadn't gone away. Love never leaves us, no matter how we sometimes might wish it to. Jace stumbled to his feet, knocking over the lounge chair. He hurried around the water rather than wading through it, climbing along the rocks to the largest waterfall—the only one likely to have anything behind it.

Sure enough, he found a cave, and what he saw beyond nearly broke his heart. They weren't just kissing. That would have been bad enough, but their bodies were pressed together, the swimsuits failing to hide their arousal. Jace stood in the entrace—the water breaking over his shoulders—and wished he had stayed in his dream.

"About done?" he asked.

Ben turned, eyes registering panic. Then he shoved Tim away, hard enough that he fell backward into the water. "I'm sorry," Ben spluttered.

Saddest of all, Jace could see that Ben really was sorry, in the same way Jace would have regretted kissing Victor had the dream been reality. The kiss wouldn't have been the source of regret, but rather the pain it would have caused Ben. What Jace would have wanted then was understanding, if not forgiveness.

They needed to talk.

"Maybe you should wait for us outside, Tim," Jace suggested.

Tim left. Maybe he slunk out or maybe he strutted, Jace didn't know. He kept his eyes on Ben, trying to decide what to do. Be understanding? Or throw it all away over one slip-up that was just as much his fault as it was Ben's? Jace had allowed things to get this far, when he probably should have shut the door in Tim's face when he first showed up.

"I'm so sorry," Ben repeated. "It just sort of happened. I don't know—"

"It's all right." Jace's throat burned when he said it.

Ben's jaw dropped. "What?"

"I said it's all right." Jace sat on a stone slab next to the entrance, an unwelcome question surfacing. Was this the first time? Ben and Tim had met when he was out of town. Could they have—? "I knew something like this would happen eventually, if it hadn't already."

"I didn't do anything with him before!" Ben said. "Just now, I promise."

Jace shrugged. What did it matter? Ben loved Tim. Anything they had done together wasn't because Ben didn't love him too.

Ben's brow came together. "Aren't you angry?"

"Not really. Old feelings don't just disappear overnight. It's normal that you and Tim still find each other attractive."

"That's it?" Ben was scowling, his chest heaving. "I wish you *were* pissed! At least then I could tell that you care."

"I care," Jace said, starting to feel angry himself. "I just thought I'd give you the benefit of the doubt!"

"What's there to doubt?" Ben demanded. "You saw everything. I did something stupid, and you should hate me for it."

That extinguished the flames. The thought was unthinkable. "I'd never hate you."

Ben's jaw clenched in the way it did when he was trying not to cry. Jace could only imagine what he was feeling, how conflicted he would be in the same situation.

The roar of the waterfall broke as Tim reappeared. He was grinning. The bastard was actually grinning! The furnace in Jace's stomach sparked back to life. He felt like grabbing Tim's face, pointing it toward Ben so he was forced to see how badly the man they both loved was hurt. There was nothing remotely amusing about this situation!

"Hey," Tim said to him. "It's my fault. I grabbed him and started kissing him. He wasn't even kissing back. Really. Please don't blame him."

Jace had seen enough to know this was a lie, but he didn't care. Any word out of Tim's mouth that wasn't begging Ben's forgiveness would have infuriated him. That's why Jace's fist was already swinging to shut him up and wipe that winner's smile from his face. Tim didn't see it coming and must not have expected it, because his head whipped back with a crack. The rest of his body followed.

This time Tim didn't catch himself as he fell, his head submerging. Not wanting to add manslaughter to the other miserable events of the day, Jace grabbed him by the shoulders, lifted him up, and shoved him against a wall. Then he turned to Ben, eyes still blazing with heat. "How's that for angry?" he said. "Come on, we're going home."

Jace saw red as he marched across the park, hearing very little. Ben was beside him, endless apologies spewing from his mouth, but Jace couldn't concentrate on the words. He was heading for the exit when he remembered their clothes. The locker rooms weren't far. When they reached them, he dressed hurriedly, pulling out his cell phone and dialing information to find the nearest place to rent a car. That was another miscalculation, letting Tim drive them down here, putting him in charge of when they could leave. The operator informed Jace of a rental car location just down the road. Once Ben was dressed, Jace wordlessly led them out of the park's gate to the parking lot.

"Stay here," he said. "I'll get a car and pick you up."

"I'm sorry," Ben said again. "I was stupid."

"We were both stupid!" Jace snarled.

Then he spun around, heading for the street. He'd promised himself after Victor died that he wouldn't argue again. Their parting words had been so ugly. At least the ones Jace had uttered. He still regretted that's how it had ended. Maybe that was why he dreamed of Victor still—one more chance to say goodbye properly.

As Jace stomped down the side of the road, he was glad to have time away from Ben. He needed space to think, to decide what to do, which was hard when his head was still clouded by emotion. When he did get the rental car, Jace sat inside of it instead of driving back to the park.

He loved Ben. But did he love him enough to put up with this? With a sigh, Jace knew the answer. Of course he did. Hell, he'd been through worse. He didn't believe for a second that Victor and Star weren't— But Ben wasn't Victor. That was one of the many reasons Jace loved him. He had to admit that Victor was right again: Life would be so much simpler if people were allowed to kiss whomever they wanted to.

Love was love was love. Spread it around, share it, give it away. What a nice thought. What a wonderful idea! But that's not who Jace was. Maybe he was selfish, a miser with his feelings. Sometimes Ben said in wistful tones that Jace was perfect. He disagreed. A perfect person would tell those they love that of course they are free to love and *be* loved. The more the merrier. Right?

They say history repeats itself, but only if you let it, and Jace wasn't about to go through this again. An open relationship didn't work for him. If that cost him Ben, then so be it. Jace put his forehead on the steering wheel and sighed. That was bullshit. If this cost him Ben, it would be devastating.

Starting the car, he drove back to the park. Ben's relief at seeing him again was transparent. The car interior was quiet as they merged onto the highway, Jace lost in thought. He was torn between two sides of himself—one with a very specific idea of a relationship, and the other that understood Ben's plight all too well. It wasn't just Victor. Kyle, his terrified passenger—Jace had wanted to kiss him too, and he hadn't even felt strong emotion for him. Human biology drives the body to reproduce, no matter how futile the chance of success. Mankind's survival had depended on this urge for millennia. Of course that just didn't go away. Perhaps it was time to stop fighting and embrace the inevitable.

Then again, cavemen used to smash in each other's heads with rocks. Mankind used to kill each other for having different ideals, and sometimes still did. Violence had served a purpose once too, but now had no place in civilized society. Jace had no intention of embracing those urges. All he could do was recognize them and set them aside.

"I'm sorry," Ben whispered from next to him.

Jace pressed his back against the seat, exhaling the tension he'd felt. "I had a close call once."

"Close call?"

"About six months ago. On a flight to Boston."

Jace told Ben about Kyle, deciding to be honest about everything, including how he felt. Jace had wanted to kiss him. There was nothing wrong with that. "He was hot, and I won't lie and say that I didn't want to, but I made my choice when I decided to be with you."

"So you didn't?"

"No. I didn't."

Ben sighed in relief, which comforted Jace, because it meant he too was uneasy with the idea of an open relationship.

"There's a difference though," Jace continued. "You were once in love with Tim. You probably still are to some extent. You two have a history, and that complicates matters."

"I still shouldn't have kissed him."

"Get over it," Jace snapped. "What's more important to me is what you're going to do now. You're stuck with an old-fashioned guy. I like monogamy. I don't want to have a threesome or share you with anyone. So now you need to decide if you can handle that or not."

Ben didn't take long to answer. "I think I can."

"Good." Jace said, bracing himself. "The next thing you have to figure out is what you're going to do about Tim. I'm not going to forbid you to see him. I'm not going to say you can't be his friend. I'm going to trust you now as much as I did before. There's no point in going on otherwise. But I want you to ask yourself if you can resist doing something like this again."

Now Ben was quiet. For most of the ride home, he thought in silence. Jace knew this would be a big decision. While he couldn't forbid Ben to see Tim, he knew it was all or nothing between them. Friendship between former lovers is an exercise in restraint, not a relaxed camaraderie. What Ben and Tim once had—shared even now—couldn't be contained by the bonds of friendship. This was something else Jace understood from his time with Victor. Had Victor miraculously come back, and had Ben asked Jace to make a decision, it would have been very difficult. In the end, though, he would have chosen Ben. In his heart, there wasn't any contest.

"I've made my choice," Ben said.

Jace's throat felt tight until Ben reached over to take his hand. Then he exhaled, squeezing Ben's fingers and showing just a little of the desperation he felt. They felt the same way about each other after all.

Two months of gloriously normal life. The threat of Tim Wyman had come and gone, like the big hurricane of the year, this one not having done much damage. In fact, Jace felt closer to Ben than ever. He respected him too, especially after Ben had done the hard thing and said goodbye to Tim. Hell, Ben had even given Tim a puppy, something Jace felt was an inspired move.

What a way to break up with someone! No more of the "it's not you, it's me" nonsense that never worked. Instead, a relationship could be ended simply by saying, "Sorry, can't stick around, but here's a puppy to lick up all of those tears."

Not that Ben and Tim had broken up and not that Ben had been so crass. The important thing was that it was over, allowing them to resume their lives. A lot of exciting things awaited them too. Ben was set to graduate in a few weeks, which had all sorts of implications. Dual income would be nice. No more pinching pennies, especially since Jace planned on inviting Ben to move in. They could also move back to Houston, be closer to their families and to Jace's home base. That would make commuting to work easier, since many of his routes left from there. The future was full of potential, which had him very excited, but Jace kept a tight lid on all of this. He knew the kind of stress Ben was about to go through with finals.

As if to prove this, when Jace returned home from the supermarket, Ben opened the door with a miserable expression.

"Hey!" Jace said, hoping his good mood would be contagious. "You ready for dinner?"

"A note just came for you," Ben said, not returning his smile.

"A note?"

Ben gestured for him to go inside. Jace did so, spotting the note on the hallway floor of all places. He set down the groceries on a side table as Ben picked it up and shoved it into his face. He read it, half-distracted by Ben's behavior. The letter was handwritten, but Jace didn't recognize the penmanship.

Surprise! Bet you didn't expect to see me so soon, huh? My parents sprung for a ticket. Guess I should have called ahead to tell you I was cumming. At least I hope I will be. How about a rerun of what we did in your hotel? Then again, maybe not. I'm still sore!

Jace glanced up. "Is this some sort of joke?"

Ben crossed his arms over his chest. "Come on. Where were you last week?"

"A lot of places," Jace replied.

"Including Boston?"

"Yeah. So?" Jace finally understood. "You think— No, this isn't from that kid. I haven't talked to him since."

"Since what, exactly?" Ben said, voice laced with accusation.

"You know the story. Nothing happened. This is—" Jace waved the note at him. "I don't know what this is."

"It's perfectly clear what it is," Ben shouted. "Or is there another gay guy next door named Jace, and Aaron just happened to pick the wrong door?"

Jace wanted to shout in return, but he knew that would make it worse. Instead, he set down the note, took a deep breath, and looked Ben in the eye. "I've never cheated on you."

Ben's angry expression wavered. "Then how do you explain it?"

Jace shrugged, but it didn't take him long to find an explanation. "If I had to guess, I expect Tim thought this might—"

"Tim?" Ben's scowled. "Get a grip, Jace! He's not Moriarty! I saw the guy who put this on the door, and it sure as hell wasn't Tim."

Now Jace was angry. That Ben could get so worked up about Tim, still defend him like he was a saint, pissed him off. That Ben was pointing the finger at Jace when he was the one who had cheated… "I don't know what's going on," he said evenly, "but if anyone deserves to be under suspicion, it's you!"

"I admitted when I fucked up," Ben said. "The least you could do is the same!"

"*You were caught,*" Jace said. "You didn't heroically confess that you were horny for Tim. In fact, you didn't mention it once before it happened. You're telling me you weren't tempted?"

"Fine, throw all of that back in my face!" Ben spun around, heading for the living room.

Jace grabbed the note and followed him. "You're the one who brought it up," he said, rereading the letter, but this time looking for evidence to defend himself. "This letter is signed Aaron."

"So?" Ben said, flopping down on the couch.

"So the guy in Boston was Kyle. I told you that!"

Ben shook his head. "Did you? I don't remember you ever saying his name."

Jace's head was spinning. "Then why do you think Aaron is the guy in Boston?"

"So maybe it's a different guy!" Ben shot back. "You probably have a hookup at every major airport!"

"Are you serious?" Jace shouted. His anger was rising, but he was past the point of caring. "After everything I've done for you, all the love I've given you, you honestly think I could fuck around on you, come home, and still look you in the eye?"

"I don't know," Ben said. "I honestly don't. You know what I keep thinking of? How you were hardly angry when you caught me kissing Tim. Not really. You forgave me *way* too easily, and you know what that tells me?"

"What?"

"You forgave me because you've been doing the same thing this whole time."

"No." Jace clenched his jaw. "You're fucking crazy, you know that? Just because I didn't fly off the handle and make you beg for forgiveness, you think that means I've been cheating? It's called love, Ben! That's why I forgave you!"

"Then what's that?" Ben said, gesturing at the letter. "Do you call that love too?"

"I don't know what this is!" Jace shouted in exasperation. "You know what? That's not true. Use your brain, Ben! You know exactly who did this!"

"Don't drag him into this," Ben said warningly.

Jace dropped his arms to his sides. "Why?" he said. "Why can't you even think of him being the bad guy? The guy who hurt you so bad when you were young is a saint, but I *love you*! And yet you can sit there and accuse me of cheating on you! Fuck Tim! He did this, and he's a piece of shit!"

"Shut up," Ben said, his voice a growl. "I gave up Tim for you. I looked him in the eye and said we couldn't be friends because that's what you wanted! He's fucking gone, so don't try to demonize him further!"

"I asked you to make a choice," Jace said. "It sounds to me like you regret the one you made."

"Maybe I do," Ben said defiantly.

"Fine!" Jace crumpled the letter and tossed it at him. "Go back to him if you want. I don't care anymore. Do whatever you want, Ben, fuck whoever your heart desires, because we're done!"

"Damn right we are!" Ben stood, face crimson as he headed for the door. "Have fun with Kyle and Aaron and all the rest of them!"

"I will!" Jace shouted.

When the door slammed shut, he winced. Then he sat on the couch, face in his hands. After a while, Samson came out of hiding, tail poofy in fear. Jace shook his throbbing head and wondered if two years had just gone down the drain.

Chapter Twenty-nine

"Love ain't easy." Greg raised a glass to his lips, nearly turning it upside down to get the last drops of beer.

Around them, the airport buzzed with activity, full of passengers excited about their trips. Jace felt like twisting off their happy little heads. He had a much easier time being around the more nervous travelers who were drowning their fears at the bar. He often met Greg here, when his schedule permitted, since it was an easy way to catch up with each other.

"Another round?" Jace asked.

"Don't you have to work soon?" Greg asked.

Jace shrugged. "So?"

"Uh, no thanks. I'm fine." Greg slid his glass away from him. "Listen, I know it was a bad fight—"

Jace snorted. "That's putting it mildly. It was Armageddon. We were one police call away from being on one of those trashy cop shows."

Greg snorted. "It wasn't *that* bad. I've had worse with your sister, believe me. Things only get more tense when kids are added to the equation. Do you know how many nights I've had to sleep on the couch?"

"How many?" Jace asked.

"Twenty-three," Greg said matter-of-factly.

Jace expected a vague answer, like dozens or hundreds. "That's a very specific number."

"I keep count," Greg said with a straight face. "I have a file on my computer that I update."

"Seriously?"

"Yup. That same file also has the exact day me and your sister first, uh... I'll spare you the details. My point is, every time we have a serious fight, that file also reminds me how far Michelle and I have made it. We've been together thousands of days. Only twenty-three of them have been bad. Perspective is important. In two years, you and Ben have had a couple of really bad days. How were the rest of them?"

"Amazing," Jace admitted. He finished his beer and sighed. "So what does Gregory Trout do after a night on the couch?"

"He gives Michelle Holden her space, but when she does

come around, he makes sure to wave the white flag."

Jace nodded. "You know what makes all of this worse? Ben has his finals over the next couple of weeks."

Greg sucked in air through his teeth. "Ouch. Yeah, you might have a few nights on the couch then. That's rough."

Jace gave him a look. "You say that now."

"What do you mean?"

"You did the same thing to me when I was close to graduating."

Greg thought about it, then smiled. "You mean when I brought Victor down to see you?"

"Yeah. I keep thinking about that. Adrien and I argued about that indirectly. We sort of used the stress of finals as an excuse. I skipped town on him, and when I came back, he kept begging for us to patch things up. But it was too much for me." It was clear that his friend didn't see his point, so Jace added, "History repeats itself."

Greg shook his head dismissively. "You and Ben, that's something completely different."

"I hope so," Jace said, "but maybe it's better to let him get through graduation first."

"I don't know, man."

But Jace did. The last thing he wanted was to push Ben away with good intentions. Besides, there was another outcome of that reunion with Victor, something vitally important, and part of him wondered if Ben needed that too. He couldn't bear to think of it, though. Not now.

Over the next few days, Jace threw himself into his job. It took all of his willpower not to call Ben, but he persevered, letting Ben decide when he was ready to speak. When Jace was settling into his hotel room one evening, his cell phone rang. Ben. Sitting on the edge of the bed, he answered it, eager to hear the voice on the other end.

"Hey," Jace said. "I'm glad you called."

"Where are you?"

"Chicago."

Ben's voice hesitated, uncertain. "Are you flying back tonight?"

"No. Not for a couple of days."

"Oh." Disappointment.

Jace took a deep breath. "Look, Ben, I think we both said things we didn't mean, but I think we should take a break."

The other line crackled in silence.

"You have a lot going on right now with school," he continued with a tight throat. "I understand how much pressure you're under. I remember. Focus on your finals and your thesis and make sure you graduate. Once that is out of the way, then we can talk. Okay?"

"I guess."

Those two little words sounded hurt, but Jace felt this was the right thing to do. "Good. I love you."

"I love you too."

The line went dead. Jace set down the phone. Then, hunched over and staring at the carpet, he let himself consider what could happen. Getting back together with Victor had been exciting, but it had also reminded him why they weren't compatible. If Tim was somehow involved... Jace shook his head and sighed. He could only hope that Ben was a quick learner.

The weeks that followed were hell for Jace, a self-induced purgatory of waiting and wondering and wanting. As Ben's graduation day drew near, Jace couldn't help himself. He was sure most or all of Ben's finals were out of the way. Now, in the calm before the storm, was the time to sweep back in and make things right. But when Jace called Ben's cell phone, only voicemail picked up. When he called the duplex, Allison answered, tersely telling Jace each time that Ben wasn't home.

Jace didn't believe it. Once he called past midnight and she told him the same thing: Ben wasn't home. Jace had to wonder if Ben had found somewhere else to spend his nights. When he was in town again, Jace drove over to the duplex, holding a single rose as he waited for Ben to answer the door.

He didn't. Once again, the duty of sending Jace away fell to Allison.

"He's not home," she said.

"Then can I come in?"

Her eyes widened, giving away the game. "No," she said. "It's not a good time."

Jace swallowed. Maybe he had been foolish again. He had thought, if given the chance, Ben would see Tim for what he was.

Instead, maybe they were as happy as two love birds in a nest.

"Is he okay?" Jace asked. "Just tell me if he's happy."

Allison's expression was pure sympathy. She glanced toward the interior of the house, then leaned toward him and whispered, "Duncan Park. Noon." Then, in a louder voice she said, "Sorry! I'll tell him you came by!"

Jace stared at the door after it was shut, then left the rose on the doorstep. Back in his car, he checked his watch. Two hours until noon. But what would he find there? Would Allison bring Ben so they could serendipitously run into each other?

The prior weeks had been hard enough, but waiting for noon to roll around was grueling. Jace went to get his hair cut, just so he was looking his best, then wasted time at a department store trying on clothes until he settled on a pale green dress shirt. Feeling and looking like he was going on a date, he arrived at Duncan Park half an hour early.

The park was mostly a big empty field providing space for a picnic, Frisbee, or similar activities. Trees walled in one side; a creek created a natural border on the other. Across 9th Street, the park was much more interesting. Paths wove around and connected mounds of dirt, kids racing their bikes along these and launching into the air. Jace stood in plain sight, watching from across the street as they shouted gleefully with each self-induced risk to their health.

When he spotted Allison's car parking along the side of the street, his body went tense. Disappointment helped him relax again when he saw she was alone. He walked over to meet her, Allison nodding toward the concrete path that curved toward the creek. Walking together, Jace repeated his question.

"Is he okay?"

Allison exhaled and shook her head. "No. Tim's out of the picture. That's the good news. Tim was behind the letter taped to your door."

Jace's jaw clenched. He felt vindicated, but couldn't celebrate yet. "Then why isn't Ben talking to me?"

They left the path, walking down a sandy slope to the edge of the creek. Allison was watching the water flow by to keep from looking him in the eye.

"Allison," Jace prompted.

"Ben made some mistakes."

Jace's throat felt tight. "He was tricked. I wish he had trusted me when I said I hadn't cheated, but I'm not holding that against him."

Still Allison wouldn't look at him. "You two were taking a break, right?"

"Yes," Jace said, his voice hoarse. She didn't need to say more. He knew this had been likely to occur, figured maybe it even needed to, just so it was out of the way. But now that it actually happened, it hurt more than he expected.

"They were together," Allison said gently, glancing at him to make sure he understood. "But I want you to understand that Ben always follows his heart. Even when it leads him in the wrong direction. He's never been the kind of guy who—"

"I know," Jace said. Ben didn't have sex for fun or conquest. He hadn't slept with Tim because of his good looks or his body. There was an emotional connection between them. Or had been. Now Jace felt he was being tested. How strong was his love for Ben? Could he forgive him? Could he ever get over this?

Does love cease to exist the second you kiss another person? Is love that fickle?

Victor had been right about a lot of things. Not everything— Jace still believed that a relationship had to be a commitment. But Victor had understood love very well, because what Jace felt for Ben wasn't diminished. Yes, it hurt, and no, he didn't like the idea of Ben being with anyone else—even if Ben did care about that person—but that didn't change the love Jace felt.

"Why isn't he taking my calls?" he asked.

Allison seemed surprised he still cared about that. "He's kind of burnt out on everything. Tim hurt him. Again. Finals have been a nightmare, and… He thinks you won't want him anymore. Because of what he did."

Jace laughed bitterly. "Well, he's wrong."

Allison stared. "He is?"

"Yes! Of course I still want him."

After a moment of disbelief, Allison threw herself at Jace, hugging him. "You're a saint," she said. "An absolute saint."

Jace didn't feel that way. What kind of man allowed the guy he loved to get hurt, just to teach him a lesson? Still, Jace had paid a price for it too. "The only question that remains," he said, "is if Ben still wants me."

"He does," Allison said, releasing him, "but I know him. Ben will wallow in his own guilt and say he's not worthy of you anymore. Even if you bust down the door, he'll just run out the back, thinking he's doing you a favor. So if we're going to do this, we have to do it right. Also, you and me talking? What I told you today? That remains a secret."

Jace nodded. Whatever it took, he would do it.

Allison's plan was simple. Too simple, Jace worried at first, but as he waited outside the stadium, graduates pouring in, he began to reconsider. When Jace graduated, he had felt two things: nostalgia for the past had been one, which was ironic considering how often he'd wished for college to finally be over. The other had been an almost overwhelming excitement about the future. Once the diploma had been placed in his hand, Jace had felt like anything was possible. He could go anywhere and do anything, and yet part of him had already mourned the past. Maybe that was the right combination of feelings to bring Ben back to him.

When he heard the graduation ceremony begin, Jace took the bouquet of roses from the back seat of his car and walked to the entrance. Allison had said she and Ben planned on leaving right after getting their diplomas. With the family names of Bentley and Cross, he wouldn't have long to wait. Jace strained to hear the names as they were announced, feeling a surge of pride when Ben's was called. When he heard Allison's name, he stood at attention, waiting for them both to appear. Despite his vigilance, they nearly got away. Only Allison calling his name alerted him.

Jace realized he'd been standing at the entrance instead of the exit. That didn't matter though, because he spotted Ben, nearly unrecognizable in his cap and gown. Allison was saying something to him, patting him on the shoulder, before she returned inside the stadium. Jace's long strides were already closing the distance between them. Ben didn't walk to meet him. Instead he stood there, watching Jace with vulnerable eyes.

When Jace reached out to touch him, Ben began to cry.

Jace dropped the roses to the ground, taking Ben in his arms and kissing him. Ben shook his head, as if it would be wrong, but then he kissed Jace back, still crying. "You shouldn't— I'm not worth— I have to tell you—" Ben's words were interrupted each time by sobs.

Jace hated seeing him so hurt, took no pleasure in the state Ben was in. "You're fine," Jace assured him. "Everything's fine."

"Take me home," Ben managed at last.

"I thought I'd take you out to eat."

Ben shook his head, face crumpling. "I want to go home."

"Okay." Jace picked up the roses and dusted them off. Then he handed them to Ben, who accepted them, but clearly felt he had no right to. Good. Not good that Ben was hurting, but good that he loved Jace enough to feel bad about what had happened.

By the time they were in the car and underway, Ben had calmed down enough to speak.

"Congratulations," Jace said, starting easy. "Are you excited about graduating?"

"Yes." Ben's focus remained on the roses. He looked embarrassed.

"Are your parents in town for the big occasion?" Jace asked, knowing they weren't.

"I asked them not to come," Ben said. "I don't feel like celebrating."

"You should," Jace said, trying to show that all had been forgiven. "I'm proud of what you've achieved."

He glanced over to see Ben on the verge of tears again, so Jace remained quiet until they pulled into his apartment complex and stopped.

Ben looked up, surprised by where they were. "I meant my home," he said.

Jace resisted the urge to reach out and touch him. "I know what you meant."

Ben was solemn as he entered the apartment, didn't speak to Samson when squatting down to pet him. Jace tossed his keys and wallet on the table and waited for Ben to stand again. When he did, he wore a familiar expression of determination. This was it. Jace braced himself to hear what he already knew, because hearing it from Ben's lips would be the hardest.

"I was with Tim. We slept together."

Jace fought down the lump in his throat. "I figured. Got it all out of your system now?"

Ben nodded.

"Good."

Ben probably expected Jace to drive him home now, or kick

him out. Instead, he took off his shoes and loosened his tie. Ben stared in disbelief, so Jace nodded at him. "Don't you want to get out of that doofy gown?"

"I don't understand."

Jace sighed. "My love for you doesn't stop just because you make a stupid mistake. An extremely stupid mistake, I might add. I love you, and if you promise to trust my word in the future, then I'll trust you again too."

Ben looked as though he were about to cry again, but thankfully, he laughed in the way of someone overwhelmed by relief. Jace smiled in return, stepping close to help unfasten Ben's graduation gown. Beneath he wore a plain white T-shirt and a pair of shorts. Jace took off the jacket he was wearing, tossed it aside, and held out his hand. When Ben accepted it, Jace led him to the bedroom.

They wouldn't sleep together. Not today. Jace felt it was too soon for either of them. Instead he wanted to start over, to begin again in the same way they had two years ago—by talking. But the intimacy between them wasn't gone. Jace held Ben from behind, sometimes placing gentle kisses in Ben's hair as he told Jace what had happened and how sorry he was. As Ben talked, Jace found the details didn't matter. He loved Ben. All that had changed was that Ben was now free to love him back.

Part Four:
Austin, 2004

Chapter Thirty

Winter's purpose was to wipe the slate clean. No matter how perfect a year was, or how disappointing it had been, once winter came along it was time to say goodbye. First autumn disassembled what summer had supported, forcing flowers to give up their petals, plucking the leaves from the trees, and blowing it all away with the same winds birds took flight on. Then came winter's white blanket, returning the world to an empty canvas so a new spring could begin. Even Central Texas had its share of snow in the most recent winter, cementing Jace's feeling that they truly had a fresh start. All their sins had long ago been absolved, all past indiscretions forgiven.

Now warmth had returned to the world, and Jace couldn't think of anywhere else he wanted to celebrate than where he and Ben were now.

"Paris," Ben said, breathing in air moist from the river they sat beside.

"I know," Jace said, sighing at the wonder of it all.

They were below street level, feet dangling over the stone walkway that ran along the River Seine. Above them cars raced by, and tourists strolled along carrying maps folded in origami shapes. The two towers of Notre Dame stood cold and gray against a perfectly blue sky.

Ben scooted closer to Jace, the faint smile signaling that he hoped for a kiss. Jace was happy to comply. They were good now. The bump they had hit was nearly two years behind them. Sometimes it felt like it had never happened at all.

"So should I go first, or do you want to?" Ben said, unzipping his backpack that had been empty an hour ago when they had split up. Now it was positively stuffed with all manner of things.

Okay, so maybe Ben did go a little overboard at times, like he was still trying to compensate.

"Please tell me that's not all for me," Jace said. "We agreed to buy one present each."

"Of course it isn't all for you," Ben said. He opened the backpack wider and peered inside. "Okay, so maybe it is, but I couldn't decide what to get."

"So you bought everything?" Jace said incredulously.

"Yes. Well, at least everything that I was considering.

Besides, what's the point in working two jobs if I can't spend any money? And don't say you're proud of me. I wasn't fishing for compliments."

"I *am* proud of you," Jace said. After a year of floundering in the post-college void, Ben had found his way. First he suffered temp work that offered him nothing in the way of benefits or satisfaction. Finally, Allison landed Ben a job at the hospital where she worked as a counselor. Ben worked in speech rehabilitation, helping people recovering from strokes or other misfortunes, utilizing the vocal training he had received as a singer.

Typically this was only part-time work, Ben being called in when he was needed and leaving him with time to spare. More time than Ben liked, in fact. Jace had finally gained enough seniority to take on international routes, usually to Italy, since he spoke enough of the language to get by. This meant more money and benefits, but longer layovers too, leaving Ben wondering what to do with himself.

Allison had come to the rescue a second time. Or her husband, Brian, who was part-owner of a dinner theater. Allison had met Brian during her internship and gotten swept up into a whirlwind romance. But the relationship had substance as well. When she suggested that Ben audition for a new musical—

"You're thinking of me being on stage, aren't you?" Ben said.

"How could you tell?"

"Because you get this dreamy look on your face, just like when you watch me perform."

"That's because you *are* so dreamy," Jace said, nudging him. "You should be the centerfold of a *Tiger Beat* magazine."

"I'm not that young," Ben said. After a moment he added, "Do they really have centerfolds?"

"Yes," Jace said, thinking of Michelle's ceiling. "I'm surprised you don't know this. What did your sister decorate her room with when you were growing up?"

"Mostly photos of herself," Ben confided. "Anyway, enough stalling. Open your presents."

Ben thrust the backpack into Jace's lap, so he slowly started unpacking it. The first item was a calendar of Parisian cats.

"Ugh!" Ben said. "Calendars are the worst present. Buyer's remorse!"

"It's fine," Jace assured him. Reaching into the bag, he pulled out two paper bags. He started with the smallest. Inside was a lapel pin of a cat's sleek silhouette.

"I figured you could wear it on your airline uniform," Ben explained.

"I love it!" Jace said. The pin was elegant and simple in design, not gaudy and tacky. He'd wear it with pride. In the other paper bag was a handful of macaroons in various colors. His mouth watered at the sight of them. He knew from experience how delicious they were. These had an added detail. Thin lines of frosting made the top of the cookies appear like round cat faces. "I'm starting to detect a theme here."

"It only gets worse," Ben said, "but I deserve extra credit for the macaroons. They were behind the counter, and I had to play charades to get them, since the woman at the bakery didn't speak English. You know what else? They didn't have croissants."

"No!" Jace cried as if scandalized.

"Seriously! We've been here three days and haven't had a single croissant. You promised me croissants!"

"You'll get your croissant," Jace said. Not from a *patisserie*, where Ben had surely bought the macaroons. He needed to go to a *boulangerie*—a bakery—instead.

Next in the backpack was an art print of a woman overwhelmed by pets. Dogs gathered around her feet while cats covered a counter near her head. On it were written the words *Clinique Cheron*, whatever that meant.

Ben leaned over and pointed at the fattest cat. "That one reminds me of Samson," he said.

"I can see why!" Jace said with a chuckle. "Man, I miss him."

"Me too," Ben said longingly. "I adore him. I really do. Ever since I moved in I feel like..."

"What?" Jace prompted.

"Well, like I'm his dad too."

Jace shook his head. "He's already got a dad. You can be his mommy."

Ben laughed. "Fine. I'll be his mom. Uh, you should probably skip the rest of the presents. There are some cat socks in there that I can't bear to look at again. There also might be a hideous T-shirt. We probably shouldn't split up again."

"Maybe not," Jace said.

Ben grew solemn. "It'll never be enough."

"What?"

Ben nodded at the pile of souvenirs. "I could buy you everything in the world, and it still wouldn't show how much I love you. It's frustrating."

Jace chuckled.

Ben shook his head. "I mean it. I wish there was a way to communicate it so completely that you couldn't doubt it. I think sometimes about all the times I've messed up, tallying them up in my mind—"

"You shouldn't," Jace interrupted.

Ben shrugged. "But I do. If I could turn back time, do everything right the second time around, maybe then you would see."

"I do see," Jace said. "You have plenty of ways of showing me. I don't remember the last time I had to clean the apartment, or worry about Samson. Every time I've come home from work and bitched about passengers, you've sat there and listened, always finding a way of cheering me up again. And I haven't felt lonely since we met. Some nights out of town, sure, but when I'm with you, I never have any doubt. I know you love me, Ben. I feel it." Jace pulled out the socks covered in cats and shook them. "If I had any doubt, these would have banished it from my mind."

"Now I wish I *had* bought the cat-patterned underwear," Ben said, regaining his humor.

"It's not too late."

"But first," Ben said, already grinning in anticipation, "what did you get me?"

"Brace yourself," Jace said, reaching into his jacket pocket. He pulled it out quickly, brandishing it proudly.

"A candy bar?" Ben said, his smile fading.

Jace beamed at him. "Isn't it great?"

"Yeah!" Ben said, trying to muster enthusiasm. "It's just—"

"What?"

"It's a Snickers bar. It's not even French."

"I thought you'd be homesick by now," Jace lied.

The truth was, he had split up with Ben to buy something very specific. By the time he had found and bought the right thing, no time remained to grab a decoy. He wasn't ready to give Ben his real present. Not quite yet. Luckily, Ben had just given him an idea of when and how he was going to do it.

"Now I'm thinking that cat calendar isn't so bad," Ben said, taking the candy bar. "You know I hate Snickers."

"Yup," Jace said shamelessly.

Ben shook his head. "You're so weird."

"Oh wait, I *did* get you something French," Jace said, leaning toward Ben.

"Oh?" Ben said. "Oh!" he added a second later when he caught Jace's meaning, eyes half-lidded when they kissed. A few minutes later, near breathless, Ben said, "God, I love Paris!"

The little apartment they had rented was in Montmartre, a hill in the northern part of Paris that afforded an excellent view of the city. While the area was famous for being the former haunt of artists like Picasso, van Gogh, and Monet, what Jace really found appealing about it were the cobbled streets, the village atmosphere, and the little pathways lined by old street lamps. Naturally this meant it was overrun by tourists, but in the early morning, such as now, it was easy to pretend that they lived in a sleepy French village.

Speaking of sleepy, Ben was still in bed, even as Jace set the table. Their one-room apartment included a balcony, one so narrow that all Jace could fit on it were two chairs. He dragged over a small table, even though most of it had to stay inside, but enough of the edge jutted onto the balcony for them to use. The commotion made Ben stir, but that was okay, because breakfast was ready: orange juice, fresh fruit, a wheel of oozing Camembert cheese, butter, jelly, a selection of toasts and pastries, coffee, and most important of all, croissants.

Just one croissant, actually, and that was on Ben's plate. Jace considered it, heart pounding. Was he being stupid? Was this the right way to do it? Of all the romantic potential Paris provided—

"Is that breakfast?" Ben said, sitting up and yawning.

Too late now! "Yes."

"Good, I'm starving." Ben got out of bed, fully naked and half-hard, and strolled to the restroom, smiling slyly at Jace before he disappeared. When he eventually reappeared, preceded by a flushing toilet instead of royal trumpets, Ben was wearing a bathrobe and looking amused.

"Bidets are weird!" he said mischievously. "Why don't they just hang their asses over the bathroom sink? It's basically the same thing."

Jace smirked. "Feeling refreshed?"

"Yes, thank you very much." Ben considered him on the way to the table. "Look at you! All showered and dressed. What time did you wake up?"

"Early enough to go shopping," Jace said, taking a seat. He took a swig of coffee, but his throat still felt dry as he realized he had no special words prepared.

"A croissant!" Ben said, hopping into the chair across from him. "You're my hero!"

Jace smiled, watching as Ben poured himself some orange juice, unaware that their entire future was about to be decided. Ben even glanced out at the quiet streets, an old woman sweeping in front of her door as a cat ran diagonally across the road.

"Didn't you say you were hungry?" Jace prompted.

"Yeah," Ben said, returning his attention to the food. "It's just so pretty here."

"Wait!" Jace said when Ben picked up the croissant, one end already pointing toward his mouth. "In France, you're supposed to tear it in half."

He had no idea if that was true, but luckily Ben always trusted him on such things. Jace had more experience traveling and... Oh god, none of that mattered now! As Ben tore the croissant in half, something small and hard fell out of it. Jace worried it would bounce off the table, fly over the balcony rail, and be swept up by the old woman. Instead, the ring clattered noisily to the plate.

Ben stared in surprise. Then he looked up, a question on his lips that Jace could read. *Is that what I think it is?*

The words came to Jace then. There wasn't enough room to kneel, so he reached across to take the ring from the plate and held it up. "You're my heart, Ben. My soul. You complete me. I can't imagine living my life without you, and you'd make me the proudest man alive if you would agree to be my husband."

Ben's cheeks flushed, his eyes darting down to the ring. Then he started laughing. Jace looked at the ring in puzzlement, spotting a big croissant flake stuck to it like a ridiculous diamond. Grinning, he plucked the flake off and shoved it into Ben's mouth, which only made him laugh harder.

"Smell it," Jace said, holding the ring up to Ben's nose. "It's the most deliciously buttery ring in the history of the world. You can't say no!"

Ben laughed harder, eyes filling with tears. Down below, the sound of sweeping stopped, but Jace's eyes remained on Ben, who was calming down. The table still separated them, which frustrated Jace, so he stood, walked around it, and took Ben's hand. Now he was able to kneel.

Ben looked down at him, eyes still wet with joy. "Yes!" he said, bending over for a kiss.

"Not so fast," Jace said, dodging this attempt.

He held up the ring until Ben offered his hand. Then Jace slid it on Ben's finger with surprising ease.

"It's so greasy!" Ben said, getting worked up again.

"Just like our love," Jace said. Then he stood, picked Ben up, and tossed him on the bed.

"Hey! You haven't married me yet!" Ben said. "Save it for the honeymoon."

"Not a chance," Jace said, crawling on top of him and untying the bathrobe.

"I haven't taken a shower," Ben protested, trying to hold it shut.

"You think after all these years I haven't gotten used to your stink?" Jace said, kissing his neck. "I love even that part of you."

Ben laughed again and gave up, allowing Jace to pull back the robe like ripping open a curtain on a magnificent view. Sometimes he wondered if he would ever tire of Ben's body, crave hard muscle instead of soft skin, bulky curves instead of lean lines. What Jace discovered so far is that the more he loved Ben, the more enamored he became with his body. Jace had no doubt that when they were both old and covered in loose wrinkled skin, he would still find Ben just as sexy.

Right now, everything about him still radiated the perfection of youth, something Jace appreciated more since turning thirty last year. He rocked back on his knees, just so he could stare at Ben's naked body.

"Still want to marry me?" Ben said teasingly, but with a touch of insecurity.

Jace shook his head. "You have no idea."

Ben reached for him. "Then show me."

Jace bent over him, kissing Ben's lips, his chin, his neck. Then Jace rubbed his hands up and down Ben's body. The robe flowed around Ben like he was a half-opened present. Jace kissed him, tasted him, made him moan and gasp. Then, very gently, Jace rolled him over, removing the robe completely before standing to undress himself.

Ben watched him over his shoulder with a wonderful mixture of anticipation and nervousness.

"First time?" Jace asked.

"I was saving myself for the man I marry," Ben replied, playing along.

Naturally this wasn't their first time doing this, but it remained as special. Grabbing the travel-sized bottle of lube from the side table, Jace brought it back to bed with him, lying alongside his boyfriend—no, his fiancé!—and chuckling when Ben winced at the cold liquid poured between his cheeks.

Jace played at first, kissing Ben's back as his fingers explored, but then he couldn't wait. Lubing himself, he positioned his body above Ben's, sighing when he slid inside. He watched Ben's back closely—muscles tensing. Or his profile on the pillow as Ben bit his bottom lip, a sharp breath escaping his mouth. Jace used these cues to guide Ben away from pain and toward pleasure. Soon he didn't need to be as cautious, every motion of his hips causing moans of pleasure.

Needing them to be closer, Jace wrapped his arms around Ben's torso, rolling over to feel his whole weight pressing on him while he continued to thrust. He let a hand wander down to take hold of Ben, their breathing becoming heavy, shorter, rougher until they both groaned and growled at the same moment.

Afterwards, Jace rolled them both over on their sides, holding Ben close and remaining inside him. After a few minutes like this, Ben spoke.

"You've got me facing the balcony," he said.

"Worried someone can see you?" Jace asked.

"No, but I'm staring at all that food. I *still* haven't eaten a French croissant!"

Jace laughed. After a quick trip to fetch a towel, he made sure Ben was comfortable in bed, sitting up with the sheets hugging his hips. Then he dragged the table over for a proper breakfast in bed. Soon Ben's mouth was happily stuffed full of flaky pastry.

"When should we do it?" Jace asked.

Ben looked concerned.

"I mean the wedding, silly. When should we have it?"

"Oh!" Ben took a sip of orange juice and thought about it, but he didn't need long. "Summer," he said. "It has to be summer."

Jay Bell

* * * * *

"But it's not legal... is it?"

Jace smiled at Ben's aunt. He'd fielded this question countless times since their engagement. Most people seemed embarrassed that they had to ask, which he appreciated. He couldn't blame them for their curiosity, even today, just moments from the ceremony. They needed to know, and Jace was happy to answer.

"No, it's not legal in the State of Texas. That it *is* legal in a few states still doesn't mean marriage between two men or two women is recognized on a federal level."

A strong hand grasped his shoulder. "And it doesn't matter," Bernard said. "No law can force two people to love each other, or keep them from growing distant and getting divorced."

Jace glanced over at him with an appreciative smile. Bernard wasn't getting any younger, but he still had fire in his eyes. A light summer breeze blew through his wispy white hair, the world around him in the peak of life. Trees were in full bloom, birds winging through the air at full power, and the roses...

Ben had spent a fortune on them, used them to cover the pillars and rails of the strange gazebo they had reserved. The little shelter had a heavy Asian influence. Ben kept calling it a pagoda, and Jace supposed that fit well enough, since its roof curved upwards at the tips. Now, decorated in roses, it looked like something from another world.

"I think it *should* be legal," the aunt said, making up for the question she felt compelled to ask.

"As do I," Jace said. "Obviously. For now, what matters is the commitment we're making to each other. A wedding is just a very showy declaration of love. It's hardly better than bragging," he jested. "But when it comes to Ben, I just can't help myself."

He cast his eyes over the mingling guests until he found Ben near the parking lot, standing next to Allison. Ben looked sharp in a black tuxedo. They'd laughed and joked about Jace wanting to wear white as if he were the bride. As if either of them were, but the nice thing about going against the grain is how liberating it could be. There was no common concept of how a gay wedding worked. They could have worn grass skirts and waded into the lake together, if that's how they felt their wedding should go.

As it was, they weren't too far from tradition. No church, which was why they stood in a park. And no clergy, either, since they had both agreed they didn't need someone telling them what

371

to say. As for God's blessing, they figured they either had it or they didn't. That they had made it this far was a hopeful sign.

Ben met his eye. As good as he looked on the outside, Jace could tell his insides were anything but calm. The empty-handed guests were probably Ben's biggest concern. No appetizers or flutes of champagne, thanks to the caterers being late. Ben loitering by the parking lot wasn't going to make them arrive any quicker, either. Jace shook his head, as if to say *What have we gotten ourselves into?* Then he turned his attention back to the relatives surrounding him.

With the exception of Bernard, they were all Ben's family, but they were nice enough. Half of them seemed to be spinsters or widows, from the way they were sizing up Bernard. It didn't help that his fingers were too gnarled to wear a wedding ring. They'd be disappointed when they saw him dancing with his wife later.

"So any poor woman born under this certain star or whatever," Bernard was saying, "is said to be cursed. Whatever man she marries will die an early death. So what they do is marry the woman to a tree. Then they destroy the tree, both fulfilling and breaking the curse."

"Where's this?" Jace asked.

"India," Bernard answered.

"Funny, because we have the same tradition in Texas. I made Ben marry one of the bushes outside our apartment last week. They really hit it off too. He cried and cried after I hacked it to pieces."

The titters of laughter that followed were drowned out by blaring music. Once the volume was adjusted to a more civilized level, Jace recognized the song. He and Ben had chosen it as the one that would accompany their walk to the altar—or weird Asian gazebo thing. Except it wasn't supposed to happen yet. Jace turned to the DJ, who gave him a thumbs up.

Jace shrugged. Who was he to argue with fate?

"Excuse me," he said. "I'm supposed to get married now. Uh, Bernard, can you make sure everyone gets seated?"

"I'll do my best."

Jace strolled over to Ben, who was clearly mortified.

"He's playing it too soon!"

"It's okay," Jace said.

Ben pointed at his watch. "Half an hour too soon!"

"Ben," Jace said firmly. "Everyone is here already. I've spent the whole day setting up chairs and talking to strange people, most of whom I've never met before, when all I really wanted was to be with you. That we can be together now, ahead of schedule, makes me happy."

Ben's posture relaxed as he laughed at himself. "Okay, okay. Sorry."

Jace offered his hand. "Are you ready to marry me?"

Ben's nervousness returned with a vengeance. His palm was sweaty when Jace took it, his legs stiff as Jace walked him to the seats and up the division in the middle that acted as an aisle.

"Remember to breathe," Jace murmured when he thought Ben looked unstable.

"You might have to carry me," Ben joked. "Or drag me up there. Whatever you've got to do."

"You're fine," Jace said, smiling.

When they reached the gazebo and climbed the three steps, Jace suddenly understood why a couple would want someone presiding over their ceremony. With all the nervousness and overwhelming feelings that come with weddings, it would be so easy to simply freeze. But Jace felt calmer than ever before. He wasn't nervous because this is what he'd always wanted. This was a dream come true. He took Ben's hands in his, and when the song ended, he spoke.

"I love you. I know most wedding vows probably end with those words, but that's the most important thing for you to know. We're standing here today because I love you, Ben Bentley, with all my heart and soul. Giving myself to you is something I did a long time ago, so if anything, us being here is a mere formality. And to make sure all these beautiful people here know how serious I am."

The guests laughed.

"Since we're here anyway, I have a promise I've been meaning to make: I will always be there for you. Even if I'm halfway around the world because of my job, I'll be with you in spirit. Think of me when you're lost or scared, and know that no matter what happens, everything will be okay when we're together again. That's how it will always be. Forever. I want to grow old with you. I want us to look at each other one day and laugh at how shriveled we've become. I know we'll still be laughing, because no matter what life throws at us in the future, we'll face it together. And we'll win. Love is the greatest force in the universe. Especially when that love comes from you."

Ben stared at him with eyes full of wonder. Then he grabbed at the rings, shoved one into Jace's hand, and kissed him. After a moment of confused surprise, the audience burst into applause, Jace laughing through the whole kiss.

The next song started, which was just as well because Jace didn't think Ben would be up for making any speeches, not from the way he was trembling. But it was good. He knew Ben well enough to know when he was upset, sad, or afraid. Ben wasn't any of these things. Right now he was overwhelmed, Jace feeling very much the same.

Jace took Ben into his arms, gently swaying to the music. Halfway through the song, Ben pulled back a little, tears of joy in his eyes.

"So we're married?" he asked

Jace smiled. "Yup."

"Simple as that?"

"Simple as that." Jace chuckled. "Just a promise and nothing more. Hard to believe that anyone makes a big deal out of it."

"It *is* a big deal!" Ben protested.

"In that case, we should probably put the rings on. It might not be official until we do."

Ben's eyes went wide, as if they were on a time limit. He opened his clenched fist to reveal a ring pressed into his palm. "I was a little nervous," he explained.

"I noticed," Jace said. "I would have thought performing on stage would prepare you for something like this."

Ben shook his head. "Nothing could prepare me for this. I just felt… everything!"

Jace smiled and took the ring from his palm, replacing it with his own. "You first," he said, holding the ring by the edges. Ben presented his hand, cheeks flushed as Jace slid it on. "I was tempted to rub a little croissant grease on it," he said.

"Knowing me I probably would have swallowed it," Ben replied. "Now you."

Grinning broadly, Ben slid the ring on Jace's finger. Then they kissed, and the few who were still paying attention applauded— along with a catcall that sounded suspiciously like Greg. They resumed dancing, not ready to end their private moment. The caterers had arrived, so the guests had food and champagne to keep them occupied. All Jace wanted was Ben. He finally understood those weddings on TV where the bride and groom rushed from the church and into a limo. He'd like nothing more than to run away with Ben right now.

Still, there would be time. Days, weeks, years and decades. All for them. With that in mind, Jace took Ben's hand. Together they walked down the steps onto green grass, Jace proudly introducing everyone to his new husband.

Chapter Thirty-one

"The master bathroom has a Jacuzzi," Greg said, sounding very professional as he led the tour. "Double sinks, as you can see, which makes getting ready in the morning much less stressful, as does the separate shower. Walk-in closet. I love the window above the bathtub. Great view of the backyard. That's a school-quality playground out there, with enough room left for a pool. Come look!"

Jace stayed where he was. In the bathroom mirror, he could see that his poker face had slipped. His reflection showed a man under strain, despite holding hands with the most adorable creature in the world. Sorry, Samson and Ben. Jace waggled his eyebrows at Emma in the mirror, causing her to giggle. Ben, who was holding her other hand, sucked in his cheeks, making himself look like he'd just eaten a lemon. This made Emma howl with laughter.

"You don't like it?" Greg said, lowering the clipboard.

"I love it," Jace said. "But I told you, we're looking for a small house."

"It's only three bedrooms," Greg said, clearly not understanding.

"You've been in Houston too long," Jace replied. "Three bedrooms is huge. Especially for us. What do we need that many rooms for?"

"Well, just look at you guys." Greg gestured to all three of them. "You'll want to adopt someday. Hasn't Michelle talked to you about that?"

Jace and Ben glanced at each other. Then down at Emma.

"You're going to adopt me?" she asked.

"No, honey," Greg said, "but someday they might want to adopt kids of their own. Then you would have a cousin. Wouldn't that be nice?"

"Maybe this was a bad idea," Jace said. "I mean, I appreciate you coming all the way out here, but I don't think you understand what we're looking for."

"It's *really* nice," Ben said, no doubt trying to ease Greg's hurt expression. "But I don't earn much and you know about all the airline cutbacks."

"Okay." Greg shrugged. "I can talk the owners down. We

can chip in too. You know Michelle and I have more money than we'll ever need."

From anyone else, the statement would have been boastful, but Jace knew that Greg meant it. He'd give them every penny he could spare if they asked, but Jace wanted to own a house because of his own hard work. He and Ben had been saving up for this very moment. To stand now in a house so out of their price range was almost embarrassing.

"I can make a few calls," Greg said.

Jace was about to thank him and decline, but Ben spoke first.

"Jace, why don't you take Emma out back to play? I'll go over what we need with Greg one more time. I'm sure he can help us find what we're looking for."

He agreed, if only to spare Greg's feelings. Once in the backyard, Emma broke free and ran for the playground. Most kids were happy to have a couple of swings and a small slide. The children who would live here had tunnels to crawl through, a bouncy hanging bridge, some kind of pulley thing to swing along—

"We would have killed to have that," Michelle said, leaning against the house. She had one arm over her stomach, the other vertical and resting on it. He recognized the pose from when she used to smoke.

Jace walked over to join her. "Ben's going to look adorable swinging along those monkey bars."

Michelle smiled wryly. "I told Greg this wasn't the right house for you."

"Are you sure?" Jace said. "Apparently we're adopting kids soon."

Michelle jutted out her lower lip and exhaled, causing the hair on her forehead to wave. "I merely said it would be nice someday. You know how Greg takes an idea and runs with it. Besides, you guys would make great parents. Every day at work I see kids who need a loving home. It's only natural I think of my brother and his lovely man-wife."

Jace appreciated the compliment. His sister worked in foster care, interviewing potential families and trying to match them to the right children. To him it sounded like a very emotionally taxing job, but it gave her a sense of satisfaction. Jace was immensely proud of her.

"I don't think we're ready quite yet," he said. "Even when we get a house, you know my schedule. I'm not home enough to be a parent."

"Ben is," Michelle said. "Remember how Greg's dad was only there on weekends? Plenty of kids grow up with one parent paying the bills while the other does all the nurturing."

Jace nodded. "I suppose. We're still not going to buy this house."

Michelle snorted. "I wasn't trying to give you the tough sell. I know my husband is crazy."

"More like you're crazy about him," Jace teased.

"That's what I tell myself every night as I hold a pillow above his sleeping head."

They laughed, then contented themselves with watching the children play. Until the glass door slid open.

"I've got it!" Greg declared. "Let's go, kids! In the car! Your uncles need to buy a house."

Jace gave him a skeptical look.

"It doesn't even have a garage!" Greg said proudly.

Behind him, Ben nodded encouragingly. Piling into two cars, they drove to an old part of Austin. The streets were lined with ripe old trees, rustling branches thick with leaves. The houses here were smaller, perhaps built during a time when the economy wasn't doing so well. The visible age of the neighborhood had charm. No giant lawns sequestered by lengths of privacy fences. Here everything was closer together, making it feel more intimate.

No garage or driveway. Greg wasn't kidding. Just street parking like at the house Victor's mom used to live in. The house's condition wasn't much better than that home, either. The roof looked solid enough, but shutters were falling off the windows, the little porch was missing boards, and everything needed to be painted.

"How many bedrooms?" Jace asked, standing in front of the steps.

"One!" Greg declared happily.

"And how much does it cost?"

"It's within our range," Ben said.

Jace glanced over at him, back at the house, and back over at Ben again. Then he swept Ben up in his arms. "Open the door," he told Greg. "I'm carrying my husband over the threshold."

"Wait until we see inside," Ben said, laughing.

Jace didn't need to. He had a good feeling about it. Once this little house got some of their love, it would be perfect.

Tim Wyman returned to their lives once more, albeit in a manner much different than the first time. Gone was the cocky self-assured guy with the body of a demi-god. Now he was broken, struggling in a dysfunctional relationship that drove him to drink. Or so Ben told Jace one night. They were sitting in the backyard, sharing a bottle of wine to celebrate one year of being homeowners. How ironic, then, that the homewrecker would reappear.

Regardless, Ben was concerned about Tim and felt he needed help. Jace, more convinced of their love than ever, gave his blessing. As he had done the first time, he let go. Not by offering Ben a break. He simply trusted him to do the right thing.

And he did. Ben chased away Tim's abusive boyfriend—doing so in a manner Jace wasn't particularly fond of—and after much thought, Ben decided that maybe Tim could be his friend. Jace allowed this too, even hanging out with them on occasion.

Ben was right. Tim had changed. Life hadn't been particularly kind to him, but maybe this was for the best, since he had gained humility. Despite everything that had happened in the past, Jace found himself hoping that Tim would do better. Tim still struggled with expressing who he was, or with revealing the near-mythical good side that Ben insisted existed. It did, though. Jace began to see glimpses of it too.

Friendship is a poor remedy for love, and when it became clear that the feelings between Ben and Tim had merely faded into the background and not disappeared, Jace began to worry. He wouldn't ask Ben to make a difficult decision this time. Jace wouldn't lecture him on how all of this was normal, before repeating his needs. Ben knew them by now. Jace believed in monogamy and commitment.

Jace was doing dishes one night, window open to humid air since the weak air conditioner couldn't keep up, when he discovered Ben missing. The television was still on, the sensory assault of commercials rendered impotent by a lack of audience. Jace shut off the TV and walked from room to room, finding each empty. Then he went to the backyard and waited, watching the fireflies blink in the grass, hoping to attract a lover.

The atmosphere between Ben and Tim had been thick lately. Jace only pointed it out once, but the way Ben looked at Tim… Jace supposed such things were obvious. Shortly after they moved in, when they'd been unpacking, Jace had stripped away newspaper to find a primitive carving of a lion. The shock of seeing it unexpectedly, the emotions it conjured, must have been transparent because Ben had stopped what he was doing and stared.

So Jace didn't blame Ben for having a heart that could love more than one person. Jace had one too. Everyone did. He just wasn't sure what he would do if Ben didn't come home again, mostly because he didn't have a home without him.

Samson stood at the screen door, meowing plaintively at not being allowed out. Then he stopped, bounding off through the house. That meant Ben was home. Jace stayed where he was, scared of what he might see. He tried to have faith, but he was still human. Imagining the worst was all too easy. Still, Ben had come home.

When the screen door slid open, then closed again, Jace turned in his chair. Ben's cheeks were red, as were his eyes. Had he been crying?

Jace stood and went to him. When he asked his question, he kept all traces of accusation from his voice. "Where did you go?"

"I drove over to Tim's house," Ben said. His chin quivered, but then he steeled himself. "To say goodbye."

Jace placed his hands on Ben's shoulders, making eye contact. "You didn't have to do that," he said.

Ben shook his head. "I did. Believe me, I did. I love you, Jace. Don't think this means I don't, because I do!"

Jace nodded. "You having feelings for Tim and having the strength to turn away… Remember in Paris when you felt so desperate to prove your love for me? I didn't feel you needed to then, and you don't need to now, but the sacrifice you're making—it's tremendous."

"I love you both," Ben said, swallowing against the confession. "Is that wrong?"

"No," Jace said. "Love is never wrong. What you choose to do about it, well, that's debatable. But never apologize for feeling love."

Ben held up his left hand, brandishing his ring. "I made a promise, but only to one of you."

"Any regrets about that?" Jace asked, trying a tentative smile.

To his relief, Ben smiled back and shook his head. "None at all."

Some mornings felt like hell. That was just part of getting older. Jace tried to remember ever waking up as a teenager and feeling like he'd gone ten rounds in a boxing ring. These days, if he slept in the wrong position, he'd wake up with an aching neck or back. Naturally he couldn't consciously control how he lay while sleeping, so at times the bed seemed more like a roulette wheel. Would he land on red and wake up feeling fine, or on black and start the day in pain?

Black, as it turned out. Just sitting upright made Jace's head hurt, which was ridiculous. He was thirty-three, not sixty-three. Jace sat on the edge of the bed, waiting for the blood to stop pounding in his ears. When it didn't, he decided to give caffeine a try. He used the restroom first, then picked his flannel boxers up off the floor and went to find Ben.

Both things that he wanted were in the kitchen. Ben was seated at the table, half a grapefruit in front of him, which he insisted was slimming. Of course Ben added a heap of sugar to make it palatable, but Jace wasn't worried. Ben looked as slim as the day they'd met. He padded over to the coffee machine, which Ben had thoughtfully run for him, a clean empty mug waiting next to it. Jace poured himself a cup and went to the bay windows, blinking against light that seemed much too bright. Was this a migraine? Jace had read about them but never experienced one.

Once his eyes adjusted and he could see the backyard needed cutting, he turned to find another sun shining on him. Ben had that look in his eyes, the one that said: *Oh my gosh, I love you so much and I really want you to take off those boxers.*

Jace held back a smile. "I thought I wore you out last night?"

"I slept well." Ben's bedroom eyes suggested they head there now.

Why not? Maybe the endorphins would help his head. A fresh throb of pain shuddered through his skull. Jace pictured his head cracking open, like the ground in an earthquake.

Ben's amorous expression turned to one of concern. "Are you all right?"

"My head is killing me," Jace admitted.

"You didn't drink anything last night."

"No, but I'm beginning to wish I had, especially if I'm going to have the hangover anyway." Jace sat at the kitchen table across from Ben, rubbing his temples. This had to be a migraine. "Grab me a couple aspirin, would you?"

"Sure." Ben stood, watching him a moment before he rushed from the room.

Jace closed his eyes while he waited, the usual dark of his inner eyelids now red, hot, and burning. He could almost see a singular flat line, searing with heat, like the glowing metal in a toaster.

"Maybe it was something you ate?" Ben said on his way back in the room. "Is your stomach okay? You could be coming down with a bug."

Jace shook his head, holding out his hand for the aspirin. He tossed them into his mouth, sending them on their merry way with a hearty swig of coffee. God speed, little pills! He was trying to set the cup on the table when his hand spasmed. He heard the cup break on the floor, felt some of the coffee splatter against his leg. When he looked down, it seemed like there were two cups, two puddles, two messes.

"So clumsy," Jace said. He needed to clean up and get back in bed. When he stood, his head responded with fury. The red line in his mind intensified, the glowing heat translating into screeching pain that threatened to cripple him. All he could see was the red line, growing thicker at an alarming rate, his pain increasing to impossible levels as it filled the horizon.

Then nothing. Sweet blissful nothing.

The sensation of spinning. Nothing. Bright lights, white rooms. Nothing. Detached eyes above light blue masks. Nothing.

Then the same scene, over and over again. A dim room with curtains pulled shut, in front of them many faces, all wearing the same expression of concern. Ben. Michelle. Jace's father. Ben. Jace's mother. Bernard. Michelle. Ben. Greg. Jace's mother. Ben. Ben. Ben.

Finally the faces slowed, settling on Ben, who was staring off into— Where was he? Jace glanced around the room. A clutter of tubes and bags stood vigil on one side of his bed. In front of him, a television was mounted on the ceiling. A hospital? Jace rolled his head back over to face Ben, catching his attention.

"Why am I here?" Jace asked.

Ben took a deep breath, as if disappointed by the question. "You're in the hospital," he said as if reading from a script. "You had an aneurysm, but you're okay now. You just need to get better."

Jace exhaled, looking back up at the television, staring at the confusing reflections on the darkened glass. Then he glanced back over at Ben, who didn't look hopeful.

"Is that the truth?"

Ben sighed, squeezing his hand. "Yes. I promise."

Jace tried to remember what had happened. He and Ben had stayed up late making love. No, there was more after that. A morning that was too bright, and the headache, but it was a blur. "I don't remember how I got here."

"I know," Ben said. "We have this conversation a few times every day. They say it's your short-term memory. You wake up, ask what's going on, and once you close your eyes again, you seem to forget. They say you might get better though. I think you'll get better."

Ben's face crumpled. Jace wanted to comfort him, but he was tired. "Tell me one more time," he said. "This time I won't forget. I promise."

Ben took a deep breath. "You collapsed in the kitchen and lost consciousness. You wouldn't respond—"

Ben's voice became a squeak, and he needed a few minutes before he could continue. Jace felt like closing his eyes, but he'd promised to remember. Instead he focused on the sliver of daylight he could see between the curtains.

"An ambulance brought you here," Ben said. "They operated on you for five hours. Your parents flew down immediately and arrived just when you were coming out of surgery. Everyone's here. We all love you. Okay?"

Jace nodded, feeling tired. He needed Ben to hurry up and finish so he could go back to sleep. "What else?"

"Nothing," Ben said. "You've been here for a week, and the last couple of days you and I keep having this same conversation.

I don't care, though. It doesn't matter if this is all we have left because I love you, and I'm so glad you didn't die!"

Ben was crying, and Jace felt a pang of guilt, but he couldn't find the energy to comfort him. His eyelids were so heavy. He needed rest. All he could do was give in...

When he opened his eyes again, the television was on, the sound muted. A police officer was shoving a suited man into a car, cameras flashing, capturing every angle. When Jace turned his head, Ben was there, frowning at a book. The line of daylight between the curtains had gone. How long had Ben been sitting there? All week, night and day? Jace could imagine his mother making Ben leave if only to get some sleep, but aside from that, he knew Ben had been there, waiting for him to get better, to come back to him.

Next to Ben was a tray of uneaten food. Only the juice box had been touched, punctured by a straw. Considering Jace's condition, he doubted the food was for him. Suddenly he wanted to see Ben eat, to see him smile or laugh or do anything besides sitting there in the gloom like a flower without sun.

"I'm sorry about all of this," Jace said.

Ben looked up, his face registering surprise. "About what?"

"All of it," Jace said, managing to gesture with one of his hands. "The hospital, the aneurysm, scaring you like that."

Ben was still staring. "You remember?"

He did. At least when it came to the morning of his headache, taking the aspirin, and dropping the coffee. After that everything was a blur, aside from the previous conversation he and Ben had shared. "Of course," Jace said, smiling gently. "I've got a memory like an elephant."

Ben laughed in disbelief, tears streaming down his cheeks. Then he tossed aside the book and covered Jace's face in kisses. By the time he was finished, Jace's face was wet, although whether it was from Ben's tears or slobber, he didn't know. Nor did he care. He was just happy to see Ben smile again.

Chapter Thirty-two

"I'm going with you," Jace said, ready to throw a fit worthy of a toddler denied a new toy.

Ben stood by the front door of their home, car keys in hand. "I'll be back in half an hour. It's just the grocery store."

"Which sounds like the most fun place in the world!" Jace said.

Ben considered him like an amateur doctor trying to make a diagnosis. Was the patient feeling well? Was this behavior one of the many side effects? Over the last month, Jace had seen this expression countless times, not just from Ben but from the reflection in the mirror as well. Jace was doing better, there was no doubt about it, but he also felt like someone else had moved into his mind while he was being operated on. Jace was possessed by a side of himself he still struggled to understand.

"I guess if you really *really* want to tag along," Ben said, sounding anything but certain. "But what if you—"

"Freak out," Jace finished for him.

He wished Ben hadn't voiced this concern, especially since Jace shared it already. Sometimes, like now, he felt perfectly fine. A little more on edge, maybe, but generally the same as he'd always been. Other times, lights were too bright for him, just like on the morning he'd had his aneurysm. Or sounds were too loud. That was something new. Sometimes Ben had to whisper to him. Naturally being in public when that happened wouldn't be good.

"I can't live my whole life in this house," Jace said. "All I've done the last month is sit around here or go to physical therapy."

"You only have two weeks left," Ben said. "After that you can go where you please."

"Two weeks!" Jace said, stressing it to make it sound like an eternity. "That's it! I give up. If my whole life is going to be spent in this house, I might as well embrace it by staying home and getting repulsively fat. Better buy a bucket and mop while you're out to scrub my hippopotamus body with."

"I'll add it to the list," Ben said, a smile tugging the corner of his mouth. "Oh, fine! You'll only slow me down, but let's go."

Jace felt like shouting with joy as they got in the car. What he wanted most was to feel like an adult again. Recovering from his surgery not only meant physical rehabilitation, but seeing a counselor. Jace found this unnecessary. Most of the time he was just so happy to be alive that he didn't feel sorry for himself. Then again, other times he felt like he wasn't in control, especially when he snapped at Ben or lashed out at the world for having so many things to remember. But mostly he was fine.

Ben, on the other hand, still acted like Jace was fragile. Often Jace would find Ben watching him, braced for the worst to happen again. When they touched, Ben treated him like a china doll. That they hadn't had sex since the aneurysm was the ultimate example of this. Even now he kept glancing over, as if driving Jace anywhere but rehab was somehow endangering him.

"Two more weeks and I'm done," Jace said.

"I know."

"And then I want you to treat me like a normal human being again."

Ben nodded and exhaled. "I'm sorry. I will. In fact, I have some news in that regard. It was supposed to be a surprise, but my parents rented a cabin for us."

"Really?"

"Yup. To celebrate you making it through physical therapy. And hell, you might as well enjoy the time off from work."

Which Jace didn't, but he let it slide. Talking to Ben about how eager he was to return to the skies would probably give him a heart attack. "Where's the cabin?"

Ben grinned. "The Ozarks."

Which wasn't too far from Warrensburg. "They want me to see my parents, huh?"

"Yeah, I think that was part of the idea. I guess they're thinking about how they'd feel if something happened to me."

"It's very thoughtful," Jace said. Then he started looking around, commenting on anything he could see, no matter how mundane. Every conversation as of late led back to the stupid aneurysm. He was quickly tiring of it dominating his life. In the parking lot, as they were walking into the store, he found the perfect distraction: a grocery list tumbling across the concrete.

He picked it up and glanced over it. "Interesting what a grocery list says about someone," Jace said. "Why would they need ten pounds of chicken? A giant chicken salad for a party?"

"They could have dogs," Ben said, glancing over his shoulder.

"Some people make their own pet food. I've been thinking about trying that for Samson."

"He's fat enough already," Jace said.

"That's the point. Lean chicken has to be better than whatever they put in those cans."

"Hm, let me see our list for a second."

Once Ben handed it to him, Jace crumpled it and tossed it in a trashcan by the door.

"Hey!" Ben spun around, as if to dig it back out.

"Nope," Jace said, grabbing his arm and dragging him in the store. "We're using this list now. It's the only way to figure out the kind of person who wrote it."

Ben looked skyward. "*This* is why I can't take you anywhere. I had meals planned. What are we going to do with ten pounds of chicken?"

"Make cat food," Jace said as if it were obvious.

"Fine," Ben said, taking a grocery cart. "What's first on the list?"

"Marshmallows."

"And then?" Ben asked, craning to see.

"Hot dog buns."

Ben shook his head and pushed the cart. "Dinner's going to be interesting tonight."

Jace grinned. "I'm enjoying this. I think I'll do the grocery shopping from now on."

"In that case, I'll be eating out more often. Isn't there any fresh produce on the list?"

"Uh," Jace scanned it. "A watermelon."

"Great!" Ben said. "Something fresh between mouthfuls of marshmallows and chicken. Do we really have to do this?"

"Yes," Jace said. "Keep your eyes peeled. The person could still be here."

"The one who dropped that list, you mean?" Ben glanced around. "You're right. Maybe there's a reward."

As they continued shopping, they not-so-casually peered into every cart they passed, trying to assess if any other shopper was collecting the same items. Everyone became a suspect in the biggest case of the century. Did the overweight man in the frozen foods section need marshmallows *and* chocolate? Or the skinny woman loitering in the canned goods aisle? Maybe she bought the foods she wouldn't allow herself to eat, staring at them all night without partaking.

"She *does* look hungry," Ben said, running with this theory.

"But she wouldn't need three boxes of graham crackers," Jace said. "One would do."

"S'mores!" Ben declared, loud enough that Jace would have winced even without his recent health problems. "The person is buying ingredients to make s'mores!"

"Could be," Jace said, scanning the list. "Most things on here aren't perishable, which is good for a camping trip."

Ben looked thrilled. "We cracked the case!"

"Maybe," Jace said. "Although chicken doesn't keep well in the woods."

Ben's shoulders slumped. "True."

Jace stopped the cart. "Hold up. Saltines are on the list." He reached for one of the long boxes of crackers with his left hand—a mistake since it was still so unreliable. His whole hand was shaking as he tried to put the crackers in the cart, but his fingers wouldn't unclench. Ben looked torn between panic and tears.

"I'm fine," Jace said. "Happens all the time."

Jace grabbed another box of crackers, this time with his right hand, and although it was steady, he started shaking it too. Soon he was moving his shoulders and hips to the rhythm as he shook the crackers like two maracas.

Ben tried not to laugh but couldn't help himself. Jace grinned in return as he danced around the cart, ending with a flourish by tossing in both boxes of saltines.

"Pretty sexy, huh?" he asked.

Ben's smile became more demure, which was good, since it meant he had taken the hint. *This* is exactly why they needed to do normal things together, so Ben would start viewing him that way again. Normal. Sure, maybe Jace had mood swings, strange sensitivities, and a twitchy left hand. But he was still Jace.

They gathered the rest of the items. Then Ben insisted they get kitty litter, even though it wasn't on the list. Jace agreed. The game was fun. Smelling a dirty litter box wasn't. They were heading to the front of the store when Jace checked the list one more time. "We didn't get marshmallows," he said.

Ben pointed to the cart. There they were. Of course.

That was another side effect. Jace's short-term memory wasn't great. He glanced over at Ben, dreading the sad expression he'd see there, but instead Ben's eyes remained bright. "Looks like you need me more than ever," he said.

"God help me," Jace muttered, as if this was a terrible fate, but of course he couldn't be happier.

They were rolling up to the cash registers when Ben nudged him, nodding meaningfully at a man waiting in line. After a moment, Jace saw it too. The man's cart was filled with all the same items they had just bought. Jace put a finger to his lips. Then they got into line behind him.

Ben kept laughing as Jace put everything on the conveyer belt, doing his best to place them in the same order as the man ahead of them had. Chicken first, then the hot dogs and buns, saltines, and so forth, until the items were perfectly duplicated. Almost. Jace tapped the man on the shoulder.

"You forgot the graham crackers," he said.

The man looked panicked when he realized this was true, then puzzled when he noticed the conveyer belt. "Are you having a grill party too?"

Ben and Jace glanced at each other. "Of course!"

The man considered them, unsure about their curious behavior. He was soon comforted when Ben offered him the graham crackers. "I just remembered. I already bought some last week."

The man's face lit up. "Thanks!"

They waited until the man had paid and left before they burst out laughing.

"What are we going to do with all of this horrible food?" Ben asked when they were wheeling the cart out to the parking lot.

"Grill party," Jace said.

"We don't own a grill."

"Then let's go buy one."

Ben shook his head, but he was smiling. After stopping to pick one up, along with charcoal and lighter fluid, they drove home. Ben didn't want Jace carrying anything heavy, which meant he couldn't help bring in the groceries. He contented himself by putting away everything they wouldn't be needing. Then they went to the backyard, working together to assemble the grill and laughing that neither one knew how to get it going.

After checking the instructions and the Internet, they eventually got it started. When the coals turned white on the surface, they were ready to cook their food from below.

"We did it!" Ben said.

"Yes, we did." Jace glanced over at him, at the way the light of the setting sun caught in his hair. "Are you hungry?"

When Ben turned to him, it was if he saw Jace clearly for the first time in a month. "Not for food," he said.

Jace smiled. "Good. Me neither."

"Bedroom?" Ben asked.

Jace nodded. "Bedroom."

The hospital parking lot was the last place Jace wanted to be. Unfortunately, Ben was staring at the steering wheel, as if he no longer comprehended how a car functioned. Jace resisted the urge to lash out at him, to demand that he be taken far away from there. Instead, he said, "Do you want me to drive?"

Ben glanced over at him like he was crazy. Maybe he was. After all, Jace was a ticking time bomb. He was the last person who should be behind a wheel.

"Maybe they were the wrong results," Ben said. "Maybe they belonged to somebody else."

"Does this mean we're not going out for burgers?" Jace said, but even he didn't laugh at his humor.

They were supposed to be celebrating right now. Neither of them had thought the day would turn out like this. "Just a routine follow-up," the doctor had joked yesterday. "We'll scan that head of yours and make sure everything was put back in the right place."

They had laughed, which seemed extremely naïve now.

"Two more aneurysms," Ben said.

"I know," Jace snapped. "You don't need to remind me. Even my fucked-up short-term memory won't let me forget this."

"I'm sorry, I just—"

"I know," Jace said, pinching the bridge of his nose. "How do you think I feel?"

"I'm sorry," Ben repeated.

Jace felt guilty for acting this way. "There's no reason to panic," he said. "You heard what the doctor said. This isn't like an emergency room visit. Unruptured, the mortality rate is less than one percent. We're probably more at risk eating fast food. Which we'll still be doing. You can't take away my burgers now. That would be cruel."

Ben started the car but didn't pull out of the parking space. He was probably thinking the same thing Jace was. Between now and the surgery, two tiny little things could go wrong, both of them in Jace's head. If one of those aneurysms should rupture... Jace had beat the odds once, which still felt like a miracle. His chances of doing so again seemed beyond unlikely.

"Shouldn't you be in the emergency room now?" Ben asked, but he already knew the answer.

"If the doctor doesn't think it looks bad, then it's not bad. Otherwise I *would* be in the ER. And it makes sense that he wants me to finish recovering from the first before the other two are taken care of, right?"

Ben nodded numbly.

"We'll call tomorrow to set up the appointment," Jace said.

No response.

"Ben!" Jace shouted. "Fucking look at me! Stop acting like I'm still in intensive care! Right now we're going to get some food. Next week we're going to the Ozarks, and sometime afterwards I'll go in for a low-risk surgery. During all of that, you can either freak out and make me feel like I'm ruining your life, or you can act like you love me."

Ben turned to him with tears in his eyes. "I do love you!"

"Then show me I still make you happy!"

Ben unbuckled his seat belt and practically threw himself into the passenger seat to get at Jace and kiss him. After a moment of shock, Jace exhaled through his nose and kissed Ben back.

"It's not easy," Jace said. "I feel like life is getting harder by the day."

"I know how that is," Greg said.

Greg was sitting on the trunk of his Porsche, wearing a tank top and shorts despite it being the first cool day of autumn. Sunglasses in his hair, he looked like he owned the world. Hell, he still got carded when they went out drinking. His career had taken off years ago, Michelle was crazy about him, and the kids adored him.

"Care to explain what you mean by your life being hard?" Jace said.

Greg winced. "I was aiming for empathy."

"Well, you missed. Anyway, I'm not trying to throw a pity party here. I just need you to listen."

"I can do that," Greg said. "We still have time?"

Jace checked his watch. Another twenty minutes until his appointment with the lawyer. He glanced around the parking lot of the office building, then motioned for Greg to scoot over. Once perched on the most expensive seat he'd ever sat on, he began.

"It's Ben. All the medical stuff, the fear of death, it's nothing compared to how I feel like I'm failing him."

"*Failing him?*" Greg said incredulously.

"Yes. I'm supposed to take care of him. Not vice versa. Plus, I'm not exactly the guy he married. I get moody all the time. I can't count how often I've yelled at him lately. It's getting to the point where I'm sick of myself."

"Everybody understands the mood swings," Greg said. "They don't bother Ben, and they don't bother me. Did you hear me complain on the way over here?"

"Huh?"

"When I ran that red light. You snapped at me."

Jace shook his head. "I don't even remember that. See what I mean? I'm losing it."

"That's putting it a bit strongly."

"Is it?" Jace frowned at the office park around them. The perfectly pruned trees, the glass buildings that reflected sky. All of it planned, all of it perfect. "Remember when we were teenagers and I had just broken up with Victor? We got super-trashed that night. Do you remember?"

"Yeah," Greg said. "Except I drank so much that I blacked out and still can't remember half of what happened."

"And it drove you crazy. You asked me for days to tell you what we'd done that night, and I kept making up stories to screw with you. Eventually, you got upset at not being able to remember and made me tell you the very boring truth."

"Flipping through the yearbook and pointing out who we wanted to sleep with, right?"

"Yeah."

Greg sighed. "Okay, I can see how the memory thing must be upsetting to you."

Jace nodded. "I don't trust myself anymore. The memory loss

and personality change alone ensure I'll never work again. Not as a flight attendant. Lord only knows what else will happen to me. As much as I hate having two unruptured aneurysms, I'm more scared of who I might wake up as once they are removed. The worst, though, is what all of this is doing to Ben. I've been researching online, reading personal accounts from people who have gone through the same thing. That was comforting until I started reading ones written by spouses of aneurysm survivors. Past the initial fear and relief, many of them begin to feel resentment."

"That's not Ben," Greg said strongly.

"Maybe," Jace said. "You have to think in the long term. More than just this last month or the next year. Picture decades of me snapping at him, of not being able to remember the simplest things. He'll never stop worrying, wondering if another aneurysm has formed that we don't know about. I don't want to do that to him. This isn't what he signed up for."

"Yes, it is," Greg said. "It's called marriage. Would you abandon him if he developed a disability? You're better than that, and so is he."

"Okay," Jace said. "But I still don't know if I want to put him through this, even if he's willing."

"There's no alternative," Greg said. "Don't you dare suggest one. Like it or not, you guys are spending the rest of your lives together, even if I have to lock you up somewhere."

Jace smiled. "Just make sure it's somewhere nice."

"How about that banana-filled gay island of mine?" Greg bumped shoulders with him. "You know what you remind me of lately? When we were teenagers. You were moodier back then, and half the time you didn't know what was going on because all you could think about was Victor. Now you're angsty again and obsessing over what Ben thinks about you. Well, you know what *I* think?"

"What?"

"That whatever happened to your brain knocked you back a decade or so."

Jace groaned. "You think I have the brain of a teenager again?"

"Why not?" Greg shrugged. "Stranger things have happened. Anyway, that means you'll grow out of it eventually."

"How embarrassing, if true."

"Nah. Most guys our age are gearing up for a midlife crisis. You'll fit right in."

They shared a laugh together, Jace thinking about it. Maybe he just needed to mentally go through everything he had before meeting Ben, relearn from his life experiences. How ironic, then, that he was about to visit someone who had been crucial to his development.

"I'm worried about the surgeries," Jace said. "There's little chance that I'll die, but I might come out a different person again. There's just no telling."

"You'll be fine," Greg said dismissively.

"If I'm not," Jace said, silencing any protest by raising a hand. "I need you to take care of Ben."

Greg shook his head. "He doesn't need me. He needs you."

"Regardless, he'll need support."

"He's family. Of course we'll be there for him, but only you can give Ben what he needs."

"That's what I'm worried about," Jace said. He checked his watch. "Time to talk to my past about my future. See you soon."

Jace hopped off the car, feeling nervous as he entered the office building. When he'd spotted the ad in the phone book, he scarcely believed it could be the same person. He still wasn't sure—wouldn't be until they were face to face. Just the idea made him edgy. He was glad Greg had agreed to drive him out here. Jace didn't trust himself to drive, not when he could cause an accident if another aneurysm ruptured. Until he was given a clean bill of health, Jace would make his peace with being chauffeured.

The office Jace entered was elegant and smelled of success. Jace was the only one in the waiting room, so he didn't need to be seated. The secretary, keeping an interested eye on him, called her boss.

"Mr. York? Yes, Mr. Holden is here to see you. Okay, I'll send him in."

So formal! Jace had a hard time not smiling as he opened the door. He did so quickly enough that he caught Adrien fixing his hair in the window's refection behind him. Then he spun around in his chair to look Jace over.

After a moment of uncertainty, they grinned bashfully at each other.

"I couldn't believe it when I saw the name," Adrien said, standing and offering a hand.

Jace took it, feeling like they should hug or something, but a very professional desk stood between them. "I couldn't believe it either," Jace said. "How did you end up in Austin?"

Adrien sat back down, making sure his tie was centered. "I'm a gay Texan. We all end up in Austin eventually. Have a seat."

Jace sat. Another few moments passed as they eyed each other, taking note of the differences and similarities. Age suited Adrien. The hair at his temples was receding, but this only drew more attention to his eyes, which were just as shrewd as before. The light crow's feet made him seem more experienced, and—

"If you say anything about the gray streaks, I'll murder you," Adrien said in good humor.

"Your hair is going to look awesome when it's all gray," Jace said truthfully.

"Thank you. Is that a wedding ring?"

"Oh." Jace held up his hand, which naturally chose that moment to tremble. "Yeah. Over two years now."

Adrien narrowed his eyes as if furious, and at first Jace thought he'd made a terrible mistake in coming here. Then Adrien winked, smiled, and held up his own left hand. On one slender finger was a diamond-studded ring.

"No way!" Jace said.

"Don't sound too surprised," Adrien replied. "At least, not until you find out who I married."

On the desk was a picture frame, which Adrien flipped around so Jace could see. The photo was of an Asian man built like a brick house. Not muscular like Greg, but a real body builder, someone who made it their life's work to be as huge as possible. Despite his size, his smile was friendly. There was something familiar about that face, but the last time Jace had seen it...

"Is that Caleb?" he asked. "The chubby freshman who followed you around in college?"

"Yes," Adrien said. "My shy guy. He's still that way. Quiet and soft-spoken, even though he could give Conan a run for his money. After you dumped me, he started working out like he had something to prove. Turns out he did! And let me tell you, he's not shy in the bedroom."

"That's awesome! About the marriage, I mean."

"Thank you," Adrien said, looking a little red in the cheeks. "And what about you?"

Jace's smile faded. "That's why I'm here, actually."

He told Adrien a little about Ben before he launched into the story of the aneurysm. For once, the person hearing the story didn't interrupt to express sympathy. Adrien was in professional mode now, listening to a client and trying to discern his need.

"Of course we're not married in the legal sense," Jace explained. "I'm worried that if something does happen... Well, both our names are on the house, but we have separate bank accounts. I don't want him getting screwed over by the state or anyone else, which is why I'm here."

Adrien nodded. "Your family would automatically inherit, but making Ben your sole beneficiary won't be difficult. You were right to come here. They treat us like second-class citizens in this country. It's getting better, but there's still a long way to go, and I'm sick of waiting. I'm thinking about getting into politics."

"Do it," Jace said. "I always knew you'd take the world by storm."

Adrien blushed at the compliment. "I always knew you'd find the right guy. I never meant what I said, you know."

Jace shook his head. "When you said what?"

Adrien swallowed. "When we were breaking up. I said that you were going to die alone or something cruel like that. And then you said you hoped I'd find someone who made me feel loved." His smile was sad. "You were always so sweet. I always thought about that later, how you were classy even after I'd said something so awful. I regretted saying it. I still do. Especially now."

"I'll be fine," Jace said reassuringly.

"You'd better be," Adrien said. "I loved you, you know." There was a thick silence, Jace wondering if he was expected to say it back, but in the end Adrien smiled. "We'll take care of this lucky husband of yours. We should be able to get most of the paperwork together right now. There will be a few things I'll need you to get. When we're ready, you'll both need to sign. And you'll have to bring him in, of course."

"Ben? For legal reasons?"

Adrien shrugged. "For whatever reason. I just want to meet

him! How about we all go out to dinner? Caleb can show you this trick he does where he crushes walnuts with his bare hands."

Jace laughed. "Now *that* I have to see." A second later, he had an idea. Greg would never forgive him, though. "Hey, you know who drove me here today? Actually, just wait here. I'll be right back."

When Jace dragged Greg into the office, Adrien screamed like a little girl. Literally.

Chapter Thirty-three

Adrien was either cunning, had become sympathetic, or was simply very good at his job. Perhaps all three. Of course Ben hated the idea of a will, but Adrien made it about them both. Rather than preparing only for Jace's potential departure, the will covered the possibility of Ben dying too. That way it became more about being prepared for any eventuality, something that made sense after the recent scare. That the wills were signed over dinner was another stroke of genius. There wasn't time to ask awkward questions or get emotional. Not when trying to make room for the paperwork in between plates of appetizers and rounds of drinks.

Afterwards, the occasion felt more like a celebration than a time to sadly reflect on losing each other one day. When the meal was over and they had said goodbye to Adrien and his husband, Jace and Ben stumbled out into the night air.

"There's no way either of us can drive," Jace said.

"I can't believe they're staying for another round," Ben replied.

"I've seen Adrien out-drink lumberjacks before. True story."

Ben laughed. "Should we call a cab?"

Jace considered the twinkling stars in the clear sky above. "Let's walk a little. I want to enjoy the weather."

"Okay."

Plus, they weren't too far from a location special to them both. Taking Ben's hand, Jace chose the direction they strolled in. A few blocks later, they reached the park where they were married.

"Hey!" Ben said.

"Is there something special about this park?" Jace teased. He realized the joke was ill-conceived when Ben looked at him with concern. "Let's go find the pagoda. Maybe one of our wedding guests is still there, sleeping off the champagne."

Smiling in relief, Ben picked up the pace. When they spotted the strange gazebo, they ran to it, laughing when they finally reached the stairs and sitting on them.

"Should we repeat our vows?" Ben asked.

"That'll be easy for you since you didn't say anything."

"I spoke using a higher language," Ben said, demonstrating by kissing him with a passion equal to that day.

"Wow," Jace said when they broke away. "That's exactly what you said, verbatim!"

"Word for word," Ben said proudly.

"Does this mean I really need to repeat what I said?"

Ben shook his head. "No need. I remember it all."

"Really?"

"Yes. The important parts, at least." A smile spread over Ben's face. "Okay, so maybe I can only remember one word."

"And which would that be?"

Ben glanced over at him, his face a mixture of shadows and orange light from a distant streetlamp. "Forever."

Jace swallowed. "That's right. I meant it too."

Ben rubbed his nose absentmindedly, lost in thought for a moment. Then he dropped his hand and turned to Jace. "Do you believe in God?"

"Which one?" he asked, trying to keep the mood playful.

"Any of them," Ben replied. "I guess what I mean is, do you think there's more to life than this? Do you think that when we die, we live on somehow?"

"I don't know," Jace said. He considered the trees rustling in the breeze, the sounds of traffic and laughter in the distance. "Sometimes that seems like wishful thinking, like ideas mankind came up with to push back against our fears, or help us deal with loss. But then I think how I feel about you, how our love is something almost tangible, like something we created together that doesn't have a physical form. Then it's very easy for me to believe in a soul."

Ben nodded in understanding. "I was thinking about it the other day, how I was unsure if I have a soul, but when I think about you it's obvious. I know you have a soul because I can feel it." Ben laughed, as if embarrassed. "I don't mean that literally, but you're the one person I don't have any doubts about. Maybe that's how it works. Maybe loving someone means being able to see their soul, to know that it's real."

Jace smiled. "In that case, I can see yours too."

"Really?" Ben looked mischievous. "What color is it?"

"Brown."

"*Brown*?" Ben said incredulously.

"Yeah. Not a becoming brown either. Kind of a dirty poo brown, like something Samson would cover up in his litter box."

"You're cruel," Ben said.

"I know. What color is mine?"

"Golden," Ben said in all seriousness. "The best of the best."

Jace nudged his nose against Ben's cheek, kissing him there. "Now you're making me feel bad."

"That was the plan." Ben said, turning his head for a real kiss. When he pulled away, his eyes were searching Jace's. "Did we do the right thing tonight? I feel like we're tempting fate."

"By signing the wills?" Jace shook his head. "If anything, being prepared ensures it'll never happen. And if something does, at least there will be less to worry about. That having been said, a will only covers so much. There are things I need you to know."

Ben turned his face away, as if he didn't want this discussion to happen, but it had to.

"If something should happen to me," Jace continued, "I'd want you to be happy. I know you wouldn't be at first. If I lost you, I'd be devastated. Eventually, though, I'd want you to move on."

Ben raised an eyebrow. "You're drunk."

"I'm not," Jace said. "Okay, so maybe I am, but I've been thinking about this lately. A lot. I'd want you to find someone else, Ben."

"No." There was no thought, no delay. Just a simple flat rejection.

"Yes. You're too young to spend the rest of your life alone."

"I'd have Samson," Ben said flippantly.

"I'm serious!" Jace felt his temper rising, which he didn't want, so he took a deep breath. "You're a wonderful person, and you have so much love to—"

"Would you?" Ben interrupted. "If I die first, do you really see yourself being with somebody else? Honestly?"

Jace thought about it. "No," he admitted. "You're the only one for me."

Ben's response was soft. "Then don't ask me to do something that you're unwilling to do yourself."

"Fair enough," Jace said, taking his hand. "Just know that no matter what happens, be it today or in a hundred years, I'd want you to be happy. Whatever it takes, I'd be okay with it."

Ben nodded. "Anything else? If so, please tell me now because I don't think I could have this conversation sober."

Jace exhaled. "Samson. I'd want you to take care of him. And I'd like you to stay in touch with my sister and her family. She'll miss me when I'm gone, and I think it would help if you could fill in for me. Travel some more, if you want. See the world for me. Most of all, keep living. And don't do anything stupid, okay?"

Ben squeezed his hand in response.

Jace glanced over to see tears running down his cheeks, so he stopped. He wanted to promise Ben that all of this was just a mental exercise, ideas that they would never have to act on, but he couldn't. Even if he made it through the minefield of aneurysms unscathed, eventually one of them would be the first to go.

"Is there anything you'd want me to do if you die first?" Jace asked.

Ben thought about it. "Yes. I want you to rent a bus and invite everyone I love out for a ride. My parents, your entire family, Allison, Samson, everyone. Take a nice trip together up to the mountains, stopping somewhere along the way for a picnic. Afterwards, you should all get back in the bus and drive over the tallest cliff you can find."

Jace's jaw dropped. "What? Why?"

"So you can all join me in whatever comes next."

"That's very... selfish."

Ben turned to regard him, face dead serious. "I know."

Jace was the first to laugh, then Ben joined him. As crazy as the idea was, there was something romantic about it. That's how death should work. Everyone who loved each other making the journey at the same time—one final trip together into eternity.

Jace woke up with a headache.

At first he wondered if he was dreaming of that morning again, since he occasionally had nightmares about it, but the morning light was too bright, the details of the world too real for this to be a dream. He tried blaming poor sleep. His next surgery was just a few days away, and he'd spent more than one night tossing and turning. Of course this left him tired and cranky, and sometimes a little achy.

He glanced down to where Samson was sleeping, the cat's eyes opening instinctively before blinking shut again. Beyond him, Ben slept with his mouth half-open. He always looked younger when he slept, the muscles of his face relaxed, lending him an innocent quality. Jace wasn't feeling so innocent. He reached over, put a finger on Ben's chin, and gently closed his mouth for him.

Now the muscles of Ben's face came to life, the brow knitting in confusion, the eyes squinting against the day. When he saw Jace watching him, he smiled.

"What time is it?" he asked.

"No idea," Jace admitted "Time to get in the shower?"

Ben stretched and nodded. "Okay."

Samson remained in bed, as usual, only willing to wake up when a can of food was opened. Ben got in the shower first, getting the water warmed to the right temperature. Then Jace joined him. The funny thing about cohabiting was how normal things like this could become. The idea of showering with another guy would have driven him wild as a teenager. Now Jace still enjoyed seeing Ben nude, being able to help wash each other, but sex didn't drive his every need anymore. Intimacy was another matter. Jace exhaled in relief as Ben went from scrubbing his back to kneading the muscles of his shoulders.

"You're tense," Ben said.

"I think I slept on my neck wrong," Jace said, rolling it back and forth.

"We need to get you a new pillow," Ben said for the umpteenth time.

"Okay," Jace conceded. "We'll go shopping later today. Maybe get something to eat."

"Pizza," Ben said, slapping him on the butt.

"Again?"

"Yes. I'm out of here before my whole body turns into a prune."

Jace stayed to let the water run over his neck, but it didn't do much to relax it, or relieve his headache. By the time he got out of the shower, he had the bathroom to himself. He looked at himself in the wiped-away circle Ben had made in the steamed-up mirror. If there was a god, days like this one made him wish he could send his body in for an exchange. Or at least repairs. Jace closed his eyes.

That's when he saw it. A red line, thin and dim, but definitely there.

Panic shot through him. One of his aneurysms was rupturing.

His head throbbed as if in confirmation. Jace rushed into the bedroom, heading for the dresser.

"Ben?" he called out as he pulled on underwear and socks. There was no answer. Jace hurried to finish dressing. Ben could drive him to the hospital, and if they were lucky... Jace hesitated, fingers still on the top button of his jeans, his left hand trembling. There would be another surgery, if he even made it there. The odds of him dying on the operating table were high. Fear tingled down Jace's spine at the idea of being cracked open, surrounded by strangers in a cold white room as he took his last breath.

Jace sat on the edge of the bed, trying to decide what to do. Even if he lived, he wouldn't be the same person. He'd be changed again in unpredictable ways. Maybe Ben would have to spoon-feed him the rest of his life, or do other more personal things. The very idea made Jace shudder. But he had made a promise. He had told Ben forever, so he had to try, had to take that risk. Jace stood up, his head raging in response. The pain was so great he almost fell back. When he blinked, the dim red line was a raging inferno.

As he entered the kitchen where he thought Ben would be, his vision doubling, he knew he was out of time. This was it, whether he liked it or not. His time was up.

Oddly enough, this realization helped to calm him. No more fighting. No more indecision or fear. His path was decided for him. Ben sat at the table, attention focused on a script for a play Jace would never see him perform. Jace leaned against the doorway to stabilize himself.

"Come here," he said.

Ben looked up in puzzlement, so Jace held his hand out to him.

"Come to bed with me."

Ben checked his watch. "But we just got up."

"Come," Jace said, more insistent now.

Ben didn't smile as if Jace were being seductive. As he stood, he studied Jace, trying to figure out what was wrong, but Jace couldn't tell him yet or he knew Ben wouldn't go along with his plan—with what he needed. They walked into the bedroom and he sat on the edge of the bed, Ben staring down at him.

"We're okay," Ben said, maybe hoping desperately at this point that it was true.

"No, we're not," Jace said, grasping tighter to Ben's hand

and pulling him into bed. Usually he was the one to hold Ben, to protect him and make him feel safe, but part of Jace was a little scared, needed back some of the comfort he'd always given. To have Ben spooning against his back felt unusual, had almost never occurred. But it felt good too and helped slow Jace's heart.

"What's going on?" Ben asked.

"My head hurts," Jace admitted, fighting back tears. "Just like last time."

He held on tight as Ben tried to get up, knowing he'd run for the phone, get lost in panic for their final moments together. He didn't want that.

"Just stay with me," Jace pleaded. "It was a miracle I made it last time. I'm not going to again."

"You don't know that!" Ben said, his voice weak.

"You know the statistics as well as I do." Jace closed his eyes; the red line had become everything, swallowed up his entire world. But in a strange way, it didn't feel angry anymore, like it knew they were in agreement. "Please, I don't want us to argue. Not now. I don't want to die in a hospital."

"Jace."

"Please do this for me. I love you, Ben."

"I love you too." Ben's body shook with tears. Jace felt kisses on his neck, on his ear. "I love you so much."

Jace gritted his teeth against the pain, the grimace becoming a grin. He was loved. That's all he'd wanted, ever since he was old enough to need someone else to make him feel complete. Someone to be there for him in his darkest hour, to transform it into the most beautiful moment of his life.

"I'll always love you," Ben was saying. "Forever. I'll never stop. I promise. I promise."

Samson stood up, lay himself against the curve of Jace's belly, warm and purring. As the quiet warmth overtook Jace, he remembered the time Greg had held him like this, or the times he spent lying between his mother and father as a child. But just before he drifted off completely, he felt Ben's fingers intertwine with his own, felt a kiss against the back of his neck, and heard those three little words whispered with so much meaning that there was no room for doubt.

He was loved.

Author's Note

When I was fifteen years old, I tried to kill myself. I had gotten into a lot of trouble and felt that my life was over—that the mistakes I had made were too big to ever recover from. This was the culmination of three very difficult years in my life, and since I didn't see anything getting better, I thought it might be wise to check out before things became even worse. After swallowing a fistful of pills, I started to have second thoughts. What followed was a very uncomfortable hospital visit and a night in juvenile hall followed by one of the worst days of school ever. Life wasn't exactly trying to convince me that I had done the right thing when choosing to live. And yet, all these years later, I think about the wonderful adventures I would have missed out on if my attempt had been successful. The pets, friends, lovers, and even colorful enemies that make life so interesting. I never would have met Andreas, seen the world with him, or written any books. All because I was too short-sighted to see that there was hope, no matter how distant.

A few years ago, a friend of mine took his life. The method he chose didn't allow for second thoughts. Once the trigger was pulled, it was too late for him. I was devastated. This friend and I hadn't talked in ten years, but still his death took a terrible toll on me. When we knew each other, he was young, bright, beautiful, and wild. I had a crush on him, and loved him in one way or another. I never forgot him, never stopped thinking about him and wondering how he was. I suspect most of us don't realize how much we mean to others, how we make an impact on the lives of countless people, even if we aren't aware of it. Committing suicide does more than just end a life. Like a stone dropped in a pond, suicide spreads ripples of consequence outward, shaking up those more distant and threatening to drown those closest to us.

I'm not trying to judge. I had my reasons for attempting suicide, as did my friend. Nobody is perfect though, and often we make decisions that we regret later. With suicide, there might not be a chance for that regret. That's why it's important to talk. Tell those closest to you, tell anyone you can. Talk, listen, and then think very carefully. I know how trite "it gets better" is starting to sound, but it really is amazing what a difference a decade, a year, or even just a week can make. If you are contemplating suicide and feel you don't have anyone you can talk to, please consider calling one of the numbers listed below. The people manning those phones are there because they care, and I bet many of them have been in a similar state of mind. They are reaching out to you. All you have to do is take hold of their hands.

-Jay Bell, June, 2013

In the United States:

National Hopeline Network
http://hopeline.com/
1-800-784-2433

National Suicide Prevention Lifeline
http://www.suicidepreventionlifeline.org/
1-800-273-8255

For the deaf: Contact the Lifeline via TTY by dialing 800-799-4889

The Trevor Project: serving lesbian, gay, bisexual, transgender, and questioning youth.
http://www.thetrevorproject.org/
1-866-488-7386

In Canada:

National Suicide Prevention Lifeline
http://www.suicidepreventionlifeline.org/
1-800-273-8255

In the UK:

Samaritans UK & ROI
http://www.samaritans.org/

+44 (0) 8457 90 90 90 (UK - local rate)
+44 (0) 8457 90 91 92 (UK minicom)
1850 60 90 90 (ROI - local rate)
1850 60 90 91 (ROI minicom)

PAPYRUS – Prevention of Young Suicide
0800 068 41 41
email: pat@papyrus-uk.org
SMS: 07786 209697

In Australia:

Lifeline
http://www.lifeline.org.au/
13 11 14

To find a help line in your country, please visit:
http://www.suicide.org/international-suicide-hotlines.html

The story continues...

...in the *Seasons Series*, each book written from a different character's perspective, the plots intertwining at key points while also venturing off in new directions. The quest for love takes many different forms, changing like the seasons. Which is your favorite?

Current books in the series:

#1: *Something Like Summer*
#2: *Something Like Winter*
#3: *Something Like Autumn*
#4: *Something Like Spring*

Also by Jay Bell
Something Like Spring

Nothing in this world is permanent. Friends, lovers, even family, can all disappear in the blink of an eye. Without these anchors, it's all too easy to find oneself drifting.

Jason Grant doesn't have much, aside from a beat-up old guitar and knack for getting kicked out of foster homes. His latest placement is set to be just another in a long line of failures. Then he meets Caesar Hubbard, a handsome guy who lives down the hall. For the first time in his life, Jason wants to stay, which means learning to be part of a family, and not letting his feelings—or his actions—ruin his first real chance of falling in love.

Something Like Spring introduces a new character to the *Seasons* story, one with a troubled past and an equally turbulent future. Jason must traverse a winding road fraught with emotional conflicts and tough decisions… a road that might just lead to a certain couple in Austin.

For more information, please see:
www.jaybellbooks.com

Also by Jay Bell
The Cat in the Cradle

To set out into the world, to be surrounded by the unknown and become a stranger. Only then would he be free to reinvent himself. Or fall in love.

Dylan wanted one last adventure before the burden of adulthood was thrust upon him. And to confront the man he hadn't spoken to since their intimate night together. Stealing a boat with his faithful companion Kio, their journey is cut short when they witness a brutal murder. A killer is loose in the Five Lands and attacking the most powerful families. Dylan—a potential target—seeks sanctuary from an unpredictable bodyguard named Tyjinn. Together they decide to turn the tables by hunting the killer down. Along the way, everything Dylan thought he knew about himself will be challenged, but if he survives, he stands to win the love he never dreamed possible.

The Cat in the Cradle is the first book in the *Loka Legends* series and features twenty-five original illustrations created by Andreas Bell, the author's husband.

CPSIA information can be obtained
at www.ICGtesting.com
Printed in the USA
LVOW11s1515270617
539543LV00003B/604/P

9 781484 814772